NUWORLD AT WAR

A SteamPunk Universe

WILLIAM BARRONS

Chula Vista • Columbus

The tall, muscular and young Duke David Odin Bushnell, stood on a ridge watching the painted savages. They were dancing around fires down below, by the Ohio River, to the beat of war drums, and were far west of Pennsylvania Colony's western frontier, at the time.

It was Thursday night, September 2nd, 1756.

The Duke knew those stomping warriors were boosting up their courage, by bragging of past and future acts of daring. They were gaining a kind of battle madness — as they called it—which they sometimes got more quickly, and easily, from alcoholic "firewater"— if they didn't drink too much.

To the Duke's surprise, there were many fires, to the right of the Delaware tribe's disorderly village of Kittanning. The 30-year-old and make-shift town, of perhaps 50 or so wigwams, log cabins and teepees, was down the cleared-of-trees slope, next to the Ohio River. There were also a few wigwams, on the other side of the Ohio.

Actually, the Delawares called themselves "Lenni-Lenapes." They had originally lived along the Delaware River, near the present site of Philadelphia, thus getting named after the river, by the newly arrived, White immigrants from Europe.

"Lord Andrew, please come here," the Duke called to the man, who was also observing the scene below, from several paces to his right.

Arch Duket Andrew Montour, the Duke's second in command, ranked just below Duke.

"I know what you're going to ask," Lord Andrew said. "Why are there so many warriors down there, Overlord? Our intelligence said there'd be maybe 150 to 200 warriors here; but there might be close to 300 of them down there now, I'd say."

"That would be my guess also, Lord Andrew. So, you had best get over there to Overlord Croghan (say Cro-an, meaning in the ancient Gaelic of Ireland, "Crown"—of Royalty) and help him get his Battle Force down there, to reinforce Overlord Armstrong's Battle Force."

"So there goes our reserve already. But that's what it's for, to take care of the unexpected. I'll see you on the river after the battle," Duke Odin added.

With a quick "Yes, Milord," the Duke's Overlordet disappeared in the darkness, to the right along the ridge.

Arch Duket Andrew Montour's famously remarkable mother, was fathered by a French-Canadian trader, to an Ottawa tribe woman; and Montour's father was of the Onondaga tribe. But Montour looked like a handsome European man, "gone Indian," as they said those days.

Lord Montour was especially intelligent and was fluent in several languages. He had been an associate of George Croghan, "King of the Indian Traders," before the vengeful French Army robbed Croghan's stores and killed, captured or drove off, all of his employees.

Those vicious attacks on Croghan's stores, by French soldiers, had been the beginning of this third "French and Indian War," against the English Colonies in the Nuworld.

By about 10 o'clock that night, the slice of moon in the sky was to be down, and not much starlight would shine between the clouds. Then the Duke's Forces would only have the savage's fires, and noisy drums, to guide them into their assigned, dawn attack positions.

In a moment, Mr. Ezra Stiles came up to the Duke. He was the owner of—and presently the "war reporter" for—the NUWORLD NUZ, a new and quickly famous newspaper, based in Stratford, Connecticut Colony.

Stiles was also one of the Duke's 13 rich partners, in the Nuworld Company. They had formed their company in April 1754, to gather Spanish treasure off the Caribbean Sea floor.

"Duke Odin," Stiles whispered, "I was wondering what your dispositions might be; just for the record."

That was the way with his friend Ezra; always so curious.

Stiles was the only one of 369 Nobles on the mission, not carrying a weapon. He was also their Chaplain, as he had been on the 6-months long Caribbean treasure voyage. That Yale graduate was licensed by Connecticut Colony, as a Congregational Preacher, and as a Lawyer besides. Although 30 years old and rich, Stiles still hadn't married.

"Mr. Stiles, it's really quite simple," Duke Odin said. "I sent Overlord William Trent, and his *Invincible* Battle Force to the left, nearly a mile. That is where he said he had waded across the Ohio River easily, some years before.

"At dawn, his Force is to come upstream, and destroy whatever enemies there are on the other side of the river. Also, Trent's Force is to prevent any of the enemy over there, from escaping in any way whatever.

"Overlord John Lamb's *Defiant* Battle Force is to go behind the *Invincibles* and come sunup, sweep through that big cornfield to the left of the village. They are to make certain no enemy escapes down-stream, on this side of the river.

"You can see a few fires burning there in that cornfield, Mr. Stiles; that's to ward off mosquitoes, for those making love there, I'm told," the Duke told him.

"Really? Love making in a cornfield?" Stiles asked.

"Many of those with us are quite familiar with the practices of these Indians.... excuse me, I do mean 'Asians,' rather than 'Indians,' of course.

"Yes Mr. Stiles, *we all know that Indians, only live in India*. You've made it plain that we Whites are correctly called 'Euros' and these folks we now call Asians, had ancestors who had to have canoed east over the Pacific Ocean, here to the Nuworld. Well, as you said, they are now properly called *Asians,* and not *Indians* at all.

"Amazingly," Stiles said, "in the 264 years, since Columbus got his geography, and these peoples so very wrong, folks have kept on with that same mistake, insisting on calling these Nuworld Asians, *Indians.* What of your other 3 Battle Forces, Duke?"

Although they were quite certain, no enemies were near; the men kept their voices low.

"Overlord Daniel Morgan's *Gators* Force, is just below us, hiding in those bushes you can barely see," the Duke pointed. "He's to attack straight on down into the village, at first light.

"You can see nearly every tree has been cut down along that slope for building and for firewood, over the 30 years of the village's existence.

"Overlord John Armstrong's *Braveheart* Battle Force is to attack from the right of the village. They are to keep anyone from escaping upstream.

"Lord Andrew and I could see there are more warriors over there than we anticipated. I had him get Overlord George Croghan's *Valiant* Battle Force, there to reinforce that right side.

"Comes the dawn, Mr. Stiles, all those warriors—and any French soldiers with them—are going to pay with their lives for murdering our frontier families," Duke Odin said.

"Thanks, Duke; you've told me what I wanted to know," Ezra Stiles said.

"I sincerely believe your revolutionary OdinGun, will be a world-changing invention. This first test of your marvelous weapon and your organization for battle ought to prove that.

"Milord," Stiles continued, "I will never get over the great swell of emotion, each of your Noblemen and Noblewomen exhibited, when you laid your golden OdinGun, on their shoulders, in that ceremony of yours. You then made them Noble Commissioned Officers. It was especially emotional when you loaned them your OdinGun and placed it in their hands.

"It was truly touching," Ezra Stiles added.

"Yes sir, it was," the Duke agreed.

"It was brave of you to style them as Nobles," Stiles went on. "The British will be offended and hate you for that, but I can't see that it matters much. Personally, I shall forever be grateful for you escaping from the English Navy. Now we'd both better get some sleep, Duke."

As Stiles disappeared, the Duke supposed the war drums were beating louder. He knew the drums provided rhythm for the war dancing, in an age-old tradition, on the "stomping grounds" for just about all of the Asian tribes. But those savages present would need no further rhythm, come morning. He expected they would all then be very dead.

He heard the melody of a feminine voice asking for him. A few steps closer in the darkness showed it was Grand Countet Annie Willing. She was the Overlady to the 35 Noblewomen, serving as Healthors, record-keeping clerks, cooks, and bakers for the Duke's 5 Battle Forces.

At the moment, the Noblewomen were caring for the 27 pack horses, that had carried mostly food, foldable ovens, and grills, plodding over the Alleghanys, to this place.

The strikingly beautiful, 23-year-old leader of the Noblewomen, was a wealthy Philadelphia socialite. She proved to be a superb, self-confident leader of women. Besides, she was an anti-violence Quaker. The Duke had to respect a person, who would put their religion aside, to attend the gravely important mission they were about.

And although she had never even held any kind of gun before, she proved to be their third best sharpshooter!

Annie Willing was a remarkably pure blonde beauty. She was seemingly perfect in every way, and she reminded the Duke of his little sister's porcelain doll, made in England. However, she jiggled and wriggled nicely when she moved, and baked clay dolls do not do that. But she was five years older than him, and anyway, he had no interest in a possible romance, during this intense effort at war.

He had been told that she remarked how handsome he was, with his curly black hair and unusual great height of 6-feet-4-inches. But he was sure; his friends were exaggerating.

The Noblewomen wore similar uniforms to those of the Noble-men, of yellowish, so-called buckskin; although that deer leather could also come off of does.

All of the Nobles' first and last names, were boldly painted in large black letters, on their jacket arms – below the 3-inch circular Nuworld flag sewn on there. Their names were also painted on the AndyPaks, strapped on their backs. Their AndyPaks had been designed by Lord Andrew Montour, and of course, named for him.

The word "HEALTHOR" was embroidered on the Noble-women's 3-inch-high collars, and their rank was spelled out, and embroidered on flat sleeves, slipped over their shoulder straps. Those rank sleeves added a little padding on their noble shoulders.

Each Noblewoman wore the same deerskin "trouzer," of the Gaelic language (not the plural "pants" or "trousers") as the Noble-men, with a covered button front "fly." Their garments were a new design by clothier Cypriot Dudley – thus, a trouzer was often called, a "Dudley."

The Noblewomen wore the same brass hats, which also had their names neatly painted in black letters on the front, below the Equator part of the Nuworld half-globe... which covered the Western Hemisphere from a bit beyond the North Pole to the Equa-tor. The continent and islands were pressed in, and the Great Lakes were indicated; otherwise few features were shown. A 2-inch wide brim was all around the hat, to ward off the sun and the rain.

They also wore calf-high, lace-up-boots. They all carried their holstered OdinGun, with a belt-like leather tether, at the rear of the gun. The tether wrapped over the right shoulder, or over the left shoulder, for the left-handed Nobles.

All Nobles, male and female, also wore full undergarments of cotton, as deerskin feels clammy against the skin. That was espe-cially true when perspiring or getting the leather wet.

But tanned deerskin was the only washable leather known.

The clothier Dudley had bought an entire shipload of those deer hides, from South Carolina Colony merchants, since their ware-houses had large stacks of them. European workers had recently switched to cloth clothing, instead of the imported deerskin they had used for years. Thus, large quantities of that fine leather, beautifully tanned by Asian tribes in and near, South Carolina Colony, was available; and cheaply, too.

"Milord Odin, may I speak to you briefly?" Overlady Annie Willing purred quietly as she came up to him.

"Overlady Annie, I'm surprised you'd come up here. Is there trouble with your Healthors?" the Duke asked.

"Oh, no Duke, that's what I wanted to tell you; to reassure you we're alright, and that all 27 of our horses are well fed, watered and quiet.

"Also, I've set up a perimeter – I think you called it – all around them. There's no chance I can imagine that any savages could come in, unnoticed, to steal our horses," she said.

"That's good to know; but you should be getting some sleep, Milady. The morning will surely bring casualties for you Healthors to attend to. And I expect there will be released Euro captives, needing your care," the Duke said.

"Yes Milord, I know I should, but frankly, I'm rather excited. But I want you to know; I am not afraid. I'm still surprised I'm carrying an OdinGun, but you must know my Healthors, and I will use our weapons if we have to. By the by, I've heard dogs barking down there in the village; might they give us away?" she asked.

"That's not likely," he told her. "The Asian's animals are no good as watchdogs, so nobody pays any attention to their barking. They're only good as winter food. I tried some dog meat once, and it's quite tasty."

"Excuse me Duke, but I can't believe I'd try it," she said with a grimace he could barely see. "Anyway, that's the reassurance I wanted to give you, so it's a bit less worry for you. Also, Lord Doctor Gale is some better. I think the long walk climbing up and down all those mountains was a little much for him.

"Oh yes, and I've assigned the 12 Healthors to accompany you downstream on the morrow. Now, you too had better get some sleep. Good night, Milord Odin," she said as she silently glided away.

Lord Doctor Benjamin Gale, was another partner in the Nuworld Company, and had been the ship's cook and "Healthor." He had kept all 14 partners so healthy, they needed hardly any doctoring during the six months, of their Caribbean treasure-hunting adventure. He also was their fisherman and kept them well fed during the entire voyage. He used fish guts as bait, mostly.

Duke Odin had never known that big medical man to be ill, so it must have been the extraordinarily long hike, as she said, along the narrow trail up and down the Alleghanys—the "mountains-many," as the Asian word meant. The amiable Doctor taught the Noblewomen much about sanitation, hygiene and treating wounds, as well as cooking and baking in quantity.

The Duke recalled that during the long walk up and down those mountains, there had to have been a huge cloud of human odor on the ground, all around the Nuworlders; they spotted no deers, bears, wolves or other animals then. Oh yes, there were chattering squirrels high in their trees, and birds in flight beyond counting, for they felt no danger from the sweating humans.

Overlord Croghan had recruited two other doctors from Pennsylvania; Hugh Mercer, who was born in Scotland and was said to be a graduate of a medical school there; and John Cochran, born of Scots-Irish parents in the Colony. But Cochran was really only an apprentice doctor.

Those two doctors would accompany the Duke downstream, after the morning battle.

Four others of the Duke's Nuworld Company partners were with him. They were listed as his "aides" and ranked as Lords and Barrons.

One aide was Barron David Rittenhouse, the brilliant Pennsylvania scientist. He was experimenting with sending electrons through the air, for messaging. "Ritts" and "ritting" was what Ezra Stiles dubbed such messages; from the brilliant man's name, and from "writing."

Barron Elias Tully, at 5-feet-4 inches tall, an entire foot shorter friend of Odin, since childhood schooldays, came along to assist Lord Rittenhouse. He had been a busy businessman, getting some of Odin Bushnell's inventions made and sold.

Barron Tully also prepared the "Health Kit" that went into everyone's AndyPak. That kit contained a comb, bar of soap, washcloth, towel, toothbrush, toothpowder, and an OdinRazor. As was the custom of the time, the soap was also used for shaving. Only 20 scissors were handed out, and only to those who said they knew how to cut hair.

Every Noble also got a small, printed calendar book and a pencil, to keep a personal record in their AndyPak, of their experiences and observations. Some of them were unable to write but could read their calendar anyway. The majority who were literate were encouraged to make friends with less educated Nobles and help them.

Lord Tully was no scientist, but he was a shrewd and an especially smart businessman. He was unusually handsome, despite his short stature, and had told the treasure hunters many bawdy tales of "bedding widder wimmen," throughout Connecticut Colony.

Barron Tully had married a pretty girl named Mercy, three weeks before sailing away for the six months it took, to gather treasure in the Caribbean Sea. And now he was away from his wife again, and his newborn son, in this new cause of fighting the evil French, and their savages.

Lord Tully had suggested that the Duke change his name, from the "too-cold and common Biblical David," to the "very unique and friendly-like, Odin." So, Odin Bushnell, it was from then on. He took it as his middle name, from his Mohegan great grandfather, Odin.

The Yale graduate Ezra Stiles had informed the Duke that "Odin," was the name of a Viking War God, and that his extremely old Mohegan great-grandfather, surely had acquired that name, by it being passed down from visiting Vikings, perhaps long, long before the present.

"Well Mr. Stiles," the young man had said, "if that name was good enough for a Viking God and especially for my own kin, it surely is good enough for me!"

The young Bushnell's given name was David – named for the young fellow who fought Goliath in the Bible – but he rarely used his first name.

The partner and artist, Barron John Singleton Copley, of Boston, had been pushed by Odin, into experimenting with making pictures with light, on silver-fogged glass plates. Copley had persisted like a bulldog to success with the phenomenon, they both had seen as gleaming white silver, turned dead black when exposed to light, in the slightly acidic, salty Caribbean Seawater.

Another talented artist and partner, Barron Benjamin West, of Pennsylvania Colony, had been talked into becoming an architect, instead of spending his life painting pretty pictures. West came to help Copley, in making "coppix," as Stiles called Copley's pictures-from-light.

Lord Rittenhouse had made the lenses for their "coppix boxes," used to hold and to "expose," the silver-fogged glass plates.

One other aide was the Duke's secretary – his *"Secret Arie,"* from which the word had been derived—Arch Barronet Charles Thomson, of Philadelphia. Thomson had a fair education and had been a private tutor to wealthy children, in that growing city. He was also to help teach the less literate Nobles, at every opportunity.

The soft and plump Sir Charles was not hardened with manual labor as the rest of them were. Indeed, Sir Charles had vomited earlier that same evening, when he saw the torn-up bodies of the 2 French officers, and their seven savage companions, carelessly guarding the trail to the village. Those "outguards" had a huge fire going, and were jabbering noisily when the Duke's Nobles, splattered their brains. The Nobles' shots were drowned out by the booming of war drums, in the village at the time. They knew those guards weren't to be replaced until dawn.

None of Odin's aides were expected to actually fight, but they all carried OdinGuns, as did the Noblewomen Healthors, "just in case."

Although all the Nobles were expected to be well paid, none could be termed "Mercen-Aries." Odin insisted every Noble must shave regularly, and keep their hair trimmed; and of course, *bathe* whenever they could. Odin had been astonished to learn many of their recruits, had never before had a toothbrush. Bathing then was rare for people to do, let alone regularly.

Before the Caribbean voyage, Odin Bushnell had owned a fancy French-made musket, and a French pistol; both of them had been prettily cast in brass. Odin's father, Militia Captain Nehemiah Bushnell, had captured some French Army weapons in 1745, eleven years before. That was when New England Colonials, had conquered France's Fortress Louisbourg, on Isle Royale, at the entrance to the Gulf of Saint Lawrence.

But with the powder-and-ball paper cartridges they used, 5-feet-long-and-longer muskets very often failed to fire. Dishearteningly, such muzzle-loading weapons refused to shoot, in about 1 in 3 tries. And when the powder in those paper cartridges were rain-wetted, muskets were pretty much useless... oh, except for the nasty bayonet on their muzzles.

The first unexpected discovery of the Nuworld Company partners in the Caribbean, on February 1st of 1755, was what proved to have been a Dutch pirate ship.

From dated coins found in the wreck, they knew it had been coming in the year 1662, from the Indian Ocean near India and the island of Ceylon and was heading to New Amsterdam—which became New York City in 1664. That pirate ship had been loaded with chests of captured pearls, 12 other kinds of gems, and captured gold and silver coins. It was sunk, as a result of having the pirate ship's bottom ripped open when it hit a reef, east of Jamaica Island.

Those pirates had also kept a great number of assorted brass cannons, and brass ships bells, from their nine pirated victims.

One of the small cannons on that ship was a one-of-a-kind "breech loader." Near that cannon, were 3-inch diameter, 15-inch-long, 2-handled brass "cups," originally filled with gunpowder, and a cannonball. That cup stuck only part way into the breach of the cannon. Having some of those cups loaded with powder and ball on hand would have made it possible for the cannon to repeat firing, more rapidly than the usual loading, from the muzzle of the weapon.

Odin Bushnell's instant reaction was they should have made the cup thinner and stuck it *all the way* into the bore.

Thus, began the invention of his OdinGun, as Yale man Ezra Stiles named it.

The key idea was to replace the flimsy paper cartridge, holding powder and ball, with a ½ inch diameter, 2 ½ inch-long, brass cup.

And since the brilliant Paul Revere, silver-and-gold-smith of

Boston was a partner in the Nuworld Company, Odin knew he could precisely make, absolutely anything. Lately, Revere had been turning out OdinGuns, at the rate of nearly 100 every day! His many men had actually managed to step up production of those guns, to almost 600 a week. Revere's arsenal, and other Nuworld Company businesses were back in Stratford, Connecticut Colony.

All of Europe's armies of that time had their soldiers carrying very inaccurate muskets. Rifles had been invented and were far more accurate than muskets. But they were also muzzle-loading and were far, far slower to reload than even the slowest muskets were.

The word "rifle" came from the Dutch who, when looking down the barrel of a gun, grooved to make the ball spin, thought they saw "ripples" (or for them, "rifles"), as in a stream.

Together, Odin and Revere devised complicated iron molds, into which molten brass was forced to make the twenty-one inch long and strong OdinGun. The OdinGun was a brand new "bolt with an operating handle" type. The bore of the barrel was narrowed from 5/10ths of an inch to 3/10ths of an inch at the muzzle. That "squeezing-down" of the shot, greatly accelerated it, like water through a hose nozzle. The effective range of a musket was no more than 50 yards. For the OdinGun, the range was *at least 400 yards.*

When you were to reload, you pulled up and back on the lock handle. That brought out the empty brass cup. You grabbed the cup and put it back in the jacket slot it came from, just inches away from the gun. You then took another fresh ammo, laid it by the bore, and shoved it in, turned the handle to lock it, and you were ready to fire again. A Noble could repeatedly fire very, very much faster than any musket on earth could be fired.

Odin made the barrel, merely 17 inches long. That was about half the barrel length, even of the shortest muskets, oddly called "carbines."

He also made the pointed "shot" cylindrical, instead of spherical, and only a ½ inch in diameter. Musket barrel bores and balls were mostly ¾ inch in diameter.

It was like putting a nozzle on a hose to speed up the water coming out. They had done that very thing, when diving in the Caribbean, to move the sandy bottom off of treasure.

None of the very precious brass in the ammo cups was thrown away. Those fired brass cups were kept in jacket pockets, and could be re-filled at their arsenal, and fired again.

The lod shots had three angled surfaces on the rear. The very high-pressure gas pushing against the shot rears, down the barrel, made the shots spin just enough for stable flight. That was rather than use grooved rifling in the bores. Rifling, Odin reckoned, slowed the shots down.

A hollow vertical handle was cast midway, at the bottom of the barrel. It had a screw-on cap on the bottom of it, so an oily cleaning rag and cord could be stored inside. The rear handle was similar, and both handles were leather-wrapped for comfort.

Cast onto the rear part was a rectangular ring to hold the adjustable leather belt tether that wrapped around one's shoulder. Not only did that tether hold the OdinGun steady, you rested your cheek on it to aim, and to fire the weapon. No heavy wooden "stock" was needed.

A pull on the lever-like trigger would bring a firing pin inside to where it would push a dent in the soft copper covered primer, on the base of an ammo cup. That dent pushed the center of the dried-hard tiny button primer, of ground glass and gunpowder, to ignite into the main charge in the brass cup – *ka-boom!*

The gunpowder Revere had developed also was somewhat less smoky, and more consistent and powerful, than other explosives of the day. And unlike paper "cartridges," the brass cupped ammos, were moisture-proof and could be fired in even the rainiest weather.

Although most Nobles let their brass hats tarnish to a light green color, they kept their brass OdinGuns shining, as though made of solid gold!

Each Noble had rows of slots on their jackets to hold 48 ammos. Additional ammunition was carried in their AndyPaks.

The Noble*women* only carried 12 ammos, on their jackets – just in case.

Ezra Stiles said *l-e-a-d* is what *leaders* do; *l-e-d* is what leaders did;

and *l-o-d* is the correct English word for the heavy, soft metal used in ammunition.

To fire, you pushed forward on the handles, rather than pulling the weapon against one's shoulder. That helped control the recoil of each shot. That leather belt tether around the shoulder, rather than a wooden stock, made a surprisingly steady rest for your cheek while aiming.

The leather holster on one's hip supported the OdinGun, along with the Noble's shoulder, by the belt there. That left the hands free while eating—or whatever—until a Noble was actually ready to shoot. The clumsy, overly long musket had always seemed to be a bother to carry.

Ezra Stiles said the word "pistol" came from the French word "pistole" which in turn, oddly came from a French word meaning "whistle." Duke Odin Bushnell's weapon, was no pistol, and certainly not a whistle; it was an *engine of war; a gun; an OdinGun!*

From 4 Spanish galleons sunk in 1609, in shallow water during a voyage from near Panama to Havana, Cuba, the 14 Nuworld Company partners recovered huge amounts of gold, silver, and emeralds. Very importantly, they also recovered many tons of precious brass, from those olden vessel's great armament, of exclusively huge brass cannons.

More recently, warship armament was mostly switched to cheaper cast iron cannons.

From the brass of each of the largest of those cannons, Revere could make nearly 1,000 OdinGuns! So, they had on hand more than plenty of brass for those guns, ammo cups, and the Noble's much-loved brass hats.

As the Duke lay down on the grass to sleep that night, he thanked the stars above as he did every night, for allowing him to escape enslavement by the English (so-called *Royal*) Navy.

With his OdinGun holstered, he removed his brass hat, a creation mostly by Paul Revere.

The good-looking hat was shaped like a half world globe, but "spun" in a spinning hollow iron mold, from a flat, oval, brass sheet. The sheet was clamped down all around, oiled and the brass was spun, and stretched with a tool, gradually down into the mold. When it fits tightly inside the mold, sand was poured in, and pounded, to force the brass against the inside of the mold, to create a view of the Nuworld, embossed on the hat. A 2-inch wide band went all around, and an adjustable leather band circled inside the hat, to fit various sized heads.

You could not do such things with felt or cloth hats. It was actually quicker and cheaper to make them of brass than the complicated manufacture of felt hats, with expensive beaver pelts, and poisonous mercury.

❄ 2 ❄

Someone was touching the Duke's arm. Ah; he saw it was Sir Charles Thomson.

"Milord, it's getting close to dawn, I think," his secretary said. "I see down below in the village, the women are lighting fires outside their wigwams, for the morning feed."

The Duke thanked him, realizing he had surprisingly slept perhaps, 6 or 7 hours.

He rose, stretched, did those morning things, and drank some cold coffee from his canteen. He also ate some "rope cake" from his backpack.

That cake had been concocted by Overlady Annie. The dough had been rolled out, sprinkled with raisins, walnuts, and cinnamon; it was then coiled, twisted, cut to foot-long lengths, and baked. When done, it was dipped in sugary "frosting," cooled and wrapped with paper, for carrying in their AndyPaks. After about a week's time since it had been baked, Overlady Annie's concoction still seemed fresh to him; and it was still delicious.

The Friday, September 7th, 1756, morning breeze was cool, and the sky was yet cloudy.

There were no more fires in the cornfield to the left of the village; nor were any fires lit to the right of the village. He could see only a few cooking blazes around the helter-skelter jumble of log cabins, wigwams, and a few teepees.

The two doctors, Ezra Stiles, his four aides, and Sir Charles gathered around the Duke.

Except for Stiles, they each had "FORCE GROUP" embroidered on their high, stand-up collars. All other Nobles had their Battle Force name in that place. Stiles' collars appropriately had NUWORLD NUZ embroidered on them, with its "brand nu" spelling.

A dozen Healthors were to run down the slope, joining the Duke as the shooting stopped.

The sun was taking its good old sweet time, lighting the morning sky.

"Gentlemen," the Duke whispered, "as soon as there's any shooting, I'm going through the village to the left a little, to get quickly to the river. We must make certain we have all the canoes we need. All of you are to stick close to me."

They waited, straining to see something; just anything. Finally, the sky did lighten up.

The first shots fired were across the Ohio, by Overlord Trent's *Invincibles*. Then the thunder from over 300 OdinGuns, plus that from uncountable muskets, filled the morning air as the Duke and his entourage sped down the slope.

Part of the way down that slope, the Duke spied 2 Asian warriors in a small clump of bushes; and they were raising their muskets up to fire at him and his aides.

At about 20 yards, Duke Odin blasted both of the enemies in very quick succession; BANG! BANG! The two painted warriors were knocked flat on their backs. Crimson streams of blood were gushing from a little hole, in each of their chests. The Duke had practiced reloading his OdinGun so many times; he was lightning fast at it by then.

He held his OdinGun with both hands, at the ready, as he cautiously approached the painted bodies in the yet dim light.

He saw a form on the ground, in a black and red striped blanket.

Reaching down anxiously, he yanked the blanket apart to see that it was a young, naked Asian maiden. She was so young; she was barely "in bloom." She was anything but pretty at the moment, what with her face contorted in terror.

"Sir Charles!" the Duke roared to his secretary whose eyes were as big as dinner plates.

"Wrap this girl up, and get her up there to the Healthors. Then meet me down at the river!"

"Damn!" Stiles exclaimed, looking over the two dead men with bloody chests. "Look at that brandy jug! They must have been having a drunken sex orgy, here in the bushes all night!"

"Follow me!" Duke Odin shouted, and they continued on down the slope to the village.

The Duke wondered to himself how Overlord Morgan's Nobles, had missed those savages in the bushes – ah, because of the faintness of the light, he assumed.

Duke Odin Bushnell thought, what every military leader must think: *You cry havoc, you let loose the dogs of war, and you can never know for certain, what the result will be.*

Overlord Morgan's *Gators* had fought nearly through the entire village, before the Duke and his aides reached the nearest edge of it.

To his left-front, there were two small log cabins near the river, with their roofs of tree bark, and tanned animal skins, burning. Those two fires made an amazingly loud, crackling racket, and produced much stinky smoke, adding to the clouds of gunsmoke.

Just as Duke Odin got to the edge of the village, Overlord John Lamb's *Defiants Force,* rushed in from the large cornfield on the left.

They were herding about a dozen Asian women, who naked from the waist up. The Duke ordered those women, to be taken up the hill.

Bodies were everywhere, lying about in every conceivable contortion. They were mostly leaking blood out of countless holes, caused by those deadly, squeezed down shots, that tumbled when they poked through flesh. That was 1/2 ounce of extremely deadly lod metal.

They had been "knocked over," a term the Duke used instead of

"killed," to salve the consciences of those, who took the Bible literally, on the "Thou shalt not kill" commandment. But he figured
those words actually meant, "Thou shalt not commit cold-blooded
murder, in the first degree, except, of course, much murder is the
necessary thing to do in war."

He had emphasized that to his Nobles. "Our enemies would
happily murder us if we don't murder them first," he had told all of
his Nobles, men and women both.

Smoke and awful stink from the two burning cabins filled the air.

Women were wailing miserably, and children were whimpering in
fear, mainly on the ground where they were ordered to sit.

Odin only noticed a few Euro captives, shivering in the shock, of
the overwhelming chaos around them.

Doubtless, from what the Onondaga warrior Lord Andrew had
said, many an Asian warrior would much prefer to sing his death
song in his home; the enemy be damned.

It was surprising that gunfire had continued to the right of the
village. But then, it suddenly stopped.

Duke Odin glanced at his companions. They were taking in the
horror, the carnage, and the confusion of battle, with their eyes full
of wonder.

Barrons Copley and West had their picture-making coppix boxes,
tight to their chests.

Barrons Rittenhouse and Tully had their heavy messaging equipment, all of it stuffed in their AndyPaks.

Stiles had a pad of paper in one hand, and a pencil in the other.
But he had yet to put down a single word.

The doctors appeared almost numb, gaping at the turmoil all
around them.

The Duke jogged further to the left near the burning log cabins,
heading quickly toward the river, as the others followed. He had
made sure every Noble knew how to paddle a canoe, back in the
training camp, of his newly purchased Cornwall iron mines. That
huge iron ore pit was about 100 miles west of Philadelphia.

He had instructed them to secure every canoe here possible, for a
speedy trip downstream to the French Fort Duquesne (say

Duquesne), the very center of the evil French effort, to destroy all English settlers within their reach. The Nuworlders hoped to surprise the French there.

Near the Ohio, those two small log cabins were burning furiously.

The roof of the cabin to Odin's right was fully collapsed. The roof of the cabin on his left seemed ready to cave in.

Suddenly, a few paces away, an apparition rose up directly out of the flames and the smoke, of the fire to his left. It was two painted savages, garishly splattered with color for war. Their faces were blackened with soot for death. One warrior was close behind the other, both of them screaming gibberish at him, and aiming their muskets straight for him.

Duke Odin got off a shot at the first of them just as fire and smoke, billowed from the second savage's flintlock!

He could see that the first Asian warrior's primer pan puffed smoke, so his musket luckily misfired! But a ball from the further musket whistled past the Duke's ear! Duke Odin's second quick shot, got the second man in the forehead and down he went!

Then he could see that both of them were down, flat on the ground. The closest savage collapsed onto the second, whose feet were jerking, as he reached for his throat, which was gushing blood! That first warrior had actually turned around in falling, but his neck had been almost cut off! His head was on backward! That shot had begun tumbling, when it first touched skin, and very nearly cut his head right off!

Duke Odin and his companions, gaped at the ghastly scene, of the savage staring up at them, from atop the other dead man—while his body was chest down!

The Duke then spied a movement, inside the cabin to his right, and saw a child's eyes peeking in terror, from under a blanket. That cabin was almost totally engulfed in flames.

Sir Charles Thomson caught up with the Duke just then and saw the child at the same time, and he dashed through the doorway. He put his shoulder against a rafter to lift it, as it was pushing down on the child. The secretary grabbed the child and yanked him out of there.

It was a naked boy, maybe five years old, and although apparently not much injured, he was crying hysterically. The Duke had Sir Charles, hand the boy to Barron Tully.

"Lord Elias, you won't be going with us, so please take this boy up to the Healthors," Odin told his friend.

"Yes Milord!" the Barron said and took the child.

The Duke with his reloaded OdinGun hastened to the river. It was very good to see there were plenty of canoes on the banks, on both sides of the Ohio River.

Only the lighter and faster birch-bark canoes, were to be chosen for their use, because the also common, elm-bark canoes weighed more, and were not so fast. The square-ended, and much too heavy, French oak bateaus (boats) he saw there, were far too slow for their purposes.

The Duke was gratified that only 2, of the perhaps 50 cabins, wigwams, and teepees, in Kittanning, had been destroyed. The Nuworlders remaining in the town would need the shelter; to say nothing of the stores of food, of stolen tools and cooking kettles, that would be there. The Delawares and other Asian peoples, joining the French, had killed a great many of the owners, of such English-made goods, along the frontiers between French and English claims.

In short order, the 12 Noblewomen Healthors had joined the 260 male Nobles, who were quickly aboard 36 canoes, and were paddling downstream.

Fort Duquesne (as preacher Stiles liked to spell it in his NUWORLD NUZ, referring to the Biblical bad man, Cain), was something like 40 miles down the Ohio, from the village of Kittanning. It was estimated the trip would require paddling nearly the whole day.

They would briefly stop mid-way to stretch their legs, do their duties in the bushes, and eat a snack. Also during that stop, each Band Overlord would be exchanging rank sleeves, on his Noble's shoulder straps. The Band Overlords would be promoting only the

Barronets, to the next higher rank of Grand Barronet, after their first battle.

Sir Charles, in the Duke's canoe, would go from Arch Barronet to Barron, and be styled "Lord Charles" forever after; he would be declared a "Lord of Battles."

Noblewomen would go from "Dames" to "Ladies," upon becoming Barrons.

Other ranks were not necessarily promoted after a battle. The courtesy "ess" after a title, was only given to the wives, the life partners, of Noblemen.

Without stopping their canoes, reports came to the Duke.

Overlord Morgan's *Gators,* had 2 Nobles wounded badly enough, that he had sent them to the Healthors to be tended. Overlord Lamb said not one of his *Defiants* was hit, although they had "knocked over," over a dozen warriors in that big cornfield. Overlord Trent reported, only 3 or 4 of his *Invincibles* were barely nicked.

Overlord Armstrong had no casualties whatever, and Overlord Croghan, according to Lord Andrew Montour, had but slight hurts except, 1 Noble was killed; he had seen it himself.

The Duke mused to himself: *What great luck!* The French and their savage allies had not a prayer of a chance, in such a surprise attack, and when facing the firepower of the OdinGun! The ability to fire, to reload lightning fast, and fire again with extreme accuracy, he knew had to be a "war-winning" invention of his.

That weapon – and Odin's other inventions—had been conceived in an age, when invention was a really rare thing. For many centuries, there had been almost no innovation in the world. Odin Bushnell had proved humans could be – and actually were – creators, but hardly anyone on earth seemed to realize that, except for himself and his Nuworld Company partners.

Lord Andrew Montour brought his canoe again, to alongside the Duke's.

"All that shooting over there to the right, was because maybe, 150 warriors of the Seneca tribe were there, Overlord," he said. "None would surrender. Every one of them was slaughtered; every one of them. They mostly stood up there, those drunken fools, getting themselves killed. They simply could not grasp how deadly our OdinGuns are, Duke."

Lord Andrew had great gravity and sadness in his voice. Of course, he would, since the Seneca tribe, was also a part of the League of the Longhouse—the Iroquois—the same as Lord Andrew's, Onondaga tribe.

The Duke touched his arm as a condolence gesture. He got a nod in return that Montour appreciated the meaning.

"Lord Andrew, what Noble was killed?" the Duke asked. He simply had to know.

"It was that Turbutt lad, Milord. A French soldier stuck his musket out a cabin window, and put a ball exactly through Turbutt's left ear, right there in front of me. That boy never knew what hit him; he dropped like a stone. Bunch of us then shot the Frenchie in that cabin. Too bad; Turbutt was a truly nice lad. Everybody liked that boy, Milord."

Duke Odin felt like crying, but he durst not. Dukes, he knew, durst not cry.

As the paddlers kept the canoes moving down the Ohio, the Duke thought about them arriving at the training camp, at his newly acquired Cornwall iron mines. That was on August 2nd, 1756, and it was about 100 miles west of the Delaware River.

George Croghan and Andrew Montour had accomplished miracles ahead of the Duke's arrival. They had bought horses, supplies, and of greatest importance, they had recruited mostly frontiersmen – Irish, Scots-Irish and English, to fight the French, and their Asian allies.

The Nuworld Battle Forces, had only three very intense training weeks there because it was learned Fort Granville, on the Pennsylvania frontier, had been tragically surrendered, to the enemy French and their savages. They learned that those White – Euro – people, captured in the fort, had been taken to the Delaware Asian's village of Kittanning. Other victims of raids along the frontier, they knew, had also been taken there.

On that first day in camp, Duke Odin had stood on a large stump, before the whole crowd of volunteers. He gave them a long speech, and in it, he told them why they would be called Nobles instead of soldiers. He also showed them the buckskin uniforms; they would wear.

By far, the most important thing for the recruits was that he demonstrated the formidable-looking, OdinGun. He had looked as though, he had more than plenty of ammunition on his chest, ready to shoot.

First, Odin had blasted three young, tied-to-stakes pigs. He had fired repeatedly, at about 50 yards, with extreme rapidity. Fifty yards was about the maximum range of a musket. The surprisingly quick shooting he did, was a stunning thing, for all of the rugged frontiersmen to see.

Next, Duke Odin Bushnell killed a 200-pound hog, at about 300 yards. He then killed another big hog at 400 yards. He killed each of the big pigs with a single quick shot each.

They would eat pork for some days, because of that demonstration.

Most interesting was the amazement in butchering those animals, to see how their interiors were chewed up. The longish shots obviously tumbled and went every which way, once the tough skin was poked through. What the horrific effects on an enemy human's body would be, was more than obvious.

Well, the skinny lad Francis Turbutt was brought to the Duke, by George Croghan, the next morning in the camp. That was before the ceremonies of commissioning men and women, as Nuworld Noble Officers. Then, with a bit of pomp, touching their shoulder with it, he put into their eager hands, a loan – it was to be strictly a *loan*—of his OdinGun.

Croghan said the boy somehow got to the camp from 100 miles east, from Philadelphia. Croghan also said he learned the lad was not the minimum of 17 years old, but merely 15. He told the Duke too that he had learned the lad, was escaping his responsibilities, of getting his family's maid pregnant.

"And, he's too young for this business, Duke," Lord Croghan said.

"So am I too young for this business," the Duke replied.

Duke Odin was then but 17 years of age, himself. Later, he turned all of 18 years old, on the trail through the "mountains-many" – the Alleghanys—to the Ohio.

David Odin Bushnell had been born on August 30th, 1738, in the West Parish of Old Saybrook, in Connecticut Colony. That was exactly 100 years after English settlers had arrived there, to seek religious freedom and certainly, opportunities for prosperity, not then available in the home country.

Although yet a pink-cheeked youth, everyone seemed to accept Duke Odin Bushnell's leadership. Probably it was because he was clever enough, to invent the OdinGun and that he was the tallest fellow at 6-feet-4-inches, for miles around. He was a self-confident speaker, and if you're rich, you must somehow be smart – or even better, lucky. Lucky leaders are much appreciated by every sort of warrior.

"Do you know how to shoot?" Duke Odin had asked the lad.

"Never have shot a gun Milord, but I can learn," Turbutt replied.

"Then you have no bad shooting habits to overcome. Tell you what Turbutt; if you put yourself into it 100%, you might end up in the top 5% of the shooters, and you'll get a Gold OdinGun Badge for your chest. If you do that, you can stay," the Duke had said then.

Turbutt went away grateful, and in fact did well enough on the firing range, to earn a Silver OdinGun Badge, but not the gold one.

Amazingly, Overlady Annie Willing had won a Gold Badge for her well-formed chest. She had topped by a little, even the Duke's own score.

But the Duke could not have turned that boy away, for he knew all their secrets, including where they were going to fight, and what with. And in their very first battle, *Barronet Sir Francis Turbutt was the single Noble killed.*

Overlord Croghan with his 63 Nobles in his Battle Force *Valiants,* was left behind after the Kittanning battle, to hustle the Asian women and their children out of there. He was to send them on the way to the French Fort Junandat, at Sandusky Bay, on Lake Erie.

All of the Asians would, of course, know the forever self-confident Croghan, of the great trading and diplomatic skills. He was to explain the Nuworld flag for them and chide the Asian women bitterly, for allowing their men to be so rashly unthinking, as to aid the French, in their fight against the English. And now, with all their men dead, the French could feed and house, those refugee Asian women and children!

Overlord Croghan's *Valiants* also had the awful duty, of burying the many enemy dead.

They were in addition charged with guarding their 27 pack horses, the trail back over the Alleghanys, and the 24 Noblewomen, remaining there.

Importantly, the *Valiants* would be giving encouragement, and safety, to the redeemed Euro captives, taken by the Asians and French, from along the frontier.

Barron Rittenhouse was paddling in the front of the Duke's canoe, while Lord Tully was left behind at Kittanning, to hopefully send and receive ritts, with the brilliant scientist.

Barron West was in Odin's canoe also, while Lord Copley had been left with Croghan, to make coppix, of the devastation created at Kittanning.

Along with the Duke in the canoe was Lord Charles, Mr. Stiles, and three other "borrowed" Nobles. All 8 of them were paddling a smallish, truly ingenious birch bark canoe, that barely kissed the surface of the pretty blue Ohio River. The lightweight boat moved along easily. But it was easily tipped over, so they had to be careful.

It would take most of the day to get to Fort Duquesne, and in that time, the Duke would visit all of the 35 other canoes with him.

Since every Noble had their name painted on their buckskinned arms, and on the front of their brass hat, it was easy to call each by name. The name of their Battle Force was shown on their collars, and their rank was plainly embroidered, on the slip-on padding, over both of their left and right shoulder straps.

It was Odin Bushnell's idea that no Noble, at any time, had anonymity. Each Noble was therefore completely conscious, of needing to be responsible for their own honorable actions – *indeed, to be truly noble, at all times.*

Duke Odin felt his great luck continued. For the slightest movement to that second black-faced savage's musket, could have meant a ball in the brain, instead of a mere whistle, and pop sound by his ear.

The word Ohio means exactly, "beautiful river," in the Asian Algonquian tongue (O! Hio!—about like the Spanish "Rio," for river.) Stiles told Odin he thought the occasional similarity of Nuworld, and Old World words were too much of a coincidence. Stiles said there had to be some ancient connection between the people of Europe – the Euros – and the original people of the Nuworld – the Asians. It was quite probable, Stiles said, that Vikings had visited the Nuworld. Possibly, others might have done that, too, before the recent arrivals of Euros.

The slow Ohio River current was smooth, and fairly wide, where they were hurrying along. They were churning that clear blue water, with a great many paddles, dipping into it.

All Nuworlders were instructed to shoot any, and every warrior, seen along the river banks; but they saw none. It was an Asian warrior's business, of course, *not to be seen*.

The Duke looked down to examine his jacket, noting he had only fired four times to "knock over" those four savages. A Noble wearing his own jacket could tell easily which ends of brass cups had dents in them, from being fired. To an observer in front of him, it would look as though all 47 of those brass cups sticking up, were still deadly.

Odin noted to himself that his father, 11 years before – and now himself as well – had made good on the family name of Bushnell: To go into the *bush* and deliver the death *knell*, to an enemy. His "Pops" had fought at the capture of the French Fortress Louisbourg, by New England colonists, in 1745. That extremely important fort and the town had guarded the entrance to the then-called Gulf of St. Lawrence. A few years later, incredibly, the English government traded that fort and town back to the French; they did it for an advantage to English merchants!

The Bushknell name came to a distant ancestor, in Sussex England, as an honorable Saxon title, for actions against invaders. That was after the year 1066 conquest of Britain, by William the Bastard, the Duke of Normandy, and his French *k-naves*, called by Saxons, *k-nig-hits*. With their long *k-nives* (swords), they had been evilly killing, robbing, and raping, the Saxon inhabitants of Britain. So, that long-ago ancestor of Odin's had delivered the death *k-nell,* to some of the enemies, near his village, out there in the *bush.* This latest of the *Bush-knell* clan was doing the same thing, Stiles was to report, in his NUWORLD NUZ.

The extraordinarily learned Ezra Stiles had told him, that when they gave out family names centuries before, a man might build houses and be called "Carpenter." The name would stick, even if none of his descendants, male or female, never hammered a single nail.

Stiles told Odin if a worthy Irishman was given a title by an English Monarch − such as being made a Barron − no Irish person could inherit it as a Noble Title. But they could inherit that title as a family surname, as generations of Bushnells had done.

The goal of the 4 Battle Forces Duke Odin was leading, going down the Ohio, was the notoriously infamous, yet piously-named, "Fort Duquesne of the Blessed Virgin, on the Beautiful River." The hastily built fort was named for New France's Governor-General at the time, Marquis Duquesne.

Duke Odin Bushnell used instead of "Marquis," (in Britain, the feminine-sounding "Marquess"), the Noble terms Duket, Grand Duket and Arch Duket. All six of the Noble ranks could have Grand or Arch appended, to show increased status.

That fort at the confluence of the Ohio and Monongahela Rivers, was the very center of the French effort, to urge Asian savages to viciously murder, completely innocent frontier folks, of the English Colonies. The Asian warriors were also to kill, or steal, their livestock. They were instructed as well to burn the English settler's cabins and barns, to run off with their children, and rob them of all their worldly goods. That's how pious, were those Catholic French!

The French had a believable assertion to arm the Asian's will to do those dastardly things; that the English were intending to take all their lands, in the Ohio Valley, and drive them away, or destroy them. Of course, that was precisely what the big land speculators had in mind − such as Virginia's "Royally Chartered Ohio Company."

The brave Major George Washington was among the Ohio Company members.

Duke Odin had heard that, and much else, from Lord George Croghan. That man had a virtual library of knowledge, about the frontiers and even beyond.

The goal of the Ohio Company members was to acquire huge tracts of land, for little or no cost to themselves. They planned then, to sell that land in small parcels, as dearly as they could, to the "lesser men"; those men hungry for land to support their families; men without the "connexions" of the land-grabbing-and-land-hogging speculators.

And just naturally, it was not the distant speculators, and their families, that were at all endangered, by the raiding war parties. Oh no. The French organized, led, supplied and encouraged their Asian allies, in their horrendous attacks, on those of the vulnerable "lower orders," along the frontiers.

The Duke had good intelligence of the French fort and even a fair map of the place. The map had been smuggled out by an English-friendly Asian, from a Major Robert Stobo, held captive there, for a while.

Major Stobo had volunteered to serve as a hostage with the French, when Major Washington's small force was surrounded, and badly beaten. Washington had then surrendered his "Fort Necessity" to the French. That had occurred two years before, in the summer of 1754.

Shortly after that time – from February to June of 1755—was when the partners in the Nuworld Company, were bringing up tons of Spanish treasure, from the Caribbean Sea.

Fort Duquesne was hardly a large fort. It was unlikely to resist cannon fire for long, but the Duke's Forces were bringing *not a single cannon*.

Nor had they brought the secret rockets; the "OdinRocks," as Ezra Stiles had named them. Odin had of necessity invented that deadly weapon before the partners sailed to the Caribbean. With the OdinRocks, they felt they could destroy any pirate ship, or warship, that threatened them. But such a deadly encounter had not occurred, during their treasure-seeking voyage.

Unknown to his Nobles, the OdinRocks would be employed against the French at sea, during the coming winter of 1756-57.

The French had built Fort Duquesne, after chasing Washington and his Virginian militiamen away, back in the summer of 1754. English colonists had barely begun construction at that spot, under the supervision of a half-brother of George Croghan's, Ensign Edward Ward. Then the French completed the fort.

It was at the point where the Monongahela River meets the Ohio River – which some mistakenly called the "Alleghany River," up to that meeting. The Asian word Alleghany actually means "mountains —many," not a river. ("Alle," as in the English altitude, meant high or mountains and "ghany," meant many.)

Since the completion of their fort though, the French had also built some sort of extension of it, to house more troops, and maybe Asian warriors as well. But the Duke didn't know how large, that extension was.

The Nuworlder's greatest concern was that the French were known to hold captive there, an unknown number of captured fron-tiersmen, and their women and children.

During the trip downstream, the Duke was told, that probably 24 to 36 French soldiers were killed at Kittanning. The French killed, were in addition to a large number of warriors of several tribes, whose lives were taken. Did that mean the force at Duquesne was depleted?

Also, how many cannons could the fort bring into action? Some of those cannons mounted on that fort's walls were British-made, as a result of the English General Braddock's debacle. Braddock lost his battle, about 9 miles short of Fort Duquesne, with the French, and mostly "ignorant savages," the year before, on July 9th, 1755.

Although such cannons at the time were notoriously inaccurate, the iron balls they sent flying, could cut a man in two, one-half mile away. Cannons were *something to respect!*

Overlordet Andrew Montour pointed out to the Duke, one of Overlord Croghan's properties, next to the river as they canoed by.

Croghan's farm was said to be only 4 or 5 miles distant from Fort Duquesne. Montour told the Duke it had been a pretty place, some 2 years before. His farm had had a cabin, a barn, and vast cornfields. But they could see that by then, it already was overgrown with weeds and brush.

🕸 3 🕸

C louds had been threatening the whole day, and the air got cooler as a bit of rain began to fall. By the time they rounded a bend near the French fort destination, they could hardly make out the fort, because of the rain.

The Duke hurried his canoe ahead of the other canoes, with the fort looming up to his left-front.

There was at the time a small island next to the fort, splitting the Ohio River. But it seemed quite barren of anything but sand. So, the Duke shouted at Overlord Trent to ignore the island, and to follow his plan—to attack the fort with his *Invincibles,* from the point of land, at the junction of the Monongahela and Ohio rivers. It was where the Duke figured had to be, the weakest part of the fort defense.

Overlord Lamb's *Defiants* were to attack up the bank, on the Ohio River side of the fort. The *Defiants* were to use whatever might be at hand, to bash in the stockade gate.

Other Nobles were to use their canoes as ladders, to climb up and shoot over the twelve-foot-high, wooden posts of the stockade, into the fort.

Overlordet Arch Duket Andrew Montour was to direct Overlord

Morgan's *Gators,* and Overlord Armstrong's *Bravehearts,* in assaulting the place from the land side. They were also to attack especially, the mysterious housing extension to the fort.

Fort Duquesne seemed to the Duke, to be remarkably small, to have created so much hell and torment, for so many innocent frontier people, as it did.

Suddenly, men were seen running to the fort madly, from adjacent fields. Some of them were near-naked Asian warriors, obviously caught out in the open, unaware of advancing danger.

Those enemies were being shot down as they ran. That indicated 2 of the Battle Forces were ashore, and using their shots quite effectively, especially at fast-running targets.

With the great advantage of surprise, and the rain perhaps wetting the French gunpowder, in muskets and cannons alike, the Nuworlders began their direct assault.

Duke Odin joined Overlord Lamb's *Defiants,* helping to lift up a heavy French bateau, that had been lying upon the Ohio River bank. Fourteen or more of the Nobles hoisted the heavy oaken boat up in all haste. They were slipping and sliding in the rain-soaked mud.

That bunch of Nobles, slammed the large boat, against the stockade gate once, CRRRRRACK! Then again, CRRRRRACK! And down the gate went, flattened on the ground.

Shots rang out all around them, as Nobles climbed their canoes as though ladders, against the 12-foot-high stockade, made of pointed logs stuck into the ground. The Noble Nuworlders were firing into the fort itself.

The Duke and other Nobles strained mightily, with the heavy-weight, of that water-soaked wooden boat. They had carried it across the yard to the gate into the fort itself, ready to bang it down, when lo! The gate magically opened, and there grinning broadly at them was Overlord William Trent!

Odin glanced up to his right then to see many of Trent's *Invincibles,* on the roof of what he knew to be, the "Officer's Quarters." They were shooting rapidly down into the fort.

Just then, Odin saw 2 Nobles, tumbling off the rain-slicked, wooden-shingled roof. Blood was spurting out the mouth, and both cheeks of one the Duke recognized as Maryland's, Barron Samuel Springer. Surely, his tongue had been severed. He was the top sharpshooter with the OdinGun.

Springer had bested Lord Montour and Overlady Willing. He even bested the Duke himself, who had much more practice. He had been given his rank, because of his exceptional, best-of-the-Nobles, marksmanship.

The other Noble fallen from the roof, was the vaunted Band Overlord, New Hampshire Colony's Arch Barron Nathaniel Folsom. That Noble jumped up off the ground, holding his chest, with blood redding his jacket. He was not only shot but had broken several ribs in the fall. The splintered rib bones probably punctured his lungs further.

Neither of those prized Noble Barrons would live through the night. No one could help, and they each died a miserable death.

Five other Nobles were wounded, but none of them so seriously. All of them were attended by the two doctors and the 12 Healthors. The Healthors also comforted the freed captives, and sent the Asian women away; they would have to fend for themselves.

The uneven "battle" was over in only 10 minutes – that being the estimate of newsman Mr. Stiles, who was noting such details of their entire expedition.

They learned the fort Commandant, had been the dead Captain Jean Daniel Dumas. His second-in-command, also killed, was Captain Coulon de Villiers.

Captain de Villiers was known to be the officer, who led the destruction of Pennsylvania Colony's Fort Granville, in July. That was the disaster that caused the Duke to cut short his Battle Forces training time, of the rugged frontiersmen to only three weeks; then hasten to the Ohio.

There was not the slightest chance for anyone to surrender at Fort Duquesne if they had been so inclined. The tally of French killed was only 88, of the regular French army, and the Canadian militia. They had been much understaffed, possibly because of those urging deviltry, at the Kittanning village and elsewhere.

Also, 20 Asian warriors were killed, of various tribes. Twelve of them had been caught out in the open, shot down by Overlords Armstrong's and Morgan's Nobles.

All 5 Asian women in the fort survived and were given some food to take with them, as they were sent away to find their tribes, as best they might. Three of those 5 were "with child." Euro women in the Nuworld were far rarer than men, so inter-breeding was common, between the native Asian women and the love-hungry, eager Euro males.

Amazingly, none of the 27 English captives were hurt. They consisted of 2 men, six women, and 19 children, from ages 4 to 15. But not one of those captives were in good shape.

Many other English colonist captives had been "given," by the French, to various Asian tribes to adopt. Those captives were supposedly, replacing those of their tribe, "lost in battle."

Those Asian warrior losses could hardly have been numerous before the Nuworlders came along. Of course, Asian warriors intelligently attacked by surprise, with clever stealth and with slight risk to their own hides or hair.

Just before dark, the Duke, and others looked into the fort magazine, to see scores of small "barrels"—kegs—of gunpowder. That explosive was on hand mostly to encourage Asians in their murders. None of the Asian peoples had any idea of how to make gunpowder. Nor could any Asian make the muskets and pistols, to use the noisy, smoky stuff.

None of that explosive in the fort would aid in the slaughter of innocents again.

Arch Duket Montour, who was fluent in the French language, busied himself studying the French officer's papers, found in the fort. He told the Duke that there were copies of orders, inventories, personnel lists and several maps of French holdings, with many notes on them. The maps especially interesting were those showing the Canadian, and the Louisiana territories of New France. A surprise was that there was a lot of information, on Spanish territories, as well.

The Duke could eat no supper, because of the dying Nobles, Springer and Folsom. Once again, late at night, he thanked Mother

Nature for saving him from the clutches of England's Navy. Then he slept fitfully, because of the painful passing, of the two highly valued Nobles.

Dawn brought clean air with a bright sun drying everything. The rain had tapered off during the night and finally stopped.

The famished Duke ate some rope cake. That cake was fully sealed, in a hard-crust coating of sugar frosting, before being wrapped in paper.

Besides the valuable maps and other papers, the Healthors found a supply of coffee beans and sugar, in the French officer's "quarters." The Frenchies' coffee proved to be quite good. The captured silver coffee pot was remarkably fancy, and it did make really good coffee.

Those who had begun as first rank Barronets, and promoted after the first battle to be Grand Barronets, were then promoted to Arch Barronets. Once more involved in such a fight for those Nobles, and they would be styled Barrons, "Lords of Battles."

The Duke washed himself in the Ohio. That was something none of them had done the day before. But the Duke did not have the beard he expected to have at age 18. There was no point in shaving the tiny "peach fuzz hairs" scattered on his face, nearly invisible.

He knew the lack of facial hair, was because of the Asian blood in him. His mother's grandpa was the now-deceased Asian Chief of the Mohegan's Pochaug Band, Odin. Duke David Odin Bushnell was 1/8th Asian, 7/8th Euro, and now went by his middle name of Odin.

Every Nobleman was glad to receive a gift of the Duke's invention, of a 4-sided razor, it being far superior to the "straight" razors in use for centuries.

Odin thought the wonder was, that it took so long for someone to think of simply stamping a thin sheet of 1½ inch square steel, and to angle down the edges about 10 degrees. The OdinRazor Mill where the razor was made, sharpened the four edges. The blade was mounted over a similar sized, 4-sided "comb." With both comb and blade screwed onto a vertical handle, the OdinRazor was easy to keep sharp. Men shaved their whole face with it quickly and safely, before swirling it around in rinse water. They would then spin it, to dry it.

Elias Tully had been selling OdinRazors, and the very bright OdinLamps, all over.

The OdinLamps got their bright light from having lime powder, infused into the cotton wicks. Odin had noticed the brightness of limelight, in the smelting of iron ore, and thus applied it to the molded glass lamps, with glass "chimneys." Whale oil was held in the base of the lamps. The limed wicks brought the oil up to the chimney to burn, and throw light all around, far better than did the oil lamps, that had been in use, absolutely unchanged, for countless centuries.

Overlord John Armstrong and his *Bravehearts* Battle Force canoed down the Ohio that Saturday morning, to Logstown, a Shawnee Asian village, about 18 miles distant, as the Duke had planned.

Many of the Logstown's cabins, were said to have been built by the French, which doubtless gained some gratitude, from the Asians. The Euro's steel-bladed axes were a huge advance for the Asians, whose stone axes were far inferior, for chopping down trees. But for splitting enemy heads, the made-from-stone axes, had been quite satisfactory.

At Logstown, Armstrong was to retrieve every possible captive, and if he could not acquire any, he was to totally destroy their village, their cornfields and every Shawnee warrior within the long range of their OdinGuns. He was to use his own good judgment and also to raise and explain to them, the beautiful Nuworld flag if he could.

The Duke directed Overlords Trent and Lamb, to determine how best to destroy Fort Duquesne the next morning when they were to return upriver to Kittanning.

Those Nobles were also to bury all of the dead, down the fort's deepwater well, in the center of the fort. They would shovel dirt over the bodies, and then pile into the well, every possible bit of metal. That would include muskets, pistols, cannons, plus lod and iron balls. That was for the occasion later when the well could be "mined" for those metals. They would, however, bring back right then any unusual, or fancy weapon souvenirs they could find – including offi-cer's swords—for their future Nobility Museum.

They were also to raise, on a pole, the Nuworld brass flag at the juncture of the rivers.

They had brought half a dozen, 2-foot-diameter round flags, with them to lay claim, to the territories they conquered – *with all those speculating, land grabbing hogs, be damned!*

The flags were made of circular brass sheets, instead of cloth, and designed by Nuworld Company partners and artists, Paul Revere, Benjamin West, and John Singleton Copley. They only brought the 2-footers with them, because of the problems in hauling the brass sheets, and the equipment needed, to hang them on poles. Two sheets pressed to show rises in land and islands from waters, and some places raised further to show mountains were held back to back by bending the edge of one sheet over the edge of the other. By pressing both sheets to bulge out a few inches, people could get the idea of a half-of-a-world-globe, duplicated on each side.

The view was of the Western Hemisphere, from the North Pole, exactly to the Equator, as supposedly seen from the moon. All the land was "gold" (the lacquered brass of the sheets), plus the lacquered-on blue waters of the Pacific, the Atlantic, the Caribbean, the Great Lakes, Hudson's Bay, the Gulf of Ohio (instead of Gulf of Mexico), the Gulf of Canada (instead of Gulf of St. Lawrence) and a few of the known larger rivers.

Although no names were shown, the raised Caribbean Islands were plainly seen.

Since the "Earth was tilted," in the view, one could see from a little beyond the North Pole, to just beyond the Equator. Beyond the Equator, and to the edges of the maps, was a bit of South America, a little of Africa, Europe, and Russia; those lands were painted dark brown.

That view was understood to be, by Odin Bushnell and his 13 partners, what their Nuworld ought to consist of... someday when it was made free of foreign controls. When they sailed in the coming winter, to attack French ships in the Caribbean, they would have four-foot diameter, round brass flags on their OdinRaft.

On that Saturday, the mission the Duke set for Overlord Daniel Morgan, and his *Gator* Battle Force, was to accompany Lord

Montour, and the Duke himself, to the battlefield where General Braddock's British soldiers, and some few Colonial Militiamen, had been thoroughly thrashed, by "ignorant savages," 14 months before. That calamitous battlefield was about 9 miles up the Monongahela River, from Fort Duquesne.

They brought along French shovels from the fort, noting that not one of those shovels, had been well made.

Barron Rittenhouse was asleep when they left, so the Duke didn't know if he had succeeded in signaling back to Kittanning. From past experiments, Lord Rittenhouse had said he could ritt far better after dark, and had no idea at all, as to why that would be. The Duke could offer him no insight on that matter if he had been asked, and he had not been asked.

Barron Benjamin West came along, lugging his coppix box on a tripod, hoping to get some pictures of the battlefield of British defeat.

Publisher and war reporter Ezra Stiles came along, of course.

Arch Countet Daniel Morgan was two years older than the Duke and very intelligent. He radiated physical strength, as well as being an excellent leader. He was born of Welsh parents in New Jersey Colony but lately had been a Virginian. Morgan had been a teamster – along with Daniel Boone – driving horses pulling wagons, on new-made trails, during the English Army General Braddock's, march to disaster.

During that trek toward Fort Duquesne, Daniel Morgan had been nastily called *"a son of a bitch,"* by an English boy-officer, gravely insulting Morgan's mother. And just naturally, Morgan flattened the foolish curser, with a quick fist to the jaw.

For that, Major General Edward Braddock sentenced Morgan, to be whipped with 500 lashes. That seemed to be the only way the cruel British oligarchy could think, to maintain some degree of discipline. But keeping careful count, Morgan found they only delivered 499 lashes. So, they owed him one lash, and he owed the British, 499 lashes!

Morgan was a rough and tumble man. Some called him "half

horse and half alligator," so the Duke named Morgan's Battle Force, *"The Gators."*

Outside of Fort Duquesne, were nine healthy hobbled horses, and four milch cows tied to stakes. All of them were grazing contentedly, and unmindful of the defeat befalling their former masters. The Healthors would do the milking, and others would roast 1 of the cows that day.

They would make use of those nine horses, to add to the 27 left at Kittanning.

They hurried along the path adjacent to the cornfield, planted to supply the fort. The corn was ripe, so they could look forward to a supper of that, and of roasted beef.

The French and English alike learned from the Asian tribes and grew besides corn, beans which curled up the stalks, as squash proliferated between the rows. That was the "Three Sisters," as the Asians called them, sustaining the tribes. The three foods were their long-time "Staff of Life," in addition to bear meat, but mostly venison—deer meat.

On the way to Braddock's battlefield, just beyond the fort's area cleared of trees, to build the fort and stockade, the Nuworld Nobles entered the woods.

They had gone but a short distance in the forest, when they clearly heard metal-clattering noises, and men's voices on the path ahead. So, the 68 Nuworlders ducked into the bushes.

They presently saw a French officer and 8 painted Asians. Each one of them was carrying several muskets and other loot. The Frenchie and the warriors wearing frightening war paint were quickly shot all to pieces, by so many OdinGuns.

The only way Lord Andrew could tell which tribe the Asians were from, was by their footwear! They were Chippewa's from far off Lake Superior, Montour declared. The Chippewa tribal name meant, he said, "they make their moccasins, puckered up."

Those few warriors had joined the French, no doubt, to get in on the easy plunder.

Those nine had apparently killed as many as 18 settlers to get those muskets, powder horns, bullet molds and, bullets. Also, the bloodied red-haired, and blonde-haired scalps, of the previous owners, were on those warrior's belts. Then the dead French officer and those Chippewas were buried with their victim's scalps, by the Nuworlders.

They piled up the iron muskets, and other metals, to later take back to the fort for burial. The Asians also had stolen four good axes, three well-made shovels, and an iron pry bar. To the Duke's astonishment, those Chippewas possessed eight arrows, with shiny red *copper* points, instead of the usual, *stone* arrowheads.

"Copper! Where would they get that metal?" Duke Odin wondered out loud.

Lord Montour responded, "I've heard, Milord, they sometimes find copper rocks lying on the ground, which they can pound into arrowheads. Also, I saw a note on the papers in the fort there, that in that Lake Superior area where the Chippewas reside, compasses sometimes go crazy, as they do around iron mines."

"Aha!" Odin said. "That means there must be deposits of iron ore and copper ore there. Unfortunately for us, it's a long way from any of our settled areas. But we'll be up there sooner or later," he said, ending with a mere whisper.

Later that morning, they came upon Braddock's battlefield. They noticed that the path they had been following deviated to the left, and up over a rise in the ground.

Lord Montour explained that Asian warriors would consider that battlefield haunted forever after, with the spirits of the fallen. Therefore, the place was to be avoided.

Human bones were scattered all over the place. Carnivorous animals from brain-hungry badgers, to bears, and mountain lions, plus insects beyond counting, had been feasting on those unburied men. The bones of slaughtered soldiers had laid on the ground there, for 14 months.

Most were British and newly arrived in the English Colonies, a month before their deaths. A few of the dead were Colonial volunteers. Braddock himself was killed, and of his roughly 1,400 to 1,500 soldiers involved, less than 1/3rd of them escaped unhurt.

Both sides in that fight had shot at each other with the same, very-slow-loading muskets. The Asian savages had been paid for their beaver pelts, and other furs, with muskets and ammunition, by both the French and the English.

The disrespected "ignorant" enemy, fought with a much smaller number of warriors, than did Braddock's Force. They shot from behind trees and bushes and had but trifling casualties. The exact numbers of casualties would never be known, but that field of 1,000s of scattered bones was telling enough for the Nuworld Nobles.

Arch Duket Andrew Montour – who, with George Croghan, had led Braddock's English Army, through the forest to that battlefield – insisted the savages could easily have killed every Britisher, but for their greed in too-hastily reaping booty, and scalps from the dead. That undisciplined Asian greed was what allowed most of the defeated living, to flee in mad retreat. Major Washington had taken General Braddock's place and led them to safety.

On this day, the Nuworlders got busy making up rough litters, of poles and ragged scarlet cloth. They gathered all the emptied, chewed-on skulls, and other bones, they could find.

There were no weapons to be found, nor shiny buttons, nor gold lace. Such items had been snatched from the dead immediately, along with their hair-laden scalps. Even their white-haired wigs were taken. Every one of those dead soldiers had worn the fashionable wigs, since their never-washed natural hair, was so awfully unmanageable.

The Nuworlders worked hard through much of the afternoon, digging a trench, and burying every human thing they could find. They buried even shoes, with their brass or silver buckles missing.

Ezra Stiles worked along with the rest of them, but made many notes for future stories, in his *NUWORLD NUZ*.

Afterward, Connecticut-licensed Congregational Preacher Ezra Stiles, led them in the mumbling prayers for the brave departed, urging the Almighty to take them Unto His Own.

Barron Benjamin West got to make 14 coppix pictures of those scenes.

The Nuworld Nobles got back to the captured Fort Duquesne, with the dead Asian's iron muskets and axes, right at sundown.

Overlord Armstrong and his Battle Force had returned from

Logstown shortly before. He brought with him 26 Colonial English captives, gained from the Shawnees there. He also had a most interesting tale, of his Force's adventure.

The Nuworld flag was shining beautifully, on a tall pole, at the junction of the Monongahela River, with the "Beautiful River"—O! Hio!

Barron David Rittenhouse was smiling broadly. "Milord Odin, it would seem my ritt system works pretty well, at that. I ritt them in Kittanning, what happened here. Now, let me read to you, and Lord Andrew, the ritt I got from Lord Elias at Kittanning, during the night. Mind you, that's from about 40 miles away:

"Captives released: 52.

"Enemies killed: 354; including 37 French, 68 Delaware, 17 Mingo, 14 Ottawa, 22 Shawnee, and 196 Seneca.

"Asian women and children ordered to Sandusky: 114.

"Nobles wounded: 9; Noble killed: 1.

"I had Elias – I'm sorry, I mean Lord Elias, of course – repeat all of this twice to make sure. And my friend Duke Odin, my ritt system has proven itself!" the scientist said.

"Barron Rittenhouse, you are to be most heartily congratulated, on your brilliant achievement!" the Duke said. "But of course, we must keep your ritt system secret, for some time, as it is a very great advantage for us."

"Oh yes, Duke; I agree. Even my hand-cranked electricity maker, worked fine," Lord Rittenhouse said. "But just that my ritt system works at all, is one terrific thrill for me!"

The Duke reviewed the ritt with Lord Andrew, who was not only saddened, but much alarmed to learn that so many Senecas—his fellow Iroquois—were killed.

"Duke," Lord Andrew said gravely, "this could mean big trouble for us going back over those many mountains. They are going to want those OdinGuns, more than anything in the world. I tell you this Milord Odin; you can count on it."

"You and I will have to think on that some, Lord Andrew," the Duke said.

The Duke had long admired the clever Rittenhouse apparatus.

One part was the "concentrator," an umbrella-like foldable brass disc that the inventor said, concentrated the pulses of electrons, being either sent or received.

Out of 1,000s of countrymen thought possibly to have been captivated by the French and Asians during the last couple of years, the Nuworlders had only released 105 thus far. But surely, the Duke surmised, other tribes would see to it that their prisoners were returned, rather than face deadly retribution from his Nobles.

Asian leaders were not fools at all. They were realists, and they very much understood the power of guns. They would all understand the power of the OdinGuns; that was certain.

Three Force Overlords, Lord Andrew, and the Duke met with Overlord Armstrong, as they supped on roast beef, with corn and beans mixed as "succotash," as the Asians called it.

Then they listened to Overlord Armstrong's report.

Arch Countet John Armstrong was born of Scots parents away back in 1717, making him then, to the Duke, an almost ancient, 39 years old. He was balding and almost as old as the Duke's own father. Armstrong had come to Pennsylvania Colony in 1741, from Scotland, and was a very polished, impressive leader. He had been made by the Colony Assembly in Philadelphia, a Colonel of Militia.

Overlord John Lamb was 21, a New Yorker, and well-educated. That Lord wrote and spoke well, but had not before, been on any of the English Colony frontiers.

Overlord William Trent, born in 1722 in the town his father founded – Trenton, New Jersey Colony – was a wonderfully ambitious, 34-year-old, and seasoned leader.

The Duke respected them all highly and, except for Lamb, they all had had much frontier experience. Importantly, they were thus familiar, with the cultures of the Asian tribes.

"I could see Logstown was deserted," Armstrong began telling the others. "Of course, the Shawnee would know we were canoeing downstream, and all about us taking Fort Duquesne.

"Dammit, we saw some Asians up there yesterday, watching our fight," he pointed up the mountain overlooking the Monongahela River and the fort. "They could almost throw rocks on us from up there! What a place this is for a fort! It would be a ridiculously hilly terrain around here, to try building a large city in this place.

"Now that Logstown, it's not like other Asian villages, all helter-skelter, because the French laid it out sort of neat. It has a wide space down the middle.

"And that's where the big Shawnee Chief was; old Hokolesqua himself. He's the Asian leader most English call, 'Cornstalk.' He was sitting cross-legged on the ground, arms across his chest, bidding defiance to the world. That's the way with him, and he was all by himself.

"It so happened, as we put up our canoes on the bank there, I spotted a gigantic huge thick cloud of Passenger Pigeons, coming toward us, from the south. It was a truly large flock of them, as usual, flying just above the trees. That flock must have been 1/4-mile-wide, and at least 1-mile long. No one knew how thick it was, with many 1,000s of those birds."

All of the Nuworlders had seen such impossibly large, and dense flocks of the pigeons, blocking out the sun, even in the Alleghany Mountains.

"Anyway," Armstrong continued, "I got me an idea right away. So, I told my Nobles, 'We'll all have our OdinGuns loaded, and when I give the order, each of us will fire exactly three times, as fast as we can, up into that flock of birds. Immediately after shooting those pigeons, we must all be sure to re-load our weapons,' I emphasized to them.

"Duke Odin, we did just that, and we never saw such a rain of birds, falling out of the sky, in our lives! I reckoned it was maybe some 180 of our shots speeding up there, in no more than 3 seconds. And what with every shot capable of killing, or of maiming, several birds – well, that's why it rained down so many.

"The ground was actually covered with squawking, squealing, dying pigeons, all around the horrified old Chief. Maybe 10 or 12 of those birds, dying and flapping their wings, actually struck him. You can imagine old Cornstalk, was mightily amazed, with *the big magical medicine* of our OdinGuns.

"The old Chief pretty quick called in his people, and the captives from the woods.

"Milord Odin," Armstrong continued, "I speak some Shawnee, and I told him you would be blowing up this fort, and we would be leaving – *but only temporarily.* I told him his people would be welcome, to have those cows, and the corn, but not the horses out there. I hope that was alright with you, Milord."

"Absolutely, Lord John; that was a truly good gesture toward better relations. Also, we'll put all the fort things out there on the ground, that we figure they might find useful; that is, everything but weapons, which we are going to dump down that well. Did you try to explain our flag and our 'flag-hats' to them, and the reasons for doing them that way?"

"Yes, I did Duke, and some of them seemed to understand what I told them. I'm sure none of them were familiar at all with maps, let alone world globes. Even so, I pointed to where we were at that moment on the map, and they seemed to be impressed. We left our beautiful flag up there on the pole, and I hope they will not abuse it. Really, the Nuworld shiny brass flag looked to be pretty up there on a pole at Logstown," Lord Armstrong said with pride.

"Thanks very much, Lord John, for that. You know from the Book of the Nuworld Nobility that you each have," Duke Odin continued, "and from the display of them in the training camp, that I've provided Badges for Sharpshooting, and medals called Campaign Shields, plus Crowns for Leadership, for Courage and for Merit.

"But Lord John, I must confess I failed to come up with a medal for shooting pigeons!" Duke Odin said with a smile. That brought a roar of laughter.

"Dammit Overlord John Armstrong, all I can favor you with for the brilliant handling of that situation, is an 11-feathered Gold Crown for Merit," the Duke told him.

The Crown awards were designed by artists West, Copley, and Revere, to resemble Plains warrior's headdresses – the French called them "war bonnets"—in miniature.

Gold-plated Crowns, about 1½-inches overall, had 11 metallic feathers (for the top 5%); Silver plated crowns with 9 feathers (for the next 15%); Bronze crowns with 7 feathers (for the next 30%); and Blued Iron crowns with 5 feathers (for the last 50%), of those deserving awards.

The Duke had emphasized that they would be awarded as fairly as humanly possible, and that to argue about such awards, was forbidden – that it would be *ignoble* to do so.

Battle Forces *Defiant* and *Invincible* had been busy the whole day, spreading out kegs of French gunpowder. Those kegs would be ready to open up, by earliest light of morn. The Nobles would spread that explosive about, on everything burnable.

Every piece of metal found in the fort would be thrown down the fort's well, atop a layer of dirt over the bodies buried there.

They had also put outside of the fort, items useless to the Nuworld Nobility. Included were such tools, pots, and pans as were thought useful to the Shawnee. But they kept the Frenchie's gorgeous silver coffee pot and the excellent coffee. They also collected for their future Nobility Museum, artfully-made, English and French officer's swords and pistols.

Everyone was up and eating a hearty breakfast before dawn, on Sunday morning.

When the sun rose up over the Alleghany Mountains as a huge yellow ball, the Nuworlders were mostly in their canoes.

The cattle had been moved to safety. Overlordet Montour with eight other Nobles was astride the nine horses to ride upriver. The rest of the Nuworlders and the former captives canoed.

Since Overlord Trent's *Invincibles* had been the first Nuworlders in the fort, they had the honor of lighting the long fuses to blow it up. They lit them and paddled in haste upstream, to where the rest waited, for the show to begin.

Sure enough, the Nuworlders could see Asians, were high on the cliff overlooking the fort. Those folks would get a surprise!

Barron West had his coppix box and tripod on the shore, to get his pictures.

It was a fort burning to remember! There were numerous, thunderous explosions followed by the most extravagant, roaring fires any of them had ever seen.

That show of a lifetime ended forever the evil terror that had been emanating from that piously named, French "Fort Duquesne of the Blessed Virgin on the Beautiful River," for the past two horrible years of murders.

Well, the way they mounted their flag with extreme care, he thought it should be alright, leaving it there near the fort. Unlike cloth flags, it was held to a pole with a foot-long capped tube, being slipped loosely over a pole, a bracket extended out and attached to the circle at the top, and a few-inches-long attachment to the middle of the brass. All of that made it withstand strong winds and move about easily with the changing wind.

4

P addling the Ohio River upstream back to Kittanning, was slower than the other way, especially with the added burden of 53 released captives. Not all of those who were freed seemed happy with their new fate.

Paddling along, the Duke thought of the 354 enemies slain in their Kittanning battle. It was roughly one "knocked over" for each Noble, in the battle. He had killed 4 of them himself. Many of the enemy, of course, had been hit numerous times, by more than one deadly shot coming out of the Nobles' OdinGuns.

The Asian women sent away after the battle at Kittanning, would surely tell tales of the great disparity between the single death, of a Nuworld Noble, with the 100s of their own men killed. And they would possibly tell of the wonder, of the Nuworld flag.

But nearly 200 of those casualties had been the supposedly English-friendly Senecas; the largest of Asian tribes known, east of the Mississippi. The Duke had heard from Lord Andrew, that the Seneca had about 1,000 warriors. Well, they *formerly* had that many.

Lord Andrew told him the tribe would be in the deepest mourning, shocked at the loss of so many of their menfolk − husbands, sons, and brothers. But he didn't know for how long.

And anyway, were the Senecas simply visiting Kittanning, because the French were offering gifts, as they sometimes did? Or were they there to get in on the fun, and the excitement of butchering English settlers, and plundering their possessions, with the smallest risk to their own hides and scalps? None could guess, but the Seneca were certain to claim their innocence.

The sun was nearly down in the forest when they got back, to the former Delaware (properly, Lenni-Lenapes) Asian village of Kittanning.

Waiting on the Ohio River bank was Overlord George Croghan and his *Valiants* Battle Force. Overlady Annie Willing and her lovely Healthors were leaning out to see. The Duke's dear friends and partners, Barrons John Singleton Copley, Elias Tully, and Lord Doctor Benjamin Gale, were waving eagerly. Many released captives they, of course, didn't know, were also crowding the shore as well, to see them.

Their beautiful Nuworld brass flag – 2 feet in diameter—was flying up on a high pole.

Overlord Croghan was "all over" the Duke, bubbling with congratulations, and acting as though they had been separated a long time. But it had only been three days and two nights.

"Duke," Lord Croghan said right off, "that first savage you shot near the river—that was the notorious Ottawa-Frenchman, Ensign Charles Langlade. You remember, he was the brute that cut out the heart of Chief' Old Britain' at Pickawillnany. He cut that Chief's heart out and ate it, right then and right there. Langlade was the most brutish human being imaginable.

"The fellow behind him you also shot? That was another Ottawa, named Pontiac. It took only your two shots to kill those two beasts of men. Both of them, I knew, were very, very bad men," the most knowledgeable man of Asian affairs said.

At least 12 fires had been lit – an easy thing then with the Odin-Flamers the Duke had invented, and that Lord Tully had seen to, they were made and sold all over.

The Overlady urged the Duke to join her on a log by a fire, so she could tell him what had happened, while he was away.

"We were told by Overlord Croghan," she began as they both sat down, "that there was a danger our dead might be dug up, and scalped, so we had to bury Sir Francis Turbutt really deep. But it's so sad we had to leave him, in an unmarked grave. All the enemy dead were buried too, but not so deep. I'm told the Asians will forever avoid this place, because of their defeat.

"We saw those two savages you killed, up on the slope. The young Asian girl you had Sir Charles bring up to us Healthors, promptly ran off. We don't know what happened to her. It didn't seem right to shoot her in the back, as she fled. Possibly she left because of shame? Do you suppose so?" Overlady Willing asked.

"I have no idea on that one, Overlady," the Duke sighed.

"We Healthors were horrified to see so many dead men, all torn up from being shot; some of them had been hit lots of times. Those that you shot near the river, Milord – oh dear, that ugliest one was glaring up at us, with his head on backward. That was so terrible, so very chilling. But we understand Milord Odin, that this is war, and that these very men who were killed, have had no hesitation to kill, and mutilate, and cruelly torture, our innocent frontier people; even sometimes little children, we're told.

"And the tales we were told by the captives that were saved – well, such cruelty is hard to understand. Yet those same Asians can be as loving as any people, as we saw when we gave them the little boy, Sir Charles Thomson saved from the fire," she said.

"Milady, he's Lord Charles, now," he said and then added, "These people should not be our enemies. They should be part of us, Euros and Asians united for the benefit of all. I expect to help make that happen, so that our universal human genius, won't be wasted so terribly.

"Everyone has been given genius of one kind, or of several kinds, by Mother Nature, and it seems hardly anybody understands that. We are all miraculous geniuses. We are all creators. There can absolutely be no question about that fact; it seems to me," the Duke told her.

"That's an amazing statement, that everyone really is a genius, and a creator," she said.

"There's easy proof, Milady. Our Nuworld Company has 14 partners, and with encouragement, every single one of us has proved to be a profound genius, including myself. Even my Pops, a poor farmer, turns out to be a genius at getting men to do their best, working first in our iron mill, and then in our steam engine mill. It is truly amazing what my Pops has done, as it seems he's an ingenious manager – or leader—of men," he said.

"Lord Tully told me, Lord Rittenhouse is a genius, too," she said, seeming to have missed his mention of a steam engine mill.

"See what I mean? That ingenious fellow even discovered that water is not one single atomic element, but 2! Over and over again, in an exquisite experiment, he took water apart and put it back together again. He named the two elements – with Mr. Stiles help – Oxygen and Hydrogen. That bit of added knowledge proved immediately to benefit me, in designing our iron blast furnaces," the Duke said.

"I hope someday I can get to see what you, and your partners, have done over there in Stratford," she put in. "Oh, and I've noticed that Lord Montour, married to 2 lucky Asian girls, that he's a very handsome man, and could have come from England. Yet he's 3/4 Asian, I hear."

"And I assure you, he's a genius as well, although he had to be persuaded of it," the Duke told the Overlady.

"What about Overlord Croghan?" she asked.

"Oh, definitely! That man's a true marvel; really, a true marvel. He seems never to have met a human being; he didn't like. I've learned a lot from him, as I try to learn from everyone I meet. Oh I.... speak of the man.... here's his Lordship now," the Duke grinned.

Sure enough, Overlord Croghan came up just then with deliberation and said it was high time, both of them had something to eat.

"And anyway Duke, what are your plans for the morrow?" Lord Croghan asked.

To Duke Odin Bushnell, George Croghan, an immigrant from Ireland, with that "royal Irish name," was one of the most remarkable men on earth.

Partner Benjamin West had gone from Stratford to Philadelphia, in 1755, to recruit a very successful builder named Rhodes, to help build their city; to build it up from a Connecticut Colony village named Stratford. But the experienced builder rebuffed West, not wanting to take directions from a boy architect, who was just learning his way in the building business.

In a Philadelphia tavern, West was telling someone the tale of a legendary Asian named Hiawatha, who united the Iroquois tribes, and at the table next to him, were Croghan and Montour. Those two were both knowledgeable about the story, and they wanted to know how West knew. That meeting soon led to those two men being employed to help build mills, homes and so forth in Stratford. Both of those men had great ability "to get things done."

Croghan's Mohawk Asian wife had died, and his mother was then twice widowed, and taking care of his little daughter "Suky," back in Stratford.

Overlord Croghan verified the figures ritt by Lord Tully to Lord Rittenhouse. Amazingly, those messages went right through the air 40 miles away, over the earth's curvature. But oddly, ritting seemed to work well, only after dark.

Odin had invented a ship promptly dubbed an "OdinRaft," because a part of the square bottom of it was extended forward to just beyond the prow. That flat surface under the sea very much lessened the vessel pitching and rolling in a sea gone crazy. Also, the rudder was attached to the vessel's prow, instead of at the usual rear "steering end," the "stern."

On the OdinRaft the Duke had invented, and on which they sailed to and from the Caribbean, Rittenhouse had fastened close-together strips of every kind of metal he could find, onto the wooden side of it. That was to see what sort of reactions there might be between the metals in mildly acidic salt water. From this experiment with many metal strips, he deduced electrons flowed best from one lod plate to another, when in acidic seawater. From this came Rittenhouse's invention of electricity-storing "E-cells," which he continued to experiment with.

The Duke was asked by Overlord Croghan to tell again the tale of Nobility, as the 107 former captives had never heard it. Also, the

Nobles could do with hearing it again. After the Duke had eaten a bit of supper, they all gathered near a large tree stump which he jumped up on. Campfires were burning nearby, to light both him and the crowd.

Odin reminded himself again, to emulate the famous English actor-turned-preacher, Reverend George Whitefield. He and his Pops had witnessed that man twice, throwing out his nonsense oratory to huge crowds. But his hour or more of hollering out threats, of eternal hell after death, to his terribly, terribly sinful audience, didn't make sense to them. Many in Whitefield's audiences actually cried, from taking such a verbal beating, by that man's roared-out words.

His Pops had said it was unlikely most people would remember what that famous man said, but they could never forget the man who said it.

"He was like a woodsman swinging an ax," his Pops had said, "for he speaks from the toes up." That was how the Duke intended always to speak to crowds; from the toes up.

"Dear people!" Odin roared, with his tiredness suddenly gone. "You civilians should know why we call ourselves, the Nuworld Nobility.

"Everyone can see the Nuworld map at the top of our arms, as though we are seen from the moon, just above our names – *so that no Noble will ever forget that his or hers, is the sacred trust of being one, to do away with wrongness; for we are each a Nuworld warrior.*

"I must tell you, that some seem to think that I invented the Nobility, and I wish to assure you the idea of Nobility, was invented long ages, before there was any writing to record it.

"But in the centuries past, the idea of Nobility has been perverted, twisted, and unbelievably corrupted, by European regimes. Wow! Even babies can inherit titles over there, that they could not possibly have earned.

"I've read that in snobbish France, no Nobleman is recognized as such until seven undeserving generations have elapsed, since the first one may, in fact, have earned a title; I've been assured that this is true. And that – please excuse the very old but crude expression –

that is strictly B.S., and everyone knows what it means! A Nobleman or Noblewoman must be forthright, truthful, faithful and more – NOBLE – NO... BULL!

"When the partners in the Nuworld Company, agreed to back me in forming our Battle Forces, I decided not to form an 'army', for that term comes from using weapons that are extensions of men's arms; such as spears, clubs, javelins, pikes, swords – weapons we will never use.

"Nor would I create a 'navy,' because that word comes from regarding Rome as the belly button of the world – the navel – and ships going to and from Rome, as their navy. But I say the earth has enough belly buttons already!" he shouted with a big smile.

The whole crowd reacted with laughter to that "belly button" statement.

Duke Odin went on: "Digging in many books, it was fascinating to find that most army and navy titles, are in truth, insulting.

"The title 'General' is said to have come from Spain; the King there finding a far superior leader, that he logically should have made a Duke or even a Prince. He instead said perhaps, 'You're in charge of my forces in general, speaking generally, so we'll call you 'General.' Why? Simply because that very good leader, was born as a mere commoner, and the King didn't wish to disturb the political backing, of his inherited aristocracy, by giving a Noble title to someone who actually deserved it. *This was, of course, a large pile of B.S.*

"To give an idea of the worth of the title of General, France has in its army about 200 'battalions'—which is Italian for 'big battle'—with about 500 soldiers in each battalion. Since France has about 25,000 career officers, that's 125 officers for each battalion!

"And 3,000 of those French officers are Generals; of which 12 are Marshalls of France! There are 15 Generals for each and every battalion! A plain General tops other Generals, even Major Generals. And all European countries copy the French, especially the English.

"The title of General, *incredibly, and all other Officer titles* can actually be purchased – and is, from their King; even for children. Merit has nothing whatsoever, to do with it. *All of us can see this is more, of that awfully smelly B. S.*

"What of top-ranking navy men? 'Admiral' comes straight from the Arabic' Emir-al,' a leader of pirates, who still do capture European Christians as slaves, in the Mediterranean Sea. Such a compliment! Is a Vice Admiral in charge of vice? How naughty! Does a Rear Admiral have much to do with rears? So nasty! *So much more bull!*

"What about Captain? As the head man – which the word means – he might command on a warship, 1,000 men or more; or like my darling Captain father – I call him my Pops—he might command a gigantic militia company, of 50 or 60 men!

"And Colonel? That title is pronounced 'kernel,' which is from 'coron-el,' meaning little crown; that was what bodies of fighting men, long ago, awarded a successful leader. We now have crowns for leadership, for courage and for merit, which we award, to our deserving Nobles.

"But the King who wore then, the really big crown, wished to have no others wearing any crown at all, so he changed the title "Coronel" to 'Colon-el,' meaning 'little column.' Certainly, that is *more B.S., for Colonel could mean nothing more, than a porch post.*

"The title 'Major' comes from 'Sergeant Major' and officers don't like to be called a lowly servant – which sergeant means in French – so the title was pushed down to the lower ranks, leaving only 'Major.' *But Major what? We needn't say it, but we know what that is.*

"Then you have 'Lieutenant,' the 'lieu' part meaning instead-of and the 'tenant' part meaning the same, so a Lieutenant is really an 'instead of – instead of'!

"An Ensign is a little flag; not exactly a flattering title for a leader of men.

"Sergeant, as I said, means servant and all of us should be servants of others, some way.

"Corporal comes from Latin, meaning a body; and since everybody has a body, it's hardly an appropriate title.

"Then comes 'Private'; and in an army, the least private person possible. It makes no sense except that in Europe, the 'King's Privates' is what they are called, and it is definitely meant to be degrading.

"King's Privates are considered to be the very scum of the earth, as dirty as their whore-bedding monarch's unwashed, filthy private parts; as dirty as their King's own privates!

"We all know the right words to use here!

"Oh yes, I mentioned Marshalls of France, but the French spell it more correctly as 'Mareschal,' meaning horse servant—a stable groom—a high honor indeed!"

The Duke paused, looking over the mostly surprised faces all around, for he had only told all of this before, to his partners and to the recruits, in the training camp at his Cornwall mines.

"Also, the word 'soldier' comes from old Rome," he continued. "Those very rich Patrician, slave-owning, land-hogging, Roman Senators, were belittling the men of their Legions. Their men finally insisted on being paid, instead of with cheap salt as their 'salary' (from the word salt), they wished to be paid in gold coins, called 'Solidarius.' Soldiers were wrongly named as though mercen–Aries... for the coin, they should have been paid with.

"As they paraded by, those rich men again insulted them by referring to the complainers as crybabies, merely infants: 'infantry'! Infantrymen are, therefore, 'crybaby men'!

"A 'Company' used to be a number of mercenaries, organized to fight for the highest bidder, for profits, of course, the same as civilian men in business.

"A 'Platoon' means a big plot of ground, 'squad' means square which it, of course, is not, and squadron means big square, which it also is not. I'd have guessed 'regiment' means Regio's men, but it only means 'governed by rules.' Even 'legion' merely meant, a collection of men.

"What about 'sailors'? Why, anybody can be a sailor, a mariner, a marine; there's no distinction to it at all. Even the title 'Knight' is hardly flattering, for it came long ago from the Saxon sound 'k-nig-hit,' bringing night – eternal darkness – death – to some innocent, by a k-nave with his deadly long sword, his k-nife.

"So just naturally, knowing the contemptuous meanings behind those titles, I refused to use any of them. Rather, I have established the Nuworld Nobility with 18 ranks for the excellent, and honorable, *very Noble-men* and *very Noble-women,* who dedicate their precious lives to destroy the evil snakes of wrongness. *Noble, all of us can believe, means no-bull.*

"None of these titles shall ever be inherited or purchased at any price. We add the 'ess' onto a title strictly for the wife of a Noble, with no one else to be affected.

"Someone asked me why the double-R in Barronet and Barron? I know it's correct because it's carved in stone that way, over a church entrance in Leicestershire, England. That church was founded in 1653, by Robert Shirley, BARRONET.

"Also, Queen Elizabeth, in about the year 1583, made an extraordinary judge a Barron. But as he was Irish, the title wasn't inheritable. So, he passed the honorable title on to following genera-tions, as the surname Barron. *No bull."*

The Duke wound up his "little educational speech" then:

"Now that I hope to have cleared up the fact, I absolutely did not invent the idea of Nobility; and I see the sky has cleared, and Mother Nature's stars are shining down on us, so we should all get much-needed rest.

"On the morrow, we shall head upstream. The Nuworld Nobility has combed away the nest of snakes here at Kittanning and combed them away at the fort full of vipers, called Duquesne. We must also comb away Fort Machault at Venango upstream; then Fort LeBoef further on and lastly, Fort Presque Isle at Lake Erie. Only then shall we go back over those 'mountains—many,' the Alleghanys.

"One more thing: We Nuworlders understand you released captives have lost all of your possessions, so I want to assure all of you, that you will be given enough money when we reach Phil-adelphia, to start a new life.

"Have a good rest!" Duke Odin said and stepped down off the stump.

The Duke laid down later, to sleep on the grass, but not before thanking Mother Nature, as he did frequently, for allowing him to escape the sinful brutality, of the English navy.

$$\begin{array}{ccc} \text{❦} & 5 & \text{❧} \end{array}$$

Duke Odin Bushnell woke well before dawn, from his farmer's habit.

It was Monday, September 6th, 1756.

By starlight, he took a quick bath in the Ohio. He put on clean underwear and fresh stockings. Just as the dawn broke, he drank freshly-made coffee they had got from the French and ate newly baked bread. The bread was particularly satisfying, as it was loaded with raisins, walnuts, and cinnamon. The bread was almost as sweet as the cake, invented by the Overlady.

Overlady Annie Willing had told him the folding ovens, and the grills, hauled on the packhorses' backs, were quite satisfactory.

"Also, Duke," she had said, "we have about enough food, with the captured stuff here from Kittanning—enough left, I think for two weeks. That is even considering the added 105 former captives to feed."

She showed him a list of wheat and corn flour, dried peas, dried beans, raisins, walnuts, sugar, two full jugs of molasses, coffee, salt, pepper and cinnamon, the pack horses were still burdened with. In addition, they had gained from the various dwellings, and storage of the Delawares in Kittanning, considerable corn on the cobs and three kinds of beans.

The pots and pans for cooking and baking were also plentiful. The Nuworlders had recaptured many varied utensils, stolen from murdered frontier folks.

Then he was told several of the best canoes, needed patching before they could leave. Several canoes had been damaged when used as ladders, against the stockade at Fort Duquesne.

They had a 2-day trip upstream ahead of them to Venango which Lord Andrew said was nearly 60 miles on the wandering river. But most likely, it was about 40 miles or so, as the goose goes, to the envy of all mankind, on his pretty wings.

No one had to tell the Duke that some of the newly released men and women, would wish to hurry back over the mountains, what with the French forts being none of their concern.

The delay in leaving gave him a chance to inform them of the dangers. He put out a call for all who weren't busy with the canoes, to gather around the stump, he had spoken from before.

"Dear people!" Duke Odin boomed again, "I believe everyone here is entitled to know why we are going to continue upriver.

"First of all, it is why the Nuworld Nobility was formed, and what so many brave and outstanding men and women, have dedicated themselves to do.

"But another thing is this mighty OdinGun," he said, pulling it out of his holster at his hip, and holding the pretty, gold-like, brass weapon up for all to see.

"All of us Nobles know the power of this gun, that we can shoot deadly shots great distances. And we can shoot 6 or 7 or even eight times, while an enemy is reloading his terribly inaccurate, and weaker musket, once.

"We knocked over nearly 200 Senecas here the other day, but a few of that tribe were seen to slip into the woods, and disappear. So, we can be sure Seneca war chiefs are well informed of what happened. I've been told they will be in deepest mourning for their losses, for perhaps a week or 2; nobody knows how long they might mourn, for sure.

"Certainly, they will desperately want to get possession of these weapons of ours, for they are easily as smart as us, and they understand the power of our OdinGuns very well. If we were to go back over those mountains trails now, stretched out single file for 1½ miles, as we must, we'd be extremely vulnerable to ambush, again and again, and again. We all know those Asian warriors have sharpened great skills in the woods, over the centuries.

"So, we shall continue on as planned, and I expect we shall pick the time, and the place for a reckoning with them, instead of allowing the Senecas, their deadly advantage. We might just ambush the ambushers! Now, onto your assigned canoes or horses!" he shouted.

They were soon on their way upstream, 471 of them, mostly by canoe, and some riding along the river bank.

At noon, they stopped at a meadow, in a loop in the river, which was easy to defend. They rested, ate, and proceeded upstream after a while, to a similar spot by evening. That spot was said by Overlord Croghan, to be more than half of their way to Venango.

Only the ovens were set up for the baking of bread for supper, and molasses sweet cakes for breakfast.

Deer, elk, bear, buffalo, grass-eating geese, and other creatures had grazed in that meadow, from times unknown.

The 5 Battle Forces made a ring of Noble guardians, around the encampment, with Healthors and civilians in the center.

Duke Odin and Arch Duket Andrew, toured the circle to reassure themselves, and the others, of their security for the night.

During the day, "eyes in the woods" had now and then been spotted, and the Nuworlders were very much alert, to being watched.

Asian warriors supposedly never attack at night, for the very good reason they couldn't see what they were doing. Some snickered in disrespect of their prowess that besides, too many scary spirits were out and about, after dark. But it would be utterly stupid to assume the Asian warriors never would attack during darkness if they thought it was somehow to their advantage.

Beyond the meadow, the dense and eternal forest was right there. So, some men's imaginations were thinking that, in hiding there, were every savage on the continent, and perhaps whole French armies. *The Nuworlders kept wary.*

They had thought to bring only six small tents for the wounded. But not having that need, women, and children, were housed in them at night.

Overlady Annie Willing brought the Duke a cup of coffee, well-sugared, and two slices of the usual delicious, freshly made bread.

"Milord," she said, "you explained again last night, that you didn't invent the Nobility; very well, I'll accept that. But I've been told that most of these former frontiersmen that you've made into Nobles were the roughest, toughest, hell-raising rascals on earth. They were forever using God's name in vain irreligiously, wrestling, fist fighting, getting drunk – all that and more. Now they are completely different. They seem to me to be truly Nobles, in every respect.

"And I must say, our Noble*women* are equally noble, with no naughtiness about any of them. I'm so very, very grateful to you, Duke Odin, for giving me the wonderful opportunity to serve this worthy cause, with such good people," Overlady Annie Willing said.

For no reason at all, the Duke felt uneasy when she came so close. He was wary of her as Lord Elias had told him, "Those women who are so perfect and beautiful, they seem to cast spells on men. It's maybe not witchcraft exactly, but awfully close to it. Homely women are the truest kind."

He mumbled an answer to her, about that. "It is I who should be grateful, for you've been a great help. I still can't get over your shooting skill. Do you suppose your blue eyes see better than my brown eyes?"

She smiled as she rose up and walked away. "My, my Duke; I'm surprised you noticed I have any eyes at all!"

Eighteen-year-old Odin Bushnell puzzled over that remark while bedding down for the night. Women – especially porcelain dolls – were, well—they were beyond understanding.

Then he thanked Mother Nature again, for saving him from the English navy, as he sought some sleep.

The next afternoon, September 7th, 1756, they had got to but a few miles from the old Asian village of Venango, when they saw dark smoke billowing into the sky ahead. That was much unexpected.

When they got within sight of the village, and of the French Fort Machault, they saw everything was afire; even the few wagons and carts there were aflame.

Taking Overlord Morgan, and some of his *Gators* on a scout with him, the Duke forded the Ohio easily. They rode their horses all around the fires, finding not a person present. The French had left them nothing to do, "saving their honor" by destroying their own possessions.

The Nuworlders galloped back over the river, with the satisfaction that their enemy understood the power, of those handsome brass contrivances, on their hips. The Nuworlders had only to put up their beautiful Nuworld circular brass flag, on a tall pole.

The Frenchies had done the hard part.

At that place, the Ohio River bends nearly 90 degrees, to the north. There was a grassy pasture used by the French for their horses, and where wild things had no doubt grazed for centuries. It was a defensible space in which to set up camp. An extensive and well-dried split rail fence made by the French would provide plenty of excellent firewood.

The Duke called the 5 Battle Force Overlords, Overlady Annie and his Nuworld Company partners to a meeting.

"Overlordet Montour will be in charge here, during my absence," the Duke told them. "Lord Andrew, you are to set up a defense perimeter of Overlord Morgan's *Gators,* Overlord Armstrong's *Bravehearts,* Overlord Trent's *Invincibles* and Overlord Lamb's *Defiants.* You may be here for several days. All of you must keep watch for those 'eyes in the woods.'

"No one but Barron Rittenhouse thought to bring a spyglass, but all of you can use it. So, I want someone at all times to inconspicuously scan that forest, with that telescope, to try and estimate how many enemies there might be to attack us.

"I noticed one of the packhorse mares, is getting more and more lame. We need the meat, so she must be turned into roasts. We know there are animals in the area, but we durst not hunt. Overlady

Willing, your Healthors will need to bake lots of bread, and sweet cakes, for the journey back to Kittanning; and then back over those many mountains, we must trek to the east.

"Overlord Croghan with but a few of his *Valiants* will go with me to make sure the other 2 French forts are destroyed; either by them or by us. We'll leave at sunup, and we will be gone for at least two days; but longer, if we must burn those forts ourselves," he said.

There was no thought of taking Lord Charles Thomson as he was a poor rider. Nor could they use the ritt system, to send messages, as the E-cells were too heavy for fast riding.

Barron Copley would go with them, however, bringing his coppix box to make pictures.

Knowing some – especially Overlord Morgan – would feel slighted at not being asked to go along, the Duke pointed out their danger.

"Lord Andrew, you Nobles defending these precious people here, have by far the most dangerous task. You are more likely to be attacked by the vengeful Senecas, with some Nobles gone. That's why I've selected those with great fighting spirit for this duty here. Let us hope the mourning period of the Senecas, might last until we return. Then, with fully five strong Battle Forces together, we can deal with them," the Duke said.

They had enough time before dark to tend their rides for the next day. They set aside for them, some of the remaining supply of oats.

Then when the sun buried itself gloriously in the forest to the west, most Nobles bathed and shaved in the river. The OdinRazor was easier than the old straight razors, to shave with at any time, but especially when they had no use of a mirror. Duke Odin had forbidden any degree of facial hair, to be worn by any Noble. Nor could any Noble wear their hair long. The Noblewomen could wear their hair, any pretty way they pleased, he had told them.

The Duke thanked Mother Nature again, for his freedom from slavery, in the English navy. He rested for the hard days, he knew were ahead.

All 35 Nobles for the expedition were mounted at first light. But instead of fording the Ohio, they first charged hell-bent-for-break-fast into the woods where spies had been seen.

Sure enough, they rousted four young Senecas, painted for war, who were too slow coming up with their muskets. They were instantly torn apart, with the Noblemen's shots.

The Nuworlders then swung their mounts quickly, back through the camp, and over the river. Several fires were still burning, where Fort Machault had been.

Overlord Croghan was familiar with the territory, along their route beside Buffalo Creek. He pointed out things to the Duke that he might have missed, being wary of ambush.

There were salt springs, and salt was extremely important for human use, especially for the preservation of food. And here was salt brine, coming right up out of the ground!

The Duke had noticed iron ore and coal occasionally, along the Pennsylvania Colony roads. And there were more of those invaluable minerals along the Buffalo Creek they were following. It was a creek that pretty much dried up, he was told, for much of the year.

Croghan pointed out a mysterious gas flame, burning in a marshy field. At another spot, oil springs were bubbling up amazingly, out of the earth. The Duke was very impressed with these sights and made mental notes about them. He figured the value of them to the future nation, could very well be extremely important. Petroleum was coming right up out of the ground, and to him, that meant there must be a lot of the stuff below, that could be pumped out. Petroleum, he speculated to himself, could possibly be, just about everywhere under their continent.

It was said to be about 40 miles from their Venango camp to Fort LeBoef. The French had named the fort after the creek they were riding along. It was an area known for the animals that lived near the creek – buffalo or bison; but to the French, boef = beef.

Lord Montour had said the local buffalo, which mostly hid in the forest, were rather smaller, than those which spread over the far away western plains, in impossibly large herds.

Forty miles is a good day's ride on the back of a bounding horse anytime, but doing so constantly wary of danger, making it more of a strain. Even so, they were careful to water and rest their horses, to graze them a bit at noon, and to not push them too hard.

However, the French had lavished much attention on that rather good dirt road they were following. There were no hills along the way to climb, that would slow them down.

It was clear their mission was well-known since they saw no sign of humans; not even eyes in the woods. There were fresh tracks aplenty though on that road, of horses and wagons, since the French had skedaddled the day before.

By mid-afternoon, clouds of smoke were well-formed, ahead of them a few miles. And arriving at the site of Fort LeBoef, they found an inferno. Even the outbuildings were ablaze.

Overlord Croghan rode to the other side of the fort and reported the French had left about half a day before. They had burnt both carts and wagons, so as to ride well ahead of the Nuworlders.

The Duke had seen on maps captured at Fort Duquesne, that Fort Presque Isle, at Lake Erie, was perhaps 12 or so miles further on, and pretty nearly, straight north. Not one of the Nuworlders had ever been there; not even Overlord Croghan.

Ezra Stiles voiced his opinion that if they rested, and watered the horses, and let them graze for about an hour, they could reach that place by dark.

So, that is what they did, with Overlord Croghan telling them about his experiences further west along Lake Erie, back in his trading days. Those times were when he had much happiness, dealing with a variety of Asian tribes. The various tribal peoples were equally happy to purchase things, impossible for them to make, and which were superior in quality, and lower in price, than the French offerings.

But the French army had destroyed Croghan's businesses and killed or captured many of his employees. That had been the beginning of this latest, "Third French and Indian War."

Lake Erie had been named for the large tribe, which occupied the territory south of that pretty body of fresh water. However, that tribe had often called themselves, "Arragahas." Stiles said he had supposed they didn't wish to admit they were partly mixed with the

Eastern folk of Siberia *(that is, Sib-Aria – siblings to Aries, the Whites.)* Perhaps that tribe had not been so very much mixed with tan people and called themselves "Eries," meaning "Aries" – white people. Asian peoples did vary considerably, in the lightness of their skin. That was despite being their whole lives, exposed to the sun.

The name of that tribe became the name of a Great Lake. To the Euro Nuworlders, all of those folks whose ancestors came from Asia in the Old World, an awfully long time before, were properly called Asians.

But 100 years or so, before the Duke and his Nobles came to this spot, the Iroquois had surprised, and utterly destroyed that tribe, called "Eries." They then took over all the females and slaughtered their males. They did this dastardly thing supposedly, because of the Eries (or Arragahas) being neutral in the Iroquois war, with the Huron tribe, across that very lake. But more probably, they surprised and slaughtered the men of that tribe, simply because they could.

The Iroquois thereby eliminated a potential competitor, in the profitable beaver pelt trading business, with the newly arriving Euros, from Europe. An added benefit to them, was the increase in child-bearing females, to greatly increase the numbers of Senecas.

That Iroquois demonstration of their great power sent a chill of fear running down the backs of every other Asian tribe, for great distances around.

Surely that had happened countless times before, all over the continent. Only the wariest, strong *and lucky* tribes, survived over time, just as had happened, everywhere in the Old World.

The Duke and his Nobles lit out for the last of the French forts. As they neared it, the sun was beginning to set through lacy, frilly clouds over Lake Erie, putting the western sky fabulously ablaze. Being reflected on the tranquil Lake Erie made the sunset even more spectacular.

As they charged on, mindful of using the last of their horse's energy, they could see Fort Presque Isle was still standing.

But then they saw men in boats and canoes, approaching Lake Erie, from the bay defined by a long, embracing, left-arm-like sandbar.

The Duke and his Nobles slowed down cautiously, and sure enough, when they were within half a mile of the fort, the left-behind fuses blew.

The fort exploded with a tremendous blast, with fire shooting up into the sky to their front. It was as though that fire was trying to equal, the fantastic show Mother Nature's setting sun was putting on at the same time to the west, over that next-to-smallest of the Great Lakes.

Duke Odin stopped his Nobles right there. They had actually destroyed 3 French forts without so much as unholstering, their gold-like OdinGuns!

Merely by their presence, by the threat of the deadly brass they carried in their holsters, those evil-harboring forts, had vanished from their Nuworld earth.

And the French had somehow, in each case, preserved their very great "honor," by destroying those places themselves.

Tired as they were, the Duke organized guards for the usual 2-hour stints during the night. They erected their flag and hobbled their horses, to feed on the abundant grass. The French had apparently driven their own horses into the woods, for they were not to be seen.

Dawn found the Nuworlders riding hard to the south, and then east, with the morning air cool and dry.

A 50 or maybe 60-mile trip on horseback – their bodies already racked from the same ride the day before – was a challenge to each of them. That was to say nothing, of the well-worn animals, that bore such demanding burdens.

But the terrain was flat, with no hills or even slight rises to contend with, and the road was rather good. Fresh, clean water and nicely green grass for their 35 horses was available next to the trail, the whole time.

The French had lavished considerable effort on the road, for hauling things back and forth between Lake Erie, and the Ohio River. Using the adjacent Buffalo Creek was more efficient for hauling things like cannons, but the water was often too low to float the heavy French bateaus, let alone with those oaken boats, loaded with cargo.

There was a real urgency to the Nuworlder's galloping, as they worried about their people, left at Venango.

They paused fairly often during the day, caring for the horses, coming down out of their saddles now and then, and of course, always on their guard.

They passed Fort LeBoef, with its fires still smoldering. They saw their beautiful circular Nuworld flag was yet swinging this way and that, in the wind, as the breeze picked up speed.

Near dark, 3 of their 35 horses gave out. They simply stopped in their tracks, unable to proceed. Stiles told the Duke they must stop awhile, and then walk those beasts slowly, the last 5 miles or so. Otherwise, those horses would surely die.

They had great need of those animals, as they were a long way from safety, over the Alleghanys. The weary men walked their horses into the camp and were greeted by blazing fires and welcoming friends.

The exhausted Nobles of the hard riding were allowed to rest the night, with no guard duty. They could bathe in the river, wash some clothes, and of course eat heartily.

They put on clean underwear and stockings, but they had no change, in boots or buckskins.

There was plenty of freshly baked bread, from the flour brought along, and from the captured stores from Kittanning.

They also had roasted "horsey-beef," as a little boy called it. The horse meat did indeed taste like beef, to the non-squeamish.

The Duke and Overlordet Montour exchanged reports. The camp had not been disturbed those past days. But they had spied plenty of "eyes in the woods," especially across the river.

There was a slope going up to a forest, on the other side of the river, that the French had mostly cleared of trees, to build their fort. They had built their stockade, and split rail fencing, from those cut-down trees, several years before. Above that slope, the woods were untouched, and observers had been seen up there.

Lord Andrew told the Duke, that he was feeling certain, because of the number seen, that the Senecas had mourned their losses, long enough.

That fairly close slope had interested the Duke before. There was a few years' worth of new growth there. It was by then, more or less covered with bushes. So, the Duke supposed, a wise old Seneca war chief would think it a great place to hide his warriors for an attack. Aha!

As the Duke the next morning dunked his bread in hot coffee, Overlady Willing came by.

"Milord, we've learned a new song while you were gone. Would you like to hear it?" she asked him.

"A new song?" he asked in surprise.

"Yes Duke, and I should introduce to you, the young man who taught it to us. Sir Francis," she called out to a young Noble lad, standing nearby, "would you come here, please?"

She introduced him as the very first graduate, of the brand-new College of Philadelphia. He was 18 years old, and the son of a lawyer in that bustling city. He seemed a little nervous, about average height, and was a good-looking fellow. He was in Overlord Lamb's *Defiant* Battle Force, and the Duke had, of course, seen him many times.

"Sir Francis Hopkinson," Overlady Annie said, "please tell the Duke about your song."

The lad had begun as a Barronet, but with the two battles he had been in, he then had "Arch Barronet" sleeves over his shoulder straps. One more fight and the lad would be a Barron; a "Lord of Battles."

Soon there would be no more Barronets, male or female; and no more Sirs or Dames, until new Esquires were recruited, and made into Noble Commissioned Officers.

"Yes, Milady," Hopkinson nodded to her. "Milord, I began to write this song back at the Cornwall Mines. But it's not entirely original with me. The melody is based on that old English tune, "God Save the King." Would you like to hear it, Duke?"

"Yes, of course," the Duke told the lad.

"Overlord, I taught the Healthors to sing that same lovely

melody, to my lyrics. So, if they may, they'd like to sing it for you now," Hopkinson said.

It was a surprise to the Duke as Overlady Annie formed a semi-circle of 4 Noblewomen to her left, and 4 to her right. Sir Francis stood in front of them to direct.

They started the song, singing in the same spiritual-feeling way, the "God Save the King" tune was sung, by the English; including those English in the Colonies:

"This is our Nuworld, our very free Nuworld,

"Our Brightest Rich Part of the Whole World.

"So Nobility, Nobility, protect us all from harm,

"And honor us, with righteousness,

"In city, sea, and farm!"

Everyone nearby applauded heartily for it was sung very well. The Duke could hardly carry a tune himself, and rarely even hummed, but he thought he could handle that one. He asked them to sing it twice more; and they did so, *beautifully*.

"Milord," Hopkinson said, "I've been working on other verses, but that's as far as I've got so far. Do you really like it, sir?"

"Like it, Sir Francis? I certainly do, and you've just won yourself an eleven-feathered Gold Crown for Merit! I hope you'll teach that song to everyone. Now, I must call a meeting for we have some other, fairly important business today," the Duke told the Arch Barronet.

As a Secret-Airie, Barron Charles Thomson was proving worthwhile after all. The Duke had him make a note about the Hopkinson Gold Crown for Merit, and to call Lord Andrew, and the 5 Force Overlords to a meeting, off to one side, by the Ohio River.

6

When they arrived, the Duke had them stand with their backs to the water and facing him.

"Lords, you should look over the scene behind me now, and also during the day," he began, "without being obvious about it.

"Where the river turns abruptly north, you will notice on the other side of it, the extensive slope that's been cleared of trees. It now has a lot of bushes all over it.

"We are going to entice the Senecas to attack us, from those brushy hiding places, on that slope, tomorrow morning. We'll make it easy for them to decide to do that. About mid-afternoon today, we will start back for Kittanning, to take the trail back over those Alleghany Mountains. That is, we will all start back except for one Battle Force, which will stay the night, and canoe up the Beautiful River at dawn. Then we will...."

"Yes Milord, Duke!" Arch Countet Daniel Morgan burst out. "We *Gators* will be the bait! Yes, Duke Odin! We'll do it!"

"Overlord Morgan," the Duke scolded, "I was going to have you gentlemen draw straws for this very dangerous mission. But I'll tell you what – when you hear the remainder of my plan; you may change your mind, and not be so generous with the lives of your Nobles."

"Oh yes sir, I understand what you're saying," he actually smiled as though he had given himself great honor, "but I tell you, Duke, my *Gators* are spoiling for a fight!"

"Dammit Overlord Morgan, we all are! Now then, as I had begun to say, we are being watched," the Duke continued. "The Seneca tribe supposedly has now, about 800 warriors. We can bet that every one of them, is probably ready to risk his neck, to gain possession of an OdinGun, and the ammunition to go with it.

"Lord Andrew thinks it unlikely they'll get other Iroquois tribes to join them, as they'll want to keep the war power of our golden guns, to themselves.

"So, all of this put together, means we bring catastrophe to them here, and soon, or we will likely have disaster brought upon our heads, when we're spread out single file for 1½ miles, going over those Alleghanys, those mountains after mountains.

"We mustn't tell the others of this plan. Keep it secret. We will be all set to leave later today, and I'll stand up on that log over there (he pointed), and speak to everyone.

"I'll be extremely animated, making wild gestures and so forth, so that those watching from the woods, will hopefully grasp the meaning of what I'm saying.

"Then we will leave downriver, some by canoe, and some horsed *except for the hasty volunteer, Arch Countet Daniel Morgan, and his feisty Gators.*

"As we leave, Overlord Morgan's Force will have to make themselves as secure as possible, for the night. They will do that because at dawn; they are to paddle around that bend, and north up the Ohio. They'll be making themselves vulnerable, to a rushing attack, by 100s of screaming devils coming at them, with muskets blazing, and tomahawks, and arrows, and spears, and axes flying at them like hail in a windstorm!"

Amazingly, Morgan was grinning at what the Duke said.

"However," Duke Odin continued, "during the night, 3 of the 4 Forces downstream will return, on foot and as quietly as possible, to this spot, and take positions over there up that sharp grassy bank, rising on this side of the river.

"I imagine that little ridge has been pushed upon the bank, about 7 or 8 feet, in a single year, or over many years, by ice piling up short of the river bend. Anyway, it's a pretty safe place to face the Senecas from, where grass has grown on it.

"My estimate is that we can pretty easily hide, 190 Nobles along that ridge, ready to fire the instant all hell itself, begins to fall, on our gallant *Gators*.

"Please now, during the day, take stock of that place without being obvious, and mind the markers I give you to guide your Nobles by.

"Overlord Croghan, your *Valiants* will spread out on the left of that ridge, shoulder to shoulder. Overlord Armstrong, your *Bravehearts,* will take the center. Overlord Lamb, your *Defiants* will keep to the right.

"And Overlord Trent, just about the fightingest Noble alive, will have the very great responsibility, with his *Invincibles,* of guarding our precious Healthors, and those civilians. Have you any questions, gentlemen?"

Later, wouldn't you know, the muscular Welshman just had to confide in the Duke.

"Naturally Milord Odin, I knew you'd have a clever scheme up your sleeve," Morgan smiled at the Duke.

"Oh? Really, Lord Daniel? Let's hope that scheme isn't so clever; you end up just awfully dead," the Duke told him most soberly.

Nearly everyone relaxed during the morning, more or less lazily making preparations for leaving. It would certainly be obvious from the forest, that they were doing so.

Lord Andrew reminded the Duke that 200 years before, "He-who-combs" – "Hiawatha" had a vision up that Ohio, at the beginning of the Beautiful River, in a beaver pond, and the man united the five Iroquois tribes.

At mid-day, all those hungry people had finished off the last of the meat, from the unfortunate packhorse mare.

By mid-afternoon, figuring the timing to be somewhat reasonable to those "eyes in the woods," the entire entourage was gathered around the chosen log.

Morgan had his Nobles a little separate, with 5 of the larger, gleaming white, birch bark canoes directly at hand, so the Duke could point to those Nobles, and their canoes, as he spoke. There would be 12 or 13 Nobles to each of those largest canoes.

As the Duke stood tall on the log roaring out not much sense, but waving his arms and pointing as though, in high drama, everyone was staring at him, as he intended. He indicated with his gestures, that the *Gators* would be paddling around the Ohio bend, and upstream for some distance. Some of the children watched the Duke in wonder, thinking he had gone quite mad with his silly gestures. But the intent was anything but humorous.

That was on Friday afternoon, September 10th, 1756, and all but Overlord Morgan and his Nobles moved out.

But they were having much less than perfect weather. There were thick clouds forming, but at least there was no rain; anyway, there was no rain coming down just yet.

The Duke reckoned that stopping about 5 miles downstream, in a defensible loop in the river, was far enough. They rested and slept, including the tired Duke.

A touch on the shoulder woke him. Ah; he saw it was Lord Andrew.

"Seems to me," his Overlordet said as the Duke brushed away the sleep, "it's about time to leave, Duke Odin. It's a couple of hours past midnight, and that gives us 3 ½ to 4 hours, 'til first light of morn."

"Right you are, Milord. You got some sleep?" the Duke asked him.

"Not much. Worried about Morgan. Hope he wasn't too rash in volunteering," the handsome man of 3/4 Asian blood said.

"Don't worry about Daniel Morgan, my friend; he's a sharp one. It does no good to worry anyway. Morgan instructed them that at the instant they are attacked; they must jump into that river because the water is about 4 feet deep there. Even if their OdinGuns get wet, they can still shoot, and they should be fairly safe from enemy fire while barely showing themselves above the water," Duke David Odin Bushnell said.

The 3 Nuworld Battle Forces sneaked back in the darkness whence they came, with the utmost caution, and in utter silence. All of the Nobles would have their OdinGuns loaded and ready to fire.

Odin estimated that their shots could reach lethally far beyond the other side of the Ohio River at that point and some way up that brush-covered slope.

Of course, very few of the present Nobles had, before coming to the training camp at the Cornwall Mines, any experience with marksmanship. No muskets in use in any Army, even had sights on them, since you could only more or less guess, where a musket ball might go, beyond about 50 yards.

At the camp in the Cornwall Mines, Odin had them measure off with large stakes, 200 yards, then 300, 400 and even 500 yards. That was so everyone could get a feeling for those distances. The rear open sight on his OdinGun was stepped, to mark off the distance in yards the weapon would shoot. Actually, even at 500 yards, the shot dropped surprisingly little, because of its high velocity, done by the tapered bore of the OdinGun.

A light breeze from the west cleared the sky of possible rain clouds. So, they had the barest amount of starlight to find their positions on the short, sharp, grass-covered ridge. The ridge was roughly 7 or 8 feet nearly straight up, from the river's side of it, but sloped well on the other side as they climbed up the grass.

Then began the seemingly long wait to dawn as they maintained absolute quiet. They strained to listen to the rustling of leaves, from the westerly breeze. They could also hear the gurgling of water rippling by, in the O! Hio!—"The Beautiful River."

At last, they could hear Morgan's *Gators,* splashing their canoes into the water. Then they could just barely make, out the nearly silent dipping of paddles.

Peeking over the top of the ridge, with grass tickling his face, the Duke strained to see the canoes. Morgan apparently became a little anxious, pushing off as the sky began to lighten.

Odin could no more than sense that they were in the river, but could not see.... oh, there they were, the dim outlines of canoes and men.... ah the sky was indeed a tiny bit light.... and distant clouds to their east began glowing red with dawn... *BANG!*

A musket shot rang out directly across the river! Then Seneca warrior's muskets belched fire and great smoke all along the opposite river bank!

There was a solid mass of painted savages, shoulders tight to shoulders, on a narrow strip of the opposite river shore. Ah, and they could see more warriors, coming down off the slope!

Those Asians had snuck in before the Nuworlders did, and the bit of wind had carried away the odor and sounds, of so many unwashed bodies!

The Duke hadn't expected so many enemy to be there; he had been very much surprised!

The roar of about 250 OdinGuns, along with with hundreds of muskets, and blood-chilling war-whoops, and deafening screams of those being struck with uncountable searing, and seemingly red-hot cylinders of lod... all that thunderous racket drowned out, any instructions anyone could have given.

The hopeful savages were quickly hopeless. They were being unexpectedly punctured, fractured, shattered, battered, and splattered, by those remarkably-quick-to-fire-again OdinGuns.

Across the river also, a human cascade of whooping, hollering, devilishly-painted warriors rose up and came down the brushy slope. Of course, each and every one of them had the absolute determination to kill a Noble and relieve him of his unmistakably powerful weapon.

Once their downhill charge had begun, they seemed unable to stop. They were incapable of grasping the fact; they were facing many times the number, of OdinGuns they had anticipated.

Just as in every battle, chaos reigned.

And anyway, Morgan's 63 Nobles were not in their canoes. They were at least armpit-deep in the river, fairly safe from most musket shots. They stood there blasting away as fast as their right or left hands, could trade empty-for-full-ammos, the short inches from their jackets to their weapons. Their quick to reload, and fire, really accurate OdinGuns, were dealing death to those screaming devils, on the far side of the river.

Firing at the astonished savages just across from him, Duke Odin saw some of them simply wilt in place, and a few tumble into the river; dead before getting wet. The living targets were so close that the Nobles on the ridge could hardly miss with their quickly aimed shots.

The slaughter of so many, so very near to them, was truly ghastly! It was the damnedest of massacres! The garishly painted Seneca warriors had no chance whatever!

Every gun spewed a small cloud of smoke, but the fair breeze blew it away, to the east. Those on the riverside ridge then could see through the thin haze, even those savages across the river, who attempted to conceal themselves, while firing from bushes. For the muskets, they had purchased from European traders in exchange for beaver pelts, that long range made their weapons, almost useless. Only those savages, at the very top of the slope opposite, were perhaps beyond the range, of the Noble's weapons.

Those highest up that slope were probably war chiefs, the Duke assumed. Several were seen to fade away into the forest, doubtless in utter shock, at the unforeseen scene.

The shooting didn't gradually slow down as one might have expected, but rather, it seemed to suddenly stop. There were simply no more living painted devils, for any of the Nobles to shoot. Even the twitch of an enemy in pain had brought more lod shots plowing into him, from the fevered Noble shooters.

And of course, no hands were ever raised in surrender; never; not a single one.

Overlord Croghan's *Valiants* were the first to dash down to the water's edge to assist Overlord Morgan's *Gators,* out of the much-bloodied river.

Some of those coming off the riverside ridge, leaped into the water, to help the wounded. Others grabbed drifting canoes.

Overlord Morgan was wading toward shore, carrying a Noble in his arms when the Duke first spotted him.

Then he noticed blood coming out of Morgan's right shoulder

and running down his sleeve. Bright red blood was literally washing over the painted words, "DANIEL MORGAN."

The Duke raced over to him as he got to the river bank, and took the Noble out of his hands, with Morgan showing wonder at his move.

"Your wound, Milord!" the Duke shouted at him. "Get it taken care of!"

"My wound?" Morgan asked in surprise.

"Yes, your shoulder! Your shoulder's bleeding!" the Duke told him.

Then the Duke turned to see Doctor Hugh Mercer, just behind him.

"Doctor! Get that musket ball out of him!" he shouted.

Staggering under the weight of the heavy Noble in his arms, the Duke laid him down on the grass. Only then, did he realize his left hand, was awash with blood. And the man was limp. He was not breathing.

As he put the man on the ground, he realized his own left sleeve was covered with blood. He then saw that the Noble had been shot in the neck.

He was dead, the spine of his neck apparently cut through, by the ball of a savage's gun.

Of course, the Duke knew him. He was Arch Barron William Montgomery, two years older than Odin, born near Philadelphia, and an excellent Overlord of his Band.

There were other losses. The Duke found out that even with all the lod flying through the air, not one Noble on the ridge had been hit. But Morgan and his *Gators* were under extreme assault, and 4 of those 63 Nobles had been killed. Eleven of them had been wounded, including the especially noble Nobleman, Arch Countet Daniel Morgan, himself.

One *Gator* received a wound similar to Barron Stringer's at Fort Duquesne; a musket ball had poked through one cheek, and out the other while cutting his tongue almost completely in two. He could not live long, and the man, of course, knew it. In a way luckily, that brave Nobleman lived in awful misery, only half an hour or so. He literally choked to death, on the remains of his devastated tongue.

Overlord Morgan pretended his wound hardly hurt at all, after Doctor Mercer dug out the ball, applied a film of Lord Doctor Gale's creation of mostly pine pitch, whale oil, and oat flour, that had definitely proved, to help with healing. Over that, Doctor Mercer wrapped his upper arm in a clean bandage, and put that right arm in a sling.

Lord Morgan moved his holster and OdinGun tether, to his left side; he said he reckoned he could shoot left-handed for a while.

The Duke thought the big man with the red hair, and the skin to match, was one tough fellow, and a terrific actor.

One might have thought that an intellectual fellow, Licensed Lawyer, and Preacher like Ezra Stiles, would be reluctant to count enemy dead. But without being asked to, he did just that. He did it quite systematically, garnering the assistance of Barrons Copley, West, Tully and Thomson.

Stile's count was an astonishing 681 enemy dead, that they found on the other side of the river. That was not considering some few unknowns, who had by then gone to the bottom of the river, leaking their life's blood, out many holes in their hides.

Every one of them were Senecas, said the saddened Lord Andrew —who of course knew many of them personally. More than a few of whom had been his friends.

Overlords Trent, Armstrong, and of course Croghan, also knew some of them.

The Duke asked all Nobles to report the number of ammos expended. The average turned out to be a whopping 14 ammos fired by each. The "battle" hadn't lasted long enough for any of them, to even need to dig in their AndyPaks, for more ammos. That totaled to about 3,500 ammos, shot to "knock over," some 700 enemies. Duke Odin's own count was also 14 shots, sped out of his tapered brass barrel.

He didn't ask Lord Montour his own count of shots fired, in case he might not have shot at all, at his fellow Iroquois. The Seneca tribe also belonged in the League of the Longhouse.

On the spot, looking over that truly gruesome battlefield – particularly, the dead-body-packed opposite Ohio shore—Odin decided they should leave it undisturbed, and immediately. All of the Seneca's weapons were obsolete, of use to none but the hunters of game, and were too burdensome for them to take back over the mountains with them. And he didn't feel like taking the time, having their weapons buried for future "mining."

The two disastrous battles with the Nuworlders had reduced the longtime, proud tribe of Senecas, to utter impotence. They would still have numerous women widows, girls, and boys; but extremely few menfolk, to hunt meat for them. And they'd have few men to protect them from the aggression of other tribes, who now might feel eager to get their revenge on them, since it could be safe to do so, after the Seneca's devastating defeat.

The news of the power of the Nuworld Nobility would spread over the continent like wildfire. And the destruction of the French influence in the Ohio Valley was bound to have important effects.

Duke Odin climbed back atop the ridge and roared out to his Nobles.

"Noblemen! We shall disturb the enemy dead no further! We must leave this place of slaughter now and let the proud Seneca tribe, take care of their fallen. Gather a souvenir if you will for our future museum, but then, let us fly away from here!"

They had all the wounded Nobles in 3 recovered canoes and brought the then five deceased Nobles in another. The 5th canoe used by Morgan's Nobles was then too full of holes to float.

The Nuworld's Noblemen and Noblewomen would bury their honorable dead after dark in a secluded, deep and secret grave.

Before noon, those 4 Battle Forces had re-joined Overlord Trent, his *Invincibles* Battle Force, the Noblewomen, and the rescued civilians.

Another packhorse had become lame and had to be shot, so they had more meat. But that meant one less animal to help them over the mountains. The packhorse burdens had been much reduced, but they needed a few of the horses to carry sickly civilians and wounded

Nobles. Many of them had to be doubled up on their mounts, and ride without saddles.

Nobody wished to swim or bathe in the river, so near the battle, dreading a collision with a floating, bloated body painted for war, washed down from the area of slaughter.

To remove the visages of that battle, Odin had just begun at nightfall to organize his thoughts for a speech he hoped to deliver in Philadelphia when the Overlady came by.

She sat on the ground next to him, and he supposed she'd want to know about the horrors of the battle. But she had no questions about that event.

"Milord Odin, I know you must be tired after such an ordeal, but you surely understand that I must be curious about you. That is, how did you, and your partners, find and bring home so much treasure? Lord Tully says it was strictly your genius alone, that figured how to do it. Can that be true, Duke?" she asked.

"Well now Milady, that's a far more pleasant subject, than that awful massacre, I thought you'd be asking about," the Duke replied. "But you understand, Elias has been my faithful friend since we were little boys, and he's awfully modest on this subject. As a matter of fact, it was the genius of all of the 14 good men, in the company, plus my Mohegan great grandfather, and a shipbuilder friend, that made it possible.

"You've heard of the Mohegan tribe, mostly over there in Connecticut, and in Massachusetts colonies?" he asked the beautiful porcelain doll.

"Mohegans? Yes, I recall reading something about them," she told him.

"Well, they consist of a number of bands, scattered around. 'Mo' means 'people,' as does 'Po' or 'Pol' in English, from the Greek language. Also, 'hegan' like the Latin' heathen,' means 'wolf'; so the Mohegans call themselves, the 'People of the Wolf.' Many of the Algonquin Asian words sure sound similar to European words, so that leads us to wonder again about the connections between the Asians here, and the Euros – the White people—of Europe.

"Well, when in 1638, Englishmen settled at the mouth of the

Connecticut River, to form the town of Saybrook, it was on the Pochaug Band's land, of the Mohegan Tribe.

"'Pochaug,' by the way, means 'Perfect People.' Or more correctly, 'People who are perfect.' How about that? We can practically hear the prideful Pochaug parents,' extolling their children to be proud of themselves; to *believe* in themselves as true marvels as of course, every human should. Everyone should feel that way, because every human is, under the skin, like all other humans, and an *authentic marvel.*

"Anyway, those Pochaugs were very glad to welcome the English, because the peaceful Pochaugs had been bullied endlessly, by the war-like Pequot tribe nearby. *And the reason for the glad welcome was, the English newcomers had guns!*

"Eventually the newly arrived Euros and the Narragansett tribe made war on the offending Pequots, and almost totally destroyed the whole tribe.

"But I digress; because I wanted to say an ancient Pochaug man, named Odin, who was the Chief of the few remaining in the Band, was in fact, a very close friend of our family. He was also my mother's grandfather, and that's how I got my middle name of Odin. I am, as a result, 1/8th Asian and 7/8th Euro.

Also, Mr. Stiles informed me that Odin, was the name of a Viking god and that Vikings must have visited the Nuworld, long before now. My great grandfather must have got that name, handed down from those Vikings.

"Anyway, that ancient old Pochaug Odin happened to be near, when an English Navy's 'press gang' found me dozing on a Long Island Sound beach, one sunny April Sunday in 1754. I was yet but 15 years old, and the old man may well have been over 100 years old. Someone in the gang dragged me to my feet, and another one of them knocked me on the head, and I became unconscious. The bad men threw me into their ship's rowboat, as they have done to 100s of other young men and boys, kidnapped in the English Colonies.

"Luckily, I woke up a little before that boat, got to their ship.

"Somehow, I instantly understood the danger I was in, as I woke, and I jumped up, and onto the side of the boat. As I dove off the side into Long Island Sound, the several rowers, and the boy officer, all grabbed for me. But with all that weight suddenly on one side, the boat tipped over.

"As I swam away as fast as I could, the 1/2 mile to shore, their boat sank. However many English sailors there were in that Press Gang, every one of them drowned.

"Of course, English sailors don't know how to swim, or they'd swim away from that wooden world of hell, called the Royal Navy.

"Elias Tully was on the beach, as well as the old Pochaug Chief Odin, and witnessed what happened to me, and to that press gang that day.

"Well, to shorten the story, Doctor Gale, Mr. Stiles, and Mr. Uriah Hayden – a shipbuilder—came to our house that day, to find out why my folks weren't in church, 2 Sundays in a row. It was because my mother had been ill, and my father tended to her.

"So, they were all there when the 3 of us came in from the beach.

"It so happened the old Chief – really, everyone thought he was 100 years old or more – he had walked with me to the beach earlier, and asked me to solve a problem in arithmetic.

"I did solve that little problem of arithmetic, as we sauntered along, and he thought the answer was just awfully smart. So, when we got to the house, he insisted to the others, and most importantly to me, that I was a profound genius.

"Then he reminded my Pops and Mr. Hayden, of their disastrous voyage to the Caribbean in 1741, with a small crew in Mr. Hayden's little schooner.

"The English Navy was at war then with Spain. Therefore, that navy impressed – *that is, enslaved* – all of Hayden's crew in Jamaica, except for my Pops and Mr. Hayden, to fight the Spanish then at Cartagena. That's a Spanish port on the Caribbean Sea.

"Well, the history books will tell you, it was a fiasco, for nearly all the Colonials that went down there, never came back home, because of dying from yellow fever.

"Anyway, Mr. Hayden and Pops got really sick, from that same disease also, and just the 2 of them after some time, sailed from Jamaica, in that little schooner, to come back home.

"But out of that port some ways, they became even sicker, so the 2 of them simply tied down the sail, and laid back in the schooner, rested and drifted, for day after day.

"One day, as they drifted, my Pops was leaning over the side. He noticed the surprising shallowness of the water, where they had drifted to. He saw a row of several cannons sticking up, out of the sandy bottom. As they drifted further, both he and Mr. Hayden, saw parts of more guns, and ship's timbers strewn about.

"They knew it had to be the sunken Spanish ships, that everybody in Jamaica, it seemed, talked about while they were there," the Duke said.

$\mathcal{R}$ 7 $\mathcal{R}$

Lord Andrew Montour came up just then, to interrupt their conversation.

"Milord Odin, I'm concerned about Lord Morgan. I think he's getting delirious. Doctor Gale is with him, but I wondered if you'd want to see him," Overlord Montour said.

Duke Odin jumped up, and so did the Overlady. They followed Montour to the prone Overlord of the *Gators*.

The Noble Overlord Daniel Morgan was laying on his back, stretched out flat, on a blanket, his red face appearing pale, in the light of a fire nearby.

The Overlady quickly took charge. Kneeling down next to Morgan, she purred as she talked, and felt his forehead with the back of her hand.

"Ah, that's very good. Only a slight fever," she pronounced.

She ordered another blanket to be rolled up for a pillow. She had him turn over to his left side; then she removed the bandage, where Doctor Mercer had dug out the musket ball.

"Ah, you're a fast healer, Milord Daniel, for it is closing over already! No more bleeding! That's really wonderful!" she announced believably.

Overlady Annie Willing was soothing to the muscular man, in a way men could not be.

Duke Odin congratulated himself on recruiting women for the Healthor role, for they had proven the perfect, added the element of femininity, needed. Without women around, his Pops had said, a gathering of men sometimes became a gang of awfully coarse creatures.

The Duke and the Overlady, visited the other wounded as well, although their hurts were not as deep, nor as painful as Overlord Morgan's. Then they parted, and the Duke found a place to sleep for the night.

The Nuworlders placed the "borrowed" birchbark canoes, upside down by the Ohio River, at the still inhabitable Delaware village of Kittanning. Those truly ingenious vessels, made without iron tools, could still be useful to others, who would come by.

They figured newcomers might also find shelter there, in the remaining 48 dwellings. But Nuworld Asians would forever consider the place haunted, with their fallen fellow Asians.

They left their circular brass Nuworld flags swinging in the breeze on poles, both beside their last victory at Venango and at their first conquest, at the empty village of Kittanning.

Then the Nobles and civilians began plodding with natural impatience, back east over the Alleghany Mountains. The ridges and valleys were seeming even more "endless" than before.

They traveled mostly single file on the centuries-old trail. That pathway was well-traveled by man and beast, through the thick forest. They went on with somewhat less urgent watchfulness than they had on the way west.

They would have opportunities in little streams to bathe, and to wash clothing, including their buckskin jackets and their buckskin "Dudleys" trousers. The released captives also would be encouraged to bathe, and especially, to bathe their children. The Healthors would help much with that chore.

That first night on the trail back to the east, they found a rare open spot in the forest. Duke Odin had them settle down in that glade. He encouraged them to be quiet, so he could give them a talk, while supper was being prepared.

"Nobles," he began, "together we have all accomplished much. When we get to Philadelphia, you will see the OdinRafts that we will sail on, into the Caribbean Sea, to fight and rob the French, as Privateers. That mission will be extremely important, for in making ourselves richer, we will make the French poorer.

"But all of us should think beyond our fighting days. When we have at last driven the French authorities off our continent, we ought to be prepared for what comes next. We can be vague for a while, about what sort of government, we should have in these Colonies. But we all can foresee that small towns and large cities, will soon sprout up, all over our continent.

"During the next year or so, every one of us should habitually think of a role for ourselves, in making our Nuworld, our very own world, better for everyone living in it. We Nobles won't be fighting every minute, of every day, for the next year. We must take the slack time in those months, to think of our own personal goals.

"Goals? What goals? Well, let me spout off to each of you, a number of ideas so that each of you might take as your own, personal goal. Remember please, that every one of us is a genius, male and female, young and old. Believe in whatever religion you wish, or in no religion at all, but above all, *we must believe in our wondrous, ingenious selves.*

"All of us menfolk have grown up to be physically strong because we've exercised with an ax, a shovel, a plow and such, all of our years. But we need to exercise our brains as well.

"One way to exercise that mass of stuff between our ears is with arithmetic. That's what I began doing when I learned the numbers, as a child in school. I imagined I was adding, multiplying, and subtracting numbers on paper. But lacking paper, I did it in my head. It's lots of fun. It's called abstract thinking.

"If you add in your head four plus 4, you get 8. But of course, we don't have to say what the 4s are. If you say 12 times 12 is 144, it can be entirely in your head. You don't have to say 12 apples or anything.

It's abstract thinking, and excellent exercise that costs you nothing at all, but a little effort.

"Someone here can make our farmers far richer than they are, by inventing and producing, a better plow, a better cultivator, a better way to harvest crops, and even a better way to milk their cows.

"For our womenfolk, someone could invent ever-better cooking stoves. You'll see those I invented, on our OdinRafts, so you can add your ideas to mine. I've already invented better lighting with the OdinLamps. Someone could come up with well-insulated ice chests, to hold blocks of ice, to keep things like butter, meat and milk cold, so they won't spoil.

"Someone could invent a clothes washer, doubtless better than the one I've come up with. Mine is simply a very leaky wooden barrel on the inside of another wooden barrel that you crank to tumble the clothes inside, in soapy water. After some time cranking that way, you drain out the dirty, soapy water, and put in clean water to rinse the clothes. Then, at last, you drain all of the water out, while you spin the inner barrel rapidly, to get the stuff inside barely wet, before putting them up on a clothesline to dry. All of you will see those clothes washers on our OdinRafts. All of us will have the use of them, importantly, to keep our clothing clean.

"Some ideas on what ought to be done, in our coming cities are this: before paving the streets, hopefully with smooth concrete—not those damnable stones or bricks—there are things that should be buried under them, or maybe under the sidewalks.

"We should have pipes going everywhere to bring pure water, under pressure, into every house, and into every business and mill. We should have pipes underground to take away dirtied water from those places. That dirty water should be treated so as not to spread bad odors, at the least. Also, prest air could be piped all over, to turn fans in houses, and other places, during hot weather. Also, such air under pressure could be piped into businesses, and especially into mills, to power saws, lathes, drills, and much else.

"Cities must have Noble Police and Fire Fighters, to keep the peace, and with bold new equipment to put fires out quickly, with water piped under the streets, all over every city. All Nobles should keep such needs in mind for the future, after active duty with the Nobility. You'll naturally ask, why cannot all houses, and all buildings, be made fireproof? It is such a terrible tragedy, to have people lose their homes and belongings in fires, to say nothing of their lives.

"Of course, there will have to be courts, judges and doubtless jails, to keep offenders in tiny rooms, away from everyone else, so they can't be schooled in committing crimes better.

"Now then, that's a start, and all of you will create some ideas, on what you might possibly want to concentrate on, during the evenings, until our war is won," Duke Odin said.

He then stepped down off of a mound.

Odin followed through during the evenings as they made the long trek, with suggestions about plowing, planting, cultivating, harvesting, and even the taking of grains from their stalks.

His followers were uniformly attentive, to what he said since of course, they had seen for themselves, some of what his own genius, had so far achieved.

Overlady Willing formed most of her Healthors into a chorus and entertained everyone with songs. That included especially, the newly composed "Nobility Song," by Lord Hopkinson.

Even the Duke memorized the words before long, humming to himself, *"This is our Nuworld, our very Free World, our Brightest Rich Part of the Whole World! Nobility, Nobility, protect us all from harm, and honor us, with righteousness, in city, sea, and farm!"*

The Duke apportioned his evenings after eating, to an hour or less, speaking about what someone might invent. He also visited with Nobles and the civilians. He had another hour with Ezra Stiles, about what stories could be printed in the newspapers. At last, he had a relaxing little while with the Overlady.

Before leaving Stratford in Connecticut Colony for the adventure they were on, Odin had worked with Stiles, in developing a slick means to spread stories to all of the 24 newspapers, then being printed in the British Colonies. There was in fact, at that time, more newspapers being published in England's North American Colonies, than in all of England itself!

Those English Colonists were actually the most literate peoples on earth, mostly because it was insisted by their Preachers, that each one of them should learn English well, because all their lives, they must read the Holy Bible every single day.

Of course, in most of Europe, no newspapers were then printed at all, since the dominating authorities with the ruling classes, wished to keep news beyond the reach, of the under-classes of people. Few Europeans could read anyway since unlike the English, they were not asked to read the Bible at all. It was enough that their "shepherds," the Priests, did that, and that they passed on their ultra-careful interpretations, to their "flocks" – of humble, sheep-like peoples.

Back in Stratford, it turned out that after about 20 attempts, Odin and Stiles found they could mix paper pulp, and clay, to make a slightly wet blanket-like mat, that they could press the made-up-type of a story into. After having been baked in an oven, those rigid mats could then be sent by men on horseback, to all of the colonial newspapers.

Then a printer simply laid onto the mat, a sheet of type-metal, and held close over it a hot iron, which melted the tin-lod type metal. That made a perfect duplicate of the set-in-type story, for their own press. And the newspapers could do this far more quickly, and cheaply, than having their own typesetting men, set the type. Also, Odin Bushnell's idea was that the newspapers receiving such a made-up story on a mat, would not likely be inclined to alter the story.

Together, David Odin Bushnell and Ezra Stiles figured, they could greatly influence the people of the Nuworld, with worthwhile ideas. With the Nuworld Nobles beating the fearful French forces, they reckoned on getting every Nuworlder's attention, at least.

Each evening on the trail back, Stiles would question Duke Odin on a different subject. The Duke would do his best to answer, while Stiles made notes. Those questions and answers would be sent, one by one, to the various newspaper publishers in the pre-set "type-mats," for informing their readers of the Duke's views, on all sorts of things.

Stiles called Duke Odin Bushnell, "The Young Sage from Old

Saybrook," in those stories. He said, "The Duke wasn't merely advanced for his age; he was advanced for any age."

Among the questions was, "What did the Duke suppose would be the reaction of the various Asian tribes, on learning the outcomes of the recent battles, along the Ohio?"

"Mr. Stiles, the Asian peoples that have survived over the centuries until now, will be in very great shock. They have of necessity, had a war-culture in order not to be exterminated by other tribes, wishing to take over their territory, and their wild game – their main food source.

"We know there are many caring Euro men and women, who will hopefully act as Ambassadors, so to speak, from us Euro peoples to the many Asian peoples. We can help furnish useful gifts for them to demonstrate our sincere friendship and neighborliness."

One evening on the trail back, Overlord Croghan got Odin aside and confided that the Duke ought to know he, Croghan, had left his heart up north of Albany, New York Colony. His deceased wife, and mother of his little daughter "Suky," had been a Mohawk Asian beauty. When she died, he lost his heart to another pretty, and very good woman, of the same tribe.

"Her name is Molly Brant," Croghan said with a sigh, "but there's a problem. She seemed to be equally in love, with Sir William Johnson, as with me. But Johnson lived close by, lived in a mansion, and was then rich, while I was rather poor. Johnson is one I'd call a 'spectacular person' like Lord Andrew, and his remarkable mother – oh, and like you, Duke, and like Annie Willing.

"Johnson is one of a kind," Croghan confided, "but he's also one of those extremely greedy land grabbers, that you and all of us, don't like. And as I understand it, Molly won't let him touch her, because he's sick with syphilis. But she's loyal to him and keeps his house. Even so, I can't help but keep on loving her. I just thought you should know, Duke, my friend. That's why I'm not chasing any beauties," Overlord George Croghan confided.

The Duke never could guess, why Croghan thought he ought to know all that.

Duke Odin found himself enjoying the Overlady's questions,

about their Caribbean adventure. Each night during their trek back east, they were spending 1/2 hour or more munching their dinners together.

The Duke told her that the wise old Pochaug Odin, not only reminded his father of his sighting of the cannons, on the Caribbean Sea bottom 13 years before; that is, at the time they were meeting in the Bushnell house. That was the same day the young Odin, escaped from his English Navy captors. That was when, the ancient Odin, insisted the youngster Odin, was bright enough, to figure a way to find that spot in the sea again; and smart enough to bring home, *a whole shipload of gold*.

"Now then Overlady Annie, the truly remarkable ancient fellow Odin, was convincing enough, that they all agreed to meet a week later at our house. Being a self-confident lad then, I actually expected of myself, to have practically all the answers, on how to bring that treasure from the sea, back home.

"Frankly, I'm astounded now in thinking about it, that I did come up with a number of good ideas; firstly, about building a ship very differently, than those built at the time," he said.

"Yes," she said, "that's the Sarah BUSHNELL. I met you on it when it was in the Schuylkill River. I'm not familiar with ships, but I did notice it seemed longer and quite different, from those I'd seen docked in the Delaware River."

"Different? Well, yes, Milady, it really is so. Anyway, we had to dam up the little Pochaug River there for a sawmill, for the ship is built entirely of long, 2-inch-thick planks, laid cross-ways and diagonally to each other, in 5 thicknesses on the sides. We used seven thicknesses of those planks, on the bottom of the ship, and all of the planks were tongue-and-grooved. They're covered with Trinidad Island petroleum tar, and held there with brass, "gripping nails."

"It took all of us 14 Nuworld Company members, and Mr. Hayden, from April to mid-December to build it. When we launched and sailed it, in Long Island Sound, Mr. Hayden was astounded that it performed exactly, as I said it would," the Duke said.

"Lord Tully told me, Milord, that your most ingenious idea was 2, 'see-the-sea' scopes, mounted on the floor of your ship's prow. He told me it was dark down there, and two men could stand with an eye looking into the top of the scope's angled mirrors. The men could see forward, and left and right very well, through the ship floor, with those devices," she said.

"Well, as a matter of fact, those scopes proved their worth," Odin said. "The Caribbean Sea is remarkably clear because there's no dirty river water flowing into the sea, where we were.

"With those devices, we discovered wrecks; we could never have seen from the surface. And the first wreck was, unexpectedly, at a sharp coral reef east of Jamaica some ways.

"It seems that vessel had its bottom ripped off of it, by hitting the reef. We later determined it was a Dutch pirate ship. From some of the evidence found, we guessed it came from near India and the island of Ceylon, in the early 1660s.

"We supposed it was on its way to the easy-morals of New Amsterdam, a few years before the English took the town, and renamed it New York. But the pirate's ship snagged on that reef and left their treasure for us to find.

"That was on February 1st, 1755, that we discovered that ship, and later, the other ships I'll tell you about."

"Is that where you found the pearls I heard about?" she asked.

"Yes, Milady. Remarkably, we brought up three big bags of beautiful pearls. They were in thick leather bags, and simply sitting on the sand near the reef. The heavy things such as seven stolen brass ship bells, and I think 48 small brass cannons, went straight down onto the coral. But the bags drifted off a little.

"You'd think leather wouldn't last there for the 63 years, it was on the sea bottom, but they were alright until we lifted them. Then the bottoms would almost give out.

"Two other large leather bags held nearly a bushel each of gems of every description and color. Wow! We were all amazed to see diamonds, rubies, emeralds, sapphires, and others!

"Only Paul Revere among us had seen many of those gems before. That find right there paid for the voyage and then some. But there were also gold and silver coins, in those bags," he told her, to wind up their conversation for the evening. "It was gold and silver in large quantities we hoped to find, so we continued on."

On Monday, September 20th, 1756, they reached the fort they had left from, 24 days before, to begin their mission to clear the Ohio River valley of the enemy French Army.

The fort was called by most, "Croghan's Fort," since Croghan had built it, on his Aughwick property, at the edge of the frontier.

But the new Pennsylvania Colony Governor – an English Army Lieutenant Colonel, named William Denny – had renamed it for another English politician, come over to make a fortune from the "provincials." That was the then Governor of Massachusetts Bay Colony, William Shirley. So, it was officially Fort Shirley they returned to.

They had nearly exhausted their food supply by that time. But at the fort, they had stashed corn, and wheat flour, and other foods before walking warily, over the many mountains and valleys of the Alleghanys, to the Ohio River, and to victorious battles.

They had also left at that fort, OdinCarts, stove carts, and oven carts; they had used in the training camp, and to that point. They soon had plentiful bread and meat. The 2 Nobles left sick at the fort, had become well and had shot a buck deer, and a large and deliciously fat young bear, the day before the 5 Battle Forces' return.

Lord Montour assigned a Band of 12 Nobles, to accompany Ezra Stiles, and Barrons Rittenhouse and Thomson. They were to ride swiftly ahead, on the plentiful horses left at the fort, to Philadelphia with news of the Nuworld victories.

They had hidden a supply of silver "nu" coins, having no need to be burdened with money, west of that fort. They had decided on the name nu, for the new, Nuworld money, while still hauling up piles, of badly made Spanish gold and silver coins, from the Caribbean Sea floor.

It took 100nu (the plural nu was not to have an's' after it) to equal merely 1/2 ounce Troy, of silver. Thus, the value of 1nu was deliberately very small. With that money system, no fractions or decimals would ever be needed.

The lowest paid Noble, a Barronet, was to be paid 1,000nu a

month – that being roughly equivalent to 5 Spanish pesos (dollars) of 8 Reals. Instead of "pesos of 8," "*pieces* of 8," was the usual incorrect name for them. That was the Spanish "dollar," so widely used in the Colonies, and hard to make change for. Thus, those Spanish coins were often cut into eight inexact "bits"; so that 1/4 of that dollar coin, would be "2 bits."

Every Noble was to receive a 20% increase in pay for each step up in those 18 Noble ranks. A Band Overlord Arch Barron would be paid 2,700nu each month. Arch Duket Montour was to get 12,875nu a month; that being by coincidence, about equal to a "Colonel's" pay in dollars, of any of the Colonial Militias.

The Nuworld Company treasury minted 1nu coins in red brass, 5nu coins also in red brass and 25nu coins in yellow brass, in order to make change, for solid silver coins or notes.

The system was quickly and easily understood; especially when compared to the insane English money of pence, shillings, and pounds. The Colonies had been forbidden by the English Parliament, from coining or printing money (as it forbade the making of so many other useful things, even hats), but it had said nothing about a private company, coining silver or making *brass hats illustrating the Nuworld*, so they did.

Returning with their treasure in 1755, the Nuworld Company had immediately begun minting coins. Every coin had the Nuworld "view from the moon" map on one side, and the value and year minted, on the other side. Their coins were round, like their brass map flags.

Duke Odin Bushnell found it a pleasure to be inside a structure again, however crudely Croghan's Fort was built. He even had a private room, with a real straw bed to sleep on, and a slab of a table, with a smoothed bench on each side.

He worked on the "city speech" he hoped to deliver but was not yet completely satisfied with much of it. He thought that if you wish to move people to your cause, you most certainly had best have some thunder and lightning, in your talk.

The actor-preacher George Whitefield had come over from England to preach throughout all of the English Colonies; that was to be a "New Awakening." He had swayed crowds throughout the

Colonies with his hours-long, hell-fire-and-brimstone, and frightening speeches. He said his audiences were doomed to burn in hell's fire if they didn't obey what he said.

But David Odin Bushnell had seen other preachers, solemnly read their sermons, often putting some of their tired, and hardworking parishioner's in church, into a sound sleep.

It seemed to him that if you couldn't remember your speech to deliver it, and had to read it, you could hardly expect your audience to remember it.

The Overlady knocked on the door, and came into the room, bearing a porcelain platter. He hadn't seen one of those for months.

"These delicious-smelling sweet cakes just came out of the oven," she said. "You must be hungry, Milord."

"Right, you are Milady. Won't you join me? I have a fresh pot of coffee here," he said.

Maybe because he was a little homesick, and she was so friendly, he had a sudden desire to talk about himself, instead of the Caribbean venture. But that was enjoyable also because she was such a very good listener. She always asked intelligent questions.

He told her about his ancestor John Bushnell, coming from England in the 1630s, with his six sons. Three of his sons settled in the very new Old Saybrook, beside the Connecticut River, at Long Island Sound.

"My Pops," he said, "Nehemiah Bushnell, is 6-feet-4 inches tall, the same as myself. He inherited the original 50 acres of fair farming ground, allotted to one of those original Bushnell settlers. Being so tall, friends often jokingly called my pops, 'Knee-High.' He actually does sign notes, 'N-e-h-i,' instead of the more difficult Nehemiah.

"I was born on that farm on a hot August 30th, in 1738, with lightning flashing across the sky the whole afternoon. That's what I've been told. That was the same weather when my mother was born, and that's been said to prove she and I will live really long lives. My mother's Ingham ancestors came over, about the same time as the Bushnells," he told the beauty.

"Do you believe that? I mean, about the long lives you're going to have?" she asked with a quaint smile.

"Why not, Milady? I suppose I needn't be as fearful as I otherwise might be, in times of danger. It gives me self-confidence, and maybe courage, about the same as some men might believe some imaginary Almighty up there, hasn't much to do except to be constantly watching out, for their welfare," he said.

She simply smiled again at those assumptions, and he went on.

"Our house was built by my ancestor William Bushnell, in 1668, and it has been unchanged, except for the addition of a woodshed. I have kept that woodshed filled with firewood since I became ten years old. My Pops says our height, and our long limbs came from swinging an ax, with all our might, every day from an early age."

It was pleasant to talk to her since she seemed intensely interested.

He told her that nearly everyone in New England claimed to be a Congregationalist, but he reckoned nobody could know, what anyone else actually believed. And he could not understand why Quakers were disliked there.

At last, he had the courtesy to ask her about herself. But she claimed she wasn't much interested in her family history. Both her mother and her grandmother were also named Anne, so she liked to add the "i" to make her Annie name, a bit different.

Her father was a wealthy merchant-trader, and she had been tutored at home. It was obvious to Odin, that she had a fair education, and that she was extraordinarily smart – as well as an *absolutely perfect, porcelain doll.*

"Milord Odin," she smiled at him, "I thank you for that bit of your history."

She suddenly pushed her bench back from the table, stood, said good night, and left him to tend to her duties. He shrugged his shoulders and continued work on his "city speech."

The trip from Croghan's Fort Shirley to Philadelphia was a good deal more light-hearted than the way west had been for the Nuworlders. People now and then along the roads, watched for their arrival. Some of them cheered the victors and even offered them food and drink.

The Duke was curious to see what reactions, they would find

among those whose anti-military religion, dictated that their freedom should be bought, by the blood of other's sons.

So far as he could tell, they seemed to cheer pretty much equally, with others. They appeared not to be embarrassed at all, by their lack of fighting spirit.

But then, someone suggested to him that they considered themselves, not so much stubborn in their beliefs – and certainly not cowardly – but even brave, in refusing any call to fight those, who were murdering their innocent neighbors.

All day Saturday, September 25th, a light rain fell, but they plodded on east. That night the rain stopped. He sat off to one side of the crowd by a small fire; he barely managed to keep going, and began to go over his speech again. Then the Overlady came by.

"Duke, you only told me about finding the Dutch pirate ship, not the Spanish ones. How'd you manage to find them and get that treasure?" she asked.

"Oh. Oh, that. Well Milady, Pops gave me a good description of that extremely extensive shallow sandbank, west of Jamaica Island, where he had seen the cannons sticking out.

"So, I devised a water pump, plus a hose and nozzle, with which to wash sand away from places on the sea bottom.

"Two or 3, or even four men, could pump it, and it turned out to be the hardest work we had. Pumping that water, took persistence, while a diver on the bottom aimed the nozzle of the hose. That powerful flow of water washed sand away, from objects on the bottom. We also had an air pump for the diver's breathing hose, but that required only one man to pump.

"Oh that Paul Revere; he's the genius who mostly made those things that I designed. And, I must add; every one of us 14 men, took turns diving.

"After we sailed away from the pirate ship we first found, about mid-February, we spent more than two weeks searching, before we found the first Spanish wreck. While we were underway, 2 of us were at all times, peering through those see-the-sea scopes. That was the perfect way to see on the sea bottom, what we could hardly expect to notice, from the surface.

"By the way, I designed a kind of 2-legged crane hanging over the rear of our ship. With block and tackle from the crane, we brought up a great deal of the stuff, with what I called a 2-handed iron bucket, that we dropped onto the sand. We would close the two very large iron hands of it, as those hands dug into the sand, and with that, brought up every sort of thing; everything from coins and gems to cannons.

"We'd bring those iron hands up, and dump the contents onto a long table, shaped like a T. On the downslope part of the T, were troughs that went to the sides of the ship, so we'd pump water onto the table, and wash away the sand brought up. We'd wash that sand back into the sea, at the sides, and then sort out coins or jewels or whatever was left on the wooden table.

"We also brought up many brass cannons with that rig. Some of them we reckoned weighed over 5,000 pounds, so it required a terrific effort from all of us, to get them up. That brass is to us almost as valuable as gold. It's certainly useful such as for making OdinGuns, ammo cups, our hats, and map-flags.

"Anyway, during the six months we were gone, we found the four missing Spanish ships that sailed from Cartagena for Havana, Cuba, in 1605. Those wrecks contained many emeralds, and some pearls, and lots of gold bars, and coins; but not much silver.

"The three missing Spanish galleons that had sailed from Vera Cruz, Mexico, in 1691, had been blown down into the Caribbean, by extraordinarily strong north winds. We found tons and tons of silver, from those three galleons, and a bit of gold – oh, and lots of other things as well.

"We figured that each of those 7 Spanish vessels, must have been lifted high, right where we found them, by so-called 'rogue waves.' Those ships were then slammed back down onto that shallow bottom. We could see each one of those galleons had been split asunder. What remained of the keels, ribs, and planking, were all broken up. The crews and passengers surely drowned quickly in those storms. The sinkings were so far from any land at all, and of course, so very few people then, and even now, know how to swim.

"Eventually, much of the shattered wooden parts pretty much

floated away, but the heavy stuff stayed right where it was sunk. We supposed most of it may have been completely covered with sand for a lot of years, but apparently, a timely storm had partly uncovered the treasure, kindly waiting for us.

"All 7 of those ships had fantastic riches for the King of Spain, so those losses meant he couldn't force his people-controlling religion, down the throats of so many people as before. They were the exact ships my Pops had heard so many men speak of, in Jamaica, in 1741.

"So, Milady Annie Willing, that's the story of our gain, which we are using, hopefully, to make things better for everyone on this continent, including Asians and Euros alike. We expect of ourselves to comb away some of the bad things around us and replace them with good. That pretty much sums up our goals," he said.

"Milord, I'm so glad you told me all of that. It helps me to appreciate what the Nobility is all about, and why. Thank you, Duke Odin; thank you very much."

She left, and he worked on his speech, refining every sentence.

❧ 8 ❧

On Monday afternoon, September 27th, 1756, they reached a spot 3 miles from the bustling city of Philadelphia. It was a good place in fine weather to pitch their tents and polish their OdinGuns to look like gold. At this time, they polished their "Nuworld half-globe," brass hats.

They had been five days trekking from Croghan's Fort – or, "Fort Shirley."

At every opportunity, Overlordet Montour and Duke Odin had talked to every level of Overlord to get their opinions, on who deserved promotion, and who had earned what Crowns, during which battle.

It was difficult for anyone to say, busy as they had to be, in a particular fight, who deserved what. They could only try to be as fair —yet as generous—as possible. All of them knew it was considered *ignoble,* to complain of unfairness in such awards.

Duke Odin was to implore Stiles of the NUWORLD NUZ, and other newspapers, to print the names of all 368 Noblemen, and Noblewomen, in their papers. They should list the medals the Nobles were awarded, and the promotions they received, they so richly deserved.

The English Colonists were said to be the most literate people on Earth, and he thought it would be appropriate for the people, to read such names, and give the Nuworld Nobles, a little public recognition for their brave – *and truly noble* – efforts.

As they supped, the leaders went over the plans for the upcoming Caribbean campaign. Then they hoped during the winter, to intercept French merchant convoys, loaded with valuable cargoes. That bit of piracy was legal since they were licensed in wartime, as "Privateers."

As was standard practice in this legal-only-in-war piracy, they would then take the captured ships to friendly ports, and sell the cargoes, and the ships they took. If they captured very many, it could be a considerable financial strain on the enemy, and of course a large boost for the welfare, of those doing the capturing.

The Duke's secretary came bounding in from the city, on a galloping horse.

"Milord," Lord Thomson said, handing the Duke a note, "it's from Mr. Stiles. He said you should read it right away."

Opening the note, he was surprised to read: "Duke Odin, I bought into Bradford's print shop. So, I'm now printing the NUWORLD NUZ here, to spread the word of your great victories. Cypriot Dudley is here to furnish new uniforms for your Nobles. He's hired many tailors. Everyone here is most anxious to see you."

Besides the note, Thomson had brought newspapers, including the one Stiles had just printed. Odin was astounded to see right under the masthead of the paper, the statement he had made a year before, to his partners in the Nuworld Company:

"'We can do it; united, we Nuworlders can create a society, in which each Euro and Asian babe born, shall have an honest chance at life's great challenges, and for life's glittering rewards – in our Nuworld, our Free World, our Brightest Rich Part of the Whole World!' says our own Nuworld Nobility Overlord, Duke Odin Bushnell."

Lord Thomson saw him reading that. "Milord, many printers have up there on their paper, some old saying by a long-ago Roman, just to show how smart they supposedly are.

"But Mr. Stiles, he says, 'Why not put up there something that actually means a truly great deal, to the people of our Colonies?' Mr. Stiles Duke, has unbounded faith in your wisdom – even if you're not a Yale man like him, and his 10-years older cousin, Lord Doctor Gale are," he said as he laughed.

"Why he says they even learnt Hebrew and Aramaic grammar; everybody knows how useful that is! Mr. Stiles is a wonderful fellow, in my estimation sir," the Duke's secretary said.

"Yes Barron Thomson, he certainly is that and more. Did you pick out a spot where I can give a speech tomorrow?" the Duke asked.

"I did, Duke. I've arranged to have a brand-new, large, and sturdy oak wagon, for you to speak from. It's to be placed at Market and Front Streets, near the wharves. Mr. Stiles had posters made up, announcing your talk at high noon, and they're placed all over the city already."

"Thank you, Lord Charles. Now I'd best read this newspaper," Duke Odin said.

The Duke was startled to read of the fall, of the British forts at Oswego, New York Colony. The two forts had been located, on the east and west sides of the Oswego River, where it emptied into the south side, of the smallest of the Great Lakes, Lake Ontario.

That place had for some time been an important trading post, with the English traders there selling to visiting Asians, better prices on better-made goods, than the French at their trading posts did. So, the French authorities, hating competition, wiped those forts off the map.

When the French attacked with their cannons in mid-August, the flag of surrender went up quickly, the report said. It was said about 1,400 English and Colonial soldiers, and probably 100 women, were lost to the French Army.

Some of the French-allied Asian warriors there promptly got drunk on captured spirits, and many captives lost their scalps, and their lives, to the vicious, vengeful drunks.

So, at the time the Nuworlders were training in the Cornwall mines, for battles in the Ohio Valley, disaster was striking at Lake Ontario. Neither peoples had any news, of the other.

A search of the newspaper pages showed no victories by King George of England's red-coated generals; nor the promise of any hoped-for victories to come.

Odin was astonished next to read of some "youthful innovators – *very much like the extraordinary Duke Odin Bushnell* – who were also remarkably victorious at war."

"Alexander the Great," he read in the NUWORLD NUZ, "back about 300 B.C., was an innovator. He commanded in battle at age 16, became King of Macedonia at age 20, and conquered Greece, Persia, Egypt and much of the known world by his 30s.

"Augustus Caesar succeeded his Uncle Julius Caesar, as the Emperor of Rome at age 18. He won many battles and ruled that Empire until he died at age 77. He found Rome a city of bricks and left it a city of glistening marble. He was a real innovator.

"Sweden's Gustafus Adolphus commanded forces against the Danes, at age 16. He became King of Sweden at 17, and was a very great military leader, plus a remarkable innovator with artillery, for example.

"Czar Peter the Great became at age 17, the undisputed Emperor of all the Russias. Not only did he win battles, and expand his empire, but he built the beautiful new capital city, of Saint Petersburg for his nation – *innovatively, atop a swamp!*

"There are others;" Stiles said in his newspaper, "youngsters like Marshall Saxe of France and Maurice of Nassau, who were very successful young innovators in war. But of course, by now the reader will understand, that despite his youthful and great brave heart, because he is so forward thinking, and such a great innovator, inventor, and speaker, Duke Odin Bushnell can well be depended upon, to lead large, powerful Battle Forces, and win great fights for the all-important cause of freedom, for all of the good Asians and Euros on our continent."

The Duke was astounded at all that, for he was being compared with some extremely famous men! What a build-up for his speech on the morrow! And that touch of fame should help with recruiting good young men and women, to become Nobles, he reckoned; although it might give him a swelled head!

Ezra Stiles was making good use of his excellent education, in and out of Yale College; that was plain.

Stiles had at first been the "doubting Thomas" among the partners, for he could not initially accept, that a mere boy, could design a successful vessel, that had no keel, no ribs – a vessel different in nearly every respect, from all other sailing ships, up to that time.

The Duke had about finished reading the newspaper when three riders approached.

Overlord Croghan – who seemed to know everyone in the Colony – announced, "That's Israel Pemberton, a leading Quaker, and a rich merchant of the city. Those two black men would be his slaves, of course."

The "rich merchant" recognized Croghan and hailed him. As he dismounted, Lord Croghan made the introductions.

"And this is Duke Odin Bushnell, our Nuworld Nobility Overlord," he said.

As Pemberton extended his hand, he said, "I understand you have killed a great many men, but luckily, you've had a very tiny few casualties yourself." He said it with a half-smile.

It struck Duke Odin as not a friendly remark at all, and he did not take the offered hand.

"Sir, what proportion of our Nobility would you have preferred to suffer painful death, to protect your liberties? One quarter? One half, perhaps?" he asked the Quaker man.

The merchant scowled in surprise. He "harrumphed," turned his back, re-mounted, and rode away.

"I take it," Croghan said flatly, "you've not gained a friend in that man."

"I don't think I wish to make friends with such as him," Odin said just as flatly. "And for a human to own other humans, is an obscenity we shall one day, do something about, my friend."

No sooner had Pemberton ridden off when the Duke knew exactly what was missing, in the speech he had expended so much effort on. He knew then what he wished to speak loudly about, and got busy going over it in his tent. He finished it by brilliant Odin-Lamp light.

The Duke woke up Tuesday morning, September 28th, 1756, thinking about Nobility uniforms. Cypriot Dudley, a wonderfully talented clothier from Old Saybrook, Connecticut Colony, had said he would bring enough materials to clothe, at least 1,200 more men and women, in both formal wear and buckskins.

Dudley had accompanied the Duke, to the Cornwall Iron Mine training camp, to measure and uniformly clothe, the Nobles there. He had brought 24 seamstresses, OdinStitcher sewing machines and OdinEmbroiders, to fulfill the task. Those then returned to Philadelphia, while the Nobles went on to the Ohio, and their victories.

At the port of Philadelphia, when he returned there, Dudley had bought from an English privateer, an amazingly huge cargo of especially fine wool cloth, plus much cotton cloth. All of it was dyed with the indigo plant, to a bright, medium blue.

Interestingly, Dudley said he was certain the cloth was all English-made, but the privateer said he captured it from a French ship. But it was probable he pirated his own countryman's ship, and had to sell his booty over the sea!

Anyway, that rich blue wool cargo decided the color of their formal uniforms. The pretty blue jackets would be waist-length, as the buckskin jackets were, but with fringe on the arms made of white twisted twine. The collars would be the same stand-up type to show unit names – and to hide the ugly, black neck markings on Lord Andrew Montour! Half-globe Nuworld map buttons, made of shiny brass down the front, would be decorative.

The only other decorations were to be their names embroidered in white on their blue wool arms, and the Badges, Campaign Shields and Crowns, Nobles had won. Those awards would be displayed across their proud chests; left to right, in the order they had won them. There would be no ammo slots, as on their buckskin jackets. Nor would they normally wear their OdinGuns, or holsters, at ceremonies and dances, while "wearing the blue."

Noblemen were to have shoe-length blue pants; Noblewomen

were to have knee-length, white pleated skirts, and white stockings. They'd all wear black shoes, laced up with no fancy buckles.

After breakfast, Lord Montour got the whole Force Group, with the released captives, across the Schuylkill River, and into the city. Half of the Healthors helped with the formerly captive children; many of the children were then orphans.

The Duke took the precaution of directing, that a Band of 12 Nobles, on horseback, should be maintained north, and another 12 south, of the city, to warn of any enemy approach.

The Nobles and others rode or marched along the 2-mile width of the city, separating the rivers. The streets were paved with rough cobblestones, for only a part of that distance.

Philadelphia in 1756 had a population of 20,000 people and was growing rapidly. It was the largest of Colonial cities. It was concentrated mostly along the Delaware River, where most ships docked. The trade in Colonial produce was extensive, to the Caribbean and to Europe.

Many of the buildings they paraded past were built of red brick, and as much as three stories tall. Some of the buildings were rather handsomely done.

Because of Annie Willing's status in the city, Lord Montour placed her, and her 35 Healthors, right after the Duke in leading the parade. The Healthors were followed then by the 5 Battle Forces.

The Duke found it amusing to see mouths agape, staring at attractive young women wearing shiny brass, half-globe-plus-brims hats, and buckskin jackets, with fringe jiggling on their arms, at every move. Additionally, they were wearing Dudley trousers. A few of them were riding horses the same way men rode. And they were *toting shiny "gold" OdinGuns, on their hips.*

As Stiles had predicted in his note, there were huge crowds lining the street. They were cheering and clapping, with boys and girls running alongside, to hail the new heroes. The crowds seemed to have in them, every class of person – tradesmen, sailors, merchants, housewives, and even a few dark faces of slaves.

Duke Odin became increasingly nervous as he saw, near the end of the wide Market Street, the promised wagon to speak from. Mr.

Stiles and Lord Thomson were standing in front of the wagon, waiting to greet him. Looking around, the Duke could see people leaning out of brick building windows. He saw it was a very large crowd, all around that intersection.

Dismounting, Overlord Odin handed the reins to Lord Charles, who took his horse up to where other Nobles were organizing themselves.

The Duke had been told his voice carried far; he would soon find out if it was really true.

Stiles climbed up onto the wagon, and in his loud preacher's voice shouted: "Ladies and gentlemen, I wish to present to you, the *Young Sage, from Old Saybrook*... the brave conqueror of the Ohio Valley... a scientist and inventor without peer... and the ingenious Overlord of the Nuworld Nobility.... DUKE.... DAVID.... ODIN.... BUSHNELL!"

Stiles jumped off the wagon, and the Duke handed him the completely written speech he had finished the night before.

"Mr. Stiles, you might wish to see if I remember, what I hope these people will remember," he said to his friend.

With a mighty leap, the Duke swung his tall, muscular self-up, onto the wagon. Some people were applauding politely, while others were staring with curiosity.

To ease his nervousness, he "took charge," and pointed out empty spaces near the wagon, urging people to close up the gaps.

While they shuffled about, he took off his brass hat, ran his fingers through his well-trimmed black hair, letting it gather in curls over his forehead. He then took out his OdinGun. He showed it to some of the men close to him, knowing they had never seen any weapon ever, like his. Then he re-holstered his gun, but kept his hat in hand, the better to emphasize points.

"Dear People!" he roared out, putting his whole self into it; speaking from the toes up.

He would wave his arms, clench his fists and throw out words, with a snap of the head, so that the furthest in the crowd could hear him.

"Now, for all our agonies suffered thus far, in this blood-splattered part of our tear-stained Nuworld, war's bright red drops yet fall," the Duke began.

"Countrymen still wail helpless, bleeding 'neath enemy heels. Thus, we rest not, as we must not, until all of our goals of safety and happy prosperity, for all of our people, be gained."

He paused briefly, and a small clutter of clapping came along. But the crowd seemed not yet, to warm up to what he was all about.

"In this month of September 1756, your very noble Noblemen, and equally noble Noblewomen have combed away, the evil presence, of torturing murderers, in the Ohio Valley."

At last, some cheering erupted in response to that statement; and he continued.

"Your Nobles have destroyed those forts, where such wickedness was housed.

"The frowning French forts called Duquesne, Machault, LeBoef, and Presque Isle, no longer exist! But the French proved better at burning their own forts than we did!"

A bit of laughter came, with the clapping that time.

"That nest of snakes called Kittanning was combed right out of our hair!"

Ah, the crowd was warming up to him and cheered wildly at the mention of Kittanning being conquered. Many had surely read Stiles' printing of the Duke's telling of the Nuworld Nobility story, and his explanation of insulting rank names, and his reasons for Noble titles.

"The death knell out there in the bush was delivered to many, many of our enemies!

"Most folks by now, have read or heard about the attack on our Nobility, by most of the Seneca tribe's warriors. They clearly aimed to kill us and take our OdinGuns. They should have known better. We regret very much that that battle happened, but we were prepared to defend ourselves. The Nuworld's Asians and Euros, must never again, be enemies.

"Asians and Euros alike should understand the Asian necessity to prepare to defend themselves from other tribes, wishing to take over their women and their wild game. We should know that a continuous war culture, has greatly reduced their use of their genius, to create useful things. Religious, so-called shepherds, have done the same to retard Euros. We are all alike, under the skin. We all have creative genius. We should use that genius."

More cheers. Stiles had printed the numbers of casualties on both sides, at each battle, but the Duke hardly wished to mention the numbers of those deaths. Also, Stiles had written of the origin of the Bush-knell name, long ago, in Sussex, England.

"In our struggles by the Ohio, we suffered 36 Nobles wounded, and 8 Nobles slain. I suppose now.... I suppose now, we can see a few more glittering stars, in the night-time sky."

Sighs of wonder went over the crowd as the Duke pointed, and looked skyward.

"I was told yesterday by a rich merchant of this city, that we were lucky to have so few casualties.

"I asked him what proportion of our Noble casualties, he thought would have been more appropriate. Would 1/4 of our Nobles killed, or perhaps if 1/2 of our Nobles suffered painful death – would that have been more to his liking, as a sacrifice of other men's blood, to defend his liberties—his undoubted right to follow, his so-called principles, in refusing to risk his own skin, in fighting for what is our sacred right, to be a free and a safe people?"

He certainly had the undivided attention of the people by then. The anger in him was boiling, and it showed as he roared out:

"That man's remarks set me to thinking. If it was his own home that was being attacked, such a man would naturally hide himself, in the attic. From there, he might peek through a crack in the floor, and watch his sons being scalped, his daughters being ravished, his wife tortured to death... and of course, he would still stick to his vow, never to fight. But aha, if that enemy should discover his hidden money, and steal it,

"THEN YOU MIGHT FINALLY SEE HIM, ACT LIKE A REAL MAN!"

Oh! How they cheered him on that one, stomping on the paving stones, clapping and whistling. Thousands of those men and women had been living alongside "holier-than-thou" hypocrisy every day.

They obviously enjoyed the imaginative picture; he painted for them.

"I tell all of you here today, and I shall tell the whole Nuworld forevermore, that these true Noblemen who struggled, and fought, and died for our freedoms,

"HAVE BECOME THE SONS OF ALL FATHERS,

"EVERY MOTHER'S CHILD,

"AND THE BROTHERS OF ALL, FOR ALL TIME,

"WHEREVER OUR PEOPLE ARE FREE!"

It was a most solemn statement to make, and the crowd accepted it that way, with many a jaw-dropping in wonder. Many heads nodded their approval. Murmurs swept over them as the Duke paused for a bit, to let that soak in. Then he continued:

"They have gone through War's Hell, and their Heaven shall ever be, what they left in the loving memories of their people. That is the only Heaven, and the only Hell, there ever could be.

"And in eternal thanks to those who bravely gave their lives, we the people shall sing love melodies yet more, to Mother Nature, to Her from whom we sprang – the *source*, the *solace*, and the *genius* of us all."

He knew he'd hear complaints from sheep-herding preachers, about referring to Mother Nature, instead of some religion's imaginary God or Gods.

"It seems to me, that freedom is being able to do all our naturally-given genius allows, so long as our actions harm no one, and hopefully, benefit many. Freedom has nothing whatever to do with theology; it has everything to do with morality. Liberty is a virtue universal and timeless. It is an age-old dream, that will not die.

"Every one of us in this Nuworld has great ability to get good things done. We aim to make certain, all of our people are free to use their individual genius, *to get good and great things done.*

"Right now, it behooves us to understand who our enemy is; and why.

"When this latest war against us by France began, a meeting was called at Albany, New York Colony, for the purpose of uniting all 13 of these English Colonies, for the defense of our lives, and our liberties. Everyone knew then, and knows now, that of course, no colony alone could protect their people, from any intelligent aggressor.

"That meeting at Albany was a shameful farce, as is well known; for it seemed impossible to unite into any single purpose, all of the 13 colonies. Each colony considered themselves, little independent states, with but a tenuous political connection, to the government of the British Isles. And they feel they merely have a social connection, with the people of the other 12, weak, little colonies, and with the peoples of England and of Europe.

"And we all understand that government, and those friends over there, are 3,000 miles, and a very dangerous ocean away, from our problems.

"After reading about that meeting, I thought to myself, that we then knew who our enemy was.... *AND... IT... WAS... US!*"

That brought some to laughter, but others didn't think it was funny at all.

"By that I mean, we were politically disunited, and not much action against any common enemy could be expected as a result. But since we of these 13 weak little colonies, had that connection to the wondrously rich, and all-powerful government, 3,000 miles away, with their all-powerful army, and all-powerful navy, we could rely on them to save us, from the wicked forces of France.

"Then our proudly independent little assemblies would be spared much expense, and of course, great inconvenience. Events have shown those assumptions were not entirely accurate."

The next part he roared like an animated preacher, in love with his own trumpeting voice:

"AWAKE AND AWARE, OF OUR PEOPLE'S GREAT DANGER, WE NO LONGER LIMIT VISION, TO OUR OWN ABODES ONLY. ALIVE MIDST FREEDOM'S BLESSINGS, AGLOW IN LIBERTY'S LIGHT, WE SEE BEYOND OUR SELFISH SELVES.

"WE SEE VICTORY BY EVIL, AS DEFEAT OF MANY FOR FEW; AND DEFEAT OF EVIL, AS TRIUMPH FOR ALL; THAT MEN WHEN FREE, HAVE DUES AND DUTY; AND THAT

WE, WHO ARE FREE, CANNOT FULLY BE FREE, WHILE OTHERS ON THIS CONTINENT ARE NOT!"

To Duke Odin's surprise, a tremendous noise of approval went up, left and right and all around. He hoped they understood what he said; but perhaps they liked the rhythm, the way he bellowed it out to them.

"Thus, the partners of the Nuworld Company permitted me to organize and lead, the Nuworld Nobility, with their full financial backing, and extremely valuable help in every respect.

"Your Nobility has had good success thus far, but I must say, WE HAVE BARELY BEGUN TO FIGHT! AND WE SHALL CONTINUE TO FIGHT, UNTIL THE KINGS OF FRANCE... HAVE KISSED... THIS CONTINENT... AND OUR ISLANDS... GOODBYE!"

Oh! How the crowd responded to that; clapping, stomping and hollering out approval.

The Duke noticed Ezra Stiles, practically at his feet, was checking to see whether he left anything out that he had written so carefully. Then he continued:

"We must understand who our enemy is. Certainly, it is not the Asian peoples whose ancestors canoed to this continent, from far away Asia, long, long before Europeans came here.

"A most interesting, and possibly correct theory, says their far distant forbears, left Eden at the head of the Persian Gulf, a very, very long time ago. They traveled ever onward to the east, and blended to some extent with eastern folk, before canoeing to the Nuworld.

"They are now properly called *Nuworld Asians* because Asia was where their ancestors came from. Most certainly, they are not, and never were *Indians*. They are, of course, citizens of this continent, as well as the Nuworld Euros, whose folks came over much more recently.

"Surely not the people of Canada, nor even the people of France, are our enemies; for the French people here, and over there, have riding on their backs, the crushing triple tyranny of mind-numbing

Church, land and honor-hogging Aristocracy, and their tax-devouring King.

"The French people pour the fruits of their labor into the purses of Priest, Aristocrat, and King, and those purses seem, never to be full.

"Of course, they would love to have the freedoms we presently enjoy, and the expanded freedoms we shall hopefully have, in the future.

"As I said, 'freedoms we shall hopefully have,' but since we in this Nuworld, abound in genius, *we... can... do... it!*

"Interestingly, Priests and many Preachers, call themselves pastors – sheepherders—who tend their flocks of sheep. We must not ever be, unthinking sheep. Because human beings are pressed into being humble, by seeming sheepdogs, there has been almost no innovation in the world for centuries. We have only just begun to use our genius. We must employ our natural creativity, for the good of all of our people, Asian and Euro alike.

"I firmly believe that between each and all of our ears, male and female *is the wonder of the universe.* Mother Nature has planted in human heads, the genius to do good and great things. We Nuworlders have already proven to be innovators, and we can dream up steady improvements in our lives, and our children's, and our grandchildren's lives, to the furthest generations here. We are all creators. Does nature make us clothing? No, geniuses of creation, both men and women, create clothing. Every one of us can add endlessly, to that statement about creating.

"United, we the people can create a society, in which each Asian and Euro babe born, shall have an honest chance at life's great challenges, and for life's glittering rewards, in our Nuworld, our Free World, our Brightest Rich part of the Whole World."

Obviously, many in the crowd had already read that statement in a newspaper and cheered happily, and loudly, to hear it directly from the Duke.

Then he roared out with everything he had, the double closing of his speech:

"WE HAVE NO DESIRE TO TURN THE OLD WORLD

UPSIDE DOWN, BUT ONLY TO TURN OUR OWN WORLD, OUR NUWORLD, RIGHT SIDE UP!

"WE ALL KNOW MANY PEOPLE IN THE OLD WORLD, VIEW LIFE AS IT IS, AS THOUGH THEY WERE SHEEP, AND BLEAT: 'WHY? OH, WHY? OH, WHY?'

"WE OF THIS NUWORLD THINK OF LIFE, AS LIFE OUGHT TO BE, AND THUNDER... *WHY... NOT?*"

The applause was tremendous, with a great swell of noisy cheers and hurrahs. The Duke waved and bowed his thanks to everyone, including those hanging out all those windows.

He jumped off the wagon in front of Stiles, who was putting his clocket in his pocket.

"Well, dear friend, did I miss saying very much of it?" the Duke asked Stiles.

Stiles grinned broadly. "Milord Odin, you speak so perfectly! That was the most beautiful half hour speech ever uttered! Yes, Duke, perfection! It will certainly be remembered for a thousand years! I must get this printed right away!" he said as he rushed away.

Even though he had got off the wagon, the applause and cheers continued for some time, much to Odin's satisfaction. He reckoned Stiles exaggerated considerably, but the people there really did seem to approve what he said.

His Pops had said Reverend Whitefield's sermons were nonsense but "entertaining," and maybe that was all his speech would amount to. But he hoped not.

Suddenly, people were "all over him," extending their handshakes. He noticed right away that Lord Andrew was hovering about immediately behind him. His friend had said he worried someone might harm him because famous men attract crazy people.

The Duke barged into the crowd, finding folks happy to shake his hand – and he, theirs. To have the approval of what he said by so many, he found thrilling! It was simply thrilling!

Perhaps ten paces or so into the crowd, a fellow dressed as a "gentleman" pushed himself forward and spoke rapidly to Odin.

"I'm Benjamin Franklin, and I'm pleased to meet you, Duke Bushnell! That was the most remarkable speech I ever heard, sir!

Your phrasing, such as 'Awake and aware of our people's great danger, we no longer limit vision to our own abodes only'—Milord, that was truly beautiful! And yes, your troops deserve to be called Noble!"

"Aha! Mr. Franklin! Thank you, and I'm very pleased to meet you, sir!"

Another well-dressed fellow next to Franklin thrust his hand out.

"I'm Joseph Galloway and your partner Clark yesterday bought my Durham Ironworks! And I must say, Duke, that was an astounding speech, you just gave to us! And I must add to what Ben has just said, about that 'Alive midst freedom's blessings, aglow in liberty's light...' Sir, you have a pretty way with words, including that Nuworld Nobility story!"

"Well now Mr. Galloway, my friend Abraham Clark has been his usual busy self around here then, while some of us have been busy elsewhere," the Duke told the man.

Duke Odin would have liked to continue their conversations, but other hands were gripping his, left and right and soon, he could see those two gentlemen no more.

Eventually, Lord Andrew sort of rescued him, and they made it at last to the SARAH BUSHNELL, tied up to a wharf, near their other 5 OdinRafts.

The vessel had been named for his mother, since she had inspired him from his earliest age, to exercise his brain. It was the very Odin-Raft he had invented, and the Nuworld Company's 14 partners had built and brought back *many tons of treasure* with.

The Duke noticed that each of the 6 OdinRafts docked there, did not yet have their beautiful Nuworld flags flying. When they sailed, they were only then to hoist their doubled brass, lacquered, 4-foot diameter circular "flags." The 4-footers were large enough to allow some names of terrain and water features to be painted on them. Surely, the Duke thought, they would help to educate his Nobles, with the expectancy of their future nation's size.

Also, the SARAH BUSHNELL had been their transportation from Stratford, from the Housatonic River in Connecticut Colony, to the Schuylkill River next to Philadelphia, during the summer.

That ship had brought himself, others and carts of supplies, for the Ohio expedition.

The Nuworld Company Treasurer Abraham Clark had made that vessel his base on the Delaware River, at a Philadelphia dock, since that time.

Greeting the Duke, and Arch Duket Andrew on deck was Treasurer Clark.

He surprised the Duke by throwing his arms around him, saying, "Odin my boy! I didn't know you could be so perfectly eloquent! Such a wondrous great speech! Everyone is so very, very proud of what you've accomplished!"

"Goodness Mr. Clark, you bowl a fellow over!" Duke Odin said.

But the Duke wondered whether Clark had really paid much attention to his speech.

"Tell me, what part did you like best, sir?" Odin asked him.

"Oh, all of it, but maybe especially that bit: 'They are become the Sons of all Fathers, every Mother's Child and the Brothers of all, wherever our people be free.' That, my friend, was truly, truly sublime. And I didn't miss that reference to the plural Kings of France. Many might suppose that was a slip of the tongue, but I know better. I wonder if King George in ugly old England, will remember when, if he reads it, that he was laughably crowned King of France, as well as of England?" Clark said.

Then Clark went on to tell the Duke of a message from his Pops, that there were so many problems in Stratford that, only his son Odin could solve. His pops had said, *Odin needed to return to the Connecticut Colony immediately.*

That was that, and the Duke told Arch Duket Andrew Montour, he was to become Force Group Overlord, for the Caribbean privateering, in the winter. There was no need to promote either of them, as their ranks far over-shadowed other Nobles.

Another piece of news from Clark was that on August 30th, 1756, – *exactly on David Odin Bushnell's eighteenth birthday*—the small nation of Prussia had invaded the little nation next to them, called Saxony. That move had begun a war against Prussia, from the far larger nations of the Austrian Empire, France, the Russian Empire, and possibly even Sweden.

"Aha!" the Duke exclaimed. "That tiny country would not seem to have much of a chance, but we hope their King Frederick is a great warrior. And we have the extremely talented Paul Revere, who can turn out thousands of OdinGuns, to help them win against great odds! That means Lord Croghan must come along, to be our salesman to the Prussians."

Clark's eyes gleamed when he said that, since the Nuworld Company treasury was being drained of more silver and gold, than was coming in. That was despite the sales of OdinRazors, Odin-Lamps, and OdinFlamers. Thus far, the remarkable OdinStitchers and the OdinEmbroiders were held for Cypriot Dudley's use and were not for sale.

Soon that talented clothier came aboard, praising him for the part of the speech where he said, "We have no desire to turn the Old World upside down, only to turn our Own World, our Nuworld, right side up!"

"Duke Odin," Dudley said, "I must hurry and get several of you fitted in your new formal raiment, because Countess Armstrong (wife of Arch Countet John Armstrong), has arranged for a dance at the State House tomorrow night, and none of you will want to miss that fun!"

Dudley had brought much cloth and leather. Also, he brought foot-powered sewing machines, he, of course, named OdinStitchers, which Odin had invented. He also brought embroidery machines named OdinEmbroiders, from Stratford, and set up a clothing mill in a building, that Clark had bought for that purpose. Dudley had many tailors, shoemakers, and seamstresses, busy producing more buckskin and formal uniforms, lace-up shoes, and calf-high boots.

Abraham Clark had arranged for a celebratory dinner, on the SARAH BUSHNELL, with the Force Overlords, the Overlady, and the partners all invited. It was great nostalgia for those who had spent six months in 1755, living and working aboard that vessel, in the Atlantic Ocean and the Caribbean Sea.

They dined on "Blue Willow" dishes the Spanish had brought

from China, to the west coast of Mexico. The Spaniards then had such cargo hauled by burros and mules, overland across Mexico, to Vera Cruz on the Gulf of Ohio, for shipment aboard galleons to Spain.

Odin had declared that "Gulf of Ohio" was far more appropriate than "Gulf of Mexico." He had "unofficially" changed the name of the Mississippi (Snake) River, to the Ohio – "The Beautiful"—River. In the word Mississippi, the hisses of a snake could be clearly heard.

But those three heavily laden galleons were forced down into the Caribbean by unusually strong north winds. There, the Spanish ships were apparently lifted high up by a rogue wave, which then slammed those wooden ships down, in especially shallow water, splitting the ships asunder. The crash deposited their precious cargo on the sandy bottom, where Odin and his partners brought most of it up, 64 years later.

There were things to do. The Duke found out that Overlord Armstrong hated the sea since he had nearly died from seasickness in 1741, on the way over the Atlantic to the Nuworld.

The Duke promoted Armstrong to Arch Count. He was to stay in Philadelphia and represent the Nuworlders to Asian Chiefs, who were sure to visit, asking if there be war or peace, with them. Also, Lord Armstrong was a good recruiter and an excellent trainer of Nobles.

Armstrong was replaced as Overlord of the *Bravehearts,* by the battle-proven leader, Arch Barron Daniel Boone, also of Pennsylvania Colony. Boone was promoted to Arch Countet.

Another excellent leader was Croghan's Overlordet, Grand Countet Nicolas Biddle, of Philadelphia. Duke Odin also made him an Arch Countet, and Overlord of the *Valiant* Force.

They sent the dead Barron Springer's medals to his folks in Maryland, along with a condolence letter from Odin. The Duke saw to it that other deceased Nobles were also honored in the same way. Barronet Francis Turbutt's parents in Philadelphia were to receive his awards.

There was no way at the time to get Arch Barron Folsom's awards, to his folks, in far off New Hampshire Colony.

Barrons Rittenhouse and Tully agreed to select, and train, 20 Nobles to use the ritt code, and ritting apparatus. They were to accompany the Duke's group, going to Connecticut Colony; they would be training the whole time.

They would need 2 "Ritters" on each OdinRaft, 2 with Lord Armstrong, 2 with the NUWORLD NUZ, at least 2 with the Nuworld Company, and two more to accompany Croghan, on his mission to sell OdinGuns and ammunition to Prussia.

Force Group Overlord Andrew Montour, would not be able to sail away to war in the Caribbean until his 12 trained Ritters returned with their apparatus. But that gave him time to train new recruits, called "Esquires."

The original, ancient meaning of "Esquire," was for young men in military training. It wasn't meant to be appended to the names of such, as wished to "distinguish" themselves, by self-appointment, as did lawyers, judges, and that brave Virginian, George Washington, Esq.

Duke Odin also promoted Lord George Croghan, to the rank of Arch Count. He was to pick out 2 Noble Bands to accompany him, and the OdinGuns, to Prussia. Several of those Nobles, needed to speak German or French, since the Prussian "big wigs," used both languages.

Overlady Annie insisted it would take at least two days, to prepare the food on their new stoves and ovens, for the trip of Duke Odin, and those accompanying him east. That meant the Duke, and his companions could not leave, until Friday.

The Overlady told Odin, she thought his speech might have changed the views, of many Quakers that day. Also, she said everyone was fascinated with the Nuworld story and amazed the Nuworlders were styled as Nobles – especially so the women.

The sun had already set when Clark announced, they had important visitors, and they should all come up on deck. They saw four men by the rail, looking the OdinRaft over, with several OdinLamps, barely giving enough light for so large an area.

Clark introduced them. Duke Odin hadn't dreamed he would see "the rich merchant of the city," Israel Pemberton, so soon again.

With Pemberton, were Benjamin Franklin, and Joseph Galloway. The 4th man was short, a little plump, and Clark said he was the royally appointed Governor of the Colony, a Lieutenant Colonel in the British Army, William Denny.

"Governor," Clark said to the plump one, "this is Duke Odin Bushnell, Overlord of...."

"No by God; he is not Clark!" Denny exploded. "Boy, you may be a rich hero at the moment, but you are absolutely not a Duke, nor goddammit, the Overlord of anything!"

That was what Odin had been expecting someone to say, and that plumb fellow filled the role perfectly.

Overlord Croghan had told him weeks before much about Denny; about his corruption and nasty immorality. His gruff brashness of the moment, had a hollow ring to it, for Odin.

The Duke stepped forward so that his face was looking down, on the much shorter Britisher's ugly mug, from a handsbreadth away, shouting out every word for all to hear.

"*Who the devil are you to say such a thing?* You are no real governor, but merely the deputy, to whoever in the world, is the real governor! You have scandalized the people of our Nuworld, by bringing to our sacred shores, the whore you call a mistress, along with your wife! *Shame be upon you, William Denny!*" Odin roared.

The man stumbled backward, and it seemed he might fall. His face turned red and purple, and he was absolutely taken aback, with fear writ large. He appeared ready to faint. Franklin took one arm; Pemberton took the other. Galloway stared bug-eyed and open-mouthed.

"Milord Duke Odin!" Clark blurted, "You can be so astonishing!"

"Mr. Clark," Odin responded with sternness, "this character has no authority over me! How dare he tell me what I can, and cannot do? At least Earl Lowdown had the good sense, to leave his wife at home when he brought along with him, his pretty blonde French whore, along with 17 personal servants, and a whole shipload of wine!"

The shocked look on the faces all around was priceless, since the privileged English Aristocracy, were never spoken of like that.

Duke Odin had learned a lot about Earl "Lowdown" (Correctly with French spelling, *"Loudoun"*) – British Army Lieutenant General John Campbell – sent by King George the Second, to replace the slain General Braddock, as Commander-in-Chief of all British Forces in North America. *And the replacement General Campbell didn't arrive in the Colonies, until an entire year after British General Braddock, was shot off his horse!*

The Earl had lost several battles, as a Lowland Scot, fighting the very tough Highland Scots, in 1745, nine years before. Not one time in his life, had Earl Loudoun won any fight.

Far more important to the English government, the Earl was the fawning friend of King George's son William, Duke of Cumberland. Military ability didn't count for much in England, obviously, for the lowdown Earl was not at all, killing men well, nor winning any battles.

The visitors all seemed speechless, but Denny was the first to recover. "I...I didn't mean any offense, Bushnell," he lied. "We all realize what you have done, to the goddamn French, and their goddamn Indians."

The Duke laid a condescending hand, on Denny's shoulder.

"Yes, but you do understand; we are all under strain. The French could easily sail up this Delaware River, and destroy all this shipping, and flatten Philadelphia. The war is far from over, and to succeed, we must cooperate, and not be giving out insults. Agreed, Governor?"

"Why yes, yes!" the plump one said.

William Denny was proving to be adaptable, although lily-livered. "Do you really believe the French could do that? Why would they?" Denny asked with an alarmed look.

"Why would they? They might feel obligated, to retaliate for their losses along the Ohio. They just destroyed the forts at Oswego, in New York Colony; why not put this place to ashes? They could certainly do it easily. But as a British officer of some years, you understand war is one surprise after another; right Colonel?" Odin said.

"Oh, but of course. I understand you gave an impressive speech today. Now that I've met you, I'm sorry I missed hearing it," Denny said with an obvious lie again.

Franklin jumped in then. "Governor, my own printers are busy, at this very moment, setting Duke Odin's marvelous speech in type, for my PENNSYLVANIA GAZETTE. Mr. Stiles and Mr. Bradford are doing the same, with the NUWORLD NUZ.

"By dawn, we'll have riders on the roads to deliver our papers all over the colonies, so everyone can read Duke Odin Bushnell's amazingly eloquent speech. We did the same to report the Duke's astonishing victories, along the Ohio Valley," Franklin said.

"Mr. Franklin is much too complimentary," Odin gushed.

Then to change the subject, the Duke introduced his partners in the Nuworld Company, one by one. He did not fail, to give them much deserved praise, as he did so.

Israel Pemberton took the Duke's hand, gripping it tightly. "Your Lordship, I'm glad I made the remark to you that I did, for it set off a spark in you; you struck a strong chord with us Quakers when you spoke of that meeting. I thank you for that Duke, and for acknowledging the true Nobility of your cause, and of your Nobles."

That certainly surprised the Duke, and he felt he had possibly made a friend in Pemberton. The slavery issue could be dealt with at another time. But he had doubts about Denny, for he was surely as unstable, as Croghan thought.

✷ 9 ✷

The Duke rose the next morning a little before the sun came up, and delighted in having a civilized OdinRaft shower – even if it was cool Delaware River water, being sprayed on him.

Somehow, Barron Francis Hopkinson's song popped into his head, and he began singing it, hoping the sound of splashing water would drown out the sound of his off-tune voice:

"This is our Nuworld, our very free Nuworld,

"Our Brightest Rich Part of the Whole World.

"So, Nobility, Nobility, protect us all from harm;

"And honor us, with righteousness, in city, sea, and farm!"

Suddenly, right there in the shower, he got the answer to a coming problem. So, he quickly sent someone to find that talented young songwriter, Lord Hopkinson, and bring him to his cabin on the OdinRaft SARAH BUSHNELL.

While waiting for Barron Hopkinson to show up, he read his speech as printed in the NUWORLD NUZ, and saw that it was made much of.

The size of the crowd was guessed to be at least 12,000 eager listeners, and their enthusiastic reaction was commented on with flattering quotes, from several notables. The scene was described, even to the people hanging out of many windows, to hear the Duke.

Odin had just finished his breakfast, when the lad he had sent for, came aboard.

"Sit down and have a cup of coffee, Lord Francis," the Duke boomed, with the little fellow, having a worried look on his face.

"Your friends call you 'Happy Lord Hoppy,' I've heard. You wrote that beautiful Song of Nobility, and I am so impressed with you, that I have another project for you.

"All I know about music I learned as a youngster when I polished the few brass organ pipes in my home town church," the Duke said. "I'm from the west parish of Old Saybrook – called Westbrook by some – near where the Connecticut River, empties into Long Island Sound.

"The place was called Pattaquasett by the Pochaug Asians, who were one of many bands of the Mohegan – the 'People of the wolf' – tribe. That 'hegan' part of their tribal name is like the Latin 'heathen,' also meaning wolf.

"But then Lord Saye and Lord Brook financed the voyage of English immigrants to the place in 1638, and the grateful settlers named the town for those two men: "Old Saybrook." That was exactly a full hundred years before I came into this world.

"Interestingly, 'Pochaug' means 'people-perfect' and those gentle folks welcomed the English, because the newcomers had guns, to counter the war-like Pequots, who bullied them.

"Another Mohegan Band were the Corchaugs, meaning 'hearts-perfect'; 'cor' being an ancient Euro word for heart, from which the Latin 'coronary' sprung. You know, like the word cour-ageous for a Noble fighting with heartfelt bravery.

"Another Mohegan Band are the Manchaugs, meaning 'God-perfect." There are other Bands of them, but right now I've been digressing, from what I asked you to come for.

"We're making steam engines, which I invented in Stratford, and so far, we've used them in sawmills, and to pump air powerfully, into our iron blast furnaces.

"There are many uses; we'll be putting our steam engines to, including powering vessels to go on rivers, and to cross all of the seven seas, on this planet Earth.

"I'd like you to take charge of making – oh, what to call them – ah, why not 'Happy Hoppy Organs'?—above the pilot houses on those craft.

"I want you to invent and make, a series of short brass pipes, with brass reeds of different thicknesses and lengths, with some way to open valves, that will allow steam to flow through, and make music, *that can be seen as well as heard*. You'd use keys like those on a harpsichord.

"Oddly Barron, steam is invisible until it's released; then you can see the vapor.

"When you have these Happy Hoppy Organs being made, I should think you'd do well to make small instruments, with little brass reeds, you can blow through with your mouth, to make music. You could also make bigger ones, with a bellows, that you push, and you pull, on your chest; again, you'd have reeds and harpsichord keys. Oral organs and chest organs; you see?

"Would you like to do this for me, for your country, *and for yourself to get very rich, Barron Francis?*" Duke Odin asked the lad.

With sketches made by the Duke in hand, Lord Hopkinson left happy.

Then the Duke bent over the NUWORLD NUZ again, feeling mighty pleased with himself, and humming the pretty tune of the Nobility Song.

Lord Andrew outdid himself in organizing the Nuworld Nobility, to parade in their formal blue uniforms, before a small stand set up for the strange Governor Denny (Odin's friend, he suspected, only for the moment), and other dignitaries to review.

That Wednesday morning of September 29th was greatly pleasurable, with Force Overlords pinning on very many Sharpshooter Badges, Campaign Shields, plus Crowns for Courage, for Leadership, and for Merit. The Duke accepted with aplomb, his several "decorations" in gold, silver, bronze, and the Ohio Valley Campaign Shield, in blued iron. His awards were specified anonymously to him, by a committee of Overlords.

Duke Odin reckoned his new blue, formal jacket, to be quite lovely with all those awards pinned on carefully, in a straight row from the right of his chest, going left. He would wear that uniform proudly the whole day and to the dance that evening. His shoulder straps were covered over with bright red sleeves, and the word Duke on each was done in gold silk thread.

Such medals were fairly inexpensive to make in quantity and were received by the Nobles as though precious, beyond any measure. The gold and silver medals were plated over brass, so as to make them less tempting than solid gold or silver, for bad folks to steal.

Their rank names for their formal attire were embroidered in gold color, over the red flat sleeves slipped over the shoulder straps. That way, there was no mystery as to who was what rank. Odin had supposed it better than indicating rank, by the number of stars, or buttons, or stripes, could have done.

During the noon meal, the Duke felt lucky to have a visit from the Iron Master (manager) of the Durham Iron Works, 50 miles north of Philadelphia. Clark had bought that operation, for the Nuworld Company. Thus, Odin wouldn't have to visit the place on the way home.

He was able to tell George Taylor, a 40-year-old Irishman, with much experience in the iron business, what he intended to do with the property. Taylor agreed to stay on as manager, and to accompany them east, to learn how they smelted Connecticut Colony's Housatonic Valley iron ore. Over there, they smelted nearly pure iron, to which they then added carbon, to make an iron-carbon-alloy. It was called 'steel,' from the stick-like blades of swords.

An important innovation in smelting, was Odin's idea of making charcoal *inside the furnace itself,* instead of the tedious, and expensive way, it had been done. He had men cut mostly tree branches, into merely two-inch-thick-lengths, then mixed them in with iron ore and limestone. That mixture was dumped in at the top of the iron furnace. The heat rising through that mix "charcoaled" the wooden chunks, and that made for a hotter fire, further down. Also, he devised ways to powerfully pump air into the base of the fire. They also blasted air onto the molten purified iron, as it flowed out of the smelter, and then they added carbon to make it into steel.

Ironmaster Taylor had only been gone from the SARAH BUSH-NELL, a short while, when Lord Andrew came, to breathlessly report the Noble outguards north of the city, rode in fast to inform him a large number of armed British Redcoats, were approaching.

"Duke, what would you like done?" Lord Montour asked.

"Milord Andrew, this has an odor about it. I wonder if it might be the work of the much-too-friendly Governor Denny. You'd best get every Noble possible, organized to meet them, but no Healthors. I know; we'll wait for them right there, where I gave the speech. Tell the Force Overlords to position the Nobles in those buildings, in the windows, where they'll be fairly safe, from any lod balls; those Redcoats might vomit, from their rusty old flintlock muskets. I hope the people in those buildings, won't mind the intrusions too much," Duke Odin said.

Standing next to Denny that morning in the reviewing stand, Odin thought he stank of rum. And he offered a fawning friendship, that seemed not at all sincere. Surely, the Britisher resented the shouted, truthful humiliation of the evening before.

The Duke sent runners to find Franklin, Pemberton, and Galloway. He sensed it might be important to have friendly witnesses, to whatever might transpire.

Thanks to posting those outguards with fast horses, and the slowness of the approaching troops, they had nearly an hour of warning time.

About 160 Nobles were rounded up, and assigned to windows overlooking the street. They were all in their new formal raiment, medals gleaming on their proud chests, just as they would wear to the dance, planned for that evening.

With their formal uniforms, they would not ordinarily wear their OdinGuns, nor carry any ammunition. But their weapons were brought with them for this occasion, along with a handful of ammos for each one.

The Duke and several others gathered in the speaking place.

Curious citizens were standing nearby, having heard the Redcoats were coming and suspecting something might happen.

Eventually, the three gentlemen Odin had sent for, showed up.

"Milord, what's this all about?" asked Franklin. "I must say, sir, your formal attire with those medals really does look great. But what...."

"I believe we'll find out shortly, Mr. Franklin," Odin told him. "I'd like you gentlemen to stand over there," he pointed, "out of the line of fire."

Galloway seemed astonished at that. "Line of fire? What's going to happen, Duke?"

"I'm not sure, but you had best keep over there sir, by Mr. Stiles and Mr. Clark," the Duke told him and the others.

The Redcoats were by then only a block away. They appeared to be perhaps 1/2 battalion; about half of the usual 500-strong. They were marching in cadence with drums beating, and muskets shouldered. Four mounted officers with gold bullion dripping from their shoulders, rode horses beside the soldiers.

Sure enough, Odin saw the lily-livered Denny. He had changed into a uniform of crimson, with a frilly French silk sash across his chest, that was holding his sword scabbard. The other British officers were dressed about the same, in glaring red color, as though to make them the easiest possible targets in battle.

The Duke checked the line formed a pace behind himself; Lords Montour, Croghan, Armstrong, Morgan and Lamb were there. All of them, like the Duke, were in their formal attire, and on this occasion, had in their holsters, their brightly polished, golden OdinGuns.

Croghan had a big brass spyglass, and looking through it he told those near him, "That's Governor Denny by God, and that's Lieutenant Colonel James Prevost with him. I know Prevost is the hated foreign officer, who commands the 4th Battalion, of the so-called 'Royal American Regiment.' So that must be part of the unit those soldiers are in. They're supposed to be Colonials in that Battalion, but I've heard it's mostly British and Germans.

"Oh, God!" Croghan went on, "And there's Sir John Sinclair! He was the Deputy Quartermaster General, during Braddock's march to catastrophe. Who can forget the nasty words he had for us Nuworlders, before that battle?

"Oh, that 4th officer there is possibly Major William Eyre. If it's him, he's a good man, and it's surprising to see him with such characters. Eyre's an Engineer, and he was with General Braddock's march to calamity, too."

Duke Odin turned around and thanked Lord Croghan for that information. The Duke, of course, remembered the account very well, of Sinclair's noted outburst at Fort Cumberland, on April 6th, 1755. He "stormed like a lion rampant," to Croghan, Armstrong, James Burd, William Buchanan, and Adam Hoops, those being then named by the Assembly, as Road Commissioners.

Sir John had ranted at the lack, of Pennsylvania Quaker's support, for Braddock.

"In 9 days' time," Sinclair had thundered at the 5 notables, "instead of marching to the Ohio, he would bring his army into Cumberland County, kill the cattle, carry away the horses, burn the houses, and later, if defeated by the French, he would pass through the 'Province' with drawn sword, treating the inhabitants, as traitors should be treated. In fact," declared Sir Sinner Clair, *"he would not hesitate to impress the whole Pennsylvania Assembly."*

Even that "Sir" in front of Sinclair's name, was probably spurious, Croghan was told.

As the Redcoats slowly approached, Duke Odin thought Denny had picked some dandy companions, for his purpose. Rumors had it that Prevost's first name was "Jacques," not James and that he was most likely a French Army officer, and pretty certainly a spy! He was given a British Army commission as a Lieutenant Colonel, by King George II, because George's kin, the Princess of Orange, had asked him to do that. Some qualifications!

The British soldiers had stopped along with the rat-tat-tat of their drums, lining up to form companies. Their officers supervised the movements. All of them were in blazing red, making them amazingly, hard-to-miss targets.

Duke Odin knew his voice carried far; he turned around 360 degrees, giving instructions.

Even the British soldiers would surely hear, as well as his Nuworld Nobles far up, hanging out of 2nd and 3rd story windows.

"Noble Officers! Harken to your Duke! The British Army is supposed to be our friend, not our enemy! We have no wish to slaughter these troops here, as we did over 1,000 French soldiers and savage allies, along the Ohio! We have no wish to see rivers of blood, here on streets in the City of Brotherly Love! No Noble shall fire his OdinGun unless necessary!"

As though ignoring his shouted words, 3 of the 4 Redcoat officers dismounted and walked down the line of troops, swords swinging at their left sides. They came then directly to the Duke, as he stood rigidly tall, in the center of the intersection in front of his "back up."

As the 3 British Army Lieutenant Colonels, stopped in front of the Duke, a single pace away, Denny was in the center, Sinclair on his left and Prevost was to his right.

"As I told you before Bushnell," Denny said loudly, as though to boost his courage, "you are no Duke, and as of this moment, your organization is dissolved. I'm the Royal Governor of this Province, by appointment of His Majesty King George the 2nd of England, and I have right here the backing of 1,000 British troops to enforce what I say!" he lied.

"It's almost clever of you to hide your few cowardly men in those buildings, but it won't work. *You are under arrest!* Your men must hand over all their pistols, and cartridges forthwith! Do you understand, Bushnell?" Denny asked with a blustery red face.

"Oh yes Denny," Duke Odin sneered contemptuously at him and spoke loud enough for everyone within a 100 yards to hear.

"I understand very well that you are a blithering idiot, to endanger not just your own life, but the lives of those soldiers. Those soldiers have the duty to fight the French; not us. You had best get back on your pony this minute, and ride away before your ugly face is blasted right off your head!" Duke Odin said, roaring every word at Denny.

The obviously, alcohol-laden Denny's face, instantly turned even redder with insane rage, and his right hand reached to his left. The Duke assumed he was reaching for his sword.

But instead, he could see the man was reaching *inside his sash*, and that could only mean, he had a pistol hidden there!

With both of his hands, the Duke grabbed Denny's hand, holding the pistol, squeezed it hard, and turned it away from himself, as he felt bones in that man's hand snap!

The pistol went off into the red-coated belly, with a sickening sound, and with smoke rising up! Denny, as he collapsed, melted backward onto the street! The wounded man screamed as loud as any Asian war-whoop! His cheap iron pistol clattered onto the paving stones.

Suddenly, the Duke saw that the Lieutenant Colonels, right and left of Denny, had drawn their swords, as though to run him through!

Those two were immediately riddled, with countless high-velocity shots, tearing up their faces, heads, chests, and bellies. Blood was spurting out, from all over both of them!

The thunder of OdinGuns was amazing, including the near blasts from his "back-up."

Those two melted onto the pavement left and right, dead before becoming horizontal, while Denny still screamed unbelievably. He was flat on his back on the dirty stone pavement, holding his right hand up with his left. He was not a strong man, and Odin obviously broke some bones in his hand. It had to have been terribly painful. But the belly wound? That ball must have gone through him, and severed his spine, to leave no feeling down there.

His blood and his life were gushing out from his belly, and his back, with every tortured scream; and all Denny could feel, was the great hurt of broken bones, in his hand.

Meanwhile, the Duke had glanced to see the still-mounted British officer, was waving both of his hands to calm his soldiers, so they wouldn't fire their muskets. Wise fellow!

Although it seemed a very long time that Denny's screams filled the air, as he looked this way and that, with glazed-over eyes, seeking sympathy, it was probably no more than a few minutes, before he passed away—or at least passed out.

People began gathering then, to have a close look at the 3 bloodied Lieutenant Colonel Redcoats, lying midst the well-trampled horse, cow, sheep and pig dung, on the cobblestones.

Duke Odin had not so much, as unholstered his own OdinGun.

The still mounted officer dismounted and walked over to the Duke.

"I'm so very sorry about all this, Duke Bushnell," he said, as he looked over the three bodies. "Hell, I'm engineer Major William Eyre, not infantry at all, but I was ordered to come along," the Redcoat said.

"Major Eyre, you did a very good thing in calming those troops. Now, I would suggest you gather up these bodies, and get them to hell out of here, and properly buried.

"First though Major, can you tell me how anyone can be so block-headed, as to think they could carve me up, with those stupid swords, when they were obviously confronted with OdinGuns, known to kill men at 400 yards? It was suicide! With my own Odin-Gun, I could easily have done all 3 of them in, myself!" the Duke said.

"Milord Bushnell, I.... I... really don't.... oh, just maybe it's because they've been given to believe; to sort of have a blind faith in those swords, because they've been used for 1,000s of years and.... and maybe because they've carried them at their sides, in the army, day and night, since they were boys. It makes no sense Milord, but that's perhaps why they'd normally react that way, and draw those blades they love and habitually sharpen all the time."

"Thanks, Major," the Duke said.

He turned away, feeling ill, as both Lords Croghan and Montour, came up to talk to Eyre.

The Duke hurried back to his OdinRaft.

Just as the Duke stepped onto his weather deck, he sensed someone close behind him.

He turned to see it was the Overlady. She was dressed in her pretty blue formal raiment, polished brass hat, and a pretty "Grand Count" sleeve, covering each of her shoulder straps.

On her heaving chest, was the Gold OdinGun Badge she had won as third best sharpshooter; the blued-iron Ohio Campaign Shield; plus, Crowns for Courage, Leadership, and Merit.

Below were her many-pleated, knee-length white skirt, white stockings, and black shoes. She had an OdinGun holstered on her hip, and her pockets bulged with ammunition.

"Duke! Are you alright?" she asked.

"Guess so. Where'd you come from?" he asked her.

"That apartment building over there," she pointed. "I was in the 3rd-floor window, and I got to shoot those two snakes, that we're going to cut you up with their swords! *By God, I really did it!* You combed away over 1,000 snakes along the Ohio, and I combed away those two rattlesnakes, that wanted to kill you! Got each of them in the noggin, I did! Shot their hats a-flying! I just knew Dear God had a reason to make me a good sharpshooter!"

Her big blue eyes were even larger than usual – *and looking wild!* The Duke was so flabbergasted he hardly knew what to say.

"I.... I didn't know any Healthors were present. I gave strict orders that none of you..." he began to say.

"Oh, but Barrons Tully and Rittenhouse, allowed me in a window with them. They agreed it was my right," she said excitedly. "It was terribly obvious you were in an extremely dangerous situation, Milord.

"And what a marvelous little speech you gave to us Nobles! I'll never forget that 'Harken to your Duke' speech! Those British troops must have shivered in their boots to hear you roar as you did!"

She hesitated a moment, then erupted with, "But all I know is, I shot those two reptiles, just because, you are the most precious man on earth!"

With that, she whirled about, and hurried down the ramp, leaving the Duke thunderstruck.

He thought it would have been rather inappropriate to mention, that those men had holes drilled in their heads, chests, and bellies by many, many little lod cylinders; with of course some shots coming from Nobles, close behind him.

As she hastened away, Barrons Elias Tully, David Rittenhouse, and Benjamin West, came up the ramp, with big grins on their faces.

"She's a right good shot, Duke," Lord Elias said. "And I'd say she's got her man squarely in her sights, and there isn't any escaping for you!"

❧ 10 ❧

I n mid-afternoon, Duke Odin Bushnell and the others calmed
down enough, to have a meeting to discuss many things.
Abraham Clark would leave the next dawn, a day in advance
of the Duke's party. Clark said he was certain, folks in other towns,
would love to hear the Duke speak, so he'd make arrangements. The
Nuworld Company Treasurer, a New Jersey Colony man, had traveled that way many times before, he said, so he had no fear of going
alone.

He was also to arrange for a vessel in Elizabethtown, New Jersey
Colony, to take them to the Connecticut Colony. They all agreed; it
was best to avoid the British in New York City.

Clark gave plenty of silver nu coins and nu notes, to Lords
Montour and Armstrong, to pay their Nobles and to purchase
supplies. He also doled out thousands more, of silver nu coins and
notes, for the released captives, since most of them had no possessions left, whatever.

The meeting was interrupted when it was announced, the
parents of the deceased Barronet Francis Turbutt, had come aboard.
All of them went up on the main deck to meet them. Lord Croghan,
thoughtfully brought along the lad's buckskin jacket, with the blood

washed from it. The jacket of course still had the young Noble's name on the arms, "Barronet" shown over the shoulder straps, and the upper arms had the circular picture map of the Nuworld, sewn on.

Lord Croghan introduced them to the Duke as though he had known them a long time; although of course, he had never seen them before. It was Croghan's way.

The Duke hadn't planned such a meeting, but he somehow knew what to do.

"Mr. and Mrs. Turbutt," the Duke said, "if you would kindly hold your son's jacket, I'll pin on his medals."

As the quiet couple held the jacket, the Duke explained.

"The Silver OdinGun Badge is for his very good marksmanship in our training camp. The Ohio Campaign Shield, is for his Nobleness, in confronting our very dangerous enemies there, and the Five Feathered Iron Crown, is for the Courage he displayed, in actually going into battle there. A tiny red ruby is attached to his Iron Crown, for his shedding of blood, in defense of our freedoms," Duke Odin told them in a formal, yet a friendly, way.

As the medals were pinned on, the parents were pouring out tears. The Duke then stood back and said with solemnity: "Mr. and Mrs. Turbutt, your Noble son, Sir Francis, has become the *Son of all Fathers, Every Mother's Child and the Brother of All for all time, wherever our Nuworlders are Free!*"

The Turbutts cried a little, shook hands with the Duke, and the others, and left. Nobody mentioned a house maid's belly large with the lad's child, so the Duke didn't bring it up. But he hoped they would preserve the boy's jacket, and awards, as a memento of a life cut short, in freedom's all-important, Noble cause.

Duke Odin told Lord Andrew Montour, that such a statement was to be personally made, if at all possible, to the parents or wife, of every Noble killed in battle.

After their supper, the Duke and friends – except for Lord Andrew who said he'd have his fun later at home someday – got into a coach pulled by four horses, hired by Lord Croghan.

It was the first time any of them had been in such a conveyance since coaches were really rare in the Colonies.

They headed for the Statehouse where they found Benjamin Franklin and Joseph Galloway, waiting at the entrance for them. The two political leaders were full of compliments about the handling of the "crisis" that day.

They said Barron John Copley, had tacked up a large number of his "coppix," inside.

"I've wondered when Lord John Singleton Copley, would finally reveal his genius," the Duke murmured.

Galloway and Franklin led them into the largish room, where the tables and the desks had been cleared away, and chairs arranged around the walls.

Above the chairs, were the coppix pinned up all around, pretty much at eye level. The room was well-lit, with brilliant wall-mounted OdinLamps. The whale oil the lamps burned, stank somewhat, but in those days, everyone was accustomed, to foul smells from many sources.

The coppix were amazing. The paper pictures were pinned up, in an order beginning with scenes of the Nobles, in the training camp, the departure for the Ohio from Croghan's fort, and then followed through from battle to battle. The fires had been hand-colored in the coppix, making the burning of each of the 4 French forts, particularly impressive.

As the Duke looked up from the last coppix, there stood Lord John.

"My dear Barron friend," Duke Odin exclaimed, "you are to be most heartily congratulated, on your great invention!"

"Thanks, Duke Odin. I am learning all the time – you know, to make them better," Barron John Singleton Copley said.

"You're much too modest. What's next for your marvels?" the Duke asked.

"Now that I've proved my system works, I'm going to set up a mill in Stratford, to make the coppix boxes and all that," Copley told him. "Also, I'll get up a school, so I can teach others to have their own studios, all over the colonies, and make portrait coppix, mostly. They'll cost a pittance, to what a painted portrait costs.

"Also, Milord, I intend, with Lord Rittenhouse's help, to enlarge the coppix when I put them on paper. That way, I can make the glass negatives, hopefully, a lot smaller, and easier to carry about, and maybe greatly increase the coppix size. As you've insisted, I shall keep striving for improvements all the time," Barron Copley said.

People began to stream in and were excited to see the coppix. Some of them found it hard to believe, the revolutionary pictures, copied from the "negative" glass plates to "positives" on paper, were actually real.

The Overlady had invited scores of pretty girls to the dance, in addition to the lovely Healthors, so there were plenty of attractive partners.

The frontiersmen proved to be good "square-dance" teachers and callers, with most of the really big men, seeming "light on their feet." All of them had more fun than could have been legal, what with the dance lasting about 4 hours.

The Duke thought Annie Willing to be, far and away, the most beautiful woman at the dance, as well as a wonderfully graceful dancer. But then she surprised him, by introducing a good-looking fellow, of about her own age. He was one of the Philadelphia merchant family of Bingham. He was obviously crazy about Annie; which was hardly a surprise.

But that really, really stung! To see that man dancing with her, and holding her in his arms, stung, stung, stung!

The Duke didn't like that man at all. He was hardly worthy of Annie. But then, nobody was; not even himself. *Oh, but I could try to be worthy of her,* he thought.

That struck home with a bang, and all of a sudden, the fact she was five years older than him, mattered not a whit!

He found the Overlady chatting, with a few pretty friends.

"Grand Countet Annie Willing," he said with formality, "may I have the pleasure of taking you home in a carriage?"

She brought a lovely hand to her beautiful cheek in surprise.

"But I've already been asked.... Yes! Yes, of course! I'll tell him the plans have been changed!" she smiled.

While she went to bring the Bingham fellow, down out of the clouds, Duke Odin told Lord Croghan, he was borrowing the "coach and four."

"It's for a quite special mission, Milord," the Duke said.

Croghan smiled his agreement, and the Duke and the Overlady were soon outside.

He assisted her into the carriage and asked where she'd like to go.

"I must go tonight to my OdinRaft, since there's so much to do on the morrow, Duke."

He told the coachman which wharf to drive to, but to take his time in getting there. The old fellow seated up front winked that he understood.

She had temporarily made her "office" on one of the new, 10-masted OdinRafts, but would move to the smaller, 5-masted SARAH BUSHNELL, when it and the larger ones sailed away for the winter.

It was surprisingly dark inside the coach. The little smoky lamps on each front corner outside brought slight illumination to the passengers.

Odin sat next to her as the coach began to move. He boldly took her hand in his own.

"Annie, I must admit I was jolted when you introduced that Bingham fellow to me. I hope you aren't too fond of him as, well, I.... well, what I want to say dear Annie is, I have discovered I love you very much, and I would like you to kindly consent, to be my wife someday."

He blurted that out rapidly and was completely unprepared for her reaction. She withdrew her hand from his and moved away on the seat!

"I was beginning to think you must be as blind, like a mole in the ground! Didn't you know that from the first moments I saw you, I was in love with you? Heavens! I had been told by Mr. Clark, and by George Croghan, what a fabulous genius you were, and how you felt about your countrymen, and all that. But seeing you with those broad shoulders, and wavy black hair, and that wonderfully handsome face, why of course, I fell in love with you instantly!"

She was breathing hard and talking fast.

"You must have no idea how much it has meant to me, to have your praise, your approval, to be called Noble, to have that Gold OdinGun Badge, that Campaign Shield, and those beautiful Crowns! All of that has made me feel like a whole woman, a worthy human being. My entire life I've been reminded I was pretty, but that seems so shallow, and so unimportant.

"It's been you who gave me the opportunity, to do something truly worthwhile.... *and.... and yes! Yes! Yes! I would very much wish to be your loving wife!"*

Odin grabbed her, squeezed her, and kissed her rapturously again, and again until finally, they "came up for air."

"I must be awfully stupid Annie, for I had no idea you might have such feelings. But then, you know I have been rather busy, this past while. But I've known all along of course, that you aren't merely the most beautiful *doll* – may I say it? – The most beautiful doll in the world, you are truly a wonderful, wonderful person too, my dear. *My... dear! How sweet it is to be able to say that!"* Duke Odin said.

There were more hugs and more kisses until after a long, exhausting time; they began to talk about the future.

The Duke absolutely had to return to Connecticut Colony, to solve the many problems there. He had to be certain they were prepared, to overwhelmingly defeat the French in Canada, in the next "campaign season," during the next spring and summer. Meanwhile, her excellent services were needed to train, and to supervise, the Healthors in their Caribbean venture.

They left unsettled where, and when, the wedding would take place. Reluctantly, he had the coachman stop at her wharf, and they had their final hugs and kisses. They said their goodnights, and she was gone.

Oddly, when the coach got him to his own OdinRaft, Lord Elias Tully was waiting on the ramp for him.

"Where have you been, Duke? I was worried that gorgeous blonde had kidnapped you!"

"Elias! Guess what? That absolutely beautiful doll has actually agreed to marry me! Imagine that! Annie Willing shall be my wife, and I'll be an old married man, just like you!" Tully's boyhood friend, Odin, exclaimed.

"Well, I'll be switched! What in the devil took you so long to get around to that? Everybody's known she's just as wild, as can be for you!" Lord Elias Tully said.

"I'm so excited I can hardly think!" the Duke admitted.

"Damn, we have barrels of rings and jewelry back home, but none to give her here. You'd best get to a jeweler's, and get her one, don't you think?" his long-time friend said.

"Oh, I hadn't thought of rings," Odin said. "You're so right, my friend. I'll try to get some sleep and take care of that on the morrow, for we must leave on Friday. We're to have dinner at her folk's house tomorrow evening. I reckon then; I won't see her after that for a long, long while."

"About like me, and my beautiful Mercy," Lord Tully sighed, as he was reminded of the wife he had to leave behind, in Stratford, Connecticut Colony.

Barrons Benjamin West and John Copley, woke the Duke Thursday morning, saying Lord Elias had told them the good news, and they were eager to make a coppix of the two lovers together. They had already sent for the Overlady, they said.

They also told him, Treasurer Clark had already ridden off, on his way east.

Soon his bride-to-be was with him again, on the main deck, where the sun shone nicely for a portrait of the loving couple.

Surprisingly, the artists argued over what the best pose of them would be, and Lord Copley won. He placed them cheek-to-cheek, and hatless, with no need to show anything but their "fair faces and bright smiles," he said, and the deed was quickly done.

The Overlady rushed off to her duties, while the Duke had a hasty breakfast, and was soon away to meet with city notables.

A Mr. Robert Morris – partner with the Overlady's father in the merchant-trading company, "Willing and Morris" – offered them his country house, and estate as a training camp, free of charge for the duration of the war. But of course, Morris was attempting a bribe, for he hoped he would benefit from having first choice, of the plunder brought in, from captured French ships. But the Duke insisted they would pay a fair rent, and could not be so obliged to anyone.

But the 2 of them had a lengthy conversation though, about – of all things – the old city of Havana, Cuba, where Morris had been held captive for some months, a few years before. Somehow, Morris also got in some talk about the insurance business; a big thing in England.

The Nuworlders were assured their "Letters of Marque and Reprisal," as licenses for privateering, were still valid, despite the dead Governor Denny, being the signer. Of course, Clark had had to pay the dishonest Britisher a hefty bribe, for his signature on the papers.

Before Treasurer Clark had ridden away east, he had informed the Duke, that nearly all of the Nobles had left most of their salaries due, with the Treasury. Clark had informed them the retained monies would earn a whopping 6 percent interest, compounded at ½% each month. That alone would provide them with an important nest egg, by the time they had driven the French, out of the Nuworld.

Most of those Nobles, he said, hopefully, would earn considerable wealth, from the sale of French ships and goods; but only if they were lucky at piracy, in the vastness of the seas.

Overlord Montour and the Duke, inspected the 5 OdinRafts, with ten masts, being 250 feet long, that the Battle Forces would call home, for the next 5 or 6 months. The 6th OdinRaft, the SARAH BUSHNELL, had only five masts and was 1/2 the length of the 10-masters.

There was more than plenty of room for the expected Nobles and the kitchens. The privies were far superior to anything else afloat. Each vessel also had showers; however, they provided a drenching of unfriendly-to-soap-salt water, not the fresh kind.

The OdinRocks (extremely deadly rockets) would only be known to the Nobles when they got to sea.

Lord Armstrong would deal with the Asian chiefs, who were expected soon to call.

Armstrong said he knew of a Philadelphia jeweler, most likely to have an "engagement ring," as they were called. They found the shop with a grand total of 5 rings to choose from.

Duke Odin chose a gold ring the man said had on it a "pure diamond" of over a carat, he thought. He said it could be fitted to the Lady's finger. So, Odin paid for it in silver nu.

The Duke and his friends went to the Willing's house for dinner.

Annie's parents met them at the door, and Odin formally asked for, their darling daughter's hand in marriage. It was just as formally, consented to.

The dining room was large, and simply done, in the Quaker fashion. Mr. Willing sat at one end of the table, his wife at the other. Odin sat opposite Annie, who sat by her mother.

The Nobles all looked grand in their formal raiment, including the bride to be.

Barron Copley produced three prints of the coppix of the pair. Everyone said it was a lovely portrait of them, and so sharp and close-up, they could see every eyelash.

The Barron said he would make more prints in Stratford, and hoped to someday have apparatus to "enlarge" them also.

They had no sooner sat down when Duke Odin stood up. He walked around behind Mrs. Willing, to her daughter, and took the ring out of his pocket. He unrolled the red velvet cloth it was wrapped in and asked her to hold out her "ring finger."

"Whether or not this ring is as genuine as it appears Annie, I'd like to slip it on your finger, so that everyone will know you are dearly loved and spoke for. If the ring should turn your finger green, all of us will return and strangle the jeweler I bought it from," he said with a serious tone in his voice.

That brought a bit of laughter, as she nervously stood for the occasion.

"Oh! It is so very beautiful!" she said, surprising him with a kiss in front of everyone, while they applauded.

After they had eaten a very good dinner, Duke Odin felt he should say something.

He stood and said, "Dear Annie, Mrs. Willing, Mr. Willing, and friends: all of us understand this war has caused so much pain, and great hardship for very many people in our Nuworld, through no fault of their own. It is our duty to make certain, once and for all time, that the kings of France, do kiss this continent goodbye.

"So, while my future wife here, is training more Healthors, and sailing out into harm's way, my partners, and Lord Croghan, and I have very important other duties for the very same cause. We absolutely must ride away in the morning. But we shall all meet again, and enjoy much better days, when all our country's men, women, and children, shall be secure, healthy, and hopefully, have happy prosperity. Thank you all, so very much."

Annie decided to stay in her own bed that night.

She (and her mother, of course) showed the Duke her sleeping room, which seemed small and simple for so large a house, and for such a wealthy family.

She had a nice writing desk under her window, where she said she had spent so many hours practicing penmanship, as well as reading every book, she could get her hands on.

They said their goodbyes at the front door, with a passionate kiss, and off the Duke and friends went for one last night, on the OdinRaft, SARAH BUSHNELL.

The Duke was happy to get to bed – never forgetting his gratitude for escaping from the English navy—for he would be riding away at dawn.

There would be no chance he could return before the Force Group sailed away, about the 1st day of November. The hurricane season would be over by then in the Caribbean, and that sea would be swarming with merchant shipping, war ships, and privateers of many nations.

Doubtless, there would be some pirating going on too, if opportunities happened.

Friday, October 1st, 1756, came along rather cooler, than the fine weather they had been having. The sky was overcast with scudding huge clouds, as though it might rain at any time.

Benjamin Franklin and his political friends, many of the leading merchants, and perhaps 12 young beauties came to see the Duke's company off; they were all back in their buckskins, and in their saddles, for their trek north and east.

Israel Pemberton took Odin's hand in both of his, thanking him "for all you have done for our Colony," and for that "wonderful, wonderful oration."

The Duke reckoned it was a good thing to have the friendship of so influential a man. But those slaves of his, and others, were another matter to be settled, in some future time.

The Duke's dear Annie rode with them to about the city limit. There, they hugged and kissed one last time. Then he rode on, saddened to leave her behind.

Lord George Croghan led the way, with the two Noble Bands he had chosen.

Lord Rittenhouse had selected 20 Nobles to learn how to ritt.

Barrons Tully, West, Copley, Hopkinson and Thomson; Lord Doctor Gale plus Mr. Ezra Stiles, and the Ironmaster Taylor, were with the Duke. The total came out to be, 55 men.

They had six packhorses carrying Copley's and Rittenhouse's equipment, as well as their tents and food.

Abraham Clark was to arrange for the sale of the 61 horses, and the horse furniture, at the port village near the Hudson River, called Elizabethtown, in New Jersey Colony. That was where they expected to take ship for Connecticut Colony.

Only a few of them had been over this particular trail before.

They would ride about 35 miles north, along the west side of the Delaware River, to a place opposite to Trenton, New Jersey Colony. That was the town, Overlord William Trent's father had founded.

It took nearly 2 hours to get all of them across the water to Trenton, by ferry.

It was edging into a dreary-looking twilight in the town.

But about 1,000 people had gathered to hear the Duke speak. Included were some students, and faculty, from the College of New

Jersey. They were said to have come all of 10 miles, from Princeton, just to hear the Duke's already famous "city speech."

That school was Presbyterian; just as all other such schools in the Colonies, were associated with one religion or another; they were established primarily to turn out preachers. No schools, at least in the Colonies, were yet teaching engineering or science. Such men as Franklin, Rittenhouse, and David Odin Bushnell, were self-taught and true pioneers in that regard.

The Duke leaped up on the bed of a wagon and roared out the identical speech he had given in Philadelphia. He even threw in that bit about the "rich merchant of the city." All of the speech was applauded, just as loudly, as the first time, he painted those verbal pictures.

He wound up his speech by bellowing, "We of this Nuworld think of things as they ought to be and thunder... WHY... NOT?"

Well, the lengthy applause was again for him, *truly thrilling*.

The leaders in the town insisted the Nuworlders should not be breaking out their tents that night. They would accommodate all 55 of them in various houses. Folks were actually vying for that honor.

The Duke's party were tired and grateful. The Mayor herded the Duke, and his partners, to his own house.

They had a quick dinner and were then bombarded with questions about their noble adventures.

Clark had told the Trentonites, a lot about "them there savages what had been kilt" and they wished to know more.

The Mayor said he had taken the trouble, to go hear the famous actor Reverend George Whitefield speak four times, and the Duke's "oration" was superior in every respect.

Of course, Odin knew that was a flattering exaggeration. The English actor-preacher Whitefield was well known throughout all the Colonies, for being able to frighten and damn thousands of people to hell itself and keep them spellbound, for an hour or more.

Duke Odin's talk had lasted all of 34 minutes.

But Trenton's Mayor was insistent. "Duke Odin, one bit of your speech struck me as being prayer-like, and so beautifully lyrical. You said, 'And in eternal thanksgiving to those who gave their all, we the people shall sing love melodies yet more to Mother Nature, to Her from Whom we sprang – the *source*, the *solace* and the *genius* of us all.'

"Duke, I never once heard Whitefield say anything nearly so perfect for the occasion," the Mayor of Trenton said.

Lord Croghan was asked what life was like, on the Pennsylvania frontier during the war, and he told them of the murders, and the burnings that had been going on.... until lately.

Croghan told them no one would ever know, the total figures of all the horrors, but it was clear, that type of Asian warfare had centuries of experience behind it. That is, those fantastically painted men on the warpath, would strike quick and hard. They would then vanish.

The next morning the Nuworlders hoped, by hard riding, to cover the 45 or so miles to Elizabethtown, before darkness fell.

But they had gone only 2 miles out of Trenton in the morning when the rain began to fall. It came down slowly at first; then, with more and more fury. There was no midday meal.

The air and the rain were miserably cold, yet it was still only early in October.

Lord Croghan figured they had gone rather more than halfway when night would soon be upon them. They set up their tents, on a thoroughly soaked cow pasture, for the horses.

They dug out the bread, cheese and rope cake, Odin's sweet Annie had got up for them. She knew everybody loved both her bread and her cake.

That food was quite good, but privation of privations, they had no fire and no coffee.

Rain fell through most of the night. At least by the time the sun rose, the rain had stopped, and the eastern sky was clear. But alas, the western sky promised more rain to come.

As the Duke came out of his tent, he noticed high in the sky, the Nuworld's wise eagle, with its starkly white head and tail, circling over them. Was that a sign? He had to laugh at his imagination. More probably, that bird was wondering why humans bothered with tents, wigwams, and houses, when a large pile of sticks, high in a tree, made a perfectly satisfactory nest.

About mid-afternoon they arrived at the edge of the village of Elizabethtown. They were a thoroughly mud-splattered 55 men.

There was no more rain, and the wind changed, to a warm breeze from the south.

A rider approached, asking for the Duke by name.

"I'm Duke Odin Bushnell. What is it, sir?" the leader of the men said.

"I'm Captain John Hazelwood, and I was told by my friend Abraham Clark, to let you know, the British arrested him, and took him away. It was for treason, they said."

"*Treason? Abraham Clark? Impossible!*" they all agreed.

But it really was true. Clark had made good time, had arranged for a horse trader to buy all of their horses, and the horse furniture. He also had got his longtime friend Hazelwood, Captain and owner of a brand new OdinRaft, to agree to take them to Stratford.

Clark had wound up his business that morning, they were told. He, along with Hazelwood, were waiting to greet Odin, and his friends, in a tavern. There, about 10 or so Redcoats, with an officer, hauled Clark out and put him under arrest. They were to take him to their Commander in Chief, in New York City, it was said.

Hazelwood said Clark had told him as he was being taken, that the officer in charge of the Redcoats was Major William Eyre. Major Eyre! That was the seemingly decent British Engineer, they had seen in Philadelphia!

Lord Croghan was well acquainted with that Major, and could hardly believe his ears.

❧ II ❧

John Hazelwood was about 30 years old, born in England, but by then a "true blue American," he said. He had been sailing between the Nuworld, and London, for nine years in schooners.

He had sold his last schooner in London, and sailed as a passenger to Boston. He then rode down to Old Saybrook, and "ventured most of his fortune, on a 15-masted OdinRaft, from Uriah Hayden."

Hayden apparently had his shipyard busy, with turning out 15-masted OdinRafts, rather than produce the 5 or the 10-masters. Those OdinRafts were also the longest, and most capacious ships on the oceans, at a whopping 375 feet long.

Hazelwood had sailed to Elizabethtown 12 days earlier, to pick up New Jersey wheat, shucked corn, and pine logs. All of the vessel's cargo was destined for London. That was why he was in Elizabethtown, and happened by chance, to meet his old friend Clark.

Hazelwood said Clark had told him a lot about the Duke, including his genius at inventing, all about the Ohio campaign, and he had read "that fabulous speech." He had also bought OdinRazors, for his crew of 35, and 24 OdinLamps, for his ship.

As they came to the dock, the Nuworlders could see Hazelwood's OdinRaft was the same as other OdinRafts, in the 25-foot width and the 30-foot hull height. But it was far longer and had all of 15 masts. Inside the 16 holds would be strong double-X trusses, on the hull sides, because of the length. Under each of the 15 masts, was a side-to-side wall. That dividing wall, had diagonal planking, just as on the smaller OdinRafts. Those side to side walls designed by Odin were so the hull could not twist and "go crank," in storms.

Sailing ships built before, often twisted their structure in a storm – "going crank"—and ever after leaked, and were difficult to keep sailing, on a straight course.

Importantly, Odin Bushnell had also designed slanted "water wings" amidships, on each side, extending out 3feet, and each with a 3-foot width. They were fixed at the loaded waterline, so that when the wind rolled the ship left or right, the wings would counter that roll as they entered the water, the wings on the other side being then out of the water. That little idea kept the ships fairly level even in a stiff wind. The wings were raised up when docked.

Even though he was yet only a boy, the ingenious and self-confident, David Odin Bushnell had solved that problem – and many other problems—in the OdinRafts. The extending of the bottom forward, raft-like, helped to reduce the ship's pitching and rolling in a storm.

They turned over their mounts to the horse trader, Clark had made the deal with and received a bag of silver and gold coins, which was more than enough, to pay their way to their home on the Housatonic River.

The horse trader had a good business going; he would sell at a profit, those same animals and "horse furniture," to folks traveling west.

The Duke's party climbed aboard the OdinRaft, and Odin asked to confer with the Captain, Lord Croghan, and his partners.

"Captain Hazelwood," the Duke said, "please tell us all you know about British Headquarters, on Manhattan, and how close you can get to it with your OdinRaft."

"Duke," Hazelwood said, "I've only been up close to the Earl's quayside headquarters once. That was when I tied up there with my old schooner, to deliver mail, that I brought from London for him. They always keep that quay clear, so's Admirals can visit, I suppose.

"That Earl is just an average size man. He wears a powdered white wig as all those rich lords do, and he's got a long face. But I tell you, he's the most pompous ass of a snob, I ever did meet. And he dresses like a Scot, which I suppose being his name is John Campbell, he is. And he's the 4th Earl Loudoun," Hazelwood said.

"Captain, you can actually tie up, next to his headquarters?" Odin asked him.

"Yes, Duke, and I think he lives there, too. He's got lots of staff there—generals and secretaries and such. His troops are put up in nearby houses, and they have a barracks built next to the Battery, near Fort George. Here's a new map of New York City; I can show you just what's what on this map."

That map helped the Duke's understanding of that small city on the tip of the Island of Manhattan. To the Asians who had for a long time lived there, it was the "Island of the Gods."

"Man" was a common Algonquin Asian word for God, or Gods, or the Great Spirit, and

"-hattan," obviously meant island. Using that word Man, perhaps originated with Eden's Euros long ago, meaning actually that humans are the children of God, as of course, they were – thought Odin Bushnell. Therefore, he supposed, Men are Gods and Women are Goddesses. Odin had said that to his longtime friend, the Reverend Ezra Stiles, who was a licensed Congregational Preacher. Stiles merely nodded, he understood, but he made no comment.

"Gentlemen," the Duke said to his friends, "I don't want any mystery about this, so I'll just think out loud.

"A fiddler at the dance the other night told me he couldn't read music; he only 'played it by ear.' That's what I must do... I'll play it by ear.

"I think of Earl Loudoun as Lord Lowdown, the Lowdown Loser, for he has lost battles but never won a fight, and I aim to make sure he doesn't win this one, either.

"We hear he's been insultingly arrogant, in demanding the various

Colonial Assemblies do as he says they should. That is like his life-time of ordering servants around, in the mansion that he, of course, inherited.

"He seems not to know that a drop of honey, attracts more fly's as well as friends, than a barrel of vinegar.

"He's a pompous ass of a snob, who has yet to accomplish much, except for inheriting a title and I have to guess, a lot of wealth. No doubt, he gets great rents from tenant farmers, who are denied much chance, to have their own land.

"And now he imagines he is high and mighty, and has us in a corner, with Abraham Clark as his hostage; but he's not going to get his way this time... no friends; not with us.

"He supposes he can get some sort of revenge on us, for the deaths of those three crazy Lieutenant Colonels in Philadelphia; as though they weren't simply acting stupidly drunk.

"He almost has to have ignored in our newspapers – if he actually read any—the story of Nuworld Nobility and our Nobility's victories. That snob of an English Lord, probably sneered in reading my speech, if he bothered to look at it at all.

"He must be mystified about the OdinGun, thinking it's worth has been much exaggerated, because it was invented, and made, by mere 'Provincials,' as they call us.

"The Earl is doubtless much offended by me giving Noble titles, to men and women, who actually deserve such distinctions. He doubtless supposes we are a bunch of country bumpkins.

"So, if Captain Hazelwood can tie up his OdinRaft on the Lowdown Loser's quay, I'll walk down the ramp, to talk him into giving us our cherished friend, unharmed. That is aha, just as all our Nobles stand up, from hiding behind that railing over there (he pointed), with their OdinGuns aimed precisely, for the Earl's head.

"So now I want every one of us to shine our brass, and our shoes, to make certain our formal raiment is clean, and not wrinkled, with medals gleaming on our Noble chests. We must show the man who inherited his title, what Nobles look like who actually earn their titles.

"And one last thing; if either Clark or I am hurt on that dock –

and only if that happens—I am obliging every Noble here to blast away until they have slaughtered every Redcoat present! Is that clear?" Duke Odin Bushnell said.

"Good God, Almighty!" Ezra Stiles exclaimed. "You are a daring fellow!"

"A touch of audacity is what's needed here, methinks," the Duke replied. "Again, I say Lord Lowdown shan't win any battle with the Nuworlders. Let's get things done now."

By sunup, Monday, October 4th, 1756, all the Nobles were lined up on deck for inspection. They had showered and shaved, dressed again in their formal raiment, and breakfasted well. The Duke and Lord Croghan inspected each of the 51, and smiled their approval, with their partners included.

Ezra Stiles and George Taylor were not armed, so there would be just 53 OdinGuns available to shoot if need be.

With the mooring ropes off, the tide got Hazelwood's vessel moving out of the channel called Kill van Kull, with Staten Island on their right.

Those names had been retained, since the Dutch West Indies Company controlled those parts, nearly 100 years before. The English had easily won control of the Dutch holdings in the Nuworld, back in 1664, except for a couple of Caribbean islands.

When they were out of the Kill Van Kill into the Hudson, Captain Hazelwood pointed out several English warships at anchor, far up the Hudson River, near Manhattan. He also pointed out a speedy little pilot boat, heading that way.

Pilot boats were designed strictly for speed, for the one sailing to tie up to an incoming ship first, was sure to have his Harbor Pilot fellow employed. Pilots on the slower sailing craft could only look on... and grow hungry.

"Duke," the Captain said, "we may be sure there's a spy on that boat, to tell of your arrival. If he stops at one of those English warships or continues on, we'll know what's what."

A warm southwesterly was then blowing fair, and the little Pilot's craft practically skipped along on the surface, of the Hudson River.

The OdinRaft was well burdened to 23 feet deep, into the river, but the 15 huge sails could be easily and quickly winched, to every angle necessary, to catch every whiff of moving air most efficiently.

The Duke went up to the prow to watch the wind engine—much like a small, many-bladed windmill – above the prow, whirling away, pumping air down a pipe, and up through cracks in the raft sticking out forward, and left and right of the hull. Billions of air bubbles were pouring out, mostly from the bottom of that "raft," saturating the water with lightning air, that reduced the water's frictional drag on the hull.

The sight pleasantly reminded the Duke of what he had so quickly conceived, 2 ½ years before. It re-kindled his self-confidence. He was a fellow who could think when he had to, he reckoned.

Later in the morning, the Captain noted the pilot boat hadn't stopped at the warships but had continued on speedily, to Manhattan Island.

Gradually, Captain Hazelwood roared out his commands to winch the 15 huge square sails down. As the OdinRaft with its forest of now bare masts, got close to the dock, those on board could see the surprise, on the faces of those ashore, at seeing up close, such a huge ship.

At just about high noon, the OdinRaft was gliding cautiously, up to the Earl's quay, with 51 Nobles hidden, along the 39-inch-high "railing"; actually, it was a solid and 10-inch-thick wall that helped to strengthen the hull.

Duke Bushnell stood at the open gate, waiting for the craft to be tied fast, and for the ramp to be lowered. He had his right hand gripping the handle, of his holstered OdinGun, that was also tethered to his right shoulder.

He would keep his hand there, obviously ready to whip that weapon out, and shoot.

His left hand held a half dozen extra, brass-cupped ammos.

He would gesture while speaking, with his hands full of things the British had never seen.

As the OdinRaft came to a halt, the Duke could see on the wharf, a long-faced man wearing a Scots tam on his head, a far-too-long scarlet coat, a green plaid kilt, and plaid stockings to match.

That had to be the Lowdown Loser, Lieutenant General John Campbell, he was certain.

Behind the General, were officers with gold cords dangling from their shoulders. Left and right, were a company of red-coated soldiers, 50 or 60 men on each side, with their musket butts on the planking, feet spread apart, "at parade rest."

Odin noticed every officer, wore a ludicrous sword, hanging idly on his left side.

With each company was a Sergeant holding up a fancily made, long-handled, ax-like, and absolutely useless, "Halberd." That Halberd was merely an ancient symbol, of his authority.

The English loved tradition, he reckoned; although tradition had absolutely nothing whatever to do, with killing men well, and winning battles.

Immediately behind the Earl, was the Duke's partner, Abraham Clark. Insultingly, he was tied to a chair and had a gag over his mouth.

Two of Hazelwood's crewmen laid the ship's ramp down, from the gate in the railing, with its small wheels resting on the planking of the wharf.

The Duke signaled to the Nobles to rise up, and kneel by the rail. He then walked calmly down to the plank-covered wharf.

He noted the gasps of astonishment on the faces of the British as the Nobles leaned their shiny brass OdinGuns on the railing. Those Nobles were well-sheltered, from famously inaccurate musket fire.

With a large man's booming voice, the Duke spoke to the British, left and right.

"Every one of you must remain calm. Don't make any sudden moves, so no one will be slaughtered. If shooting starts, every Redcoat on this wharf will be shot as dead, as the planks you are standing on!

"General Campbell!" he roared to the long-faced man, looking down on the Earl from his tall stance, "Who among your staff gave you the really, really blundering idea to snatch Abraham Clark, and hold him hostage?"

Without pausing for an answer, the Duke hurried on.

"He should be hung by the neck until very dead! Mr. Clark is one of the absolute finest, and most honorable of men, on this planet earth!

"Now, if you happened to be wondering how it was, those 3 British Lieutenant Colonels became stupidly, drunkenly suicidal in Philadelphia, and so idiotically tried to do me in – with their pistol and swords, mind you—let me affirm what I'm sure Major Eyre, must have told you.

"*Are you listening to me?*" the Duke scowled angrily at the Earl, raising his voice even more.

He shouted that last because the Earl's eyes, were fluttering every which way, noting "DUKE" on each shoulder, staring at the medals on his chest, the brass ammos in his left hand, and yet nervously glancing at those OdinGuns, which were aimed at his own aristocratic head.

The Earl nodded yes; he was listening. He actually seemed unable to speak.

"You have got to know that William Denny was not only unspeakably immoral but crazy besides. If proof was needed, he demanded that I hand over our deadly, war-winning weapons to him, and disband the Nuworld Nobility! Such insanity!

"Whoever recommended him for that post ought to be hung up by his heels!" he roared.

(It was known King George's son, Duke William, had recommended Denny to William Penn's son, as their governor of the Pennsylvania "Province.")

"He actually supposed he could shoot me, with his hidden pistol. But I turned it around, and as a matter of fact, he shot and killed himself!" the Duke told the wide-eyed Loudoun.

"Those other 2, John Sinner Clair – who could hardly be counted as among the level-headed – and Jacques Prevost, the French Army officer who quite certainly was a spy and crazy also.... General Campbell, hard as it may be to believe, those 2 actually drew their utterly ridiculous swords on me, and although I could easily have killed them myself, they were completely riddled with shots by our Nuworld Nobles.

"Now, that's settled," the Duke said, taking a breath, "we have this little matter of a war to fight against the French, *and... not... each... other.* You weren't sent 3,000 miles over the Atlantic, to make war on us Nuworlders! We must make the Kings of France, kiss this continent goodbye! We must comb those snakes right out of our hair!

"General Campbell, you British may fight the French where, and how you wish, and we Nuworlders shall do the same. Do you agree?"

The Duke roared most of this right at him.

The Earl seemed surprised he was asked a question and fearfully croaked, "Why yes, Duke Bushnell, of course. Yes, Duke."

"Good. Now release my dear, dear friend Mr. Abraham Clark, and we will be out of your way. We will be out of your way, so we can all get back to our proper business. That is, we both should be driving the French off this continent, and away from the freedom loving folks, of this precious Nuworld!"

Without taking his eyes off the Duke or moving, the Earl said, "General Abercrombie, Colonel Webb—release the prisoner now."

"I am very glad, General, that you have just saved yourself, to live for another day. I wish you good fortune on the fields of battle!" Duke Odin said with a straight face.

With that, he turned to give the untied Clark, a hand up the ramp.

The older man appeared quite shaken by his ordeal.

Duke Odin noticed everyone on the wharf stayed put until the untied OdinRaft moved. The Nobles stayed at the rail, with their OdinGuns at the ready, until they were past the place.

The Duke, Lord Croghan, and Mr. Stiles helped Clark down into the dining room.

"Abraham, are you quite, alright?" Stiles asked.

"Yes, I am now! Duke Odin, what a performance you put on there! God! How scared they were of you! They all simply froze at the sight of those incredible, golden, OdinGuns aimed at them!" Clark said and then continued.

"The Earl and his crowd, they at first actually thought they had you whipped; they seemed to believe you'd give up your OdinGuns to them, and disband, and maybe they'd hang you. They're certainly not at all, very bright men, I tell you. They soak up too much wine! They don't know you as I do, but I still could not have dreamed you'd frighten them as you did!"

"Abraham," Stiles put in, "did I see the Earl pee down his leg?"

"Oh yes, Ezra, he certainly did. He peed down into his shoes and onto the planks!" the older man said. "And I noticed Duke; you didn't address him as an Earl; as a Noble. Of course, you knew he aimed to finish Denny's work with you, but you put the blame for that idea on an aide. Clever! You're a very sharp fellow, Duke Odin, as all of us know so well!"

Lord Croghan asked Clark, "I saw Major Eyre there; was he at all rough with you?"

"Oh no, but he said he'd have been court-martialed and shot if he didn't obey the Earl. The Earl was mad at him, for what happened to those 3 Lieutenant Colonels, in Philadelphia. But he couldn't have done anything about them, of course. The Major apologized to me several times, for doing what he was ordered to do. Oh Milord, how the Earl wanted your 'pistols,' as he called them," Clark said.

"Interestingly, none of them could believe Duke," the Nuworld Company Treasurer continued, "that you wrote your own speech. Some of those officers supposed it had to have been done, by an Oxford graduate! It was too well phrased, and too well composed, for a mere Provincial to have done it! Quite a compliment, I'd say, however unintended it was. And they certainly did not believe whatsoever, that you got done in the Ohio Valley, all that was claimed. They could not believe it was possible, my great friend."

"Well Mr. Clark, what matters is that you're in good health and that you are safe with us. You'll be back with your sweet wife, and your precious children soon, and we can all get on with our duties. Right now, I'm going for a little walk," the Duke added, not admitting he felt a bit drained by all that tension.

Up on the weather deck, the Duke could see New York City was fading into the distance. They were making good progress north up the East River, next to the "Island of the Gods."

Duke Odin walked toward the rear − not the "stern, the steering end," since both ends had rudders − and shook the hands of each of the 15 sail tenders. They were pleased to meet the famous young man who designed their fast and easy-to-sail vessel. Except in the fiercest winds, a single man could constantly manage each huge square sail, cranking it to its most efficient angle.

At the box-like, squared back end, Duke Odin watched with pleasure, as gravity forced the heavy water to cascade from both sides and below, to fill in the 25-foot-wide, by 23-foot-deep "ditch," the OdinRaft had plowed.

The bubble-filled water expanded, and surged in, slamming hard against the back, pushing, and adding speed to the ship. He could also see the rudder coming up from each rear corner of the raft. Those devices there, were extremely effective because of the rush of water to get into the ditch, as the vessel was steered on both ends, much better, than with a rear end rudder only.

He relaxed in the remembrance of conceiving such a vessel, but his revelry was short.

Ezra Stiles came up to him.

"To me, Duke, that scene below is more beautiful than any water-fall, because it was your genius that envisioned it, as no one else had. I want you to know sir; every last one of us is more in awe of you all the time. What you did today to poor Lord Lowdown, was truly amazing."

"Thanks, my friend, but one does what one must do. By the by, you won't print any of this in your NUWORLD NUZ, will you?" Duke Odin asked.

"No Duke; you're right. However, I did take down every single word you uttered today, just for the record. But publishing it now would make the Earl's humiliation even worse. It's hard for me to understand why the British view their Colonials so stupidly, with such contempt as they show. It's such an ignorant policy, to display poor regard for those who are valuable allies, and customers and friends," Stiles said.

"Mr. Stiles, it appears we must deal with a bunch of blockheads in their Army, Navy, and government. It seems just awfully short-sighted, for a nation as well-populated as England is, to enslave their own citizens in their Navy. They would only have to treat their men with some decency, and they'd have plenty of volunteers, I'd think. We've demonstrated how easy recruiting is when a proper attitude is shown," the young Duke said.

"Aha Duke, *when a proper attitude is shown.* Treating humans with due respect is contrary to what the ruling Oligarchy over there, thinks should be done. Those 200 families that in effect own, and rule that country.... well, there's nothing we can do about that. We have enough problems for the present with the French, eh Duke?"

"Yes, indeed, Mr. Stiles. Before we left Stratford on July 1st to go to war, I asked Pops to ask Uriah Hayden to sell his yards there, by Old Saybrook, and start a shipyard in Stratford, to build big Odin-Ship steamers in. I hope that's done. Meanwhile, in order to properly go up and conquer Canada, we'll need Rufus Putnam to build 36, of those steam-powered OdinBoats I designed. Oh; and 14 more Odin-Boats for 2 Battle Forces we'll leave behind to defend that town.

"Lord Andrew has an instinct for such things, and he's sure the British would hate to go up there. They don't like the woods, and they're afraid of repeating that parade-ground General Braddock's debacle, he's sure. So, I'm supposing; they'll likely try to take Louisbourg up there, at the entrance to the Gulf of Saint Lawrence – or rather, the Gulf of Canada, as it should be called," the Duke said.

"Well, your father and other untrained, poorly equipped Colonials, took Louisbourg on Isle Royale, in 1745," Stiles said, "so the Brit's should be able to do it. Such a shame, after all that tremendous and brave effort, the British traded Louisbourg back to the French, in exchange for a trading post in India. Such concern they demonstrate, for us 'mere Provincials'!"

Captain Hazelwood came back just then. Soon the Duke and Stiles, had him convinced to join their cause. Hazelwood would be taking Lord Croghan, and a load of OdinGuns with ammunition, to King Frederick of Prussia. They were expecting the Prussians to give much harm to the mutual enemy, France. The Nuworld Company would buy Hazelwood's cargo of pine logs, and he could sell his grain to the Prussians, probably at a good profit.

The Duke and his companions arrived home in Stratford,

Connecticut Colony, Wednesday morning, October 6th, 1756. They had left there, just 14 weeks before.

Odin quickly introduced his far-away bride-to-be, Countet Annie Willing, to his family, via the cheek-to-cheek coppix.

His Pops, mother, and 10-year-old brother Ezra, and sisters Sarah and Lydia, then 13 and 6, were thrilled to hear directly from big brother Odin, a recounting of adventures they had read about in the newspapers. Both of his parents, in particular, marveled at the eloquence, of his Philadelphia speech.

Odin had the pleasure too, of re-joining his partners and friends, Rufus Putnam, OdinBoats builder; Ethan Allen who provided the necessary iron ore, lime and charcoal/wood for their blast furnaces; Phineas Pratt who ran the ironworks; Alexander Chalker of the glassworks; and genius at art and precision manufacturing, Paul Revere, of the arsenal.

Pratt and Allen would be helpful in teaching George Taylor, their new ways of iron mining and smelting. Later, they sent Taylor back to their Company's Pennsylvania furnaces by ship, with two steam engine air blasters, for the revision of the iron furnaces there.

The Duke needed a house in which to work, and for his future bride. A row house was found for him, that was next door to Andrew Montour's townhouse, and four doors away from George Croghan's. His mother and others would see to it that it was furnished. It was more than big enough for him to rattle around in, and 1 of the three bedrooms, on the 2nd floor, was where he set up a drafting table to work on, late into the night.

At his Pops insistence, guards were on duty around the clock at the front, and at the back of his house. He was wary of the Lowdown Loser getting revenge by assassination, for his humiliation. The Duke always cautiously wore his OdinGun and kept it beside his bed at night.

It was then that he decided, based on the experiences of the Ohio Campaign, that there really was a need for an improved Odin-Gun. He would keep Revere producing the present design for the Prussians, but for the Nuworlders to beat the French, he wanted to change a few things. Of course, he expected the present design of the OdinGun, would be copied in Europe.

The Duke asked his partner Paul Revere, who produced the OdinGun, to come to a meeting with him at his townhome, in an evening.

The evening was a chilly one, so he had hot chocolate ready to serve his friend and him, to warm them up to the ideas he had in mind.

"Paul my friend," the Duke began, "you've provided a large number of OdinGuns for the Prussians, and we can bet, they'll want an awful lot more when they get good results with them. So, I'd like you not to make any changes at all, to their OdinGuns. We can bet, the Prussians and others will, as soon as they can, copy that gun, and perhaps make improvements to it."

"Very well Duke," Revere said. "I can sense you've got some changes in mind for me."

"Actually, not much, Paul," he said. "I'd like you to plan for one that you can be produced separately, for our Nuworld Nobility right away, to improve it so it will repeatedly fire, with every pull of the trigger. You'll understand why, when you consider if one of our Nobles should suddenly be confronted with, say, six armed enemies popping up in front of him. He'd be a very dead Noble if he didn't have the ability to spray them with shots," he told Revere.

Instead of having their ammunition kept in tiny pockets, on the chests of their jackets, he would keep an ammo insert (a magazine) in the gun's far larger rear handle. It would hold 50 ammos, that would be a bit smaller than at present. They'd be fired through a slightly different barrel, just 15-inches long, that would newly taper from 1/3 inch to 1/4 inch.

Several angled-back slots cut into the muzzle, to each side of the front sight, would counter much of the weapon's recoil, and mostly eliminate, the usual muzzle rise when firing.

OdinGuns presently had a bolt that gripped the ammo, with a locking handle the shooter pulled an empty brass cup, back out of the bore with, after being fired. Inventive Odin Bushnell figured a sensitive spring, could replace that human effort. The spring would retard the ammo cup and bolt going back, from the explosive force of the gun powder. When all the way back, it would move the empty cup over 1/3 inch, return to center, and push another unfired ammo into the bore, and turn to lock it there, ready to be fired by a trigger pull; *automatically and instantly.*

That would be far faster firing, that the OdinGun was capable of.

Extra "ammo inserts" – or just, "inserts"—could be kept in jacket pockets.

The inventive Duke figured to have two columns of ammos, in the inserts. As the pulled-out empty cup was moved a 1/3 inch to the right, all of the oily ammos moved the same, down, around the bottom of the insert, then up with the left-hand column to put an unfired ammo, ready to be pushed forward into the bore, and locked, ready to fire instantly again.

Duke Odin reviewed with Revere, every tiniest detail, to make sure there were no misunderstandings. He asked the Head of the Arsenal, to begin making the Odin2Gun, the ammo inserts for the handles, and the new, smaller ammunition, right away, and to give him one for testing as soon as he could. He was to keep making the OdinGun as is but only for the Prussians.

The Odin2Gun would be 2 inches shorter, than the OdinGun, have no fore handle under the barrel, and the 8-inches-or-so long leather-covered handle full of 50 ammos, would be gripped by both hands. It would actually appear to be a really large "pistol." It would yet be tethered to a Noble's shoulder, and held up by his holster.

The Clothier for the Nobility, Cypriot Dudley, was to be told soon to make many thousands of buckskin jackets, in various sizes, with four chest pockets for the ammo inserts.

There were many problems for the Duke to address, right then. Within three weeks, Lord Croghan and Captain Hazelwood, with 26 Nobles, including Ritters, were on the way to Hamburg, Germany, up the Elbe River, to sell to the Prussians. They would take all of the 13,500 OdinGuns, holsters and a goodly supply of ammunition, in wooden boxes, Revere had made to that time. Whether the Prussians carried their ammo on their jacket fronts, was up to them.

The price was 40 ounces Troy of silver (8,000nu) for each Odin-

Gun, including the holster on a belt, the shoulder tether, and a box of 100 ammos each.

Prussia's King Frederick was known to have a treasury bulging with silver and gold, so the 540,000 ounces of silver would hardly dent his resources. But that silver coming into the Nuworld Company treasury, would make Treasurer Clark really, really happy.

Lord Croghan would no longer be "poor," when he was paid his commissions by Clark.

Croghan also took, on credit, many OdinLamps, OdinRazors and OdinFlamers, to sell in Prussia on his own account. The Odin-Stitchers and OdinEmbroiders were so much needed by Clothier Dudley, that there was not enough of them extra, to sell to anyone, just yet.

Lord Rittenhouse busied himself in teaching Ritters and improving his apparatus.

Twelve trained Ritters were sent back to Philadelphia, to serve with Overlord Montour's Force Group, in the Caribbean Campaign. Two ritters were sent to serve with Lord Armstrong.

Lord Rittenhouse's Instrument Mill workmen, also made a considerable variety of instruments. They made large and small compasses, steam gauges, pressure gauges for the boilers, several sorts of brass valves, etcetera.

Meanwhile, the Duke determined he needed five full Battle Forces, for the conquest of New France, plus a 6th and 7th Battle Force, for the defense of their Stratford home base.

Each Battle Force he planned for, had risen in total personnel, from the original 63 Nobles each, to a whopping 2,000. That would mean probably 14,000 trained, and eager Noblemen and Noble-women would be required.

❧ 12 ❧

As Duke Odin Bushnell's luck would have it, a good recruiter showed up.

The Duke had just finished dinner at his family's house when a visitor knocked on the door and asked for his Pops. He said he was a friend of Captain Nehi Bushnell's, from the days of the Louisbourg capture, in 1745, about 11 years before.

He was Lieutenant Colonel John Bradstreet, who had just resigned from the British Army, and said he wished to join them in "turning our World, our Nuworld, right side up!"

Bradstreet appeared to be a powerfully built, self-confident man in his 40s. Since his Pops obviously trusted him, the Duke did as well.

The man said he had been the Lieutenant Governor, of the little port city of Saint John's, on Newfoundland Island, and had lately been a "Quartermaster," supplying British forts in the north, of New York Colony.

The Duke interrupted him. "Aha, do you know much then, about the Oswego affair?"

"Yes Milord Bushnell, I do, but first I'd like to let you know, I've read about your creation of all those Nobles, of your fabulous Ohio campaign, and your beautiful speech in Philadelphia. That speech, I must say, was truly extraordinary, and inspiring to all who heard it or read it, I'm sure. I've read it over, and over again, and I know others are doing the same.

"Also, Major Eyre told me about those – ah – events afterward, and about the Earl pissing down his leg when you scared him half to death, sir!" the man said.

"Thanks for those compliments Colonel, but I rather think it was the 50 or so OdinGuns aimed at the General's face that gave him a scare. What do you suppose caused the disaster at Oswego? Wasn't that in mid-August?" Odin asked.

"Yes, Milord, it was. But I was wondering if it's true, you actually escaped from a Navy press gang? That's a terrible fate for anyone unlucky enough to be impressed by those snakes."

"Yes Colonel, I was knocked out, but I woke up in their rowboat, jumped out, and swam the ½ mile to shore. I might not be alive today if I hadn't got away. So many 1,000s of our men and our boys have been ruined, or even killed by the evil English navy. But again; what about those Oswego forts?" the Duke asked.

"Well, the main problem it seems to me Duke, as they built a fort on each side of the Oswego River, where it empties into Lake Ontario, instead of a good, really strong fort," Bradstreet told them.

"Last May I employed about 1,000 men, to build 350 new boats, and all the oars to go with them. Building that many boats was no small enterprise believe me, Milord. And then with those boats, we went from Albany up the Hudson, then up the Mohawk River, across the Great Carrying Place, as it's called, and then down the Oswego River to the forts. It was a difficult thing to do, but I had truly excellent men with me, and they came through on delivering the goods bravely, despite the many difficulties," Bradstreet said.

Odin noticed he credited his "truly excellent men," an attitude that marked a good leader.

"That garrison was actually starving," Bradstreet continued. "We brought them huge amounts of food and other goods. On the way back, just as we got to the Great Carrying Place, we were attacked by

1,000 or so of French, and their Indians – no, I understand they're rightly called *Asians,* and not *Indians.*

"Anyway, it was one devil of a battle, and we finally drove them off. We probably killed as many of them as they did of us, which was 65 very good men, I'm sorry to say. And it may interest you to know, that Sir William Johnson's Indians – sorry, *Asians* – gave us no warning of the attack, although they had to know, the enemy was in the neighborhood. That very crooked and utterly dishonest Johnson was appointed Indian Agent, by King George, and he has much influence over those people.

"Milord, I reported all of this to Earl Loudoun," Bradstreet continued, "and he immediately discharged 400 of my men, the best fighters in the English service, it seemed to me. You can imagine the shock I felt that he would do that. And he also had the gall to question my promotion, to Lieutenant Colonel from Captain.

"But the British seem to believe all of us Provincials, must be inferior to anyone fresh from Europe. So, that's why I resigned and came to see Mr. Bushnell and you, Milord. I've kept those 400 discharged men in tow with me because I suppose you'll need some help. They're just outside of Stratford right now, in their tents," Bradstreet said.

"Wow!" Nehi Bushnell said. "Son, Colonel Bradstreet is the very best of men, I assure you. Maybe he could help with the OdinBoats business."

"Thanks, Pops. Colonel, you've built lots of boats, but these will be rather different if you'd like to join our cause," Duke Odin said.

"Definitely; I would definitely like to join your cause, Duke. I've heard quite a lot about your OdinRafts, about your 2-inch-thick planking being tongue and grooved, tarred and built up in diagonal layers for the hull, and all that; and they are even nailed together. All that is pretty amazing to me, sir," Bradstreet said with sincerity.

"Good. We will need 36 OdinBoats to go take Canada with, Colonel; plus, 14 of them for the local defenders," Duke Odin said. "Our iron ore near here is about used up, so we need to convert all the iron we get, into steel. We need that steel to build our ocean-going steamships. Ocean storms are rough on wooden ships."

"The OdinBoats will be 150 feet long and are actually moveable barracks, with decent privies, warm water showers, a laundry, fine stoves, and ovens. Each OdinBoat will be housing about 300 Nobles, somewhat comfortably. Those boats will have about a 7-foot draft when loaded. Seventeen-foot diameter, steam-engine-powered bucket wheels, will be on each side, just aft of the angled sides of the prow. Those wheels will reach down about 16 inches below the bottom. We'll do all this in such a way that the boat can go on any sort of waters, and actually crawl up out of the water, and drag itself along on land.

"Those wheels will have 15 slice-of-cake-like open-mouthed buckets. As a bucket on the wheel turns forward, it is full of air. Then it gulps up water which mixes with and compresses that air. As the wheel turns and each bucket passes the bottom of the turn, the water full of that compressed air explodes out backward, also from centrifugal force and paddle action, pushing the boat forward," Odin told him. The Colonel nodded, he understood.

"In another yard, we'll build far larger steam vessels of steel – OdinShips – to go on the seas of the world, with good speed. The much larger OdinShips were designed by me, for ocean travel, and to hold an entire Battle Force of 2,000 Nobles. Amazingly, we discovered through several complicated tests, that our high-carbon steel is nearly 1,000 times as strong as iron; but we'd like to keep that very secret," Odin told the older Bradstreet.

"You said Duke, your OdinBoats go on land, too?" Bradstreet asked, ignoring the steel remarks made by the younger Bushnell.

"Yes, Colonel; to some extent. It may be hard to imagine, but the OdinBoats will be able to traverse frozen-over lakes and rivers. If the ice should be too thin to support such weight, and one of them should break the ice, I believe they'll be able to crawl back onto it. If the ice should continue to break, they can continue on anyway, ice or no ice. They'll be pulled along, by their huge wheels, gripping water, land or ice, as you will see.

"My Pops here, Colonel, is right now building boilers, steam engines of steel, and other things, to make it possible in time, to turn out an OdinBoat every day. They will be not just for the use of our

Battle Forces, but for use on all our continent's many rivers and lakes. They'll provide a far better, and faster transport of people, and of people's goods, than anything ever dreamed of before. Even in the wintertime, they can go on frozen rivers, lakes and snow, because the bottoms will be covered with 1/2-inch-thick, slippery steel. And the wheels will have teeth to grip the earth or ice," Odin said.

"Did you say, sir; you plan to turn out one of those boats *every day?*" the visitor asked.

"Yes indeed; eventually. Our most energetic partner, Rufus Putnam, is in charge of getting them built. So far, he has cut and piled up to dry, an astounding quantity of oak planks.

"We've begun to build a 1/4-mile-long, greased-plank shipway, tented over with canvas on sturdy frames, so we can work in any weather.

"You see Colonel, we'll start with the steel boat bottom, and begin building the wooden part of the bottom, then the walls etcetera, but in about 12 stations. At about station number 4, the engines, boilers and the two wheels will be installed, so the boat can pull itself along over the greased planking, day by day. Finally, as each OdinBoat is complete, it will pull itself into the Housatonic River, ready for to be tried-out for service.

"I think men at each station can specialize, and become much faster, and more expert at what they do. That ought to speed up the whole business," Duke Odin said.

"Wow! This sounds great! When do my men and I start, Duke?" Bradstreet asked.

"Colonel Bradstreet," the Duke smiled, "don't you have any questions?"

"No Milord. From what I've heard about you, if you told me those OdinBoats could fly, I'd believe it! When do we start, sir?" he asked.

Bradstreet and his 400 men were soon in buckskins. Part of the time, they were training as Nobles, to defend the town, and part of the time, employed at the boat works. They were not yet furnished with the "ammo-insert-pocketed," buckskin jackets.

But the Duke needed 1,000 more men, and so had recruiters out during the winter – the non-campaigning season – to bring his ultimate number of Nobles-workers, to almost 14,000 men and women.

The workers, as well as the Nobles, were always very pleased to be paid in actual silver coins and silver notes, instead of questionable, and poorly printed paper currency, turned out on the cheap, by Colonial legislatures.

The Duke received ritts from Lord Montour that his Force Group had sailed at last down the Delaware River, into the Atlantic. Three nights later he got another ritt, announcing they had sunk the French frigate, escorting 14 merchant ships. They captured those 14 well-burthened French sailing ships and were taking them into the nearby harbor, at Charlestown, South Carolina Colony.

Overlord Montour would recruit a few Esquires there; and hopefully, some Asians.

Also, a ritt from Captain Hazelwood said they had reached Hamburg on the Elbe River. Lord Croghan was on his way to the Prussians, with wagonloads of OdinGuns and ammos.

Duke Odin congratulated Lord David Rittenhouse repeatedly, about his astounding miracle of ritting right through the night time air, for great distances. Odin Bushnell, during their amazingly successful treasure hunt, had urged the quiet, always-thinking Rittenhouse, to come up with some better means of communicating. Ah, that very intelligent man had out-done, even his own expectations, with his ritting system.

Lord Armstrong ritt from Philadelphia, that he had good success in recruiting Esquires, and was training them for the coming campaign. He also had successful meetings with several Asian chiefs, including a few from the Iroquois League; even including some Senecas. Arch Duket Andrew Montour's brother was among the visitors, representing the Onondaga tribe.

The Duke and his bride-to-be could not communicate with privacy, so they withheld loving words in their ritts.

In mid-December, Lord Croghan ritt that he had delivered the OdinGuns, holsters, tethers, and ammunition to King Frederick. The Prussians were already gaining great victories with them. And Frederick wanted 100,000 more OdinGuns....*100,000 more!*

Abraham Clark was the happiest man in the world, for he was always lamenting silver leaving his coffers, in excess of silver coming in. The 540,000 ounces and the next order for 4,000,000 ounces (!) of silver would swell his treasury vaults considerably. Clark's mint was kept busy turning out silver nu coins, and silver notes, in the many denominations.

The Nuworld's treasury contained a lot of gold, which had not yet been sold in exchange for the more useful silver, for coins and currency.

The added orders for OdinGuns, plus OdinRazors, OdinLamps, and OdinFlamers, were fulfilled in the winter. Thousands of Colonists had moved to Stratford, to work in the new mills. Newly arrived immigrants – mostly from England – also came to learn that work.

The winter of 1756-57 was much colder than previous winters, as though another "Ice Age" was occurring. Both Putnam's boatyard and Hayden's shipyard were buried in snow repeatedly. That snow caused terrific efforts by 100s of men, to get rid of the stuff. Three times the huge, long "tent" at Putnam's yard, had rips in it, from the excess weight of snow, and blizzards with strong winds. It seemed to be a conspiracy of Mother Nature, to confound their plans.

Late in February, they learned of a French-Canadian-Asian unsuccessful attack, on Fort William-Henry, at far-to-the-north Lake George, in New York Colony. Although the fort itself was kept secure, many of their boats and two partly built sloops on the stocks were burnt.

The Duke was told Major William Eyre had designed that fort and was in command at the time of the attack. That man certainly got around!

From English newspapers brought over by ship, they learned that on April 5, 1757, the new Pitt-Devonshire ministry of "Merrie Olde England," collapsed due to the hostility of King George's son William, the Duke of Cumberland. Unbelievably and amazing everyone, that nation of "The United Kingdom of Great Britain" had no "government," for over 11 weeks; not until June 29th! Then the Pitt-Newcastle ministry took office, with William Pitt boastfully, "taking command," and the Duke of Newcastle "supplying the votes" from Parliament, (of course by offering favors and bribes, *as in all legislative bodies, everywhere*) for support, newspapers from England said.

Although governing the 6,000,000 people of Britain, in William Pitt's many years in Parliament, never was he elected to that legislature, by *more than 25 men*. Britain's almost politically-impotent King only represented a single elector, it seemed: England's *tradition*.

The Nuworld Company partners met every Sunday noon, for a half-hour-long lunch, followed by hours, to discuss their business and politics. Oftentimes, highly-ranked Nobles were included in the secret discussions. Lord George Croghan, the most remarkable of men, who was well-acquainted with the bad governing of Ireland, was very helpful. The issues discussed, were "what's next," when the French authorities, were driven off the continent. All of them expected they could get that task done within the year and were earnestly preparing in complicated detail, for that happy day.

Importantly, Sarah Bushnell provided the lunch and stayed to listen to the discussions. She occasionally offered an idea, or opinion on the various subjects, being discussed by the men.

The Oligarchy of about 200 men, that pretty much owned, and ruled, the people and the land of the British Isles, was seen as a very unjust system of government.

Among other flaws of government over there, was the fact that the huge London metropolis – which went far beyond the single square mile of the ancient City of London – was in fact governed by over 100 separate, usually quarreling, political bodies!

What a country that England!

Amazingly, the not-just-terribly-brilliant – and obviously unfriendly—Lowdown Earl, ordered an embargo for all of the English Colony ports, beginning in March of 1757. Merchant ships could not then acquire "clearance," to legally sail away with their cargoes.

Warehouses and ships too, filled up with trade stuffs such as wheat, corn, flour, tobacco, hides, etc. that could not be sold beyond the shore. *However, those stuffs could be sold to the Nuworld Company, and cheaply, too.*

The British won no friends from this act, it costing Americans greatly because the Earl feared, some of them might be trading with the enemy, the French. But that blunder erased all problems of supply for the Nobility. Surely the Earl had not given a second's thought to that. However, he might have been told that the British Army could be cheaply supplied, as a result of his poorly conceived embargo.

The Nuworlders slaughtered many beeves, porkers, fish, geese, ducks, turkeys, deers, bears, and a great many chickens. They froze the meat in smallish pieces, as they had done before the Caribbean voyage. They found that spraying meat, sausages and even fish, with a slight water mist, and hanging them out on lines, on the coldest of nights, froze them hard as granite. That would keep them palatable a long time, when kept frozen, in the ice rooms of their vessels.

It seemed that in war, privateering was the biggest gamble of all. Hundreds of ships were involved in the legal piracy—English, French and many of the Colonials. Some of them won fortunes, although others met with naught but grief; even capture, and too often, death.

Overlord Andrew Montour's 1, 5-masted and 5, 10-masted Odin-Rafts, seemed to ply the Caribbean with but little further success, until March 25th, 1757. That was when the Nuworld ships encountered a large French convoy, out of the French-held island of Martinique. Lord Andrew's fleet took on the four escorting, large French warships, blasting each of them to smithereens, with the brand new OdinRocks. Those new weapons sunk them rapidly.

That sufficiently intimidated, the accompanying convoy of 60 French merchant vessels, that they "struck their flags" in surrender.

The use of the OdinRocks was not to be mentioned in the newspapers, and all Nobles were ordered to keep them secret. It would be *ignoble* to reveal such a secret, they were told.

Montour sent 2 OdinRafts with each captured group of 20 ships, into Philadelphia, Boston, and their "home port" of Stratford.

All of the extremely rich cargoes of molasses, sugar, rum, hides and leather, cotton, oranges, lemons, limes, pineapples, honey and much else, were "condemned" by the Admiralty Courts – of course after bribes, those courts being British.

The cargoes and ships themselves were then auctioned off, with 1/2 of the proceeds for the Nuworld Company, and 1/2 to the crews. The procedure much added to the wealth of the accounts owed, the 900 Noblemen and Noblewomen, involved. All of those transactions also very much made poorer the enemy, the French.

All that business of condemnation, and auctioning, took time, and it was not until late June, that all of the Nobility was gathered in Stratford, and returned to earning their salaries.

The recruiting had been successful, and they had then a sufficient 13,850 Nobles, assigned to 7, practically-full, Battle Forces.

There were very few "military engineers." Almost the only engineers going along would be tending the steam equipment of each OdinBoat.

At a drawing for the task of guarding the home base, Overlord Daniel Boone and his *Bravehearts* Battle Force, plus Overlord Nathan Whiting, and his new *Dreadnots* Battle Force drew the paper slips designating their Forces as Home guards. They would not likely win glory unless attacked by the French – or some other enemy. Both of those leaders were cool, brave, smart, and understood, the importance of their tasks.

Abraham Clark was made a Duke, and Force Group Overlord, for the city defenders.

Only Clark and Nehi Bushnell of the 14 Nuworld Company partners, would be left behind. The other 11 partners were to accompany the newly promoted Nobility Overlord, Grand Duke Odin, as aides. Those aides were still ranked as Barrons and "Lords of Battles."

Nobility Overlordet Andrew Montour was promoted to the rank of Duke.

The reunion of Grand Count Annie Willing and Grand Duke David Odin Bushnell was a wonderful occasion, to say the least. His family loved her, and she loved them. They vowed to marry on Saturday, June 2nd, 1757, and they ritt invitations well before, through Lord Armstrong to her parents, plus Benjamin Franklin and Israel Pemberton.

Early in June, the British made a sweep of New York City, in the dead of night. Battalions of Redcoats, hatefully rousted men from their beds, at bayonet point. The British kidnapped, and enslaved, about 800 American men, for service with the British fleet.

The Lowdown Earl proved surprisingly adept at gaining hatred for himself, and for the United Kingdom of Great Britain, from every level of citizen, in the Nuworld.

On June 20th, the Earl sailed his 100 or so vessels, loaded with 12,000 troops (various figures were stated) out of New York. They headed first for the English port of Halifax, Nova Scotia Colony. Despite attempts at secrecy, it was common knowledge that the Lowdown Loser's goal was to capture France's Fortress Louisbourg, on Isle Royale. That was the gateway to the Gulf of Canada and to Canada itself.

The Colonial "Provincials" had captured the place 12 years before, so the British, of course, should get it done even more easily, in 1757.

Since the British were aiming to capture Canada from the outside-in, the Grand Duke planned to go up the Hudson, to take Canada from the inside-out.

Many of the new Nobles had plenty of experience in previous years to the north, in New Hampshire, Massachusetts, Connecticut, New York, and New Jersey Colonial Militias. They had been serving with the British Army.

No Colonials had received any medals, or even praise, for their efforts and their bravery. Most had been contemptuously employed as laborers. They built forts, cleared roads and made encampments, *for the supposed real soldiers, the British Redcoats.*

Every Nuworlder was universally pleased that they would not have to serve again with the British. Nuworld Nobility pay was far better, the honors unreserved, and there would be no stupid, cruel punishments. And anyway, Nuworld Noblemen and Noblewomen behaved themselves nobly at all times. They had rarely been deserving punishment unless it be banishment.

There were showers of medals for those in the Caribbean campaign, and many of them had earned and had received promotions.

Overlady Annie earned an 11-feathered Gold Crown for Courage when she shot a French merchant captain. That too-daring man attempted to take back his ship, by holding one of her Healthors hostage and stealing her OdinGun. Annie blew his brains out just above the eye from a distance of about four paces, just missing the frantically crying hostage's own head!

Annie was beautifully tanned by the Caribbean sun, and her lengthy tresses seemed an even lighter shade of blonde than before.

On June 2nd, 1757, the affair seemed the grandest of weddings, with so many people there, for the occasion. Even Connecticut Colony Governor Thomas Fitch was present.

Odin Bushnell and Annie Willing were married in the new Congregational Church by – of course – the Reverend Mr. Ezra Stiles.

The bride and groom exchanged plain gold wedding bands, and he gave her a multi-strand pearl necklace and another of emeralds and diamonds. All of those luxurious gems had been taken from Spanish wrecks, on the Caribbean Sea floor, just about three years before.

The newly married couple had a rapturously loving weekend. He quickly discovered the "perfect porcelain doll" was made not from hard-baked clay, but of delightfully yielding, wondrously responding, feminine flesh. He also found Elias Tully was correct in his advice that, "All a husband has to do, is give his darling bride, all the pleasure he can dream up, and he'll get his own pleasure, in full measure!"

But on Monday, both the bride and groom were back to work, since there was so much to do.

It took some doing, but Odin Bushnell convinced Governor Fitch, that steel was much more needed than the great stock, of cannons and cannonballs, stored at Hartford. Running up the Connecticut River, 4 OdinBoats brought to the furnaces at Stratford, sufficient iron to make a good beginning in producing steel, for the OdinShips. The Governor was especially pleased that the Colony was paid for that iron, in silver nu.

Duke Andrew Montour had managed to recruit men from all 13 English Colonies, but women from only 9 of those Colonies.

Also, he got over 200 English-speaking, New England Asians to join. They were fully as Noble as the Euros, dressed and ranked the same, and to be scattered throughout the Forces. In addition to being Noble warriors, they were to help in diplomacy and inter-preting with tribes, expected to be met in the campaign. Some of them also knew the French language.

Long-time shipbuilder Uriah Hayden at the end of June figured he'd have fully 6 OdinShips ready for sea, in about two months. He was to provide the crews for them, and Nehi Bushnell was to teach their engineers, the mechanics of safely operating the steam boilers, and engines. Some of the intended crewmen had actually worked to make the ship's machinery.

The Nuworld Company appointed Captain John Hazelwood, as ambassador to King Frederick of warring Prussia. He loaded his 15-mast OdinRaft, with grains and flour, which was much needed in war-torn Europe. He would sell both vessel and cargo there and join Frederick's entourage. Noble Ritters and Guards, would accompany the new Ambassador.

Much experience was gained with the OdinBoats, on the Housatonic River. They proved easy to climb in and out of the water, on gently sloping banks, and sped along at 16 nauts (nautical miles an hour), when on the water. They might go faster when "broken in." They could do about four nauts on land, and probably somewhat faster, on ice-covered rivers.

Every Nuworlder was anxious to "make the Kings of France kiss our continent goodbye," but the OdinBoats were slower to build than had been hoped. Only at the end of July, had 36 of them been launched and tested. The 14 OdinBoats needed to house the home defense Forces, were by that time, not completely done.

All Nobles were inoculated with the mild cowpox, against the dreaded and often deadly smallpox. Smallpox was said to have sick-ened, and killed, 100s of Redcoats, and some Colonial Militiamen, in the past winter and spring months. That was because the British had not yet embraced, the new disease preventer.

At long last, on Friday morning, August 5, 1757, the Nuworld's Nobility, was belatedly off to war again. This time, they were led as before, by the young and profound genius, 18-year-old Grand Duke

David Odin Bushnell. He wouldn't reach his 19th year, until August 30th. He was especially glad that no one had seemed to care that he was such a youthful leader.

During the year before, the then very much smaller Nuworld Battle Forces had driven the French Army completely out of the Ohio valley. They had also devastated French shipping in the Caribbean Sea, during the winter.

Now this campaign, was to drive the French authorities, totally out of the Nuworld.

Grand Duke Odin Bushnell, Duke Andrew Montour, and Grand Duket Annie Bushnell climbed upon the pilothouse, of Odin's leading OdinBoat.

They were all covered with sweat, as the 1st days of August were exceptionally hot and muggy. But as the boat moved, the breeze off Long Island Sound, was a welcome relief for them.

Captain MacDougal was told by the Grand Duke, to keep the speed low, until the steam engines on all of the OdinBoats, were well broken in.

Also on board, were Grand Duke Odin's 11 other Nuworld Company partners. Only partners Nehi Bushnell, and Abraham Clark were left behind, in Stratford, Connecticut Colony.

The partners accompanying the Grand Duke were ranked as Barrons. Each had very much earned the right to join in the adventure and to help wrap up extremely important, and well-planned matters, when the conquest of New France was complete.

There was with them, Lord Hopkinson to play the Happy Hoppy Organ, atop the pilothouse. Also, 14 Noblewomen Healthors were aboard, serving as five secretaries plus nine cooks and bakers. All Noblewomen were trained to tend the sick and wounded, under the supervision of Lord Doctor Gale, and Overlady Annie Bushnell.

OdinBoat Captain, Count MacDougal, had a staff of 28 to tend the engines, etc. There were three printers for the printing press on board. There were also 3 Ritters aboard, for the very necessary messaging.

The OdinBoat's pilothouse roof was 8 feet square and surrounded by a wrought iron railing. A flag pole rose up from the rear of it, with the 4-foot diameter, doubled, round brass flag, swaying in the breeze nicely. Their "picture of the Nuworld from the Moon" flags, showed the golden lands, islands and the great extent of blue rivers, lakes, and seas, beautifully.

Barron Hopkinson's "Happy Hoppy Organ" popped up, atop the front of the pilothouse roof. That instrument consisted of a large steam pipe coming up, through the roof with a "tee" at the top of it. Various lengths brass pipes crowded along, up from the top of the horizontal pipe. Harpsichord-type ivory "keys" were there to finger the musical notes.

Those on the pilothouse roof looked back to see, 35 identical OdinBoats following. All of the OdinBoats were painted bright iron-oxide red.

The Grand Duke's boat had big white letters on each side, and the rear, proclaiming it as "Nuworld Nobility Force Group."

The others were lettered "Nuworld Battle Force *Bravehearts* – 6, for the Overlord's OdinBoat. Others were numbered 1 through 5 for the Noble War Parties. OdinBoat number 7 was the backup supply vessel for each Force.

Nicolas Biddle had resumed his role of Overlordet, to Arch Duket George Croghan, who was again the Overlord, leading the *Valiants* Battle Force.

They were to proceed southwest on Long Island Sound, to the East River, and stop at the tip of Manhattan, for the night.

They would then on Saturday, August 6th, 1757, steam up the Hudson, nearly to the end of that river, and pull up on land, ready for war... and maybe, for glory.

Twentynine OdinBoats then would each drag themselves, the 17 miles overland to Lake George, and thence on to Lake Champlain, into Canada, to conquer New France.

The 7 OdinBoats under Overlord Bradstreet, would split off from the rest, taking that Force up the Mohawk River, and go on to take on the French, on the way to Fort DeTroit.

Every Nobleman and Noblewoman carried the new Odin2Gun and had practiced with it. It proved to be ultra-fast to fire again and again. The upper center of the rear handle had a quarter-inch glass window in it. They could look through that glass and on through a now-uncovered hole in the ammo insert, to see a number on the brass cup, from 1 to 50. When the number visible was down to 3 or 4, the shooter had to decide whether it was time to replace the insert, with a full one, if it seemed there were more enemies to shoot at.

13

Much of the information they received about conditions up north came from newly recruited Nobles, with experience there. Among them were Israel Putnam – a relative of Nuworld Company partner Rufus Putnam – John Stark, Moses Hazen, Abel Spencer, Thomas Brown and quite a few others.

Some of them had for a time, been with the famous (or *infamous*; take your pick) Robert Rogers' Rangers. They had learned Major Rogers had sailed away from New York, with the Commander of all British Forces in North America, Lord Loudoun.

It seemed from what intelligence they could gather that the French Army Commander Marquis General Montcalm had at least 6,000 troops. Perhaps half of his force were Regular Army soldiers from France, and the other half were Canadian Militia.

Of course, the Nuworlders couldn't know whether more troops might have been sent to Canada from France, recently. Or perhaps some of the French soldiers may have been shifted to Fortress Louisbourg, because the secret British plans for that attack, were not in fact, very secret.

In addition, the Marquis General Montcalm was known to have sent, ambitious recruiting parties, to the Great Lakes region and beyond. They promised Asian warriors easy victories, much booty, and many bloody scalps to hang gloriously on their belts.

Why? Because the French had unlimited large, very dangerous cannons, and the Nuworlders and English had no cannons at all... or very small ones.

They also had the very believable argument, that the English wished to take all the Asian's lands, and drive them off, or most likely, kill them all.

The French recruiters would have to be very convincing, since it was surely well known far and wide, what had happened at the Asian village of Kittanning, Fort Duquesne, and particularly, the calamitous gun battle, for the nearly 700 Seneca warriors killed, at Venango.

Overlord Armstrong's demonstration of the OdinGun, at Logstown on the Ohio River, by blasting 1,000s of pigeons from the sky in a few second's time... well, that had also sent a magical buzz all over. On the other hand, surely many a cautious Asian War Chief would suppose the power of the OdinGun to be exaggerated. Yet, the Nuworlders had received much news of the wonder, and the fear among most Asians, created by those OdinGuns.

The French may also have said, they outnumbered the Nuworlders, and anyway, the enemy English were down there, like pirates in the Caribbean; so why worry?

By mid-Friday morning, a dark sky and a howling thunderstorm came upon them. It rained hard so, Captain MacDougal of Overlord Odin's leading OdinBoat, slowed it down.

MacDougal was a very nervous fellow going through Hell's Gate, the passage from Long Island Sound, into the East River.

The "East River" was not really a river, but a "strait," east of Manhattan Island.

The currents were wild and swirling, and the Captain said gigantic sharp rocks, were invisible below the surface. Many a ship had been holed, passing through that Hell's Gate.

The OdinBoats following did as recommended, staying close in line behind Captain MacDougal's lead. Luckily, none of them struck the deadly rocks.

Grand Duke Odin wished to see how many British soldiers, the

Lowdown Loser had left behind on Manhattan Island. He saw very few were present, and certainly not enough to defend the place, from even a small French fleet.

The Lowdown Lord and his 12,000-or-so men had sailed away about seven weeks before, so Odin supposed, they should have conquered Louisbourg by then.

They tied the OdinBoats up for the night. The rainstorm had let up to a slight drizzle. Odin went up to the pilothouse to look out on Manhattan.

The 14,000 people, said to be in the little city called New York, had no idea of what was ahead for that partly settled island, besides mostly, the farming going on there then.

With the rain falling, Odin couldn't see very much, so he returned for dinner, and went early to bed. The morrow would find them heading up the Hudson, and finally, to war.

The morning dawned brightly since the rainstorm had moved on east during the night. The cool night air was replaced, by the usual hot August mugginess.

As the OdinBoats began to move away, crowds of amazed people gathered, to watch the mile-long line, of bright red vessels, churning the water and gathering speed.

The people had never seen any vessels whatsoever, move along without sails, oars, paddles or poles before. The wheels were nearly hidden since about 1/2 of each wheel was underwater, and the upper 1/2, was behind the steel sheets enclosing them. Steam and smoke poured out, from the angled-back iron chimneys, near their rear ends, as a hint of the power source.

Odin asked Barron Hopkinson to play the Nobility song, for the benefit of the "Yorkers":

"This is our Nuworld, our very free Nuworld,

"Our Brightest Rich Part of the Whole World!

"So, Nobility, Nobility, protect us all from Harm,

"And honor us, with righteousness, in city, sea, and farm!"

Barron Hopkinson told the Grand Duke, "My Organs sound much like extremely loud clarinets, except that they're a bit raucous from the brass 'reeds'; so, they're not as mellow."

"Ha! Lord Hoppy, you've created a beautiful miracle in music! It's perfect!" was the answer to that one, from the Grand Duke.

The engines were not considered to be completely broken in, so the OdinBoats proceeded cautiously up the Hudson River, at about 3/4 speed.

Sailing ships would often struggle for frustrating *weeks*, fighting contrary winds, to voyage the 140 miles, from Manhattan to Albany. But the OdinBoats could steam up there, merely in *hours*. They arrived in good weather, at that growing town, nearly at sunset.

When approaching Albany, the really loud music was begun again, and that advertised their presence far and wide. People rushed to the riverbank, to see the strange red craft, with the remarkable music, that was seen as well as heard.

Among the curious folks were Albany Mayor Van Schaik and Sheriff Yates.

The Mayor wanted to know if the Grand Duke knew his son.

"Yes Your Honor, I've met him. He's an excellent Arch Barron now. Lord Goose Schaik is a Band Overlord, with Battle Force *Gators*. We don't use the inherited 'Van' in front of his name, as it seems to mean 'leader,' the same as 'Lord,' which is never to be inherited. He's a fine Nobleman, Mayor."

He thanked the Grand Duke for that news and said he had some news for him.

"We've got word that the French Army is right now besieging Fort William-Henry, at Lake George," the Mayor said. "They've got at least 10,000 men there, maybe more, including a large number of bloodthirsty savages. You call 'em Asians, we call 'em savages, Milord."

"And we understand that at the fort, there's no more than maybe 1,000 defenders, fit for duty, to try and keep the place," Albany Mayor Van Schaik continued. "There's an awful lot of sickness there, Milord, including smallpox. The French; they've got many large cannons and mortars, blasting away at the fort. Sometimes, even at this distance, we can hear them. That fort can't hold out for long. And General Webb? Why, he's at Fort Edward, sitting there with a good many troops, and won't go up there to help. That's what we hear, anyway.

"Webb was only a Colonel until he panicked, upon hearing some savages were in the area, up there on the Mohawk River. So, he burnt down Fort Bull, which had just been built, and then he retreated like a stupid coward, downriver. And for such unsoldierly actions, of course, Earl Loudoun promoted him, to Major General!" the Mayor added.

"Mayor, what about the so-called Indian Agent, William Johnson – is he up there?" the Grand Duke asked.

Sheriff Yates answered for the Mayor.

"Grand Duke Bushnell, Johnson is a very sick man. You know he's taken advantage of those Iroquois tribes, by getting them to give him sinful amounts of land. And in return, you might say, he's infected hundreds of those – oh, Asian girls, with the syphilis, and he's finally suffering from it himself. He may be dying from it, we hear. Serves the bastard right, I say!"

Odin turned to the Master of his OdinBoat. "Captain MacDougal, let's get going to Fort Edward right now. How far is it, anyway?"

"Milord, it's about 35 miles upstream, but it's getting dark already," the Captain answered. "Also, I've heard there's maybe snags in the river, north of here. The water's much shallower up here, so that when the river banks cave in during flood times, the trees sometimes fall in. Often their trunks are just below the surface, so you can't see them except in bright sunlight. Those snags might actually destroy our wheels, sir."

"Captain, Lord Rittenhouse here, has used his considerable genius to devise the two keg lights on the front of each boat! You just go as slow as you have to, but you keep those lights shining ahead, and we'll get to that Fort by sun-up! Let's go!" the Grand Duke ordered.

The wooden kegs had inside of them, large glass cones, coated with silver on the outside, as was done with mirrors. They beamed the light from the intensely bright, lime flame forward, instead of scattering most of it. They weren't perfect but were quite effective anyway.

The further north they went, the more they could hear the distant, rolling thunder of cannon fire, mortar fire, and bombshells, exploding all through the night.

The Grand Duke and friends were showered and breakfasted, by the time the sun peeked up, over the ever-present, endless forest, and Fort Edward came into view.

To their left was an island, that had some crudely built barracks on it; for the Rangers, it was said. That word "Rangers" came from England's huge estates, where the privileged Lords hired Rangers, to keep all of the hungry commoners, off of their sport-hunting lands.

To their right was Fort Edward, with what appeared to be, 100s of tents beyond it.

But the morning was not quiet, as the boom of cannons, and deadly large mortars were clearly coming south, through the 17 miles of forest, from Fort William-Henry.

"Barron Hopkinson!" Grand Duke Odin hollered, at the man gawking behind him. "Get on those pipes! Play your Song of Nobility, as loud as you can, and wake up this place!"

They pulled up to the riverbank and lowered a ramp.

Overlord Odin tramped down the ramp and stormed into the fort with his partners, and Overlordet Andrew Montour, following.

They met a young British officer in a blazing scarlet uniform. "Ensign!" the Grand Duke barked. "Where's your General? I want to see him right now!"

"Yes, sir! Oh! You're Grand Duke David Odin Bushnell!" the Britisher gasped. "Right this way, Milord. I saw a wondrous coppix of you, and I've read your remarkably beautiful Philadelphia speech, but I never dreamed I'd meet you!"

They were soon across the parade ground, in the center of the fort. They followed the excited young Ensign up some stairs, who waved them into a room, that was obviously an office. But no one was there.

"I'll tell the General's Adjutant that you're here, Milord," the officer said.

"Never mind the Adjutant! I want to see General Webb, right now!" Odin shouted.

A door opened on the right side of the room, and an old man with tousled, dirty white hair peeked out. Odin recognized him as being the Colonel Webb, ordered by Earl Loudoun, to release Abraham Clark, during the confrontation on the Earl's quay, the previous October.

"What's all the noise?" the old man asked.

He had apparently just awakened and pulled on his breeches over his nightshirt. He was holding his breeches up with both hands.

"This here's Grand Duke Odin Bushnell, General," the Ensign said to the old man.

The Grand Duke went right up to him.

"So, you're the Major General Daniel Webb, who's supposedly in charge of defending this frontier, but sitting here in the safety of this fort, for the French to come, and do you in, one at a time?" the Grand Duke hollered.

"Dammit man! Why are you not 17 miles north of here right now? That's where the fight is! Dammit General, don't just stare at me; speak up!" Grand Duke Odin roared.

Odin spoke very loudly to him, although he had heard the old man had palsy, and other problems, and hated loud noises. A life-long army man who hated loud noises... *like gunfire!* Odin was looking over one of King George's son, Duke of Cumberland William's, closest friends! A sick old man, timid, cowardly, indecisive and given command of 1,000s of men, on a dangerous frontier! Those English! Amazing, what they do, as though it wasn't war!

The General looked just terribly offended.

"You.... you mustn't talk to me like that!" he said.

Odin stepped even closer, shouting down from his own great height, directly into the old man's face.

"Webb, I want you to get all of your troops moving, right now, marching up there to where the battle is. Do you understand me? *I mean, right now!"* Odin growled.

"Oh no; that would not be prudent at all," the old man said.

"Dammit Webb, you will do it right now, or I shall strangle you to death with my bare hands!" The Grand Duke roared the lie into the old man's startled face.

"You.... you.... you would actually kill me?" the old man said with real terror in his voice.

"*Do as I say, or I shall most certainly kill you, in the coldest cold blood, anybody ever heard of!*" Odin roared, repeating the lie, into his frightened old face.

It was the most surprising thing. The man simply fainted, as though he had melted, right in front of the Grand Duke, and collapsed in a lump on the floor. He was no longer holding onto his breeches, and his eyes were closed in slumber.

The young leader whirled around to face others, who had entered the room. "Who's second in command of this place?"

"I... I am, Milord!" a red-coated man answered, the gold bullion epaulettes on his shoulders, mysteriously indicating, he was maybe a Colonel or something. That officer had just come into the room.

"And General Webb, Milord, has requested reinforcements. We expect many Massachusetts Bay Provincials here, in a few days," the Britisher said.

"*Provincials, eh?* You've done nothing whatsoever to conquer the French, but from that word, I suppose we can assume you've conquered the men, of Massachusetts Bay," the Grand Duke said, with utmost sarcasm.

"Now then, if you heard what I told this poor excuse, for a commander, get busy. Get your troops organized to march, but by waiting, you'll surely be too late.

"Right now, we Nuworlders need horses, to ride up, to where the hell the fighting is. We need.... let's see.... yes, 12 good riding horses, saddled up right away," the Grand Duke ordered.

"But Milord, I must tell you the road to Fort William-Henry, is very well guarded by countless Indian barbarians," the red-coated officer said.

"Sir, we're the Nuworld Nobility, and we know all about such little problems. But I doubt we'll see any Indians since we won't be anywhere near India. And the Asian warriors you're referring to could hardly be called unshaved – bearded – barbed Aryans, which the word, in fact, means," Odin scowled in disdainful sarcasm.

Everyone knew that Asian men never needed to shave; an occasional whisker that might pop out of their faces was immediately yanked out.

Things began happening.

Overlord Odin directed Lord Andrew, to lead 4 Battle Forces, in their twenty-nine Odin Boats, up to the lake, through the 17 miles of woods.

Bradstreet's *Resolutes* Battle Force's 7 OdinBoats, would be splitting off, to go up the Mohawk River, according to the plans the Grand Duke had previously made.

The *Resolutes* had 100s of axes, saws and other tools to clear a 36-foot-wide road for their OdinBoats, just as each of the Forces had. And the Overlord's boat in each Force had a boom upfront, to lift aside the logs of the trees, they would saw or chop down.

Barron Ethan Allen was put in charge of making certain, each of the partners had three blaster OdinRocks – weighing 18 pounds each —in their AndyPaks, with Grand Duke Odin carrying 2 of them, and an OdinRockCannon.

Rittenhouse would be burdened with his ritt apparatus, and Lord Doctor Gale, with medical stuff. Their ammo "inserts" were of course already, in the pockets on their Noble chests. Their AndyPaks were on their backs, and their Odin2Guns were in their holsters, on their hips, left or right, as each preferred.

Lord Andrew wondered why the Grand Duke was only taking, the 11 Company partners with him.

"Milord Andrew, I've heard of talk, that suggested because our partners are rich, they could avoid fights, and let poor men struggle in their place, as is so commonly done. We're to see if we're courageous enough, to go up to that besieged fort, on a scout. We'll be well equipped for that task," the Grand Duke told his second in command.

Just then the Overlord noticed the unmoving lump on the floor, that no one seemed concerned about. He asked Lord Doctor Gale to check him.

"Obviously, the General has fainted," Grand Duke Odin told the Doctor.

The good doctor knelt over the form, and presently announced,

"Milord Odin, this man is dead. There is no heartbeat whatever. You actually frightened him to death!"

"Poor man!" the Grand Duke sighed. "After all, it wasn't entirely his fault, that he was put into so impossible a situation, for such a sick, and incompetent man."

Then he proclaimed loudly to no one in particular:

"This Fort Edward is no longer to be named, for an undeserving kin of King George.

"It's to be called Fort Lyman, in honor of the tireless, and excellent Major General Phineas Lyman, of Connecticut Colony. He designed this fort, he had it built, and it must bear his name.

"Also, Major William Eyre designed and built that fort, we are heading for. It is now, therefore, re-named Fort Eyre, instead of Fort William-Henry.

"That lake north of here was named 'George,' by the wicked land hog, William Johnson. And for that nonsensical flattery, and for leading troops in the September, 1755, battle General Lyman actually won, Johnson was wrongly honored, with being called a Baronet, and given an amazing, 5,000 pounds English money!

"The man who deserves much honor was the Mohawk Chief, wrongly called 'Kendrick.' His name really was 'Tyanoga.' He was killed in the English service, during that 1755 battle, and his name shall hereafter be attached to Lake Tyanoga. *Is all of that clear to everyone?*"

He stated all of that with as much authority in his voice, as he could muster.

Ezra Stiles got busy scratching it all down, as he habitually did when Odin spoke.

Within half an hour, the 12 partners were in the saddle, and galloping hell-bent-for-halleluiah, toward the wrongly called Fort William-Henry, next to the misnamed Lake George.

After a mile or so, deep into the forest, they slowed to a trot. Their eyes strained in all directions for signs of an enemy.

Leading the Nuworld Company partners, on a fairly good horse, Grand Duke Odin kept an OdinRock loaded in his Odin-RockCannon.

The OdinRockCannon was merely, a plain 4-inch diameter brass tube, 54 inches long. It had sights on the left side, and a handle with a trigger, in the center. There was no need for anything but a thin-walled tube since the rocket blast put no pressure on the walls of the tube; unlike the powder exploding, in an ordinary iron or brass cannon.

Every Nobleman had an Odin2Gun holstered on his hip and tethered to his shoulder. Each also had 4, 50-ammo inserts on his chest, and one inserted up the handle on his gun, totaling 250 ammos. With practice in firing and in marksmanship, nearly every Nobleman could fire his weapon with great accuracy, for more than 400 yards, and *many, many times* as rapidly as any musketeer.

A Nuworld Noble might fire all 50 ammos in his rear handle, before a musketeer could reload, and fire his rusty, obsolete old musket, a 2nd time!

The Grand Duke saw a form dash across the road about 100 yards ahead; out of the bush on one side, into the bush on the other side. He halted his horse, brought the OdinRockCannon to his shoulder, and let an OdinRock go. *Whoooosh! Screeeem! Ka-booooom!*

They galloped forward with their Odin2Guns at the ready. Lord Elias Tully was first at the site, and he exclaimed, "Why Grand Duke Odin! Our great Overlord has just killed himself a teeny, tiny, little deer!"

Of course, it was somewhat humorous, since they were all fearful of attack, by bloodthirsty savages from hell itself, and what did he shoot? A yearling deer, lying on its side, with much of his torso blown away. The poor thing had a foreleg kicking the air.

Nobody laughed, for just then several painted warriors, were seen coming out onto the trail beyond them, and ducking back into the bush again.

"Everybody! Fire into that bush!" Odin ordered and instantly 12 Odin2Gun's shots were flailing the forest up ahead. They were still mounted and hurried to the site as they fired.

There had been 5 of them, curious about the big sound, and they were all riddled, with blood spurting from their wounds, as the partners reached the spot.

They rode on, ever watchful, but saw no further "bushwhackers," as Stiles termed them, for several miles more.

But then another set of savages were seen ahead, doubtless curious enough to peek out to see, about the unlikely clattering of many hooves.

The Overlord again halted his horse, and let go a blaster Odin-Rock at them, *Whoooosh! Screeeem! Ka-booooom!*

They charged up the road, some firing their Odin2Guns, to discover 7 of the unlucky painted devils, blown apart, and very dead, with four more badly wounded, and near death. Others had probably faded into the bush, perhaps also badly hurt. The Nuworlders returned to the trot and advanced along the trail.

Naturally, all of them were engulfed in the utmost tension, the whole 17 miles. But oddly, they only saw enemy warriors, those two times.

There was no way of knowing how many enemies there may have been, near that road. *Those savages had not expected something as unexpected, as 12 horsemen boldly riding along, so dangerous a trail – and thus they were surprised.*

It was easy to know they were getting close to the fort, by the explosions of bombshells, and the roaring of cannons. Not only was there much noise, but gun smoke filled the air, and the sulfurous smell, was biting at their nostrils.

As they got to the fort clearing in the forest, fanning out ahead of them, they saw hordes of savages blocking their way!

They stopped but stayed mounted. Odin let loose in rapid succession, 6 OdinRocks, while his companions were rapidly firing deadly shots, into those crowds of astonished savages.

It was gruesome carnage, a great massacre of surprised, and completely unprepared warriors, who were tumbling to the ground by the dozens, as others of them fled to the left.

To the Nuworlder's right was a little hill they had heard about. It was called "Titcomb's Mount," which Colonial militias had converted into a fortified camp.

Directly ahead of them to the left a bit, was Fort Eyre itself.

There were clouds of gun smoke rising from the fort, and from the French Army's field of cannons, north of it.

To get to the fort, they had to cross a small wooden bridge over marshy ground, almost to the edge of Lake Tyanoga. Then they had to go left along the shore, as fast as their by-then terribly frightened, tired mounts could go. They had their horses leap over a small creek and lo! As if by magic, the fort gate swung open, and they dashed inside.

But during that sprint, they suddenly noticed off to their right-front, a couple of French cannons were belching fire and smoke, directly at them.

The whistle of lod balls zipping by their ears was unmistakable. The French cannons were firing "canister" at them, which were wood-bottomed leather cylinders, filled with as many as 40 or 50 man-killing musket balls.

The French had obviously planned such a cannon response, to any attempt to get into or out of the fort. The partners hadn't expected such a reception, and thus they were surprised...*and they were hit!*

As Nobility Overlord Odin was about to leap out of his saddle, inside the fort, he noticed a sharp, burning sensation, on his right chest. Aha, a hole was in his buckskin jacket. And blood was beginning to pour out.

As he dismounted, Odin also noticed his horse had a ball stuck in his right rump, barely into his thick hide. He looked around to see how his companions fared, as the fort's gate was prudently closed.

Amazingly, only 5 of those 12 riders had been hit, charging through that hail of lod. And though the horses were so large, only 2 of them had been struck.

The huge man Barron Ethan Allen seemed to have the worst wound. He had been struck with a musket ball, in the side of his right shoulder blade. He got hit as he bent low over his horse, as they sprinted toward the fort.

Barron Elias Tully had his right-hand hit; a speeding ball plowed a shallow gouge.

Barron Phineas Pratt had a wound in his lower right leg. That ball stuck in the leather of his boot, just as one had nested in Odin's horse's rump.

Barron Paul Revere's wound was the least bad of them all. A ball had zipped by his belly, barely touching his skin, but enough to scrape it red and bleed. However, it was just enough to earn a pretty little red ruby, on his Crown for Courage.

Lord Doctor Gale declared they were the luckiest men on the continent, getting through that storm of musket balls with so few hits. But then, they were moving fast, and cannons were woefully inaccurate. They were at least 300 yards distant, and that meant the balls had scattered wildly and were much slowed by the time they burned into flesh.

Since the wounds were so minor, Grand Duke Odin directed all but Lord Allen, and Lord Doctor Gale, to get up on the walls and fire at the French.

The Grand Duke hastened up the stairs himself, lugging his OdinRockCannon, when of all people in the world, he nearly ran into Major William Eyre, coming down the stairs!

That Englishman seemed to be everywhere!

"Major Eyre!" Odin shouted over the ear-splitting din, of every size of guns going off, and cannonballs striking the walls of the fort. "The French must have a magazine, or laboratory tent, as you engineers call it. Point it out to me, and I'll blow it up!"

"Really, Milord? With that thing?" Eyre pointed to the tube on his shoulder.

"Yes! Yes! Show me where it is, and I'll throw OdinRocks at it!"

With a puzzled look on his face, Eyre whirled about, and headed up, with Grand Duke Odin and the others following.

They quickly found themselves atop the fort wall, shielded somewhat from musket fire, by a much-damaged parapet. They were soon at a sharply pointed, and partly damaged bastion, extending out from the fort, and which faced the enemy French positions.

"Milord Bushnell, that's it over there, that largest tent. It's double canvassed so's to keep off the rain. But I must tell you, sir, it's just about 1 mile away," the British engineer said.

The tent he pointed out was well beyond the many ditches dug, for the French cannons to fire from. Of course, such a tent would have to be beyond the range of the fort cannons. It was erected tight to the west shore of Lake Tyanoga, as the lake curved around. A number of bateaus and canoes were tied up next to that tent. Scores of smaller tents were inland from it.

His aides and partners put on a show of rapid-fire into the closest French soldiers, hunkered down in ditches dug within merely 100 hundred yards, of Fort Eyre's wooden walls.

❧ 14 ❧

The Grand Duke knew from the military books; he had devoured on European sieges, of towns and forts, what such a laboratory tent contained. That tent would hold many, many small kegs of gunpowder, and stacks of mortar, and howitzer, spherical bombshells – 13 inches, 10 inches, and 6 inches in diameter. Some of those bombshells would be already filled with explosive and fused, but some bombshells would not yet be ready for firing.

Besides the more numerous items in that tent, there would be *barrels* of musket "cartridges" – rolled paper with varying amounts of gunpowder and a lod ball inside.

"Cartridges" had nothing whatever to do, with *carts* or *ridges*. It was just a thoughtless English corruption of the French word "cartouche"... which itself, was a mindless corruption by the French, of their "carta-rouge"; meaning, paper-which-is-red. And the wrapping papers naturally were not red at all; the paper used was almost always brown.

The combined power of all that explosive in one place was so terribly dangerous, every commander would have men constantly standing guard, at all four corners of such a tent, in addition to those working inside of it, day and night, to prevent accidents, and sabotage.

Odin eyed the target through the sight on his OdinRockCannon, knowing the distance was practically at the limit of the OdinRock range.

He breathed deep, held his breath, and squeezed the trigger.

Whoooosh! Screeeem! His missile war-whooped through the air, leaving a trail of wispy white smoke. *Ka-booooom!* But the Odin-Rock hit the ground short of the target tent. He fired another. *Whoooosh! Screeeem! Ka-boooom!* That one hit some boats in Lake Tyanoga, maybe 20 feet off target. Then he fired a 3rd OdinRock. *Whoooosh! Screeeem! Ka-boooom! Then seemingly, there were endless Ka-booooms!*

His OdinRock obviously blasted through the canvas, of that exceptionally large laboratory tent, which blew up with a huge fire-ball inside, that set off explosives. That inferno, in turn, set off the entire mass, into a blazing cloud of flames, and smoke bursting out in all directions!

The spot kept erupting for long seconds, in the all-engulfing fire, and explosive booms. That horrific sound would travel for many miles.

Chaos reigned as iron shards, and probably 100,000s of lod balls were speeding through the air all over the battlefield. Those little missiles were knocking over the very French soldiers those same materials were intended to supply. Many tents were burning, and the close-to-shore canoes and bateaus were scattered far into the lake, with some of them also on fire.

The Grand Duke whirled around to Barrons Tully and Pratt. "Keep loading them in until there are only a few left!"

He continued to fire OdinRocks, but only at the mortar and cannon positions.

With sweet revenge, he knocked asunder, the two cannons that had fired canister at them! He also hit a big pile of bombshells, set up by a large mortar, and they also exploded with great devastation, leaving a huge hole in that field.

Everywhere, all over the besieger's field, men were running away for their lives, some of them obviously wounded. They were heading west, into the woods, beyond the cleared area.

The battle was won, and the fort had been saved, when Barron Elias Tully announced, "Milord, there's but 2 OdinRocks left!"

"Good! Save them! Now let's get our wounds tended to!" the Grand Duke announced, and he bolted for the stairs, down to the "parade," inside the fort.

Major Eyre insisted on accompanying them down the stairs.

"Milord Bushnell, those rockets are truly fantastic! You Nuworlders have very good weapons!" the British Army Major said.

"Yes, Major, we try. But these aren't little rocks; rock-ets. They're rather big rocks, and I ever-so-modestly call them OdinRocks," the Grand Duke managed with a grin. "Ah, I see our wonderful doctor is right there."

Lord Doctor Gale was tending the enormous man, Barron Ethan Allen. He was putting his right arm in a sling, after patching the hole in his shoulder.

Immediately, the Grand Duke and his aides checked through the little windows on their Odin2Guns, to see how many shots were left in their inserts. Overlord Odin had by far, the most remaining, at 24. Barron Tully had the least... only two shots! He and two other aides switched their nearly empty inserts, right then for full ones, from the front of their jackets.

Odin told the doctor that he also had a little problem. He took off his jacket and shirt. The movements caused surprising hurt, which he hadn't noticed, during the excitement atop the fort. He could see the ball was barely buried, into the flesh of his right breast. It was about as deep into his flesh, as the ball was in his horse's tough hide and Barron Pratt's leather boot.

"Hold still Milord, and I'll get things ready, to get that ball out of there," Lord Gale said.

While the doctor busied himself with his medical things, more than 12 women and children, had gathered to watch him at work. They had seemed to ignore the explosions coming from outside the fort, apparently having grown wearily accustomed, to that racket.

They were all dirty and bedraggled. Not a single one of them appeared to be healthy.

A boy of 10 years or so came up close and stared at the nearly 3/4-inch ball, barely visible in Odin's chest. The blood by then was trickling freely, down the Duke's front.

"Don't that bullet hurt a lot, sir?" the boy asked.

"Nope. I'm of the Nuworld Nobility. Otherwise, I'd cry like a baby," he told the boy with mock seriousness, as the lad smiled up at the fibbing Nobleman.

A young woman with impossibly tangled and dirty reddish hair came up to him.

"Milord; you really are Grand Duke David Odin Bushnell?" she asked.

But she didn't wait for an answer. His name was on his hat and arms, and his rank was spelled out on the shoulders of the buckskin jacket, he had just taken off.

"My husbun, he tole me 'bout your inventions and your mite purty speeches. Awful amazin', I'd say. My husbun, he's mebbe been kilt, with Colonel Parker's foray up that there lake," the woman said.

"What was that about a foray up the lake, Missus?" the Grand Duke asked her.

"Colonel Monroe, he sent Colonel Parker up the lake, with about 600 a 'em Jersey Blues. You must've heard of 'em Jersey Colony Militias. Sent 'em up a few days ago, an' only about 200 got back. Them Asians, as you call 'em, and them French; they was a waitin' for 'em. My husbun, he might be kilt, or mebbe captivated, Milord," she said.

"Missus, we are going up that way; up this Lake Tyanoga, and to Lake Champlain, and beyond. Our Nuworld Battle Forces are very powerful, and they will be here shortly. I hope we can get your husband freed if he's a captive. Don't give up hope, please," Odin advised her.

Lord Doctor Gale washed his hands and splashed some alcohol on Odin's chest. My, how it smarted! That alcohol had been repeatedly boiled; distilling it to make it nearly pure.

With pincers, the Doctor plucked the musket ball out and then probed for a piece of buckskin, and a piece of cotton undershirt, that had been driven into the flesh, by the little ball.

Such lod balls were called "bullets," meaning "small balls," such as "ballot" for voting with a little ball, and "ballet" for a small number of dancers, instead of a "ballroom" full of dancers. All of that was, of course, copied by the English from the French. Nuworld Nobles called their little missiles of lod, "shots." No one ever, ever said: "I've been bulleted"!

Doctor Gale placed a thick bandage over the wound and directed Odin to keep his shirt off for a while, to let the sunshine on his skin, on and around that site.

But he cautioned the Grand Duke, to shoo the many flies away, from his inviting wound. Such insects would happily deposit their eggs in such an injury, so that their resulting worms called larvae, would have lots of yummy protein to munch on.

Major Eyre introduced the new fort commander, British Army Lieutenant Colonel George Monro. He was apparently, like the shot-off-his-horse incompetent, General Braddock, a London parade ground officer.

"Bushnell," he said disrespectfully, "I understand you've blown up the French laboratory tent. Good. Now I've got the French, and their damnable Indians, on the run. Hell of it is though; I've got too few men fit for duty, to risk going on the chase. But you can give me some of your rockets. They probably could be useful."

"Monro, you seem to be as ignorant and arrogant, like many another British officer," the Grand Duke told him with a disgusted look.

"My advice to you Colonel is to gather as many of your troops as have not already died, because of the diseases in this filthy hole... go down that Hudson River, and back to England, where you belong. You must do this immediately before more of your men sicken and die. Goodbye," the Duke said while dismissing him with a wave of his hand.

"Who the hell are you to order me..." the Britisher managed to get out.

"Dammit Monro, we're going to burn down this pestilence-filled fort, so get your troops going before you and they get burnt with it! I mean Colonel, dammit, *right now.*"

With that, Barron Chalker came up boldly between them, with his Odin2Gun held in front of him. He told the obviously surprised Colonel, "Our Grand Duke has been wounded, in saving this fort, and he now needs rest. You'd best get going, Colonel."

Barron Tully, his right hand bandaged, and Barrons Rittenhouse and Copley also stepped up. The warning was more than obvious. Monro whirled about and left.

Odin relaxed in the sun, and never saw that disrespectful English Colonel again. Within a few hours, those Red Coats, with soldiers on litters, were marching south toward New York.

Major Eyre told the Grand Duke, he was taking out a patrol, onto the abandoned French positions. It was obvious those French soldiers, that had been left behind, were either dead or badly wounded.

Lord Rittenhouse left. But he soon returned to report his Ritters said, the OdinBoats were making good progress through the forest, and that he had told them of the French defeat.

Odin's partners gathered around the Grand Duke, to keep him from being disturbed.

Odin was lavish in his praise, for Barron Revere's precise manufacture of the wonderfully accurate, far-reaching OdinRocks, and the equally great, Odin2Guns. Lord Paul of course rightly took great pride, in the armaments, he had supervised in their being milled.

Odin dozed awhile and was awakened by Major Eyre, returning from his patrol.

"Milord Bushnell," he announced, "I've brought a very important prisoner. He's Lieutenant Colonel Louis-Antoine de Bougainville. He was aide-de-camp to the French Commander, Marquis Montcalm, who was killed from the laboratory tent explosion."

Bougainville was short, plump, and wore a white French Army uniform. As did the English scarlet clothing for war, the white color made the French wearer, a wonderfully easy target.

The French officer's uniform was dirty and much bloodied. Much of the blood on his clothing was drying and turning brown. His white powdered wig was a bit askew, his nose a little crooked, and he appeared to be about 30 years old, and just then, exhausted.

Major Eyre said he had known Bougainville years before, in London, when the Frenchman had been inducted into England's "Royal Society," for his improvements in mathematics. Bougainville had been the 1st foreigner so honored, by the English intellectuals of that Society.

The Lieutenant Colonel said he had been on a mission to King Louis XV, at Versailles, outside of Paris, in faraway France. He had gone to the home country, for General Montcalm, and had returned to the Commanding General that very day. He had brought with him, his King's grant of the Order of St. Louis, for the Commander of French forces in North America.

Bougainville said he was about to drape the medal around Montcalm's neck, in the presence of high officers, and Asian War Chiefs, when he saw the first OdinRock in flight.

"Ah, so you are the inventor of weapons, and victor over us in the Ohio valley," the Lieutenant Colonel said, but in heavily accented English. "And now Grand Duke, Major Eyre tells me you exploded our laboratory, with impossible rockets, that sounded terrifying as they flew! I saw your third rocket fly to hit our laboratory. That explosion knocked the General atop me and made me unconscious. When I woke up, I saw a chunk of iron in his head and blood all over me. Dead soldiers were simply everywhere then."

"Colonel Bougainville," the Grand Duke began, "we have large, steam-powered boats that will be here in the morning. They're coming through the forest right now. We are going to take all of New France. Believe me, sir; it's practically as good as done. I wonder whether you might like to save the lives of your countrymen, by helping to...."

"Grand Duke Bushnell," he cut in, stiffening himself and actually raising his nose in the air, "I am a loyal subject of my King, and I can grasp where you are going with this. Steam-powered boats through a forest or not, I shall in no way commit treason, by helping you to take New France! No monsieur, never!"

"Very well Colonel," Odin replied, remembering the French put

great store in their honor. He turned away from the Frenchman, to
address the friendly Britisher.

"Major Eyre, I would like to talk to you when you have locked up
your prisoner."

Lord Doctor Gale came by again, and gave Odin some "rope
cake," from his AndyPak.

Because he had thought to bring some silver nu coins, the Lord
Doctor had been able to buy a never-used tent, and unused blankets,
for the use of the Nuworlders, for the night. They were to put up
those tents on grass, away from the stench, of the badly scarred and
filthy fort.

The Doctor told them the entire fort was so dirty; it was unfit
for human habitation.

He also warned Odin, and the others, to keep flies off their
wounds; as flies lay eggs in them, and they'd soon be a-crawl with
maggots. *Warning enough!*

Among Odin's visitors that afternoon, was Lieutenant Colonel
Joseph Fry, of Massachusetts Bay Colony's Militia.

General Webb had sent him up to the fort, with 200 regular
English troops, and about 800 "Provincials" on August 2nd, as reinforcements. But the fort was too small to hold them, so they were
ensconced in the "retrenchment," on Titcomb's Mount. Although
near the fort, they had luckily been out of the range of French
cannons thus far, and relatively safe from the filth and disease of the
fort itself.

"So, you're the fellow that created this Nuworld Nobility, we hear
so much about! And what wonderful, wonderful speeches you make!"
the enthusiastic Colonel Fry said. "Grand Duke Bushnell, I am
Milord, very, very pleased to meet you!"

"I am really pleased to meet you too, Colonel," Odin said,
shaking the visitor's hand.

"Over there on Titcomb's Mount, we were astonished to see you
and your fellows, ride into view, and to see you blast and kill, all
those savages in your way! And then you actually charged on, right
through a storm of cannon fire, to get into the fort! Damn! What a

sight! Then we saw your rockets scream through the air, to blow up all those Frenchies!"

"It seemed the thing to do at the time, Colonel," the Grand Duke said calmly.

Colonel Fry was staring at the Odin2Gun laying across Odin's lap, with the leather tether still wrapped around his right shoulder. That tether assured his gun would not fall away.

"That must be the world-changing weapon you invented. It looks like solid gold, and it sells for its weight in silver, I hear. But it wasn't too terribly immodest to name it after yourself though; eh Milord?" the Colonel smiled.

"Well, the musket was named by the French, after the Muscat wine grapes, they love so much. That's because the lod balls they shoot, look much like those grapes. Well now, since my gun had to have a name, I thought it a bit more reasonable to name it, after the fellow who invented it, instead of say, calling it a 'Colonel Fry.' I do sincerely hope that makes sense," the Grand Duke said.

"Ha, ha! Guess so at that. I see there's an awful lot of ammunition on your Noble's chests, in those magazines you call inserts. Why's that, Grand Duke?" the Colonel asked.

"That's so a Noble can deliver his shots, with considerable rapidity. Also, we load our jackets with inserts on Monday, and shoot our Odin2Guns all week," he bragged facetiously.

Fry didn't ask to buy any Odin2Guns, having no money, and knowing OdinGuns were going for very high prices to the Prussians. Nor had the English Army asked to buy them; Odin reckoned they hoped, of course, to steal them instead.

Major Eyre came by again, to tell the Nuworlders of the many prisoners his patrol had picked up. Most of them were, of course, were wounded, and they probably would not live long enough, to ever return to their home country of France... away over and beyond the Great Ocean Sea. The English had no provisions for caring for so many captives, so the Nuworlders took over that need. The French, of course, were amazed at the Noblewomen helping them.

Those enemies able to do so had fled north; to Fort Ticonderoga, Eyre assumed.

Also, the Major had found Montcalm's sword, and wondered if Odin wanted it.

"Yes Major, that is extremely thoughtful of you. We'll keep it for our future museum. Now, let me make a proposition to you," the Grand Duke said.

Odin then took the time to quickly explain to the Major, what they had so far accomplished with steam engines, in their sawmills, ironworks, and in the soon to arrive OdinBoats. He also mentioned that the nearly ready-to-launch OdinShips, would also be steam-powered to pull them over the seas, also with bucket wheels; but much larger ones. He mentioned also, the 4 OdinBoat haulers due there, to gather up every iron thing they could find, to convert to steel.

After the present campaign, they expected to begin laying *beam ways,* instead of roadways, with I-shaped steel beams, ten feet apart, on steel saddles. The ever-wearing metal saddles under the beams would be nailed onto half-logs, laid flat-side-down, on the ground.

Steam-engined *carriages,* would haul people fast, and in real comfort. Because of steel wheels on steel beams, there would be but the slightest of friction, compared to horse-drawn coaches, on the rough roads of the day. Steam-engined *cars* would haul freight much more efficiently, over rather long distances, than with horse-powered carts and wagons.

They would need qualified engineers such as Eyre, to layout such beam ways and much more. Barron Allen would be in charge of transport; would the Major wish to talk to him about what was coming, in transportation for the Nuworlders?

Indeed, the Major would, he told the Grand Duke, and quickly Eyre handed in his resignation to an angry Colonel Monro, as he was about to march south. The talented Britisher was soon in buckskins and ceremoniously taken into the Nuworld Nobility, with the rank of Count.

Militiamen on Monday morning, August 8th, 1757, buried 1,000s of enemies, and their own dead, in the ditches the French soldiers had dug to assault the fort. The French Soldiers, of course, never dreamed they were digging their own graves.

Nobody made a systematic count of enemy dead, and their own dead. There were only the usual exaggerated military guesses.

The 12 Nuworld Company partners, stepped out of their tents that morning, feeling refreshed from a good sleep, to see 4 Battle Forces with 29 OdinBoats, including the Grand Duke's, chugging and clanking noisily up the trail. They had been heard even before their arrival, because of their Hoppy Organs charming everyone's ears. And then they watched the steam erupting from the brass pipes, making the pretty melodies.

Nobles in their swarms were flailing axes about, clearing the way. They also had to wet the ground to mud, ahead of the OdinBoats, so that they would slide on their steel bottoms better.

Nobility Overlordet Duke Andrew Montour ran ahead of the Nobles, greeting the Grand Duke and the others. He instantly noticed the blood-stained hole in his Overlord's jacket.

"Milord! You've been shot!" the Duke gasped.

"Lord Andrew, it was minor, and it's already healing. Did our Nobles work the whole night through?" Odin asked.

"Yes Milord, indeed they did and.... oh look, here comes your Overlady!" Montour said.

Odin's darling wife, Annie, came running to him, and leaped into his arms, hugging him, with happy tears forming in her enormous blue eyes. She squeezed him so that it hurt his chest. As she pulled back to kiss him, she saw him wince.

"What's the matter?" she cried, looking down at his chest where she saw the bloodied hole. "Why, you've been wounded!"

"It's only a small thing sweetheart, but you squeezed it...." the Grand Duke said.

"Gracious! Let me see!" she exclaimed as she hastily unbuttoned his jacket.

It was a bit embarrassing as Ezra Stile's wife Elizabeth, came running up also. Stiles had finally gotten around to marrying, and brought her with him, to report for his NUWORLD NUZ, on the Noblewomen's activities.

"Oh my, it's bleeding," Overlady Annie said, and he could see that it was.

"Annie, I want you to take care of it as soon as we get on our OdinBoat. But first, I have business to attend to," he told his loving wife.

Grand Duke Odin turned to his Overlordet.

"Lord Andrew, this is a very filthy, unhealthy place. Get all the Nobles back on board, and we'll get into the water, proceed up this Lake Tyanoga some ways, to the east side of it, where we can beach the OdinBoats until next morning. Our gallant Nobles can rest overnight, and then we'll proceed exactly as planned."

The train of 29 OdinBoats soon had their bottoms wet again and were heading up the newly renamed, Lake Tyanoga. They found a place to beach them for the night, opposite to the west shore, where it was thought enemies might still be lurking.

The new Count Eyre brought his prisoner Bougainville, and locked him in a room on the Grand Duke's OdinBoat, supposing he might in the future, be useful.

The 4 OdinBoat haulers, unlike the Noble-carrying OdinBoats, had six holds, with hinged hatches, so they could bring back the tons of iron needed. Those four would load up all the iron guns and balls they could find at Fort Eyre and the French battlefield, and take them to the head of the Hudson River. There, 2 of them would empty their iron into two others, since hauling on water provided greater capacity. Those two unburdened, would then advance again through the woods to collect more iron from captured forts north of there, and again, return to the Hudson with loads for water transport to Stratford.

As Odin and Annie entered their cabin, Lord Doctor Gale was close behind, advising her on washing the wound twice daily, with the stinging alcohol.

She did just that as Odin lay back on his bed. She once again admired his "magnificent physique," as she frequently put it. He habitually lifted weights to maintain his strength.

"But I'm so mad at you Odin; I might not give you the news," his gorgeous wife said.

"Mad at me? What for? And for my sake, wife, what news?" he asked.

"Why, you take such awful chances! You could've been killed! Don't you realize you have such a future; you mustn't get yourself killed?" she said.

"Believe me; I have no ambition whatever to do that. But as we charged toward the gate of the fort, the French surprised us, with a couple of cannons loaded with canister, as they call it, to deny entrance, of such as ourselves. The 12 of us went through a hail of lod balls, but only 5 of us got hit. Now, what news are you withholding from your loving husband?" he asked.

"Well sweetheart, I didn't want to tell you anything, when only one month passed, but now its two months," she said.

"One month? Two months?" he said, as he was obviously puzzled.

"You know; my period. I had no period when it was due, a few days after we married, and now another month has gone by without it. That means you're going to be a papa," she said.

She smiled so that it lit her up gorgeously.

"Well, beautiful woman; *why didn't you say so!*" he shouted.

He jumped off the bed and kissed her with utmost passion. It was particularly thrilling for him, as she had worried, as so many women did, that she might never have children.

They both cried with happiness; although he was happy because she was happy.

"I think you must have planted your seed in me, in the first minutes you stuck me with your love stick! Ohhhh, that hurt so good!" she laughed.

"Also," she said after more embracing, "Elizabeth Stiles.... well, rumor has it she was 2 or 3 months along when she and Ezra finally married."

"Really? You mean that licensed Congregational Preacher, bundled on the floor with his sweetheart, and removed the board between them? Well, Reverend Stiles is a little calculating, and I suppose he wanted to be sure his wife-to-be could reproduce, and....," he said.

"Now, now, Odin. I'm sure it must have been romantic, but you say Mr. Stiles is *calculating?* It seems strange you would say that, for not only has he gone to great lengths in his newspaper, to extol your many accomplishments... please don't interrupt me... he has printed up those 100s of posters, with a coppix of you... and spread them all over the Colonies, in maybe every tavern, to repeat your explanation for the Noble titles, instead of the usual insults.

"And yes; also he's printed beyond counting, your story of the Nobility. And of course, your magnificent speech in Philadelphia has been spread for reading, everywhere. And goodness, all those on-the-trail-back questions from him, and the answers you gave him, about science and all, in certainly every newspaper. You say he's *calculating*, Odin dear? I hardly think so," Mrs. Odin Bushnell said.

"Well now, just you wait a minute, my dear. I only meant in that one sense, Sweetheart; that he'd probably wish to know if his wife could produce children. He'd hardly be the first man to be calculating in that respect. It's a New England tradition, I suppose, and nearly every bride there has been pregnant at marriage. You were the rare exception. As a matter of fact, nearly every colonial farmer has had to rely on his children, for the necessary labor to make his meager prosperity possible.

"Those children," he went on, "can't possibly get the education they should have, because so much of their time is taken up, with caring for those farm animals, and all those hundreds of things, needed to be done on a farm.

"That's a fact and something I hope to do a lot about. That is, to make real prosperity possible for every citizen, without the employment of children. Not only that, darling but I...."

They had sat down on the bed as they were talking, and he suddenly realized she had heard little of what he said, for she was asleep in his arms!

Of course! She had worked the whole night unselfishly through, with her Healthors and into that day! He laid her down on the bed, covered her, and kissed her.

Rain began to fall; that would help them sleep.

Another thing his wife didn't mention, was that Odin himself had even changed the design of buttons on each trouzer and jacket, to make them of brass with the Nuworld picture-map impressed on them. Their brass hats and the top of every Noble arm had that picture-map on it. Every French soldier and citizen had very soon to be familiar, with what the Nuworld Nobility represented.

When they were gleaning treasure off the Caribbean Sea floor, in 1755, Odin had urged the well-educated, and highly intelligent Stiles, to publish a newspaper with his wealth.

Stiles resisted the notion for a while, but he finally agreed, and his NUWORLD NUZ was now educating people everywhere in the English Colonies – as well as telling them the news. Hundreds of copies were being sent also, to England and a very few, went on to Europe.

Among the publicity Stiles had given Odin, was about the furniture factory in Stratford, that the young man had been instrumental in getting started. Obviously, many chairs, tables, beds, chests of drawers and kitchen cabinetry – most especially, ice chests – were needed for all the new dwellings required in the growing city of Stratford. Not only that, but thousands of such furnishings were required for the OdinBoats and the OdinShips.

A large building had been put up, and a steam engine installed to compress air. That air was circulated in the factory in pipes to saws, lathes, drill presses, and even sprayers, to varnish the wood with. Indeed, another company had to be formed to make that machinery, in addition to that required by Nehi Bushnell's works and others.

It was the only place on earth, that actual steel was readily available, for the making of really good hand tools and machine tools. Odin Bushnell had a lot to do with inventing and improving many tools; although often, others were inspired to follow through, on his ideas. The steel came from the Nuworld Company's blast furnaces in Stratford.

Odin had insisted that in order for the furniture companies to get large loans of nu from the Nuworld Company Treasury, all of the workers there, had to be part owners. They would be paid respectable wages and added to that, they would share in the profits of their company.

Nuworld Treasurer Clark, talked to them about such things in business, like stock shares, dividends, and the importance of keeping accounts accurately. Thus far, every loan had been repaid to the Treasury, on time.

Ezra Stiles had made much of those enterprises, in his NUWORLD NUZ, where the workers owned their companies. He contrasted that with the English practice, of one rich man owning a company, and the workers there were lucky, even to get paid their trifling wages.

Grand Duket Annie Bushnell and her husband, woke well before dawn and bathed together in their private shower. She cleaned his wound tenderly and kissed it.

Of course, he could not see that fabulous body, so naked and enticing, without doing what comes naturally. So, they had some incomparable fun, right there in their shower.

They then dressed in clean clothing. He put on a spare buckskin jacket, with neither bullet holes nor bloodstains on it. His wife saved his holed (holy, she called it) jacket, as a souvenir.

B arron Rittenhouse reported he had a ritt from Overlord
Bradstreet, that his *Resolutes* Force, with their 7 OdinBoats,
had almost reached Lake Ontario, on the Oswego River.

"Oh, by the way," the ritt continued, "the notorious land hog, and
endless adulterer, Sir William Johnson, had been shot to death, by
someone recently."

Overlord Bradstreet didn't say who killed Johnson, but it was well
known, of the hatred between those 2 high-powered men. Johnson
had long been bursting with venom because Bradstreet had looked
into his corrupt land deals, and reported his dishonest trading
practices.

That was thought the probable reason, Johnson gave Bradstreet
no warning, of the French and their savages, preparing to attack
Bradstreet's 1,000-man supply force, coming from the Oswego forts,
the year before.

Johnson had had cunning, as when he claimed credit for the
Colonials victory over a French force, near Lake Tyanoga in 1755. But
Johnson was shot in the rump, indicating he was running *from* the
battle, not properly and bravely facing it. Connecticut Colony's own

General Phineas Lyman had actually directed that battle, and he was the Commander who won it.

But the crafty Johnson had smooth political connections. With his deft, yet ludicrous flattery, of naming a lake for King George, and forts for his undeserving kin, he had been extravagantly honored. He was given the English title of Baronet and enriched with the huge sum of 5,000 pounds, English money.

Beyond that news, Overlord Croghan was to be told that "Overlord Bradstreet was transferring 1 Band, 2 Healthors, 2 Mohawk guides, and Miss Molly Brant, on 17 horses, post-haste, to the *Valiants* Force. Please wait for them."

When Odin told Croghan of the message, tears actually came to the eyes of the man as unflappable, as any person on earth.

"That John Bradstreet," the Irishman Croghan sighed, "has just obliged me for life."

Bradstreet had known of Croghan's great love, for the Mohawk maiden, Molly Brant.

Overlord Croghan ordered his number 7 Supply OdinBoat, to wait for the 17 riders, while the rest of the Force Group, steamed up the lake.

They had very good information of the area because some of the newer Nobles had scouted that territory, as part of the Rangers.

Odin had made one of the former Rangers, Israel Putnam – a relation of Nuworld Company partner, Rufus Putnam – he made him an Arch Count, and Overlord of a War Party consisting of 5 Combats, with about 380 Noblemen and Noblewomen in his charge.

Putnam's War Party was a part of Overlord Trent's *Invincibles* Battle Force.

The former Ranger Israel Putnam assured the Grand Duke that the 3-mile-long, curvy Tycham River—in about a 200-foot-drop – draining Lake Tyanoga into Lake Champlain, was plenty wide enough for the OdinBoats.

But there were trees overhanging much of that snake-like river, and they would need to be cut down, and lifted aside. There were also rapids in that stream, with worn-very-smooth stones in them. But those slick stones were not a problem for the 10-inch-thick oak plank sides, and the 14-inch-thick oak, and ½ inch thick steel-covered bottoms, of the OdinBoats.

They expected OdinBoats to regularly use that passageway between the lakes, to and from Canada, and the Hudson, even in the ice-covered waters of winter. However, they saw from maps, that a canal would be a good thing, connecting the Hudson and Lake Champlain.

Lake Tyanoga is 36 miles long, north to south, and a mere 3 or 4 miles wide, east to west, in most places.

They proceeded at about 16 nauts and were thus at the Tycham River quickly.

Overlord Trent and his *Invincibles,* led the way as planned. He had a crane at the prow of his OdinBoat, to swing cut down trees, over onto the banks.

Trent let loose with 12 OdinRocks, of the blaster type, spraying the forest far beyond the head of the lake, with resounding explosions. Then the Happy Hoppy Organs were played, to make as much noise as possible.

The Nuworlders expected that racket, to unnerve any of the superstitious French and Asians, that might be lurking in the bush. The ungodly booms had the desired effect, for the thousands of Nobles swinging axes along the river, saw no enemies there.

By mid-afternoon, they had chopped, sawed, groaned, crawled, and rattled along to 3/4 of the length of the river.

That was where they could see an abandoned sawmill, and a smoldering bridge, almost completely burnt away. They had no need to knock the bridge out of the way; the French had cleared the way for them.

Beyond the burnt bridge, the river widened. Rather soon, they were within range of Fort Ticonderoga's, many deadly cannons.

Of course, that was reason for the French fort's location; to deny passage from the river, or nearby Wood Creek, up through a narrow stretch of Lake Champlain.

Odin had instructed Overlord Trent at that point, to speed his OdinBoats ahead to the right of an island there, and out into the lake to make them more difficult, moving targets. And most especially, Trent was to have all of his 125 OdinRockCannons, ready to "throw OdinRocks," in the event the fort guns, actually fired on him.

Overlord Odin and Overlady Annie climbed onto the 8-foot square roof of their pilothouse, with several of the partners following them. They mostly steadied themselves, by hanging onto the then-cool steam pipes of the Hoppy Organ, and the iron railing.

A dangerous thing about the use of those big muzzle-loading cannons, and maybe even mortars in a fort—or aboard ship—was that they of necessity had paper or cloth bags of gunpowder close by. Sometimes, open pans full of loose gunpowder was kept near the cannons, in order to more speedily re-load them. Also, boys or men – "powder monkeys," they were called – would be running from the fort's, or the ship's magazines, with more bags of the easily ignited, deadly dangerous gunpowder, in their arms.

All of that highly inflammable explosive was out there in the open. That stuff could be easily touched off by OdinRockFlamers. Each Flamer had 44 little paper packets, with pine-tar-gunpowder mix, and explosive to scatter the flaming packets, all over the place. Those little packets stuck stubbornly, to anything they touched, and burned with terrific heat.

It the fort withheld fire, Overlord Trent was to send Nobles in, to accept their surrender.

It had to have been a startling sight for the superstitious Frenchmen, in Fort Ticonderoga, to see the 150-feet long, bright red boats smoothly, miraculously, moving along on those waters.

The water was being churned wildly along the sides, and the stiff circles of brass, beautiful flags were seen atop the rear of their pilot houses. Steam and smoke were being shot up from angled iron chimneys at the rear of the boats.

Just as Trent's Force swung out into a narrow part of Lake Champlain, the fort let loose with its guns! The iron balls they sent out, were barely discernible dark blurs, speeding through the cool noon air.

Immediately, fully 125 OdinRocks were aflight, screaming with a heart-stopping cacophony of blood-curdling sounds. Some Odin-Rocks were Blasters, and some of them were Flamers.

They had been told Fort Ticonderoga was built largely of rocks, and sure enough, the place went up with a fantastic earth-shaking roar, sending countless thousands of large and small, cut stones, flying in every direction, and splashing into the lake.

And, like the ancient city of Jericho in the Bible, "the walls came tumbling down."

The French practice of storing huge amounts of gunpowder had again worked to the Nuworlders' advantage. It was an even larger explosion than that at Fort Duquesne on the Ohio.

Surprisingly, several of those rocks from the fort walls were thrown (because of the Noble's thrown OdinRocks!) so far as to hit the Grand Duke's boat. A rock crashed into the left side, taking out a window. His boat was hit, not with French cannonballs, but by French stones!

As Captain MacDougal pulled the Force Group OdinBoat, up to Overlord Trent's, they could see several Nobles had been struck, by both rocks and balls. On the left side of Trent's *Invincibles* 6, they could see those French iron balls, had done damage in 4 places. Two holes, 1 above the other, were made about in the center of the craft, and 1 was higher up near the rear.

One ball had drilled straight through the thin steel, which covered the left bucket wheel. That wheel was making a scraping sound, as it turned.

Grand Duke Odin hollered over to Arch Duket Trent, as he stood on his prow, "Better stop your engines Milord, and get that wheel repaired!"

With Trent's engines stopped, Barron Rufus Putnam swung over to supervise repairs. It didn't appear that the other OdinBoats, had been struck with the notoriously inaccurate cannonballs; only with the flung-by-explosive rocks.

But those rocks had done some damage, oddly knocking down a flagpole on one and shattering windows on others. Also, those flying rocks caused plenty of hurt to those Nobles out in the open, throwing or loading OdinRocks into OdinRockCannons.

The Grand Duke directed Overlord Croghan, and his *Valiants* Battle Force to back up the *Invincibles,* as they went ashore onto the smashed-to-hell remnants of Fort Ticonderoga. They would also gather as much iron as they could, and pile it up, for the following iron haulers.

Meanwhile, Odin would proceed up Lake Champlain some 20 miles, to France's Fort Saint Frederick at Crown Point. His other 2 Battle Forces would accompany him.

About an hour and a quarter later, the 2 Battle Forces came upon the notorious fort.

Again, this French fort was at a narrowing of Lake Champlain, with its big guns commanding passage up or down those waters.

Odin studied it through his spyglass. It appeared to be formidable, with a "bomb-proof" stone tower, rising up in the center, to perhaps 5 or 6 stories in height. A stone wall surrounded the whole fort, and it was thought to deploy, 40 or so large guns. Wooden barracks were inside.

The French had invested great amounts of money in the place. That fort had been a base for many deadly raids, into the frontiers of the New England, and New York Colonies, for years. Time and again, Colonial leaders had vowed to destroy Fort Saint Frederick. But they had never marched their Militias, anywhere near the place.

Those inside that fort, had surely heard the explosions at Fort Ticonderoga, and should have been wary of the consequences, of firing at the huge, and hugely different, big red boats.

Not a single Asian or Frenchman there would have any conception of such vessels, moving without sails, oars, paddles or poles. They moved by the turning of the big bucket wheels, practically exploding water, back along their sides.

Odin could see men peeking over the walls, and between the stones. When they were abreast of the place, and 3/4 mile away, the fort guns let loose at them!

Instantly, OdinRocks were war-whooping through the air, and within minutes, the fort was a scene of roaring fires and terrific devastation. The 60-foot-high "bomb proof" tower, collapsed in a cloud of smoke and dust. Time-dried-to-tinder wooden buildings, all over the compound, burnt ferociously. Walls disintegrated. Countless stones and a few cannonballs splashed into the lake. All of them were a bit short, of the too distant OdinBoats.

No human being could be anything but awestruck, at the result of those OdinRocks destroying the place so rapidly. Many watching the chaos could hardly breathe.

Major Eyre had brought Bougainville to the weather deck, so he could witness the Nuworlder's power. But the French Army Lieutenant Colonel, and notable mathematician, only wept at the sight, and made no offer, to help save any of his countrymen's lives.

With huge bucket wheels grabbing at the lake shore, the Nuworlders climbed their OdinBoats out of Lake Champlain, onto the land, to where the French fort had been.

Well-organized 12-Noble Bands sought to discover how many survivors there might be. There weren't many. Vague guesses were that about 4,500 persons – soldiers, militia, Asian warriors, and women and children, had hunkered down there, for the supposed safety of those stone and mortar walls. Despite the efforts of 12 doctors, and just over 100 Healthors, only 622 of them survived, to the next morning.

A few had hardly been hurt, but not a single one of them was clean of body. Their dominating priests, from the days of mixed male-female bathing in Roman baths, had been insisting that bathing was a most terrible sin.

It was told that Asian warriors were getting vengeance on the French officers, murdering them for their lies. It was obvious to the Asians, if not to the French that their war was lost.

The plunder taken from those French Army officers, such as pretty brass pistols, swords, and fancy carbines... well, they had to have seemed great riches, to those who may have never seen, such wondrous, man-made things before.

The Nuworlders spent the night there on the shore, and through the next day and night. They were waiting for Overlord Trent to make his repairs, and for the 2 Battle Forces left at Ticonderoga, to join them. They gathered great amounts of French iron to be made into steel.

The Nuworlders got out their much-used shovels. They buried the dead, and the shattered parts of the dead.

Neither of the 2 priests at the post survived, so the Congregational Reverend Ezra Stiles, sent the Catholic dead off, as properly blessed as he could, to their eternity. He expressed the belief that any Catholic priest coming by that place in the future would repeat his blessings of the deceased, to make certain they were allowed into that magical, mysterious heaven after all.

Watching those blessings being made, had Odin Bushnell wondering if it was merely a charade. It was obvious to him that in no way could that "magic nonsense" get those dead people to some imaginary place, up there in the sky, called heaven.

Stiles and his wife both spent much of the first night there ritting, to the NUWORLD NUZ – and thus, also to all of the Colonial papers—of the absolute destruction of the 2 French forts, that had for such a long time, been scourges to the English Colonists.

They were to refill their tanks from each Force's OdinBoat 7. Whale oil was only so plentiful, and for the expedition they were on, there was only the spare oil in their Supply OdinBoats. The French were known to have whaling ships out, so they would capture oil from them.

And since they were out of the water, they checked for damage, from the rough miles traversed, from the Hudson to Lake Tyanoga, and again over the rapids of the Tycham River. The steel bottoms of all the OdinBoats had held up quite well.

Overlord Bradstreet ritt that a single steam valve problem slowed his Battle Force in his journey to war. But he expected to attack Fort Frontenac on the north side of Lake Ontario the next day, August 11th. That was the same day as Grand Duke Odin would be moving his Force Group up Lake Champlain.

Odin asked Lord Andrew to speak with some of the French-Canadian prisoners, about becoming "ambassadors for peace," to save lives by negotiating surrenders. Montour accepted 6 young lads who volunteered; one of them was a quite sharp Canadian Militia Ensign. The French-Canadians bathed, shaved, and had their uniforms cleaned. With impressive Duke Montour's instructions in their French language, they were soon ready for "ambassadorial" service.

Count William Eyre, told Grand Duke Odin he looked over an OdinRock, and could not understand why it flew so accurately since it had no arrow-like fins.

"Milord, it's just a little piece of magic," was all Odin would smilingly admit.

Only he and Revere knew that gunpowder, mixed with nearly pure alcohol, and then dried hard after being extruded, became the rocket motor. Odin's insight gave him the idea of extruding a square fire hole, in the length of the center of the cylindrical "rocket motor." They twisted the square hole, which provided a steadily larger burning surface – for the few seconds that it burned—as it flew.

And since that fire hole was carefully and deliberately twisted a little in the extrusion process, the fire raging along that hole also twisted, thus spinning the missile. It was a simple matter of "action equals reaction," per one of the well-known dictums of English scientist, and Odin Bushnell's hero, Sir Isaac Newton.

Odin didn't mention to Eyre, or anyone else, that new Odin-Rocks were then being made, which were longer, had a more powerful blast and flew a bit more than 3 times as far.

Overlords Trent's and Croghan's Battle Forces caught up with Odin, having finished their tasks at the remains of Fort Ticonderoga.

Croghan's 7th OdinBoat had brought his precious love, Miss Molly Brant.

The lovely Mohawk maiden had shiny black hair, and pretty black eyes to match. She wore Healthor buckskins, as Reverend Stiles married her to Arch Duket George Croghan, in Odin's dining room. Everyone was impressed with her natural dignity.

Early on Thursday, August 11th, 1757, they crawled their Odin-Boats back down into Lake Champlain, and left Crown Point, heading hurriedly north. Twenty-eight OdinBoats followed Overlord Grand Duke Odin's lead.

Odin's wound 4 four days before, was healing well, as were the wounds of the other partners. But the tall and powerful Barron

Allen's shoulder blade was somewhat fractured, and he would need to keep his arm in a sling, for some time to come.

The next day they neared Isle-aux-Noix (French; for "Island of Nuts"), where they knew a small fort was located, to deny entrance to the Richelieu River.

It seemed a good time to experiment, with Duke Montour's selected "ambassadors." But just as the cooperating Frenchmen rowed toward the island, with a white flag flying, they saw maybe 40 or 50 men rowing away, beyond that island. Then a number of powerful explosions took place, as the fort began disappearing, in fire and smoke.

Duke Montour voiced the opinion, that those Frenchmen might meet with sad fates, in the bush, what with so many revengeful savage Asians about.

There was no point even in going ashore to plant the Nuworlder's brass flag – it would probably not be long unmolested anyway.

They proceeded up the lake about 12 miles north, to the priest-named and blessed, Isle Saint John, where there was another small French fort.

Again, they let down a ramp, slid a rowboat into the water, and the 6 French-Canadian ambassadors rowed over to the fort. They had a white flag on a pole, to show their friendliness. In half an hour, they signaled the fort was surrendering. No shots whatever had been fired.

The Nuworlders nosed their OdinBoats up onto the shore and took possession of the place. None of the newest prisoners had been well provided for, and all of them were vaguely aware of the calamities, at the big forts south of them.

All of the new prisoners ate ravenously. They were astonished that the Nuworlders had fresh fruit, vegetables, and meat aboard – stored in their OdinBoat ice rooms.

Oddly, French Colonies had depended on their home country of France, for much of their food. Meanwhile, the English Colonies exported huge amounts of grains, and of milled flour, to England, and to the Caribbean islands. This last, together with fish heads and fish guts, was to feed the 1,000s of slaves, as cheaply and as inhumanely, as possible.

Duke Montour had made sure that each Battle Force had men, who could speak and read, French or an Asian language. They were instructed to inform the prisoners of the tale of Nuworld, shown so clearly on their shoulders and their brass hats. They were to assure the Frenchmen of the stable, and rich future planned, for the conquered territories.

Venturing further to the north, was a place called Fort Chambly. Their surrender was affected in the same fashion. Prisoners were steadily filling up the spaces planned for that purpose.

The Nuworlders did not destroy the place just as they had not, on Isle Saint John. But after planting their shiny brass flag, they piled up all the iron balls, cannons and muskets found there. They had done that same thing at Ticonderoga and Fort St. Frederick, to assist the following iron haulers. Also, sheltering housing was still available in the still-standing places, for those who needed it.

They had good intelligence of the town of Montreal, on an island in the then called Saint Lawrence River.

That very important river had been named by Catholic priests, for the supposedly saintly fellow, whom ancient Roman soldiers reportedly, roasted on an iron grill. That was a very long time ago. But he got in trouble with the Romans, supposedly, for his obstinacy in believing, in the radically new Christian religion, instead of the Roman Empire religion – or of course, possibly for real, actually serious crimes.

The fairly important town there was named after a big hill on the island—Royal Mountain; Montreal, in French. From English traders venturing up the Hudson for years, and from cooperative prisoners, they knew the place was practically indefensible. Montreal was strung out along the river, with a weak masonry wall, and a ditch, plus tiny outlying forts there to discourage Asian warriors, from attacking. The Iroquois Asians, from south of Lake Ontario, had raided the place a number of times, with varying successes.

Ezra Stiles had printed in his NUWORLD NUZ, an explanation of many Asian words. "Canada," he said, came from the old Euro and

Latin word "canna," for reed. Just as was still done in the old Euro Eden, in marshes at the head of the Persian Gulf, the Asians originally built both houses and boats – canna-oes: canoes – of reeds. They stuck with that word for their boats, and their houses, and their groups of houses in villages. Of course, the materials changed, mostly to elm tree bark, or the lighter birch tree bark, for canoes; and other materials for their homes.

Thus, the Mohawk town of Canajoharie in New York Colony meant Canna – houses or many houses; "jo," as did "mo" and "po," meant people; "harie" meant Aries, white people – which they originally could have been. Also, the Asian word Connecticut meant "canna" – houses – along the cut – a valley. The Old World – Nuworld connections were unmistakable, Ezra Stiles had assured everyone.

About noon on Monday, August 14th, 1757, they traversed the Richelieu River and reached the misnamed larger St. Lawrence River. That was at a broad place named Lac Saint Pierre (Peter), by the ever propagandizing-the-faith, French priests.

Montreal was about 35 or 40 miles upstream, to the west, toward which they charged at full speed. They had the Happy Hoppy Organs making music, the whole way.

"This is our Nuworld, our very free Nuworld,

"Our Brightest Rich Part of the Whole World.

"Nobility, Nobility, protect us all from harm.

"And honor us with righteousness, in city, sea, and farm!"

Here and there the Nuworlders saw people along the banks, staring in disbelief at the unimaginable sight, of 29 big red boats speeding by.

The newcomers also saw several small, so-called "forts." Some of them were no more than loop-holed, wooden windmills, intended to dissuade Asian attacks.

Happily, the OdinBoats received no shots at all, from any of those smallest of forts.

Lord Andrew guessed the population of Montreal, couldn't be more than a few 1,000 Catholics. But he had then no notion of how many soldiers and militia might be present.

They could see several steeples beyond the town's wall, from churches and nunneries. They had sharp spires pointing to the sky; those pointed things supposedly demonstrated the great piety, of the strictly Catholic French people.

Yet rich French men and women were infamous for their marital infidelities. Their King had a string of teen-age whores, for his own sexual gratification supposedly boarded in his own private brothel. The French enslaved countless Africans, especially in the Caribbean, and they greatly abused their millions of peasants. Such piety, those French!

Like any sizeable town, Montreal would have taverns, butchers, bakeries, stables, blacksmiths, sawmills, warehouses, churches and every sort of little business, large and small.

But in French Canada, *there had to be no newspapers, no printers, and no book stores.* Whatever schools they would have, would be controlled absolutely by the Catholic Church, and for their own purposes of propaganda, in addition to praising the corrupt government of France.

All along the river were many small farms, where rents were, of course, to be paid to a privileged French Seigneur, or their Catholic Bishop, in the ancient French Feudal system. That possibly helped to explain the insignificance of their farming productivity, as compared with the much more-free English Colonials, south of them.

Duke Montour sent the "Ambassadors of Peace," rowing across the river to warn the town of Montreal, against resistance. They were to give assurance, that the Nuworlders would blast and burn the town flat if they foolishly resisted. But the Nuworlders would hardly desire to destroy the very buildings, they fully expected to occupy.

After a little more than half an hour, the Ambassadors suddenly reappeared atop the "protective" wall and were escorting an elderly man to their boat.

The old man was wearing fancy scarlet and gold clothes and had on a large, plumed hat and a starkly white wig. The wig was curled at the ends, where it reached his shoulders.

The Nuworld Nobles wore only their own, well-washed, trimmed and well-kept hair.

Duke Montour met them as they came aboard. He told the Grand Duke that the man was the senior person in the town, the "Major de Place"; the Mayor.

The Governor-General of Canada, the King's Intendant, and all French Army units, had fled to Quebec, the Duke told the Grand Duke as he listened to the old man. Only a few 100s of soldiers and militia, in very bad shape, were left behind.

The Major de place claimed many, many French had been murdered by maddened Asians, who then robbed the dead of their weaponry. And the flamboyant old man wished to know the terms of capitulation, as though he had some bargaining power.

Odin told Lord Andrew to draw up something that might salve their pride but to be certain they understood the town, and the area for a long distance around was to be occupied by Overlord John Lamb's *Defiants* Battle Force.

The other Battle Forces would proceed, to conquer the remainder of New France. The Colony would be severed from France forever. French Canada was to become a part of the Nuworld State, a new and separate nation.

Duke Andrew Montour was to inform the Major de Place, that those who wished to remain French, would be welcome to go to France and stay there. Those who remained, where they were, were expected to become peaceful Nuworlders, *in our Nuworld, our Free World, our Brightest Rich part, of the Whole World.*

There were still several hours of daylight, so all 4 Forces put their OdinBoats up against the north bank.

While those in the town were still in shock at the Nuworlders presence, they landed to take the place – again, without a single shot being fired. The nearly 8,000 Noblemen and Noblewomen strolling in, very certainly outnumbered the town's residents.

Soon, they had almost 400 more French soldier prisoners, most of them with wounds and none at all in good shape. Doctors and Healthors tended them and made them bathe, however unused to getting-wet-all-over they were. The French were repeatedly assured that it was sinful *not to bathe,* as well as dirty and dead skin, on a person, being dangerous to one's health.

The sailing vessels found in the river would serve as the soldiers' transport downstream, and back to France "on parole." Each man was obliged to never to fight the Nuworlders again.

Overlady Annie saw to it that the town's poorly stocked bakeries, were immediately given huge amounts of corn and wheat flour, bread being the "staff of life," almost everywhere. She also spread the word that raisins, and walnuts in bread, was beneficial to human health – to say nothing of adding great taste—and provided a barrel of each of those ingredients, also. Those bakers were both astonished at that generosity and appeared to be truly grateful.

By coincidence, Overlord Bradstreet ritt Odin that night, that his Battle Force, had surrounded Fort Frontenac. That fort was at the very beginning of the newly, and properly re-named, River Canada, at Lake Ontario.

The news of capturing Fort Frontenac, and of the destruction and capture of French forts south of there, were broadcast throughout Montreal, to the townsfolk, by an old-fashioned and roaming around, "Town Crier." He was carefully directed and listened to, by Lord Montour.

Bradstreet demonstrated the power of the OdinRocks, by throwing merely one of the flamers, onto a big timber pile outside of Fort Frontenac. The instant raging pyre quickly convinced the tiny garrison to surrender.

Bradstreet's *Resolutes* captured many "Indian trade goods" at that fort, and a surprising quantity, of brand new French muskets. Bradstreet would take that loot west with him, to give the 550 hunting weapons away, and make friends of the distant tribes. He would also gather up all the iron he could find, to send back with a future supply vessel.

❦ 16 ❦

That same night a ritt came from Captain Hazelwood, in the port of Hamburg, up the Elbe River from the North Sea, having been blown across the raging Atlantic, in record time. His 15-masted Odin Raft could almost fly, at 20 nauts, in favorable winds.

Hazelwood said the Prussians had just captured Vienna, the capital of one of their enemy nations, the Austrian Empire. The numerous Austrian Royal family, he ritted, had tried to escape down the Danube River, on a large Royal Barge. They had crowded onto the barge, crown jewels, golden carriages, prized horses, and apparently, tons of gold and silver. But the craft sank as soon as it moved into the stream. Every person aboard drowned, since they could not swim—especially with their persons and pockets overloaded, with that very heavy metal gold, and obviously, lots of gems. Even the horses drowned, he reported; they were harnessed to carriages.

Hazelwood seemed to gloat, as he reported the Prussians were to have divers, recover the great plunder. And he noted, those Prussians were putting to good use, the war-revolutionizing OdinGuns they had bought.

Many of the Nobles spent the 15th and 16th of August, at Montreal, refueling the OdinBoat tanks with whale oil from their number 7 supply OdinBoats. They could not be sure when they might again have a chance to replenish their fuel.

Arch Duket John Lamb was given an enormous area to administer. It went all the way downstream to Trois Rivieres, a town that got its name from the St. Maurice River which, where it joined the River Canada, was split into 3 channels – or "3 rivers"—by 2 islands.

Lord Lamb would need to mollify the priests, whose authority was suddenly diminished.

Also, some scores of French-Canadian prisoners, confined on the OdinBoats, were released to him, as they had resided in that area. Other Canadians would be let off downstream, so they could return to their farms and families.

Another brief ritt from Overlord Bradstreet said he had climbed his OdinBoats, out of the smallest of the Great Lakes, Lake Ontario. He had got to the French Fort Niagara, and found that the Iroquois, had killed the few Frenchmen manning the fort; and had plundered the place.

Bradstreet was proceeding to the Niagara River, above Niagara Falls, and thence to Lake Erie. He would go to the French Fort Junandat, at Sandusky Bay, and take it. He would then proceed with his Battle Force, to a little fort called DeTroit, meaning in French, "the strait." There he was to begin laying out Lord West's "wagon wheel plan," for a large city, and name the town, Cadillac. Cadillac was the name of the Frenchman, who was the much-admired original French founder of that fort.

The Grand Duke had instructed Overlord *Bradstreet,* to be sure the city of Cadillac, contained many *broad streets* in it. That got a chuckle from the man.

The Grand Duke and 3 Battle Forces, steamed down the River Canada, on August 17th, 1757. The 22 OdinBoats, could have easily gone the 150 miles, to Quebec in a single day, but the Nuworlders needed to more or less conquer, on the way.

The population of Canada at that time was only around 55,000 people. Most of them eked out a living on small farms, in an old-fashioned French feudal system. They had to have their grain milled at the Seigneur's or the Bishop's mills. Their little rented farms were strung along and close to the river.

The Nuworlders had heard conflicting guesses, about what remained of the French forces. Desertions were said to be rampant. The meager French strength had been concentrated at Quebec. They were, of course, hoping for miraculous reinforcements from France. The Grand Duke supposed the French might also have a powerful Navy fleet at Quebec.

The river was clear of all vessels but those of the Nuworlders, as they steamed along. But they were aware, Frenchmen hurried canoes downstream, day and night, with news of the invaders. The Nuworlders now and then dropped off Canadian militiamen, where they wished to rejoin their families.

The countryside was beautiful, with valuable forests lining the river, except here and there where clearings had been made. Occasionally, a few horses, cattle and sheep were seen grazing. There was also some iron mining going on, which resulted in a small iron smelter.

The French had control of a truly enormous territory, for 150 years. Yet there had been but little immigration from France. Only French Catholics had been welcome; the gatekeeping priests saw to that.

They could easily have flooded that French-claimed area, with 100,000, or even double that number, of prolific French. They could have, except those hated French citizens were Protestant Huguenots, evicted from their home country. But the priests would not allow them into Canada. The kingly government of France had much need to mollify the Catholic Church, since it was its staunch ally, in controlling the French people.

The problem of low population, could not have been because of the climate, for New England's climate was similar; and that settlement had vastly more people.

Actually, the city of Quebec is further south in latitude than France's city of Paris. But France – and the British Isles – had climates greatly moderated, by the Nuworld's warm Gulf Stream, as it flowed onto Europe's shores. Quebec was very much affected by Arctic weather.

Duke Montour came to Overlord Odin and said he had been approached by Monsieur Bougainville, with a question.

"Milord, he wondered if you planned to destroy Quebec if you met resistance. I assured him you had a plan if there was any hesitation in surrendering, whereby you would flatten the entire city, and push the rubble into the river. I told him you had seen maps, and sketches of the place, and reckoned what they called the 'Lower Town,' ought to be expanded, by filling in the river there, with the debris of buildings.

"He was startled to hear this," Montour grinned; for the Overlordet knew the Grand Duke had no such plan.

"Milord, Bougainville seems to me, to be quite hopeful, Canada will be returned to France in a peace treaty, just as Louisbourg had been, after the last war. There would be nothing to gain for the French, to have their lovely city destroyed," Lord Andrew said.

"Bougainville didn't mention the little matter, of a few 1,000s of his countrymen, being killed in the process. Even so, he would try to save the city. He knows nothing of your plans to form a new nation; I've made sure of that," the 3/4s Asian Montour, said.

"Lord Andrew, you've done well," Odin said. "I don't think we should trust him too much. If we send Bougainville in to negotiate, we'll also send along the 6 Ambassadors you chose, and who deserve our thanks, and plenty of rewards, for their courageous efforts."

"Yes, Milord. By the way, Bougainville insisted you should allow them to surrender with 'the honors of war,'" Montour said. "You know, to march out with their flags flying, muskets on their shoulders, and such nonsense as they do in Europe.

"But I said to him, 'You mean the honors of war, that your General Montcalm allowed the English, at the Oswego massacre, after they surrendered?

"'You know Bougainville,' I said to him, 'I'm an Iroquois warrior myself, and we have a number of Asian warriors with us, and perhaps we can get in on some good old fashioned scalping, just as your wondrously honorable Army, treated our people at Oswego.' That's what I told him, Grand Duke."

"Excellent, Lord Andrew. I'll see what's what later, and then decide," the Overlord said.

On the morning of August 19th, they pulled up at the un-fortified town of Trois Rivieres. They found the "Major de Place," at the water's edge to greet them. He had been informed, of course, by men in their swift canoes, of the Nuworlders approaching near.

The Major de Place claimed all the French military, had fled east to Quebec.

The Nuworlders continued on, noting that they had been having nearly perfect weather, since their night on Lake Tyanoga. But now the air was turning cool, and the sky was darkening.

Rain was in the air; no doubt of that. And that made the wheels begin spinning in Odin's head.

When Grand Duke Odin reckoned they were about 9 miles from Quebec itself – which they could not yet see – he halted their procession. They pulled up their OdinBoats on the north bank, at a place called Cap Rouge – French, for "Red Cape." That was where a stream flowed from the north, into the River Canada. He called for a meeting of the Overlords on his own OdinBoat, at that place.

There was still some daylight left, as Duke Andrew Montour, the 3 remaining Battle Force Overlords, and Overlady Annie met in Grand Duke Odin's dining room.

Rain had just begun to fall. The dark gray sky looked to hold, a fairly wild August storm coming their way, rather soon, out of the north.

"Gentlemen," the Grand Duke began, "one of the many illicit English traders that have made good profits trading with the French up here told me about a gorge up this stream some ways. That gorge leads to the right, up onto a plain, leading to the walls of Quebec. For some reason, that flat ground is called, the Plains of Abraham. We're going up to that 'wash,' as he called it, and pull our OdinBoats up to the flat ground, and then proceed to within 1/2 mile, from the walls of Quebec City.

"We'll be renaming the place Stadacona, as the original Asian inhabitants, properly called it. Asian temporary villages were often abandoned after a time, because of accumulated filth and flies. Stada – meaning 'stable,' as it was a permanent village—and the part 'cona,' for canna, meant a village. Quebec, Mr. Stiles assures us, was the word regarding the lower town part where becs – meaning boats – tied up at the quay. Quay was a word from way back in ancient Euro times; thus, the French assumed the town's name, was Quay-bec.

"We have even heard the leading man, the Mayor of Stadacona, was styled 'Donacona.' That's very much like the word for a Spanish leader, Don So-and-so. We can understand that there had to have been a connection between the Old World and our Nuworld.

"So, in 1535, when Jacques Cartier, and later in 1608, when Samuel de Champlain, began to take over and modify the city, there were difficulties in language, of course. But now I am ordering a correction of the town's name back to Stadacona. That's to honor the Asians who established this town, long, long ago.

"But in thinking about this for some time, I didn't know what we could do about the shipping, and warships downriver, beyond the town. I thought we'd probably have to let the big wigs getaway on their ships, with their loot. But aha! I now have a plan," the Grand Duke said.

"As all of us know, Quebec – no, let's call it by its proper name, Stadacona—is equipped dangerously, with 200 or more large cannons, plus huge, and deadly mortars. Those weapons are protected by strong stone walls. Any attacking fleet coming from the sea could quickly be reduced to matchsticks, it seems. But I have heard, that their *walls and guns on this land side* of Stadacona, are only there to ward off minor attacks, by Asian warriors.

"When we steam along on that plain, we'll make as much racket as possible, with our Hoppy Organs. Also, we'll flash our big keg lights, onto the ground, and light up their walls and practically the whole city, as it never has been before. We must avoid shining those lights onto the clouds, so as not to light up Lord Croghan's Odin-Boats, easing themselves downstream.

"We'll do this to distract them noisily, while the 7 OdinBoats of Overlord Croghan's *Valiants,* slip down river silently. They must proceed cautiously, to get below whatever ships might be there, and prevent any escape whatsoever. By daylight, I expect the Captains of those French vessels, will see their situation is rather hopeless. *They could not have expected big red, silent boats steaming by them down the river, and thus they will be very much surprised.*"

"Oh good," Overlady Annie offered, "we'll sneak up on those Frenchies, and flabbergast them with more than plenty racket!"

That brought a bit of laughter, midst the tense moments.

"Damn!" Lord Croghan exploded. "We couldn't have prayed for better weather than this for such a move. The harder the rain falls, the less likely men are to be out and about, to see us. Let's hope it keeps up until we get down there below their ships. Make lots of noise and shine up the town with lots of light, you fellows!" Croghan added.

"Good," the Grand Duke said. "Overlord William Trent, you will have your 7 OdinBoats, follow my boat, up this Cap Rouge River.

"Overlord Daniel Morgan, you'll have your 7 OdinBoats, follow them.

"Overlord Croghan, you will stay here until it is dark as can be, then glide along slowly downstream, as best you can.

"We've heard the King's Intendant, Antoine Bigot, was supposed to supervise all financial dealing in the Colony, to prevent corruption. But we hear he has instead, made himself tremendously rich, from his own corrupt theft, of his King's silver and gold. Treasurer Clark could make good use of that plunder, converting it to nu, after we capture the place."

Captain MacDougal then led the way, with Odin's boat, up the Cap Rouge River several miles, in the falling rain, to the little gorge, or wash, going up to their right. The first OdinBoat got up to the flat ground with little difficulty. But all of those following had to be helped along by their crews, struggling in the mud, heaving on ropes, to get all of them up onto the level ground, of the "Plains of Abraham."

❦ 17 ❧

By dawn's early light, the rain had completely stopped. The storm left huge white cotton balls, scudding across the brilliant blue sky. The rain had left the land well-soaked.

Lord Andrew brought prisoner Bougainville up, to see the Grand Duke, on the weather deck. The French Army Lieutenant Colonel could also see the familiar city, from a very different viewpoint than he had before.

Bougainville was astonished to see the lineup of OdinBoats, 7 of them stretching in a line left of the Grand Duke's boat, and another 7 to the right. The Frenchman counted them.

"Overlord Croghan's *Valiants* Battle Force," the Overlord told the French officer, "has slipped downriver during the night, to below the French warships, and the merchant vessels anchored near the city. At dawn, he fired 2 OdinRocks into a large windmill there. It blasted the mill into nothingness, so they understand down there, what power he has.

"They've doubtless heard of the disasters to French warships, in the Caribbean, from such missiles; and to all those French forts on Lake Champlain. I want to ask you sir; do you doubt we can level this town? We can do it in no more than 10 minutes' time; just 10 minutes."

"Grand Duke – *in 10 minutes?*" Bougainville gasped.

"In not more than 10 minutes, Colonel," Odin Bushnell said, exaggerating mightily.

"I don't mean to interrupt," Overlordet Andrew scowled. "But Milord Odin, you surely won't allow them to march out with the honors of war, will you?"

"Oh, I don't know," the Grand Duke said. "But come to think of it, in these years of French officers urging their allied savages to brutally murder our frontier folks, even women and children, and to torture some of them, and all the horrendous, other things.... come to think of it, the dishonorable French, gave our people no honors at all.

"But don't you know Milord Duke Andrew; this seems to be the time to teach some civility, to the French Army and Navy. We'll have to have some give-and-take at the peace table, and who knows who'll end up with this place, after that?" the Grand Duke said believably.

Then Odin turned to the prisoner. "Dammit Bougainville, you can tell those inside, that I'll grant you can march out as you wish, but you have only until high noon. Any attempt at foolishness will bring absolute destruction to the town and to all inside. Is that understood, sir?"

The chagrinned Bougainville understood very well. Soon he, and the 6 French Canadian "ambassadors," were on their way through the Saint-Jean Gate, to inform the authorities inside the town, of what they had to do, to avoid being exterminated.

As the morning wore on, nothing happened, except that the puffs-of-cotton-clouds drifted away, leaving a pleasantly warm day. There was no activity visible from the town, other than men on the walls, staring at the OdinBoats lined up side by side, 1/2 mile off.

Then at high noon, the Saint-Jean gate opened, and 100s of French soldiers marched out with drums beating and flags flying.

Overlord Morgan and his *Gators* Force, hurried over on foot, to accept their surrender. The French stacked their swords, pistols, and muskets. They also handed over their flags, with much pomp and many tears.

The Governor-General of New France, Marquis de Vaudreuil, and King Louis' Intendant, Antoine Bigot, had led the marchers out as befitted their stations.

While Arch Duket Daniel Morgan was occupied in accepting the surrender, of 3,428 enemy officers and "enlisted men," Grand Duke Odin Bushnell, Duke Andrew Montour, Arch Duket William Trent, and his *Invincibles,* strolled in to take possession of the city of Stadacona.

It was a tremendous capture. There were an incredible, 280 huge cannons to be taken, including those on the opposite Beauport shore. In addition, there were 18 large bore, deadly mortars (made with tons of the wonderfully useful brass), together with tons of gunpowder, and countless tons of precious, refined iron, in the form of cannonballs, and mortar shells. Many of the cannons weighed 2 or more tons of useful iron, in each. They would build many OdinShips with all the steel, that the iron would be transformed into.

Approaching Stadacona in any other way than they did, could have been calamitous.

All of that already smelted cast iron was extremely precious to the Nuworlders. Grand Duke Odin had big plans for the future use of it. Uncountable tons of steel from iron would be required merely for the beamways he envisioned, spreading throughout their nation, to say nothing of engines and ships and....

There was no damage to the town whatever. Many a Frenchman dreamily supposed it would eventually, be returned to His Most Catholic Majesty's control. They presumably imagined, the English would trade Canada, for some mercantile advantage, as they had so cynically done with the fort taken by English Colonials, at Louisbourg, 12 years before.

Overlord Croghan's *Valiants* boarded 2 French warships, of 70 guns each, below the town. No French ships would be allowed to leave, with any of their armaments, cannonballs, or gun powder aboard. The Nuworlders also confiscated many miscellaneous smaller guns from merchant vessels.

The capture of over 440 guns total, some of them very large, was well beyond the Nuworlder's expectations. Those iron and brass metals alone were worth great fortunes.

With the 5 small vessels captured at Montreal, and taken to Stadacona, there was a surprising 41, but mostly small warships and merchant ships, available to carry French officials, soldiers, and sailors back to France on parole.

But all of those ships would depart *sans guns*. Unloading all those guns, and cannonballs, from the ships, required a great deal of effort by Nuworlders, and the French disarmed soldiers and sailors as well. They actually captured *thousands of personal firearms*, including incredibly fancily made swords, officer's carbines and pistols.

A major event was the release of Croghan's trading store employees, and the hostage Major Robert Stobo. Stobo had volunteered to serve as a hostage, 3 years before, in 1754, to the French, when they defeated George Washington, at his Fort Necessity. There was a joyous reunion of them, and Croghan of course, and the happy freedom at last for Major Stobo.

Another surprise was that all of the town folk were nearing starvation. The ships supposedly bringing supplies from France, apparently had been intercepted, on the way over a war-bloodied Atlantic Ocean, by either English or Colonial privateers or English warships.

But the Nuworlders had sufficient food to give those sailing for Europe, and for the people remaining. Most especially, they could provide great amounts of flour for their bakeries. The Lowdown Earl's embargo of English Colony ships had made enormous numbers of barrels of flour, and other foods, available to the Nuworlders, that had been intended for England!

Soon, New England traders would be crowding in, as well as Nobility supply vessels.

Overlord Croghan's Nobles scoured the French ships, and found the hidden hordes of gold and silver, that Intendant Bigot had acquired so criminally from his King. It would be taken to the Nuworld Company treasury to convert to Nuworld nu.

Bigot would surely be going to prison, and Vaudreuil would have the distressful task of explaining to His Most Catholic Majesty King

Louis XV, the loss of New France after 150 solid years, of draining the French treasury, of hard-pressed peasant's taxes, with no return of profits to the Crown. But on the other hand, the French had lucked out, with their amazingly profitable fisheries, in the area of Fortress Louisbourg.

The Governor-General's Saint Louis Chateau was immediately put to use as Overlord Trent's residence. It was by far, the largest and the fanciest building, any of the Nuworlders had seen, to that time. The French proved to have an obsession with decoration, with almost every square inch of walls, ceilings, and even doors, a-wriggle with carvings or paintings or both. The artists Lords West, Copley, and Revere were endlessly delighted with the place.

That night Barron Rittenhouse, and Mr. Stiles ritt back to the NUWORLD NUZ, and to Duke Abraham Clark, about the great victory.

They got a reply from Duke Clark something like, "Our most hearty congratulations, and oh, by the way, our New York City spy rode over to inform us, Lord Lowdown returned from Halifax, without making an attempt on Louisbourg. There were 18 French ships-of-the-line, and 5 frigates, in that harbor, and he was afraid to make the attempt. We have just confirmed this. The Grand Duke would surely wish to know."

Grand Duke Odin exploded to everyone near, "*Hot damn! Fortress Louisbourg is still in French hands!* We must keep this very, very secret! The French here must not know!"

They had all been so certain that Loudoun could hardly fail with one—or more probably several—English fleets, many thousands of troops, and everything he could possibly need, to take the place. It was hard to understand that with all those years of preparation, the Lowdown Loser would simply convince himself, it was too difficult! *It was a stunning turn of events.*

Grand Duke Odin's mind whirled with excitement, as it seemed altogether certain, the English Commander of all British Forces in America, had handed the Nuworlders, a glorious opportunity! He asked Barron Rittenhouse to verify the ritt; indeed, it proved to be correct.

The Grand Duke called for a meeting of his partners, and Over-lords Croghan and Morgan for the morning, in his OdinBoat dining room. His vessel was still parked on the "Plains of Abraham," outside Stadacona's walls.

When they had gathered for the meeting, Odin began to tell them of his plans.

"Gentlemen! I could hardly sleep a wink last night, and I studied the map of Louisbourg quite thoroughly. We've beaten the French in their forts and were able to intimidate them into surrendering, at both Montreal, and here at Stadacona, without firing a shot.

"We durst not have France in control of Louisbourg, but we're going to have to fight for that one. We must absolutely take that place! *We must make the Kings of France, positively kiss our continent, and all of our islands, goodbye!*" Grand Duke Odin shouted.

All of them present jumped up and hollered, "Hurrah! Hurrah!"

"We had planned to have certain ceremonies, and make impor-tant beginnings right here, in Stadacona. But I'm postponing all of that, *until the conquest is complete, that the Lowdown Loser, has made possible for us Nuworlders.*

"Noble Lords, Louisbourg is more than just a powerful fortress. The town houses about 4,500 citizens. Most of them there are fishermen.

"I mention that because it is thought, the government of France profits more from that fishery, than all the gold and silver Spain robs, from its Colonies! Imagine! The French government gets more profit fishing from Louisbourg, than Spain steals from all its Colonies, from Mexico to the southern tip of South America!

"It is so amazing! *The King of France gains more profit from those fish-eries than all the precious metal wealth, Spain robs from the Nuworld!*" Odin repeated again. "So, that's another reason to take it away from them; to cripple King Louis, financially.

"Within a few days, we must load the French ships here, with all the French officials, soldiers, and all the rest that wish to go to France," he continued. "We will escort them just long enough to know, they're homeward bound.

"But they must not sail south, through the Gulf of Canada, past

Louisbourg. We'll send them through the Straits of Belle Isle, north of Newfoundland. We'll assure them that by going that way, they'll be much, much safer from 100s of English privateers and English warships.

"The first casualty of war is truth; so, every deceit is permissible. All of us must remember to claim that Louisbourg has by now been taken by the English. They did so with 25 ships-of-the-line, and at least 18,000 troops. Please; we must remember those figures.

"When we're sure they're headed in the right direction east, we'll swing south. It will probably take a little less than 2 days, to cover the 600 miles to Louisbourg.

"While Overlord Trent holds Stadacona, Overlord Croghan and Overlord Morgan will form a Dual Battle Force Group, under Milord Montour and me, and we shall take Fortress Louisbourg," their Grand Duke said, almost matter-of-factly.

He had pinned a fairly detailed map of Louisbourg and its harbor, up on a wall.

Pointing to it, he said, "The French are well prepared to defend themselves, from a siege of the place, coming from outside the walls. My Pops and other Colonials took the place in their conquest, back in 1745. But the French have improved their landward defenses since I'll bet.

"Conducting a siege is what all armies do and no doubt, that's what Lord Lowdown planned to do, too. *Thus, we must attack the place from the inside, instead of from the outside, and thus achieve overpowering surprise.*"

For the next hour and over the next days, the Grand Duke went over his plan with all the Overlords. He also informed all of the OdinBoat Captains.

They must begin the assault at first light, rain or shine, windy or calm, he told them.

His OdinBoat and 3 others of Croghan's, would blast away at the Island Battery, located just to the left of the entrance to the harbor. Hopefully, they would locate, and blow up the necessary magazine on that island, stocked full of gunpowder. If the magazine exploded, no Nobles need land on it right away.

They would then proceed immediately, to throw OdinRocks at the line of warships, most certainly moored in the center of that really good harbor.

Overlord Croghan would do the same, with 4 of his OdinBoats, to destroy the Lighthouse Battery, on a bluff at the right of the harbor entrance. Croghan would then proceed to blast any warships, on that side of the harbor.

Odin felt very certain the anchored warships would be well spread out, as they had to have room to swing this way and that, on their anchor cables, with wind and tide changes.

Overlord Daniel Morgan was to take his 7 OdinBoats into and climb out of, the slanting walls of a "graving dock," on the left side of Louisbourg town. The graving dock – dugout like an enormous "grave," and meant for the repair of ships – appeared quite certainly to be the only spot on the harbor shore of the town, not lined with either big boulders, or docks, that their boats could not climb over. Morgan's *Gators* would then speed on, between the defense walls and the town, conquering both walls and town as they went.

Overlord Odin had the utmost confidence in Morgan.

For the assault, the Nuworlders would have 250 Bands, with 12 Nobles in each.

Counting Overlords sure to be in the fight, the total would be almost 4,000 Nobles; surely that would be far fewer than the French would have in soldiers and seamen.

But the Nuworld Nobles had their fast-repeating, long-range, very accurate and deadly, semi-automatic Odin2Guns, plus their devastating OdinRockCannons. Those weapons multiplied their power far beyond that of the French... but only if they could surprise the warships before they could react to the onslaught very much.

The Noblewomen Healthors would tend the wounded and cheer the warriors on.

The French would have, perhaps, 1,000s of large cannon, and unlimited ammunition.

But the Nuworlders would be moving speedily, with steam-powered huge bucket wheels, on their amphibious land and water-craft, the OdinBoats.

The next days in and around Stadacona were hectic indeed. They filled their fuel tanks, from their Supply OdinBoats, and from captured and plentiful, French whale oil; it had been in use there, exclusively, for the crude oil lamps, made obsolete by far brighter, OdinLamps.

They filled their freshwater tanks, and scrounged every barrel they could find, anywhere near Stadacona, and filled them with fresh water also. The OdinBoats had been made to go on saltwater, as they did have steam condensers. However, some steam was lost from the engines, and they had a very long way to go. Caution was called for.

Odin received ritts from Captain Hazelwood that the Prussians had many more successes. They had even driven the Swedes out of Pomerania and whipped the French at every encounter. King Frederick had destroyed a huge Russian army, and taken Russian soldiers into his own army, amazingly. He had taken in some defeated Austrian and French soldiers, also.

Overlord John Bradstreet ritt that he had taken the place called DeTroit, and made the few local Frenchmen happy, by renaming the place, "Cadillac."

Everything settled, the Nuworlders moved out from Stadacona, on a brisk southwesterly wind early Sunday morning, August 28th, 1757.

Fair skies, a warm westerly wind, the 41 French vessels, plodding along at no more than 9 nauts, made the Nuworlders impatient. The sailing ships began to traverse the strait north of Anticosti Island, heading for the Straits of Belle Isle. Odin then told Lord Hopkinson to salute the departing French men and women, with the Nuworlder's Song of Nobility.

Overlord Odin's little fleet of 15 OdinBoats, turned south in the Gulf of Canada. It had been called the Gulf of Saint Lawrence, by the dominating, propagandizing Catholic priests.

The Nobles had good French pilots aboard. They were men who had made the identical voyage many times; but of course, in sailing vessels. The pilots were told they would be richly rewarded with silver if they brought the OdinBoats beyond all hazards safely; and they implied death to them if they did not get them to Louisbourg, as promised. They had many captured navigational charts, as further assurance of reaching their destination as promised.

They then steamed at their fastest, 17 and 18 nauts, day and night.

Odin went to bed that night of August 29th, glad for the rest, but his Annie didn't rest well. She expressed worry about the coming battle and had been having "morning sickness," with her pregnancy. That put her "out of sorts," although her middle still "didn't show."

Captain MacDougal woke Odin the next morning himself, saying it was well before sunrise, but he wanted the Grand Duke to know the wind was rising, as the barometer reading fell. Some sort of storm was brewing; but he didn't know how bad it might be, he informed Odin. He had been assured by his French pilot, that the entrance to Louisbourg harbor was quite close, and they might see the harbor's lighthouse, sparkling through the dark, at any time.

Annie rose, she insisted she felt fine, and would not miss the day's events for anything. She cooked a breakfast of cornmeal mush, in maple syrup, loaded with raisins, and bits of walnuts, plus toast and coffee, for her husband and herself.

Odin told her, "If this breakfast isn't a beautiful expression of love, I don't know what is!" That got a pretty smile from her.

"Oh, by the way, darling," she said with her big blue eyes flashing, "Happy 19th birthday! It's August 30th! Ah, what a perfectly, perfectly beautiful coincidence!"

"Thank you very much, sweetness and light! Just think, in merely 2 years, I'll be rated as an adult; a real grown-up!" he laughed.

Just as they finished breakfast, a wave hit the side of the Odin-Boat, making it lurch. Odin ran up to the pilothouse, to find the sky was still black and a light rain was falling.

A moderate wind was blowing from the northwest, off the land, Captain MacDougal said. He also told Odin the French pilot assured him, the Louisbourg light should be visible soon.

That harbor light was there primarily to guide fishermen in from their forays to the fabulous and nearby, fishing "grounds."

Within minutes, they could indeed see that lighthouse and found they were quite near the right side of the harbor entrance. The cloud-filled, dirty gray sky, was beginning to lighten.

They knew the harbor was about 3 miles long, to their left and right, and a single mile, to the opposite side, from the entrance.

Overlord Croghan by then had his 4 OdinBoats closely abreast and to the right of Grand Duke Odin Bushnell's 4 boats. Looking back, Odin could barely make out Overlord Morgan's 7 boats, close behind them.

"Very well, Captain MacDougal!" Odin shouted. "Let's get over there to the left, so we can blast that Island Battery first, and then go at the warships!"

The Grand Duke ran outside and climbed onto the pilothouse roof. Ha! His darling Annie was already there, wetted from the light rain, and she handed him his OdinRockCannon.

"Like I said Odin dear, I wouldn't miss these events for anything! You see, we have a good stack of OdinRocks here, just as your part-ners have on the weather deck," she said.

Grand Duke Odin knew, as every Overlord in war should know, that you cry havoc, you let loose the dogs of war, and its chaos after that. He had to trust in the courage, the determination and to the wits, of those truly noble Noblemen, and noble Noblewomen, who followed him.

They were quickly near enough to the Island Battery, to begin blasting it. They could see an alarm had been shouted, and men were running about in the still dim light. Some of them were only half-dressed. The French stared in disbelief, at the sight of the big red vessels, bearing down on them, with strange, shiny circular brass flags, swinging with the wind.

About ten OdinRocks were aflight at once: *Whoooosh! Screeeem! Ka-Booooom!* At least one of them found the Island Battery's maga-zine! It blew up in a huge, thunderous ball of fire and smoke!

Within a minute or so, they could hear and see the Lighthouse Battery, had also been blown up, from Overlord Croghan's attack!

There was no need to waste more shots on the place, so the Captain pulled sharply to the right, toward the rear of a line of warships dimly looming up in the light rain. Their masts were towering up far above the OdinBoats. The bows of another line of French Navy vessels, were to their right, dimly seen, and distantly facing them.

Overlord Croghan's 4 OdinBoats, would also be attacking warships through the ship's sterns. Such anchoring of fleets was common practice, according to books available, so there was no surprise to the attackers; only to those about to be attacked.

All of the men-o-war they approached, had incredibly decorated, massive, and squared sterns. Their bows pointed into the nor 'west-by-west wind, away from the OdinBoats.

Every inch of those French warship sterns was a-crawl, with gold-leaf-covered, wooden carvings, in the French fashion. The yellow gold glistened prettily from the rain.

The interiors of those ships would be bone dry, and those painted, varnished and tarred inside surfaces, would be easily set to blazing.

There were no guns jutting out yet on those stern ends, nor on the sides. Anyway, it was well known that such big warships took considerable time to get ready for battle. The gun ports along the sides and rear were at the moment closed. It also took time to unsecure the big guns, that were necessary to have tied or chained down, when not being fired, so they wouldn't roll on their wheeled mountings, helter-skelter, around the decks, creating deadly pandemonium.

It would take some long, long minutes to organize those French warship crews for action. Also, it took time to open the powder magazines, well below decks, and for the "powder monkey" young men and boys, to run up from below, to the 2 or 3 gun decks. They'd run up with bags of gunpowder in their arms, rain or shine, to stack next to the guns.

The French sailors would very certainly, not be permitted the minimum of 1/4 hour or more to wake up, get organized, and then make all those preparations, Odin had declared.

Annie loaded an OdinRockBlaster, into the tube on Grand Duke Odin's shoulder, to fire into the stern of the first French warship. From perhaps a scant 50 yards away, he shot that Odin-

Rock, as did other Nobles on his weather deck. Immediately, very large, jagged holes appeared in the ship's hull, through the explosion's smoke.

They then fired OdinRockFlamers through those openings, and more Blasters, as more of the 4 OdinBoats came close enough.

An OdinRock might go through the full length inside of such ships, before hitting something. There were few, or even no interior walls, on some decks.

Suddenly, the close-by man-o-war erupted in a gigantic explosion, disintegrating madly with masts, planks, cannons, and such, flying through the air! One or more OdinRocks had touched off the ship's magazine, via the human chain of powder monkey's armloads of gunpowder, in very flammable paper and cloth bags!

Even at the moderate speed, Captain MacDougal kept the Odin-Boat moving, they were quickly within easy range of the next warship, and then the next.

With each vessel, the action and the results were the same, until they had destroyed 13 large French warships, in that line.

Not all of them exploded immediately, but they all burnt with utmost ferocity, with the westerly wind helping to fan and to spread the flames, into hellish infernos. The light rain apparently had almost no effect, since the fires were primarily raging madly, *inside of each ship*.

There was insane fire and black smoke being belched out, from the poop decks on those once-proud warships, and through every opening, down to the water.

Obviously, this was an unprecedented calamity for the French Navy.

Finished with that line of French warships, Odin turned his attention to the Royal Battery. It had supposedly 40 enormous guns, plus smaller weapons, on the far side of the harbor.

Theoretically, that conglomeration of big guns could deny entry into the harbor, to any ship or even a fleet of ships and – like the ships just destroyed – could easily make toothpicks, of any OdinBoat.

But Overlord Croghan was already there. The entire line of ships he had attacked, had also disappeared, into a mere confusion of flotsam and jetsam, on the waters of Louisbourg Bay.

Grand Duke Odin could not see that Croghan was firing Odin-Rocks, onto the Royal Battery, so he assumed there was good reason not to. Odin instead turned the attention of the 4 OdinBoats, he commanded, to fishing Frenchmen out of the cold, cluttered water. Many had been seen jumping off their ships and grabbing for something—just anything—to hang onto.

As Odin turned to come down off the pilothouse roof, he noticed for the first time, that Ezra Stiles and Barron John Copley were there, in the corner of the roof.

"Lord John, did you manage to get some coppix of all this?" he asked.

"Yes Milord, I think I got every one of them; all 13," Copley replied. "But those explosions will be blurred; I'm pretty sure, just like the coppix of those forts you blew up."

"Overlord Odin!" Stiles cut in, "I timed this whole battle, from start to finish, and it was just 8 1/2 minutes. That's from the first OdinRocks into the Island Battery! And the intelligence was correct, in that I counted 18 big ships-of-the-line and 5 frigates. The French had no chance at all! Like you've said Milord, so many times: *They didn't expect the unexpected, and thus they were surprised.*"

Odin thought to himself: *sadly, again, we have killed men well and won another battle.*

Duke Andrew Montour later put all the facts together. They had come to Louisbourg with almost 2,000 OdinRocks; they had expended 492 of them. That worked out to be an *average of 23 Odin-Rocks,* thrown at each French ship.

They had shot hardly any Odin2Guns; oh, except by the *Gators,* they later found out, who found it necessary to shoot about 36 French soldiers, with that seemingly impossible accuracy and rapidity, to convince others to surrender.

For the next 1/2 hour, all 8 of the OdinBoats in the harbor concentrated on fishing out Frenchies from the water. Unfortunately, most Frenchmen had no experience with getting wet-all-over, and could not swim. Of the 9,000 men later claimed to have been aboard those ships, the Nobles only brought into their boats, the tiny number of 624. It was figured that over 8,000 French sailors and Marines, had been either blasted, drowned or burnt to death.

Nobles were sent ashore to secure the Island, Lighthouse and Royal Batteries.

A note from Overlord Morgan to the Group Overlord, told, of completing his audacious conquest of the walls, and the town, and capturing even the French King's Governor-General.

Since the French soldiers on the town walls, were thunderstruck to see the calamitous fate of the French warships, exploding in the harbor, they quickly understood the fabulous power of the Nuworlders and surrendered in droves.

About 800 French sailors and marines had been ashore, to assist the gun crews on the walls. But since the English under the Lowdown Loser, had never showed up, the French had returned to their ships... and to their doom... sailormen, Capitanes, Emir-als, and all.

Soon, the Nuworlders would mine that harbor for the stupendous wealth in iron, and some brass, now laying on the bottom of Louisbourg Bay. Those iron and brass cannons and iron balls, from the walls, and the 3 on-shore batteries, could be made use of immediately.

❦ 18 ❧

Captain MacDougal tied the Force Group Overlord's OdinBoat, up to the city of Louisbourg's quay. The boat crew then put out the ramp.

Nobles were deployed as guards, as the Grand Duke and the Overlady, came down the ramp to step on the shore, of their latest victory.

Just then, Overlord Morgan, and several Nobles, rode up on captured horses.

But the cold, misty rain was still falling, and the out-of-doors, was not at all pleasant.

"My dear Overlord of Overlords!" Morgan shouted at Odin. "I give thee Fortress Louisbourg for a birthday present, for this day, thou shalt be our Chief of State!"

"And lo!" replied Odin, "Arch Duket Daniel Morgan shalt becometh a King!"

"Milord, I have found a good place for our ceremonies," the handsome Welshman said. "The Governor here speaks a little English, and his Palace has a beautiful chapel and...."

"No, my friend; not in any chapel," the Grand Duke interrupted him. "Barron Rufus Putnam's steam boats, have made this occasion possible; we shall have our historic ceremonies in the dining room, on this OdinBoat. Overlord Morgan, would you please get the Governor, and some other French officials, to come over to witness our business today?"

Meanwhile, the Grand Duke settled down in his heart, despite the awesome casualties the French had suffered under his orders. Their mighty fleet destroyed, their thousands of men dead, and even their city of Louisbourg, had been taken. He knew that if the battle had gone the French way, they would be wildly celebrating their victory. So, why should the Nuworlders not get on with, their own celebratory events?

By mid-morning Odin's huge, very long dining table had 30 chairs at it, and most taken with his partners, and some of the high-ranking nobles. In addition, several of the French big-wigs, including the Royal Governor of Louisbourg, had been brought to the OdinBoat.

The Nuworld Company Partners, had drawn straws for the honors. Barrons Pratt and Copley, brought in a beautifully made walnut chest, measuring a cube of 18 inches on each side; it had been masterfully crafted by Barron Paul Revere.

Lord Revere had the honor of opening the Chest, of lifting out a Nuworld Crown, and then, as Odin Bushnell stood tall at the head of the table, Lord Paul reached way up and placed it on Odin Bushnell's head. Odin's wife, Annie Bushnell, was smiling by his side.

The dozen partners present then, in unison said loudly, what they had all well-rehearsed:

"*We, the 14 partners of the Nuworld Company, by unanimous vote, do declare the Nuworld State, on and about the Nuworld Continent of the World, does now and forever exist. Further, the Nuworld State, shall forever be a Commonwealth, a Democracy and a Monarchy.*

"*Also, we 13 other partners of the Nuworld Company, have elected, by unanimous vote, Grand Duke Odin Bushnell, as the Chief of the Nuworld State, and the Overlord in Chief of the Nuworld Nobility, for a term of 6 years.*"

Cheers and tears erupted at that pre-planned, and well-rehearsed pronouncement.

Odin Bushnell, and his fellow partners, senior Nobles, his

mother, his wife and a few other wives, had secretly discussed governmental affairs for the past 3½ years – since the beginning of Odin's invention of the OdinRaft. They had decided on the highest titles for officers serving the new State, and for the Chief of that State. Odin and his fellow partners, had presumed they had the power to conquer, and incorporate the entire, very large continent, formerly styled "North America." From then on, that continent and its hundreds of adjacent islands, was to be called the *NUWORLD*.

"We must never make little plans," Odin had told them in their meetings, over the previous years. "We must soar in our imaginations, as with the eagles."

They had expected their ceremonies to take place in the formerly French-owned, and pretty city, of Stadacona, a few days before. But the British failure to conquer Louisbourg, gave the Nuworlders an opportunity to take it, and take it they did.

Already in April of that year, 6 women seamstresses had been engaged in making the finely tailored blue woolen jackets and trouzers, meant for this occasion. Probably 100 yards of gold thread had been made into twine, and sewed onto collars to show Realms, on sleeves for names, and on shoulder sleeves to show ranks.

Paul Revere, although working day after day in the Nuworld Company's arsenal, in supervising the production of weapons, took it upon himself to make a Nuworld Crown. The noted silversmith and goldsmith, insisted he could do that in his "spare time," and at his home, in secret. His wife Sarah – whom he called "Sary" – was a seemingly "almost always pregnant" lady, putting up with her ever-busy husband, and their brood of children.

Revere began spare-time work on it, in October of 1756, and finished the Crown and the Crown Chest in May, of 1757. The Chest itself was a marvel of craftsmanship, being made of inch thick, polished, select walnut. The imaginative hinges were of solid gold and wrapped up and over the top, to the other side, with gold screws, to become hasps for closing it. The fancy handles on each side were also gold, mounted on beautiful gold back plates. There was a gorgeous oval plaque in the top center; that plaque of gold was exquisitely engraved, to say the Nuworld Crown and Chest, were made by Lord Paul Revere, 1756-57.

The Crown consisted of a single sheet of fairly thick, 14 carat gold, formed exactly into a half globe. The sides of the globe over-hung the inside leather band around the head, since human heads are more or less oval, not round.

Revere had worked the gold, to raise all lands "above the waters." He showed the Alleghany Mountains and somewhat, the mountains near the west coast, that were known to be there. Each of the Caribbean, Bahamas, Bermudas, Newfoundland and Greenland Islands were tooled up. All of the seas, lakes and the largest rivers known, were painted over the gold, with deep blue lacquer. The shine of the gold underneath the lacquer, made the waters glitter. He assured everyone, when the geography would be corrected, he would alter the map on the crown. With utmost patience, Revere meticu-lously penned latitude, and longitude fine lines, onto the surface.

It had taken a dedicated jeweler, 2 months to cut and fully "facet" 14 different gemstones, to represent each of the 14 Nuworld Company partners. Those stones were from a full *bushel of stones* they had gathered from the 8 wrecks. Each of the 14 members had been blind-folded as they reached in a jar to choose a gem. Odin had brought out a beautiful ruby. Treasurer Clark had pulled out a bril-liant yellow diamond, surely the most valuable of the stones.

They acquired an astounding fortune in treasure, from the Caribbean Sea floor, and were *giving fully 95% of it to the Nuworld State*.

So, Revere mounted each of those identical-sized gemstones, slightly oval shaped, 1/2-inch-thick and 1½ inches high, onto the 2 inch wide, highly-polished platinum band, fixed over the prettily tooled leather, adjustable band.

Small faceted gemstones of every color were fixed by then on the Crown, over the site of the new Region called Cadillac, plus on Montreal, Stadacona and the Ticonderoga Regions. Another gem would glitter later that day, mounted by Revere on Louisbourg. A jeweler had made exactly 100 of the small gem stones; stored in the Crown Chest and to be mounted on Regions and Islands, as they were incorporated into the nation. The jeweler had been paid in gems.

Done by another jeweler, a "Chief Lady adornment," was a neck-lace of triple-stringed white pearls, holding in the center, a 128-carat blue diamond, 1¼ inches of half a globe, on a platinum backing. The diamond was overlaid by gold, depicting the Nuworld and its islands and waters. That super-expensive jewelry, like the Nuworld Crown, would remain State property.

Then Chief Odin Bushnell, and Chief Lady Annie Bushnell, shucked their undyed buckskin jackets, Odin2Guns and holsters. They slipped into new formal dyed-blue wool jackets. Their names were embroidered in gold on their arms. Odin's stand up stiff collar on both sides was embroidered in gold with "NUWORLD STATE." The sleeves over his shoulder straps, read "CHIEF" in large letters, of gold thread.

When her be-medaled blue jacket was on, the Chief of State then draped onto his wife, the spectacular "Chief Lady adornment"; the string of pearls with the huge blue, 128 carat diamond. That diamond had been among the gemstones found in the pirate shipwreck, on February 1st, 1755. It took one's breath away to see it up close.

Only after they had seen Chief of State Odin, wearing his be-jeweled gold and platinum State Crown, would all of the Nobles happily realize, their brass hats were similar to his Crown.

Their medals gleamed on their chests. The Chief wore then only those medals earned in the Ohio Campaign; his wife had those and a few earned on the Caribbean Campaign. Those later added for the Canada Campaign would show nicely on their chests. Odin was to be awarded Gold Crowns for Leadership, for the destruction or capture of French forts and cities. He would forever prize the Eleven-Feath-ered Gold Crown for Courage, with the little red ruby on it, for helping to save Fort Eyre from the French.

In the days ahead, *bushels of medals,* would be handed out to thou-sands of Nobles for the Canada Campaign; including some beauties by a committee, for the Chief and his Chief Lady.

The complimentary rank of Chief Lady, was not to be shown on her shoulders, since she had no official authority. However, Odin expected to wear his rank on his shoulders, almost all the time, and those bold gold letters were rather spectacular. He continued the entire day, that August 30th, 1757, with wearing his spectacular Crown.

The seamstress ladies had created three-inch, by six-inch sleeves, in red-dyed, thickly-padded silk, which could be slipped over the formal shoulder straps, of whatever jacket or coat, the Chief and other administrators, might choose to wear.

Barron Hopkinson led a chorus of 7 Healthors, to sing the Song of Nobility, as a prelude to the new Chief Odin, beginning to speak his Coronation Speech.

Not surprisingly, their slow-tempoed rendition of the song on that occasion, had special emotion poured feelingly into it.

"This is our Nuworld, our very Free World,

"Our Brightest Rich Part of the Whole World.

"So, Nobility, Nobility, protect us all from harm,

"And honor us, with righteousness, in city, sea and farm!"

"Dear Nobles and friends," Chief Odin said, after a round of heartfelt applause, for the well-sung song, and the songsters.

"I have not written this Coronation Address, which I am delivering to all of the people of the Nuworld State. We have here 3 notable newsmen and 2 Noblewomen secretaries to transcribe what I say this day.

"Beginning 3½ years ago, with the building of the OdinRaft we sailed away on, to bring back riches with, the 14 partners in the Nuworld Company, have discussed how we could enrich our country-men, with that treasure. That was even before we had any treasure.

"Today is the culmination of much of that thinking, in our many of our meetings. Our Nobility has driven the King of France's forces, from this continent, with the capture of Fortress Louisbourg, after taking Canada, and we have formed a new nation, called The Nuworld State.

"As the elected Chief of that State, I shall tell you how it is to be organized.

"Most importantly, it is to be a Democracy. That ancient Greek word means exactly, *the people rule*. And the people shall rule by voting each summer, beginning next year, for those men or women, that the majority of Electors think best to serve them, as Jurors in cities, as Mayors of cities, as Judges in Regions, as Princes of Regions, as Justices of the State and as the Chief of the Nuworld State. Each candidate winning a majority of votes, shall serve a term of six years, and more if re-elected.

"To qualify as a Nuworld Royal Sovereign Elector, male and female Citizens, must be 18 years old or better, be able to read and understand the Nuworld Constitution, not be an indicted felon, and have a certified Birth Number, since there are many duplicate names for people.

"Voting will be strictly by mail, so as to give each Elector enough private time, to gauge the value of the statements of various candidates, and sometimes, of issues.

"Elector's votes will be mailed to a designated Treasury Valt, where agents of the Elections Realm will count votes, and advise the Treasury Agent there, to credit the Elector's Treasury Account, with their reward for voting. Just as we should expect everyone working in government to be reasonably paid, so too shall Electors be paid for voting.

"The first year's payment for voting will not likely be large. But each year, the Chief of State must publicly give, to the King of the Elections Realm, 10% of the previous year's operating profit, with which to pay Electors for voting, and for the expenses of that Realm.

"The Nuworld State is also to be a Commonwealth. That means every Citizen, from birth on, shall own the riches of our lands. When say, a deposit of gold is found, it belongs to all of us, not simply to some person who happened to discover it. Our State shall forever be dedicated to exploit our riches, for the benefit of all of our people, Asians and Euros alike. We have extensive forests, and those will be under the control of Regional Princes... again, for the benefit of the people, in funding Universities, other schools and so much more.

"Our State is also to be a Monarchy, in that Mayors of Cities, Princes of Regions and the Chief of State, shall not have to contend with crowds of men, as in Republics, eager to voice descent and grab for bribes, of one sort or another, in order to get things done. Assemblies, such as England's Parliament, are universally corrupt. With Freedom of the Press guaranteed, watchers can and will report any corruption seen, in our governments. The penalties for such shall be hard, indeed, on any elected official or employee, foolish enough to risk wrongdoings.

"We will begin with 24 Realms to serve our people. Each Realm is to be headed by a male or female King, appointed by the Chief of State, and serving at the Chief's pleasure.

"In no particular order, I'll give a very brief description of what I expect each of these Realms to accomplish.

"I must mention first though, the Treasury Realm, since that King – Abraham Clark – is to be a little more equal than the others, being also Vice Chief of State. He is to assess the wealth given by the Nuworld Company, to the Nuworld State, and give a reckoning to our people, of those many expenses, for such as our Nobility, before the 95% transfer of wealth.

"The Treasury Realm is to establish Treasury Valts, as though banks, throughout our State, for the convenience of our people, to establish checking and savings accounts; this latter shall hold savings at interest. The Treasury Realm shall also, provide loans for businesses, for homes and other needs, and earn interest from such loans.

"Also, the Treasury Realm shall assist the Elections Realm in the counting of Elector's votes, at no cost. This duplicate counting is to assure honest, accurate counting of those votes.

"The Metals Realm is headed by King Phineas Pratt, who has been running our iron furnaces, and making such things as nails, screws, bolts, nuts and even metal caps for glass bottles; and he's done this at a profit. Now, he is converting iron into high-carbon steel, with which we can make steel OdinBoats and OdinShips, powered by steam engines.

"King Alexander Chalker heads up the Glass Realm. Since returning from our treasure hunt, in 1755, he has succeeded in making glass sheets for windows and mirrors, and a fantastic variety of glass bottles. Some of those bottles are called jars. The Glass Realm King also has turned a nice profit.

"The Forestry Realm King is Rufus Putnam, who has provided amazing amounts of oak planks for our OdinRafts and OdinBoats... plus, to build the City of Stratford. In time, he will be turning over his knowledge of forestry, to our Region Princes and have another assignment.

"King Ethan Allen heads up the Transport Realm, which is to build steel beamways throughout our State. Passenger Carriages and Freight Cars will be pulled by steam engines; steel wheels on steel beams will have but slight friction, compared with wagons or carts on roads and streets. We expect those Carriages, to haul people in comfort, safety and speed. The freight cars, we expect, will haul things from people's letters to people's houses, and even Treasury Valts from the mills where they are built, to the places where needed. We expect many sorts of buildings to be milled inside buildings, out of harm from any weather, while being built.

"The Diplomacy Realm is headed by King George Croghan. He is to establish friendly relations with other nations, including the trading of goods and people. Immigration will be a major concern for this Realm, to bring good people to our shores.

"King Andrew Montour shall head up the Nobility Realm, which is to train Nuworld Noblemen and Noblewomen, in the protection of our lands and waters. We expect many such Nobles will join our City Police and Fire Forces, when their Nobility service is done.

"The Munitions Realm is headed by King Paul Revere. Besides armaments, he also has procured necessary furniture for our Odin-Boats and OdinShips. He has patronized exclusively, those companies which have every worker, as an owner of their company.

"King Charles Thomson heads up the Education Realm. I've assigned that Realm the task of correcting the spelling of the English language we've inherited. It is said to be by far, the most expressive language in the world, partly because of the habit of borrowing words from other languages. That Realm also shall be responsible for establishing school curriculum, and the training of teachers, throughout our State.

"The Health Realm King, is Doctor Benjamin Gale. He and his staff of Doctors have already advanced the knowledge of human diseases greatly. It is profoundly amazing, that even the function of our bodily interiors, is so little understood. It is said, religions are largely responsible for holding back such knowledge; but our Health Realm is pledged to discover those truths. They will also establish training for doctors and nurses, and hospitals, throughout the State.

"King John Singleton Copley heads up the Arts Realm. In addition to promoting the use of his Coppix invention, he is to promote all of the arts, from painting to stage plays.

"The Commerce Realm King is Elias Tully. He is to create Laws of Commerce for my approval, and to promote honest business practices. Because our State is so short of stores to display goods for sale, he will encourage companies to issue catalogues, so people can buy, by mail, what they need, and have it delivered by mail.

"The Ritts Realm King, is David Rittenhouse. His amazing invention of long-distant communications, by ritting, which we have been using, is to be much improved by him and his staff, for everyone to take advantage of, in time.

"King Benjamin West is in charge of the Building Realm. He is to improve building practices and suggest the very best plans for our new Cities and Regions.

"Our Geography Realm King is William Eyre. He and his people are to provide accurate maps of our State. They will suggest to Princes of Regions, plans for the 7 Cities we expect to establish in each Region. Further, that Realm is to eventually discover, not only what is on our State's surfaces everywhere, but in the sub-surface as well.

"King John Armstrong heads up our Fuels Realm. He is to quickly look for petroleum, and finding it, make it useful as a steam engine fuel, at the least.

"The Hunting Realm King, shall be Daniel Morgan. This Realm is to regulate the hunting of wild things on land, air and waters. That includes fishermen and whalers, who all should own their companies. Primarily, hunting on land, we can expect shall be done mostly for sport.

"The Science Realm King, shall be Benjamin Franklin, who has an especial interest in electricity. He shall try to make electricity useful to everyone, as well as establish reasonable standards of measures; many which we inherited, is nonsensical.

"The King of the Elections Realm shall be Israel Pemberton. He shall establish regulations for our elections for my approval, and his Realm shall have the duty of counting votes and making certain, our Royal Sovereign Electors are paid for voting.

"I expect our Farming Realm to profoundly revolutionize agriculture, partly by making a business of it, and by the encouragement of inventions of farm machinery. I have not yet found a King for this Realm.

"The Police Realm is to be Daniel Boone, who is at present Overlord of a Battle Force. He is to help establish Noble Police Forces for every City and Region, to protect our people where they live, as they have protected our nation from foreign foes.

"William Trent is presently the Prince of the Stadacona Region, but will soon, be the King of the Big Works Realm. He will be responsible for the design and building of bridges over rivers throughout our State, as well as shipping docks, and dams to control river floods.

"I have not yet chosen a King for our Insurance Realm. That very important assurance to the welfare of companies and people, is now handled privately, but it is obviously far better managed by our very rich Nuworld State. Insurance allows a pool of money from many people, to guarantee financial solutions, when disaster strikes to companies or to people.

"The 24th Realm – but not at all last in importance – is the Chemistry Realm, for which I have yet to choose a King. Chemistry is very little understood, but the possible benefits of combining some of the various elements in nature, could very well be spectacular, I do believe.

"We give the title of King, to the men or women heading up our Realms, because of the very great importance their services shall give, to each and everyone of our citizens.

"We honor ourselves to take the name of Nuworlders. That is, we aim for all our lives, to welcome what is new; to do what seems most right; and to stifle everything that is wrong.

"Before I go further, I must in good conscience, once again compliment our dear friend and devoted Nuworld Company Partner of some years, Lord Paul Revere, for his masterful craftsmanship in creating the fabulous Crown now on my head, and the sensational Crown Chest to store it in. We can be certain, that unequaled workmanship, and his name as that maker, shall last in this nation for centuries to come."

Chief of State Odin stopped and, turning to the blushing Revere, applauded him, as did everyone in the room. Then the Chief continued with his Coronation Address:

"While those of the Old World, take pride in their ancient, and often gory history, we of this innovative Nuworld, shall always rejoice in our forever newness. We on this continent are now entering a fabulous new age of human progress; of human innovation. This bright and enormously beneficial age for all of our people, begins right here and right now.

"We form this new State to make it possible, through the unity of all of our people, that each Nuworld Asian and Euro babe born, shall have an honest chance at life's great challenges, and for life's glittering rewards, in our Nuworld, our Free World, our Brightest Rich Part of the Whole World.

"We do firmly believe that every person is naturally born, with the desire to feel important; and that virtually every Euro and Asian, male and female, is a profound miracle, and has been gifted with one or more kinds of genius. We do believe that each and every one of us, is naturally endowed, to truly become important, by accomplishing much good, in our lifetimes.

"The basic purpose of all levels of Governments, in our Nuworld State, shall be to promote the security, justice, freedoms, education, health and happy prosperity, for all our citizens.

"The Nuworld Company, formed in April of 1754, is hereby dissolved, according to the signed agreement, of the 14 company members. Ninety-five percent of the Nuworld Company's considerable Treasury assets, are herewith transferred to the Nuworld State.

Each of the 14 Nuworld Company members, shall retain but 1/20th of the value, of their former 1/14th interest, in that company.

"That transfer of assets includes all in the Nuworld Company Treasury; such as our money called nu, of gold, silver and of gems of many kinds. Also, there are metals on hand, including iron, brass, copper, etc., to transfer. Also, to be transferred are all ships, boats and a boatyard, mines of several sorts, smelting furnaces, armaments, and the arsenal to make such armaments.

"The King of the Nuworld State Treasury Realm, shall give a full accounting to the people of our State, of the value of these gifts, by the Nuworld Company, to the Nuworld State. The total value of the gifts from that company, is expected to be some billions of nu.

"These contributions to the wealth of our Nuworld State is commemorated by the 14 beautiful gemstones, surrounding the Chief of State's Nuworld Crown.

"And I, David Odin Bushnell, do declare, as the crowned Chief and Chief Servant of the people of our Nuworld State, that those governing, are to honestly serve all of our citizens; including the not so rich and the rich, female and male, young and old, Asian and Euro alike.

"Included in our Constitution is Freedom of Religion; and Freedom from Religion. There shall be a complete separation of State and all Religions. No religious practices shall be allowed that demean or harm any person, including polygamy and child marriage. Every citizen of our State, must be considered to have unlimited potential for goodness, unless proven otherwise.

"There shall be Freedom of the Press; and freedom from Libel. There shall be Freedom of Speech; and Freedom from Slander.

"Another liberty we are to enjoy is Freedom from Slavery. Such Africans in our State who are, or have been enslaved, shall be assisted as best we can, in returning them to their natural home of the gigantic, and certainly very rich continent, of Africa. There, they can create real freedoms, prosperity and opportunities for themselves, and for their furthest generations.

"As a nation of good morality, we cannot permit the evil of slavery to persist here. Some slave-owners will be financially ruined by the loss, of their unpaid and maltreated workers. But those enslaved, were not only ruined financially, but lost all sense of self-respect, of self-worth, and of self-confidence. The Nuworld State has a responsibility to aid them as well as we can, to

cloth and feed them, to give them weapons and transport them, to where they can live in freedom and hopefully, enjoy much prosperity, good health and happiness.

"We have caused copies of our Constitution to be printed, so all can study it and learn that our Nuworld State is, and shall forever be, a Democracy, a Commonwealth and a Monarchy.

"This State shall definitely not be a Republic, *for a Republic is a state in which the richest men decide which laws, and governmental policies, most favor themselves.* Such a form of government had much to do, with the long ago collapse of the corrupted Roman Empire. We can truly expect; all such unfair governments will also eventually fail.

"In our Nuworld State, we expect the people shall rule, by choosing their administrators.

"England, for example, has a House of Commons – so called – in which 558 men – and no women whatsoever—primarily represent themselves, or someone who inherited great wealth. They are regularly bribed in one way or another, to vote for measures favorable to the 200 families, that largely own that country; that is, for those very few persons, who inherit great wealth and prestige. That is a measure of their unfairly and unjustly Oligarchical nation, with a powerless Chief of State, of about 6,000,000 people.

"It shall be the right of every Royal Sovereign Elector, of our Nuworld State, to write to the appropriate office-holder, and tell him or her of their views, on any governmental subject. The Electors may directly represent themselves, in all political matters, in our Nuworld State.

"Every elected office-holder, may be disapproved annually, as set forth in our Constitution. Any elected official disapproved, by more than half of the number, of the Royal Sovereign Electors of the election, who had voted for him or her into such office, must stand for re-election, even though not the end of their term of office.

"As a Commonwealth, our Nuworld State, and Regions, and

Cities, shall forever own all land, water and air to the center of the Earth, within its territory.

"Persons or companies may rent or lease, the land they need, paying their City that has been assigned such land. There shall be no taxes on properties. From such rents, the Cities shall build and maintain streets, roads, schools, libraries and hospitals, provide clean water and dispose properly of sewage. All of our Cities shall also provide fire and police protection by Nobles, trained in those important services.

"This is worth repeating: The Nuworld State, as a Commonwealth, and representing all its citizens, shall own all the treasures of the earth within its territory, including the air, land and waters, minerals, metals, gemstones, rocks, marble, clay, gravel, chemicals, gasses, petroleum, salt, coal and resources not now known, or mentioned at this time. The Chief of State shall assign duties to specific Realms, for the profitable processing of such produce, from our territory, for the benefit of our citizens.

"For example, our State shall gather up, and smelt iron ore, and most especially, make that and other metals, useful to its citizens. The State shall make such useful items as metal nails, screws, bolts, sheets, beams, pipes, tubes and bars; and sell such to businesses throughout our State, and beyond our State. The Chief of State may apply tariffs to imported metals, or wood of other produce as he sees fit.

"Our Regions, as delimited by the Chief of State, shall own, harvest, process forests and cultivate new forests, at the direction of their Princes. From their forests, we can expect Regions to create and sell lumber, plied wood, paper of various kinds, barrels, boxes, etc. Each Region is expected to be competitive in their forestry businesses.

"A Justice Realm of at most, 15 initially appointed but later, elected Justices, shall make and maintain, a book of Criminal Law and, with the Chief, a book of Commercial Law. Such Justices shall also act as our State's Highest Court of Appeals.

"The word *Chief*, derives from usage by the tribes in this

Nuworld. I expect we Nuworlders shall in time feel, we are all united as though in one tribe, with one Chief.

"The word *King,* we believe, means a servant to his or her *kin* – and all Euros and Asians, in our State, are to be regarded as each King's kin.

"The word *Prince,* means most usually, the Head of a Region, and who may initially appoint Judges for his or her Region, as necessary. When practicable, such Judges shall be elected.

"The word *Mayor* is an ancient political word meaning *first* in a City. He or she shall appoint Jurors as necessary, until such time they can be elected. Mayors may appoint men and women to one or more advisory councils for their city.

"You can read in our Constitution that an employee, of any level of Government committing a crime involving his or her duties, shall be penalized double that of other citizens, for a similar private crime. Elected Officials committing such crimes, involving his or her duties, shall be penalized thricely, that of private persons committing similar crimes. We expect such provisions, should reduce the temptation for corruption, which is a disgustingly common, and very immoral crime, in some nations.

"Committing corruption, while elected or employed in or by, any of our governments, amounts to criminal and immoral acts, against *all of our people.*

"There shall be almost no taxes; what our people earn, they should keep.

"An exception is that the Nuworld's Chief may from time to time, tax excessive inheritances, to keep the challenges of life, more nearly fair, for all of our citizens. The Chief may also tax things thought harmful to our people; such as alcohol; harmful if overused, and tobacco; harmful if used at all. All such taxes collected, shall be given to the Health Realm.

"The Nuworld State Constitution was made quite lengthy with details of each Realm's duties. The Chief may in the future add or eliminate Realms to serve our people. The Chief may also amend our Constitution, with the majority agreement of Royal Sovereign Electors.

"It is my duty to remind all of our citizens, that Peoples from Asia, came to this Nuworld long before European Peoples did. They have been slower to innovate, due to the constant danger of being warred upon. We must have peace among us, of course. Asians and Euros are each and all alike, under the skin. Together, we can accomplish much good for ourselves and our posterity. I shall ask our citizens to mingle and teach both Asians and Euros, the boundless possibilities, in our eternal unity. It is a good thing to remind ourselves of the genius we have in our Nobility King, Andrew Montour, who is ¾ Asian. I am myself, 1/8th Asian.

"I thank you all for your kind attention. Now I shall appoint some Kings to serve our people's and our State's very real needs."

Having finished reading his speech, Chief Odin and Chief Lady Annie moved over to those lined up along a dining room wall in the Chief's OdinBoat. Each of them had their buckskin jackets removed and were ready in undershirts, to be made Kings by the Chief.

Except for the few French guests, all of them knew what was to take place.

The Chief and Chief Lady stepped smartly to the front of each one, in no particular order, to help them on with their new formal, dyed blue, woolen jackets. Their names were nicely embroidered in gold on their arms. "KING," in yellow gold letters embroidered on thick red silk sleeves, was already over each shoulder strap.

Each "PRINCE" and "MAYOR" would also have their letters of rank on each shoulder, made up of embroidered gold letters.

Cities were expected to cover far more land even, than large counties then did. They would include farms and farmers, so that all persons in such a territory would be truly, *Citi-zens*.

With each appointment, Chief Odin shook hands in congratulation, midst much applause.

The Company Partners had agreed that such authorities should not be addressed as "Your Majesty," "Your Highness" and other flattering nonsense. None were to regard the people as "Subjects," since such authorities were the servants of the people, and not the other way around. There would be no thrones nor crowns, besides the

Chief's crown. Their gold shoulder rankings, were thought to be sufficient notice of authority.

Thus, New France was converted in a single day to the Nuworld State, with one Chief, many Kings and Princes, and yet more to come!

The Region's Princes, had the duty of appointing their Force Overlord replacements, plus temporary City Mayors, and Jurists and Judges, when those territories could be established.

Chief Odin wound up the meeting with, "Kings, Queens, Lords and Ladies, it must be obvious that we innovative Nuworlders see the future – *and we see the future is us.*

"All of us owe a debt of gratitude to our parents, whose love, nurture, and guidance, through our youths, has been worth more than all the gold on earth.

"We all also owe much to partner Mr. Ezra Stiles, for his constant wise advice over our years of friendship. Mr. Stiles is giving his matting equipment and the excellent type setters who make them, to my office, so that we can transmit to our citizens monthly, news important to every citizen; a magazine with articles by each of our Kings, the Chief Lady and myself.

"Each Realm King can thus frequently inform our people of progress. It is our earnest desire, to keep the people we serve, informed of what their servants are doing.

"By the way; Mr. Stiles is now to establish a new religion. He is calling it, 'The Church of Happiness'. His NUWORLD NUZ will promote his views on what he considers the truth, about we human beings, including that Humans are not sheep. Any one of us in any level of government may privately join his Religion, but we may not become a promoter of it. We must have separation of the State and all Religions, for we all know of the freedoms denied citizens of States, that have a State Religion. Now, I thank you, one and all, for your patient attention."

King Copley busied himself, making coppix of everyone. He had made many, many coppix, throughout the Canada campaign. Copley had also begun experiments, to possibly make mats of coppix for printing in newspapers, much as Odin and Stiles had done with text.

❧ 19 ❧

Later, at a celebratory dinner, with table and chairs set up in the Chief's OdinBoat dining room, Ezra Stiles rose to speak.

"Chief Odin, the English government will certainly not look kindly on your business of today. So be it. We know there must be a reckoning, between that Kingdom and our State.

"I must say, it was my very great good luck, to have been visiting your parents, in Old Saybrook, in Connecticut Colony, that Sunday, April 7th, 1754, when you were so brutally impressed into the evil English Navy. But then, you woke up in their boat, leaped out into Long Island Sound – from now on, Odin Bay—and swam that half mile to shore and to freedom.

"The world since would be a very different place had you not escaped from that wooden world, of hell on water. That same day we heard the inspiring praise for you, from the dear old Pochaug Chief Odin, and you began your remarkable conceiving, of amazing inventions.

"It was, at the tender age of 15 years, your truly wondrous invention of the OdinRaft – and your great many innovations on it— which enabled us to become rich, on the treasures found on the

Caribbean Sea floor. That wealth gave us the means to do so very much. Since then, you and many others under your leadership, have accomplished great things.

"This glorious day is the culmination of Noble efforts, and coincidentally, your 19th birthday, along with the birthing day of a rich new nation, on Planet Earth. While some nations have a King, we already have many Kings, and Princes, too. You have all of our most hearty congratulations Sire, but I would like to ask, what happens next?" Stiles asked and sat down.

Chief Odin put his coffee cup down. It was the first time he had been called, "Sire," meaning "Father of the Nation."

"Friend Ezra, you are always so full of encouragement. For the next several days we must all help King Morgan get organized here. We must get those of the French here, that may wish to stay French, on the way back to France. But I hope we can convince most of the fishermen to stay, and form partnerships in companies, so all of those hard-working men can share in the fishing profits. And it must be emphasized, that they must preserve winter's ice, for use year around, to keep fish fresh for the markets. Of course, as we all know, homes everywhere should have ice chests, in their kitchens to keep every family's food better.

"Then I hope to stop in several ports, on the way to Stratford, to gauge whether folks like our grand experiment," Chief Odin Bushnell said.

Just then King West returned to the dining room carrying a three-foot-wide water color painting on heavy card stock. He pinned it onto the knotty-pine-paneled wall next to the Chief and stood back.

"Wow!" shouted Chief Odin, "This is truly spectacular!"

West had partially drawn his proposed plan for a capital city.

All the Company partners knew the secret, that they intended to quickly capture – while they had overwhelming power—the entire continent and all of the Caribbean islands. That included the current Spanish, French, English, Danish and Dutch possessions. The nearly ice-covered and almost unpopulated island of Greenland, actually larger than Denmark, was considered to belong to the Nuworld, and not the Danes. Who knew what wealth might be hiding under that ice? Iceland was considered to be a European nation.

Rome, St. Petersburg, London, Paris and Berlin were some of the capital cities they thought their capital might someday, be equal to in beauty; but possibly not in size or population.

History books claimed long ago Rome, had over 1,000,000 residents at one time. It was said London had in it presently, about 750,000 humans – besides countless thousands of filthy animals. But the Nuworld capital, already dubbed "OdinCity" by the partners, might never have so many residents.

The 14 Nuworld Company partners had unanimously agreed, that a spot on the map, about 100 miles north of the Ohio Gulf, looked good for their capital city. That spot was on a great curve of the magnificent Ohio River (the name was changed from Mississippi = Snake River. *You could actually hear a snake's hissing, in that Asian tribe's word!*) It seemed perfect for a capital, being pretty much central to the expected eventual extent of the new State. It was easily reached by water, from the Ohio Gulf and all the oceans, the Caribbean islands, and by the gigantic Ohio River system, of many large rivers reaching into much of the continent.

The French had established, in 1718, a small settlement nearby that they called New Orleans. They named it after the then Regent of France, the Duke of Orleans, because their king Louis XV, was at the time but a young child.

Then Duke Odin Bushnell had discovered the site on a French map, found among the papers at Fort Duquesne. An interpretation from French comment on the map said, the area was a bit swampy and prone somewhat, to annual Spring flooding, by that magnificent river. The word Ohio – O! Hio! – from an Asian tongue, was short and meant, "The Beautiful River."

But then, the Nuworlders knew, the stone and brick city of Vienna in Italy, was built entirely over wooden pilings, pounded into the muck of islands. Czar Peter the Great's new capital, not yet 50 years old, was Saint Petersburg in Russia. Peter's great innovation, was to build a large city of stone streets and buildings, also on pilings, atop a swamp.

As a beginning, the artist/architect Barron – and now King—Benjamin West, had created a spectacular plan view of the State Compound, next to a great crescent in the river. That 4 miles-wide crescent would hold, along the river bank, the King's identical houses and the Chief's "Crown House." The central Crown House would feature a great dome, made of a welded steel "longitude and latitude" framework, upon which would be securely fashioned thick glass panels, colored to show lands, mountains and waters of the Nuworld. That dome would imitate the Chief of State's Crown, and the thousands of brass hats worn by both male and female Nobles.

That gigantic dome could hopefully be lit, from the inside every night. That sight from boats and ships on the near mile-wide river at night, was thought surely to be spectacular.

North of each King's house would be his Realm's administration building. North of that would be each Realm's college building. All of those Realm colleges would make up the Nuworld State University.

North of the Crown House, would be a large Public Plaza. Beyond that, was to be the Justice Building, including housing for Justices and the Law College, for training attorneys.

Beyond those buildings, would be a long city park, on the other side of which would be the commercial center of the city, with very wide streets radiating out to the furthest parts of it.

It seemed altogether natural to 13 of the Nuworld Company partners, that the nation's capital should be named, "OdinCity"... and so it was to be.

All of them knew it would take time to build their capital of OdinCity. However, every Realm King, and his people, would begin their service by being mobile in an OdinBoat, which were continuing to be built; and soon, of steel. Each King and his family and staff, would live on his boat and have the advantage of visiting, just about everywhere there was water nearby. Even Chief Odin would live probably for some years on his OdinBoat, or on his OdinShip, while the Crown House and OdinCity, were being built.

But to Chief Odin, the circled and radiating streets plan King

West offered, could very well be the typical layout of the hundreds of cities, to be built over the endless years ahead.

Odin said nothing to anyone else about it, but he looked forward to capturing Havana, Cuba. From what he had heard of it, from the Philadelphia merchant Robert Morris, who had been a prisoner of the Spanish there, the defenses were formidable. But he hoped to frighten the wealthy Spanish men in their colonies, into trying to ship their treasures back to Spain, so the Nuworlders could capture their fleet – and that treasure—in Havana harbor.

The Chief again reminded his friends and partners, as he had done once in a while as a Duke and a Grand Duke, that someday men would fly. Nuworlders would soon be traveling by steam-powered carriages, on steel beams, and by steam-powered ships on the seas, and steam-powered boats, on rivers and lakes. He assured them that because men had more than plenty of genius, they would also fly.

He asked them many times: *"As the eagle can fly, why not I?"*

For a long time, Odin had tried to imagine how it would be, to glide through the air, high above the land, as the eagle did. He had only reached the height of a tall tree by climbing it. But that was enough to make him guess, the delights the eagle must find, flying... flying... flying.

They had a 10-minute fireworks display that night of August 30th, 1757. Also, there were speeches, celebrating that eventful, historic day.

Fireworks had supposedly been invented in China, but were used occasionally then in Europe. Lord Paul Revere had made some fireworks in his arsenal, just for this occasion.

The next days were very busy for everyone. In the past 2 years of war, the French had captured merely 8 New England whaling ships, near Louisbourg, and imprisoned 207 men of the crews. The French hadn't treated them badly, but the prisoners were still ecstatic to be released.

The French had a really great supply of whale oil on hand, and the Nobles paid for it and refilled their fuel tanks on every Odin-

Boat, including the Number 7 Supply OdinBoats. They had also captured a good quantity of whale oil at Stadacona.

About 200 New England ships, had been out a-whaling, and were amazingly successful. They brought in yearly, a wondrous 30,000 barrels of whale oil, and tons of whale bone. The primary use of whale bone, called "baleen" was to squeeze in women's waists, in their corsets.

Much of that whale oil had been purchased, by the Nuworld Company as fuel, for the newly launched, and huge, OdinShips. Whale oil was expensive at the time, but far superior as an alternative, to burning anything else in their boilers. But Odin hoped rather soon to substitute refined petroleum oil, that came right up out of the ground.

Pumping oil seemed far better than shoveling coal, to the new Chief of the Nuworld.

France's lazy King Louis XV – or more likely, his ambitious whore, Madame Pompadour – had lavishly poured an incredible 30,000,000 French livres, in expenses on Fortress Louisbourg. They had done that since the English returned it to the French some years before. Among the "improvements," stone work on some of the buildings was richly done.

The people of Louisbourg were informed, by the conquerors, that those who wished to remain French were welcome to go back to France. No civilians whatever chose to make the voyage, since the Governor-General told them of the wonderful new nation, they could be free to gain great prosperity in. However, about 3,000 of the French military seemed to feel duty-bound, to return to their duties and families across the ocean. They sailed away, in crowded vessels, from Louisbourg, on Friday, September 2nd.

The Chief and Kings, ceremoniously pinned thousands of medals on proud Noble chests, for the Canadian Campaign. Nearly every formal Noble jacket, was becoming colorfully decorated with badges, campaign shields and crowns—and no frilly French ribbons. That was also true for the Chief and the Chief Lady.

A ritt from Ambassador Hazelwood, said the Prussians had taken the Austrian Netherlands, between Holland and France. They also held Bavaria, and 2 provinces of France itself. It was unknown how much of all that territory, King Frederick intended to keep.

A ritt from King Clark, said Lord John Armstrong, who was to become King of Fuels, Benjamin Franklin, who was to become Science Realm King and Israel Pemberton, to become King of Elections, were already in Stratford, and awaiting Chief Odin's return.

The ritt also said spies had reported the Commander of all British Forces in North America, the Lowdown Loser, had ordered all his land, and naval forces, to come to New York. King Clark supposed Earl Loudoun, was to return his Forces, then to England.

That news alarmed Chief Odin, and he ritt Clark to be doubly certain, of the town's defenses, in case the British wished to get some revenge before leaving. He told the new King Clark, they would arrive, to reinforce his 2 Battle Forces, with a 3rd Battle Force in a few days.

Many of the Nobles recalled that it had been exactly a single year, since their first and second battles, at Kittanning and at Fort Duquesne, on September 3rd ,1756. Probably not one Noble could have dreamed, they would conquer all of New France in that single year – that is, no one other than the then Duke, Odin Bushnell.

Nobles replenished the fresh water, of the 8 OdinBoats to go south. They would stop after about 48 hours, and 600 miles, in Portsmouth, New Hampshire Colony.

Before leaving Louisbourg, the Nuworlders scrounged every pound of brass they could find. Luckily, the French had been enamored of the fancy designs possible in casting some of their cannons in brass, so the walls of their huge fortress provided a few tons of that metal necessary for making OdinGuns, hats and other things. Even the bronze Crowns for Courage were yellow brass, with a little more copper melted in, to make them reddish bronze.

King Morgan and his Battle Force *Gators,* were left behind in Louisbourg on September 3rd, as Odin's boat and the 7 OdinBoats of Battle Force *Valiants,* steamed south. Grand Duket Nicholas Biddle, was again Overlord of the *Valiants*, replacing King Croghan. King Daniel Morgan still had much to do, organizing Louisbourg's fishermen into worker-owned companies, who owned their own boats and equipment. He had learned some French language, just for such dealings with the defeated people.

When voyaging south, and leaving 7 OdinBoats at the entrance, the Chief had Captain MacDougal, steam into Halifax's harbor, in Nova Scotia, so he could inform the English of Louisbourg's capture.

The only warships present in that harbor, were 2 smallish sailing frigates with their double-crosser flags, fluttering limply in the breeze. Others had apparently sailed to New York.

Captain MacDougal pulled up next to a frigate, with the presumed Captain racing up to the poop deck, who stared as though in disbelief, at the large, round, bulging brass flag flown atop the OdinBoat's pilot house. From the prow, Odin, in his formal, medal-decorated blues, and wearing his glittering Crown and his golden shoulder CHIEF ranks, hollered out to him.

"As a courtesy sir, I thought to let you English know, we Nuworlders have conquered all of New France, including Louisbourg. We have formed a new, Nuworld State. I have been elected as the Chief of the Nuworld State. Here," he pointed, "you can see by the gold letters on my shoulders, that this is true. Captain, we wish you English well!"

The man simply stared with his mouth agape, and said not a single word.

Odin waved to his own Captain, to leave and they pulled away swiftly. Steam and smoke shot out of the jauntily-angled chimney near the rear. Hopkinson's Happy Hoppy Organ blared out steam-filled music that was seen as well as heard. They were leaving a terrific froth and waves behind on the harbor water, to befuddle and amaze the English sailors; and presumably, those on the Halifax shore, who had never seen a vessel move as that one did.

On Monday morning September 5th, the 8 OdinBoats pulled into Portsmouth harbor, New Hampshire Colony. The Hoppy Organs got the town people's attention quickly, and about 1,700 Nobles got busy, mixing with the people and telling them the good news.

Chief Odin and the Kings also scattered to talk with people, to gauge their reaction to the new State – and judge whether they might be inclined to voice their approval.

The Chief brought the jacket and medals belonging to Arch Barron Nathanial Folsom, who had literally died in his arms a year and three days before. He gave them to the Mayor of the town, for Folsom's family, who lived 10 miles away in Exeter. The Mayor promised to repeat for the Nobleman's parents, "Arch Barron Nathanial Folsom has become the Son of all Fathers, every Mother's Child and the Brother of All for all time, wherever Nuworlders are Free."

The little flotilla would have but perhaps 2 hours there, when the visiting was done and they must leave.

After a while a crowd of 80 or 90 men and boys, and a few women, gathered around the new Chief and Chief Lady. He spoke of the Constitution of the Nuworld State for them. He of course knew the land ownership part would be a stickler for many folks, and would take some explaining.

"Aha, I see some eyebrows raised on that one!" he said.

"You seem to think it would be alright for the State, to own the waters but the way it's done now with land, is best.

"That is, your infamous Governor Benning Wentworth, who isn't in town today; he's a kind of political hack, they say. He was appointed supposedly by King George, but much, much more likely, by some bribed politician, 3,000 miles away. He was to come over here to grant land to his close friends, and his relatives, for good silver. And, he would make many, many large free grants of land to himself.... come on now, is that fair?" the Chief asked.

"Our idea is that *everybody, one and all, even the children, would own the land; every square foot of it. Not only that, each of us would own 1,000,000s of acres of valuable forests and the metals and minerals under all our lands – and that is no matter where in our Nuworld, each of us might live, and where that wealth could be found.*

"Cities – including the villages within its city boundaries – will be assigned many square miles of land. Every City needs income to pay for schools and teachers; for streets and roads; for Noblemen to fight crime and fires, and courts; for hospitals, and even more.

"We have lots of ways in mind for Cities to serve their citizens, getting income mostly, by renting or leasing their land. There will be almost no taxes. Good people, in the State of the Nuworld, what people earn, people can, and should, keep.

"So, each City simply rents out land, often by auction and also with long term leases. Say there's a 100-acre parcel of ground, you'd like to bid on, to raise crops on for a single year, or 5 years, or 40 years. You could do it, you see.

"How much land would you wish to have to hold up your house, and have a garden besides? You'd only pay for what you use, whether your house is small or large. There'd be no taxes on your house, or your business, or on land you don't use. Do you folks see that?

"The central idea is to make certain, every child has the best possible chance for a decent education and a good life; not just for those children born to rich and privileged parents.

"I am positively convinced every person, has some kind of genius in them; and often, several kinds. It's education that can let them know what that genius is, and how to use it. We Nuworlders will always try to comb away inequities," the Chief told them. "Please remember that we are the innovation nation. We shall never be like other nations, that do not accept change, even for the better."

King Rittenhouse came running up to the Chief just then, and whispered in his ear.

"Sire, we just got a coded ritt from Clark. A very large British fleet is under way, sailing not to the ocean, but up the East River. They have to be going into Long Island Sound," he said.

"Damn!" Chief Odin exploded. "Not sailing out through the Hudson River to the Atlantic? I feel that almost certainly means, they'll attack our town for revenge! Let's get back on those Odin-Boats!" he ordered.

In a short time, all Nobles were back aboard their respective OdinBoats.

Chief Odin conferred with Captain MacDougal.

"How soon can you get us to Stratford, Captain?" the Chief asked.

"Sire, we can avoid ocean storms by staying fairly close to the coast, and we'll cross Cape Cod at its narrowest. There's an easy flat road, about 6 miles long there, and we can slip and slide along, to follow that across and save time. I should have us in Stratford early tomorrow morning, Chief Odin."

"Well isn't that something? How lucky we are that our boats can drag themselves across land, from Boston Bay back to the Atlantic!" the Chief laughed.

When they got under way into the ocean again, the Chief had a meeting with his Kings. As they sat around the dining table, he stood to speak, as he said, sort of thinking out loud.

"There can be no reason for the English fleet to leave New York, by way of the East River, except they mean to attack us. Their spies have of course told them, of our 2 powerful Battle Forces, defending our town of Stratford.

"Mr. Stiles tells me the news of the Louisbourg fleet, being destroyed, came too late to appear in his NUWORLD NUZ. That means, the Lowdown Loser therefore, is probably not aware of the power of our OdinRocks, in destroying the French fleet. He may not have heard about the Nobles use of them, last winter in the Caribbean. But he'd almost have to know, about our triumphant blasting of forts, up north of the Hudson River and beyond.

"Is it possible they simply discount the power of those Odin-Rocks, as being mostly luck? Or that they simply cannot believe we mere *provincials,* could possess such power? What about the Odin2-Guns? They surely must know how deadly those newest weapons are.

"We know Earl Loudoun has suffered humiliations, and since he's of the British Aristocracy, he must have some degree of pride, false or not.

"That Lord of Losers has been given the means, and the authority to win a war, and has never won a single battle! *The Lowdown Loser has never, ever won a single battle!* The incident with Clark, must have burnt his guts, and so too, the failure to even attempt to take Louisbourg. So, my wonderment is, what makes Lord Lowdown, and his generals, and his admirals, suppose they can succeed in attacking our town?

"We can believe the tons of gold and silver, and barrels of gems in our treasury, and our mint, would be tempting enough, but...."

"Sire, if I may inject something here," King of the Nobility Realm Andrew Montour, said as he stood up.

"I was present when General Braddock, was told about the abilities of our Asian warriors. I swear to you, Braddock actually said, 'Those ignorant savages would make no impression whatever on my disciplined Redcoats.' It was a particularly stupid assessment, of a deadly, brave and very able enemy. He failed miserably in his attempt to take Fort Duquesne, in July of 1755. That makes me suppose, all English Generals, may be a bunch of blockheads. They may be good at politics to gain positions, I suppose, but not good at all, in making war.

"Also, they'll be coming to the battle against us, with 100s of trusty cannons on their ships. The Lowdown Loser's spies, surely have told him, we have no cannons at all. That may give them confidence, Sire," the King of Nobility said.

"King Montour, those are excellent points," the Chief said.

"But they perhaps think, they have some advantage, say with some sort of new weapon. But what? Breech-loading cannons? I'd think that impossible for them, at least to modify their guns here. Maybe exploding hollow shells, for guns and mortars? They've proven to be inaccurate, and often fail to explode; so they're not used much. It's well known, they don't trust rockets, especially since they haven't been able to make them accurate. Also, you can't fire rockets from ships because the back-blast, would set the ship's sails and rigging afire, at the least.

"We know they have great contempt for us peasants, as they love to call us. That's even though we've won battle after battle, and they've won not a single fight, in this war at all.

"However unreasonable their motives are, they could only rationalize the attack on us, to their government, if they were successful. How they could assume they could beat us, is a very big puzzle to me, my Kings," Chief Odin Bushnell said.

Another coded ritt came after dark, that shipbuilder Uriah Hayden had the 6 new, 400-foot-long, steam-engine-powered, steel OdinShips under trials. He had taken them north, up Long Island

Sound. There were no weapons or Nobles aboard, so he was told to keep those OdinShips away from the Housatonic, for a while.

One had been made for Chief Odin's use, and had been named *Nuworld OdinShip One,* LOUISBOURG.

The others were named NOS2 STADACONA, NOS3 MONT-REAL, NOS4 CROWN POINT, NOS5 TICONDEROGA and NOS6 DU CAIN.

Diplomatically, none of the ships had been named, to commemorate the battles with the Asians, such as at Kittanning and Venango. Naturally, the Chief wished very much to have the friendliest of terms, with the Asian Nuworlders, who were to be equally with the Euros, citizens of the new nation.

Odin had designed the new, largest ships in the world. They were propelled with "20-bucket wheels." The hulls were 40 feet wide. Those huge wheels, 32 feet in diameter, and just 5 feet wide, were mounted on the slanted part, on each side of the prow. Inside the hull, a steam engine separately turned each wheel. The ship could be steered by feeding more steam to one engine than the other. Even so, a rudder stood forward of the prow, but was to be held stationary, much of the time.

The private company of shipbuilder Uriah Hayden, had built 6 greased shipways, more than a whopping 1,200 feet long. That's where he had hordes of shipwrights, building 18 OdinShips at a time, in 3 stages. Other shipyards, were also going to build the new steamships.

Hayden was so certain of Odin Bushnell's genius, that he switched from building OdinRafts, to the 1st-of-its-kind steam-powered OdinShips. The basic hulls were the same, but made of steel "plates," over steel framing, and welded with Odin Bushnell's welder.

Odin felt he had only been asleep for minutes, when the Captain knocked on his door.

"We're only an hour or so from home, Sire," he said. "It'll be a little after daybreak when we dock."

After thanking him, Odin woke his Chief Lady. She claimed she felt fine, although she had been having "morning sickness," more or less regularly, during her 14 weeks, so far, of pregnancy. They dressed in their buckskins, and breakfasted on bread slathered with butter. The butter was still fresh, even after being in the ice room since July. The bread had been freshly baked.

It was Tuesday morning, September 6th, 1757.

A short way up the Housatonic River, at the Stratford docks, the OdinBoats discharged their passengers. The OdinBoats were then run further up the river, hopefully to safety. The unloading of all that valuable brass aboard, would have to wait.

The Chief and all the Kings were dressed in tan buckskins, and wore their Odin2Guns. All of them had 4 extra "inserts," giving each Noble, 5 inserts holding 50 ammos each.

On the dock to greet them were Odin's father, Nehi Bushnell, King Clark and surprisingly, Connecticut Colony Governor, Thomas Fitch.

Right behind Governor Fitch, was Benjamin Franklin, Israel Pemberton and Grand Duket John Armstrong; those 3 were to become Kings.

With them was the Philadelphia printer William Bradford, and new to Odin, Benjamin Eads, co-owner of the BOSTON GAZETTE.

"Pops!" Odin called to his father. "What's happening here?"

"Odin my boy!" Nehemiah Bushnell said as he hugged his son. "My congratulations on everything! Clark will tell you about the approaching British fleet. I've been in charge of clearing everyone out of the way, for a mile back from the river. I'm nearly done with that. Oh! I should be addressing you, as our Chief of State now!"

"You have no need to do that Pops!" the young Chief said.

His father was quickly back on his horse, to finish his task.

"King Clark," Odin said, turning to the older man, the King of the Treasury Realm, and Overlord of the Battle Group of two defending Battle Forces, "tell me what's what now."

The Governor and others stood close by, listening intently.

"Sire, I'm so glad you got here before the British did," King Clark said. "They're on the way and getting close. Luckily, there's been not much wind, but I think the breeze has lately been a little stronger, from the west.

"I've got Overlord Whiting's *Dreadnots* Battle Force, spread out along the shore, from here to the Sound. Overlord Boone's *Bravehearts* Battle Force, goes upstream from here. You'll see; they've built very good, sand-bagged, half-circle 'fortets', as they call them. They're just big enough for a 12-Noble Band in each fortet.

"Oh yes Sire, we are very completely prepared; that is, if they actually dare to attack us. You have a sense about such things, so I ask, do you think they really will?" King Clark asked.

"My King, we must absolutely, positively, assume they will. They can probably almost taste the gold and silver in your Treasury. Do you mean to tell me that your entire defense is along the river? What about land defenses? You have nobody over there?" the Chief asked.

"Oh no; I've been doubly assured by our spies, that the British are all coming by ship. There's no need to divide our Forces and...." Clark began to say.

Odin turned immediately to his King of the Nobility Realm.

"King Andrew, please help Overlord Biddle get his *Valiants* organized, and spread out on the other side of town. We mustn't take chances, just in case," he told Montour.

❧ 20 ❧

King Montour left, and Chief Odin turned back to King Clark.

"Please, let's get horsed so you can show me your thoughtful preparations. The rest of you," he said to his wife and others, "please stay here in King Clark's fine little fortet."

"Now just wait a minute, please.... ah, Chief Odin," Governor Fitch interrupted.

"I'm the duly elected Governor of this Colony, and I have a right to know what the devil is happening. I'm well aware of your remarkable victories and your coronation — all of that is truly most amazing. But for God's sake, why do you suppose the British might actually do battle with you Nuworlders?" Fitch asked the Chief.

Chief Odin had met Thomas Fitch several times. He had been a guest at his house in Hartford and found him to be a reasonable and intelligent man. He liked him. Of all the 13 English Colonies, Fitch was the only Colony Governor, elected by the people. But he was elected only by a tiny proportion of them, and of course, only by men; and only those men who owned land.

"Governor Fitch, you mean, 'Us Nuworlders.' You are one of the reasons for the attack. You've been democratically elected, and that's anathema to Oligarchs and Aristocrats. Also, you may be sure they don't appreciate our making steel from Housatonic valley iron ore, or the steam engines, or guns or the steam-powered Odin-Boats, and all that. They won't fight the French, but they think they're superior to us, and will beat us handily. Also, they can just about smell our gold and silver, which they hope to steal," the Chief said.

King Clark ignored the Governor; he put in a thought of his own. "I don't understand the Lowdown Earl and his crowd. Sire, they must be confident since they don't know you are here."

"Oh, now, I think they must have some sort of secret weapon," Chief Odin told them.

"I can't think the British commanders over here are particularly bright, but we durst not assume they're all stupid men, either. However, I cannot for the life of me, think what sort of weapons they might have come up with. Please now, let's mount up so you can show me your great preparations," Chief Odin said.

King Clark, originally from New Jersey, had been the Nuworld Company treasurer since its beginning, in April of 1754. He was naturally, a great man with numbers. As they and others rode along, inspecting the 4-foot-high fortets, the Treasury King rattled off the figures.

The 2 Battle Forces were spread out, in their protective positions along the river, for 2 3/4 miles. Each 12-Noble Band had an Odin-RockCannon entrusted to the Band Overlord. In each Battle Force, there were 5 War Parties, 25 Combats, and 125 Bands. Thus, in the 2 Battle Forces, they had 250 OdinRockCannons, with 19 or 20 Odin-Rocks with each Band. So, they had almost *5,000 OdinRocks* on hand, along the shore, ready to fire.

Nearly half of them, King Clark allowed, were the new, more powerful OdinRocks, and the new ones were being made every day, in King Revere's arsenal. In addition, there were nearly 4,000 Odin2-Guns to be fired repeatedly at enemy men, on the hips of Nobles, with a rough total of 500,000 deadly ammos for those accurate and far-reaching weapons.

The 200 Healthors in each of those Forces were ensconced in

the larger Detail fortets, ready to tend the always-expected wounded.

Clothier Cypriot Dudley had made the fortet sandbags in his factory, of a little over a square yard of light cotton canvas. He had bought it from a Privateer who said he made the capture, from a French merchant vessel, returning from India. The inventive clothier said he would be using the indigo-dyed cloth to make many more blued "Dudleys" garments when the sand was emptied out, and the cloth was washed.

As the Chief and his entourage, rode their horses, nearly to Long Island Sound, sure enough, they could see the British fleet coming toward them. The leading ship was about 2 miles distant. Their sails were somewhat full of air. Huge, "double-crosser," red battle flags were flying, and signal pennants were fluttering high up in their riggings.

Also "up in the tops" were English Navy marines, at the ready at all times with loaded muskets, to shoot to death any sailor – their own countrymen – trying to escape the brutish wooden world of hell, in the so-called "Royal" – that is, "ever-so-caring" – English Navy.

Those English sailing "men-of-war" moved slowly, of course. The top speed for such bluff-bowed vessels, even in the most ideal of strong winds, was about 9 or 10 "knots" – from knots on ropes, meaning nautical miles an hour. Odin figured the proper term should be "nauts."

They were sailing in 2 lines, a row of men-of-war towards the shore, and what were surely troop transports, out-board of them. All of their menacing gun ports were open, on their landward sides, yet no cannons could be seen jutting out yet, from those vessels.

Odin made no attempt to count them. It seemed obvious to him the plan, was for the warships to bombard the Housatonic shore. Then the Redcoats would be put ashore in boats, to shoot and stab people to death, with their bayonets, when their muskets, as usual, misfired.

The Chief's party rode back to King Clark's fortet, from which they could see up and down the river rather well.

The houses of the town began some ways behind them; Odin's, Montour's, and Croghan's were about a 1/4 mile away from the river shore. The mint, arsenal, mills, ironworks, boatyards, and shipyards, were further upstream just in case of attack; not by their supposed English "allies," but by their enemies, the French.

By and by King Montour came to tell his superior, that Overlord Biddle's Battle Force was fairly well hidden, behind a stone fence, where it curved along the road, leading into town from the west.

"But Sire, I do believe I smelt a large number of horses, in some woods down that road. So, I told Overlord Biddle to beware of riders, from that patch of forest," Montour said.

That seemed rather unlikely to Odin, but he said nothing. After all, every street, every road, and every field had the smell of horses, from their frequent "droppings." Montour was 3/4 Asian, and the 1/8 Asian, Chief Odin, found it humorous, that the new King supposed he had a better nose than other men had.

Arch Duket Whiting rode up to inform them, that the British fleet had begun to turn into the Housatonic River. He had counted 22 big, "ships-of-the-line." One was of 90 guns, he said, and the rest were of 70 to 80 guns. He estimated all that from their sizes. There were also with the big men-o-war, 5 smaller frigates of about 40 smaller guns each, and there were 2 bomb ketches. Those ketches would probably each have a single brass, 13-inch bore very devastating mortar, on their foredeck.

Besides the warships, Whiting had counted 57 transports, bowsprits close to the sterns ahead; everyone was densely packed with Redcoats. To Odin, that was proof of their mission.

"Damnedest thing though Sire," Overlord Whiting added, "is they've got cooks or bakers busy, on every one of those big warships. They've all got stoves or ovens with fires going, on those decks, right out in the open. The strange thing before a battle, to be baking and...."

"BY ALL THAT'S MIGHTY, THAT'S IT! THAT'S IT!" Chief Odin shouted with much force. "I tell you all, they intend to burn us down flat to the ground, with red-hot-shot! That's it! King Clark! I tell you, *that's it! Their secret weapon is RED HOT SHOT!*"

Chief Odin almost leaped in the air with the realization.

"What the British are doing, is not baking biscuits or cooking beans, believe-you-me! They have built brick furnaces on those decks, and are heating for hours, with charcoal, *red-hot cannonballs,* they expect to shower our town with. Those solid iron balls will be so very hot, the heat will last a long time, and will set on fire any building they plunge into.

"I've read all about that matter. It's extremely dangerous to do that, on those damnably flammable wooden ships, so it's only done rarely.

"You see, they muzzle-load those big guns, each with a powder bag, and then a thickness of rags or a wooden disc, and just before putting a match to the primer touch-hole, they will roll a red-hot iron cannonball, down the cannon bore. Then instantly, they fire those weapons.

"Their spies have told them we have no cannons, and therefore, we can't throw balls back at them, to scatter those fire-filled furnaces, and fire-making red hot iron balls, around on their decks. Therefore, the logic is by some too-optimistic lame brains, they'll be safe in doing that! And that my friends, is what has given them the encouragement to attack us. They must somehow feel rather invincible, to be possessed of such wonderfully, mysteriously, supremely clever weapons! Well, I assure you, its madness, but here they come!" the young Chief said.

"King Montour, I want you to go upstream, to the left some ways – use your own good judgment, just where you think it should be – and shoot an OdinRock, in front of the leading warship, when it gets to you. We want to let them know, we don't want them anywhere near our mills. Be sure Overlord Boone understands, the British must fire first; Overlord Whiting, you must allow the British to fire first, also," the Chief said.

"Yes, indeed, Sire!" Whiting roared, as he galloped off to the right, while King Andrew Montour, rode upstream, to the left.

Those talented leaders, would, of course, inform every Band Overlord, of the Chief Overlord of the Nobility's instructions, not to fire first at the British ships.

"Chief Odin," Governor Fitch said while looking awfully pale. "What happens now?"

"Now Governor, we talk slow and drink lots of water; we wait," the Chief said.

The newly made King Clark had provisioned his fortet with ice water, and his guests drank great amounts while they waited... and waited... and waited some more.

Those canvassed-over wooden worlds, seemed barely to move, in the fickle mild breeze. Also, the river current was then at slack tide. The warships were hardly making waves, as they pushed and piled up the water ahead of them, with the nearly-squared, slightly rounded "bows."

A warship, 170 feet long, would have 100s of men tending sails. The far speedier OdinRafts with 10 masts, would have merely 10 men to quickly, easily and precisely crank winches, to change the angle of masts, spars, and sails, to the ever-varying wind.

King Rittenhouse guessed the oncoming fleet, to be 1¼ miles long. They could see the 57 transports were tightly in line, stretching out no further than the far larger, 29 men-o-war.

King Copley was almost frantic, in getting coppix of both those on land in their little forts and the on-coming English fleet. He had 3 men assisting him with his new coppixer, as he called the tripod and box, with the lens sticking out. One of his assistants carried a large, black leather bag which held the silver-covered glass plates, before exposure to make a coppix.

No guns had been run out yet from the English gun ports, but they still looked ominous.

More and more clearly as the fleet approached, they could see busy men around the furnaces, on those ships with their towering sails. Wispy white smoke, from the fairly clean-burning charcoal, was still rising from every English man-o-war.

English sailors and marines were staring at those on the shore, from all over the ship's rigging, masts, decks, and gun ports. As well as those onshore, those men would also be "on pins and needles," for what was about to happen.

At such a close distance, the Chief could see big guns being made ready for firing. Some of them had their muzzles propped up at a high angle, so they would send their balls furthest.

He could also make out individuals on those ships. As he stared, he was quite certain he saw, gaping back at him, Lord Earl Loudoun, high up on the leading ship's poop deck. He was wearing his Scots raiment, as Odin had seen him, once before. He had a telescope, and that looked to be aimed at the Chief. Others, who were apparently admirals and generals, crowded around the Earl and were also staring shoreward.

Incredibly, Chief Odin spotted a woman next to the Lowdown Loser, whose amazingly full-skirted dress, and blonde curls were being wafted about, by the slight breeze. He had to suppose it would be the French whore, the Earl had brought to the Nuworld with him.

King Copley was coppixing that largest, leading ship, several times, from the hoped-for safety of King Clark's fortet.

That ship leading the parade of ships appeared to be a large, 90-gun vessel. But the number of guns was a nominal figure, as it might actually have more or less that number, of huge cannons aboard. Of course, in the present situation, they could only fire those guns on the shore-side; now, the port sides of those vessels.

But Chief Odin found no consolation in the fact that the English would only be lobbing solid iron balls, each of thirty-pounds and more, glowing with red or even white heat, at them from perhaps a mere 40 or more, large cannons on that particular ship!

The total of guns on those warships added up to enough power to give the dunderheaded British commanders, a measure of confidence, Odin reckoned. They must have supposed they could attack, with near impunity.

King Rittenhouse calculated the English fleet, could throw 500, or possibly more, sizzling hot, large iron balls into their town, with every broadside they fired!

Each iron ball would be heated, to perhaps 1,500 degrees or more! And then those bomb ketches, with their 13-inch diameter, deadly mortar (death) bombshells....

Two of the warships had passed King Clark's fortet, and still, King Andrew had not fired an OdinRock. Then a 3rd had gone by;

then slowly a 4th! Everyone in the waiting crowd was more than a little edgy.

Suddenly, *Whoooosh! Screeeem! Ka-boooom!*

Way off to the Chief's left, a huge, mainmast-high geyser of water shot up from King Montour's OdinRock, in front of the leading warship. Immediately, on every one of those vessels, they could see the red-hot balls being loaded, the guns run out...

"Everybody!" Chief Odin screamed, "Keep to hell down, as low as you can!"

Their ears and bodies were assaulted with fantastic booming noises, as those 100s of big guns belched out fire and smoke, at them from a mere 200-feet away!

Odin hovered more or less atop his wife, who was squatting low as directed. She turned her head and said something to him, but he heard nothing. The earth was still to him.

He had become deaf!

But the action was called for, not wonderment.

The Chief and 250 others, put OdinRockCannons onto their shoulders, and fired away with war-whooping OdinRocks, at the looming oaken walls. The enemy ships were barely visible, through the terrific clouds of gun smoke, making everyone gasp.

Within seconds, probably every one of the 250, Arch Barrons had missiles screaming through the air, and blasting away at the British. *Then 100s more! Again, more 100s!*

OdinRock smoke penetrated and added to the gun smoke! But all that smoke could not obscure the terrible fires, being set on sails and tarred rigging.... and wooden hulls and decks!

Explosions burst fierce flames roaring into the sky! Of course, on each ship it merely took one bag filled with explosives, on the deck or in a man's hand, to be ignited to explode, or to burn, catastrophically. And with a chain reaction, the thin paper or cloth bags being carried, by "powder monkeys," would also be ignited right on down, within seconds, to the great amount of explosive stuff in each ship's gunpowder magazine!

Men and chunks of men, masts, and great pieces of ships flew high into the air, and came plummeting down, to splash into the waters of the Housatonic River!

Yet more and more OdinRocks, war-whooped into those 29 blazing men of war, and those 57 burning smaller transports alike!

Through the thick gray haze, they witnessed a large, 3-gun-deck ship, directly in front of Clark's fortet, explode! It seemed to lift itself right up out of the water, and disintegrate into 1,000,000 pieces, that flew all over the Housatonic!

King Copley was actually still making coppix; now of the ships madly and fully aflame!

Odin's hearing was coming back, and he realized his Annie was shouting at him.

"Darling! For God's sake, cannot this madness be stopped?" she screamed.

The Chief was dumbfounded. He had never given a single thought to stopping a battle, once it had begun. Why you stopped when there was nothing more to shoot at! That's all! He suddenly had to wonder if he had failed to think of... but how?

Even as he pondered the question, the merest few minutes from the start of ship's gun's roaring, there were no more screams of Odin-Rocks aflight; *because there were no more whole ships as targets!*

None of the men-o-war still existed! The few transports still afloat were thoroughly ablaze! Those red-coated English soldiers were screaming, as they leaped into the river.

The still waters of the Housatonic River, because of the slack tide, was so covered with debris and bodies, a person might not have to be a Holy Man, to walk on that water, that day!

King Elias grabbed the Chief's arm, "Sire! A fortet's been hit! Over there to our right!"

A faulty or wet bag of powder in a large gun had sent a red-hot cannonball, falling very short, of the possible near-mile range intended.

That cannonball had be-headed an Arch Barron, firing his Odin-Rock, and gone completely through the chest, of the Noble loading his OdinRockCannon. Neither ever knew what hit them, but a 3rd Noble in the fortet, had his right leg smashed and burnt; but he should survive. Four other *Dreadnot* Nobles, died from shots falling short, a quite common thing then. The same sort of shot, also falling short, hit a fortet upstream among some *Bravehearts,* but amazingly, not one of them was hit.

Someone shouted, *"Fires! Our town's on fire!"*

Odin turned around to see behind him, that indeed, houses were burning.

Odin sent King Tully and King Croghan, immediately to see what could be done about it.

There was no fire department in Stratford, or any other town, perhaps in the entire world, at that time. Prayers plaintively given from people on their knees, begging some ghostly person in the sky above, was supposed to guarantee safety from town fires. Oddly, prayers didn't prevent fires from burning down every sort of building, and entire cities, anywhere.

There were only volunteers with buckets. At Stratford, there were plans to make horse-pulled fire-fighting wagons, with tanks full of water. There were also in-the-future plans, to run pressured water in pipes under the streets, to large faucets at every street corner, to make fighting fires more probable of success.

Chief Odin and Chief Lady Annie's house, plus Croghan's to their left and Montour's house next door, were obviously burning. But the Nuworlders had no means of putting those fires out, so the Chief concentrated on his business along the river.

Their townhouses, built tightly together, were virtually identical, with outside walls of brick. But all else, including interior walls – although plastered—floors, ceilings, attics, roofs and all of their furnishings – were very burnable.

Somewhat later a very excited Overlord Nickolas Biddle rode up, on a big white horse, to the Chief, to report on the battle west of town.

"Chief Odin," Arch Duket Biddle said, "we were attacked by close to 200 horsed Redcoats, and Sire, it was just about as King Montour said. They were hiding in a forest, approximately a mile down the road from where we were, and the mass of them charged out when they heard the ship cannons fire. We shot them all full of many holes, and there are no survivors among them; not a single one, Sire."

Odin mused to himself that his mostly-Asian friend Montour had a good nose at that.

"Did you fire OdinRocks at them?" the Chief asked.

"Oh no, Sire! We didn't wish to harm innocent animals; we just shot the riders again, and again. There were nearly 2,000 Odin2Guns blasting away, at not quite 200 horsemen! I had all my Nobles— Healthors and all—hiding down behind a stone wall, that curved around with the road there.

"But from the woods, they should have seen some of us there; that we were ready for them. Hard as it may be to believe, they came a-shouting and a-screaming at us, toward our town down that road with swords! *Sire! With drawn sabers!*" the Battle Force Overlord gasped.

"All of our Nobles got off at least 6 shots at those horsemen before there were no more of those damned, red-coated and green coated riders to shoot at.

"I can only think spies had told them all the town's defenses, were along the river, and they would simply charge into town, and cut everybody's heads off! It was stupid, pure stupid craziness on their part, Sire!" the Arch Duket said.

"Amazing!" Chief Odin said.

"Yes Sire, and you can see the blood here on this horse's rump. The rider on this one went right over backward, just a-spurting blood all over! Someone recognized him, even as he was bleeding all over, that he was Robert Rogers of the Rangers. That happened to all of 'em, but maybe 3 or 4 of those English, unbelievably jumped their mounts right over that stone wall. We counted 187 of those attacking cavalry; all were killed.

"One of 'em whacked away and split a Healthor's head a little, right through her brass hat. Sire; it was awful. But she will live, I'm happy to say.

"And two others got slashed somewhat but that pretty Healthor – oh Sire, her penmanship being so perfect, for the record books and all. She was awfully close to getting killed. There was blood all over, just like those butchered Senecas at Venango, Sire. Oh! I see you've had a right good battle over here, too," Arch Duket Overlord Biddle, looking at the river, said.

The Chief asked Overlord Biddle, to convey his gratitude to his Battle Force *Valiants,* and of course to write out a full report for King Montour.

Several troop transport hulls were near sinking, and still burning, with flames climbing high above the masts, and with clouds of black smoke, filling the sky, well beyond the river. The breeze from the west was wafting the smoke away from the Housatonic then.

Nobles were organized in boats, to search for survivors, in the debris-and-bodies-covered-water.

The river had been at slack tide but then began again to flow, out to Long Island Sound, taking fresh, bloodied, shark food, and well-seasoned oak timbers, with it.

The Nuworlders would later "mine" the Housatonic, for the many thousands of valuable English iron balls, English iron guns, and the rich prizes of huge brass mortars, on the river bottom. They would also thoroughly mine the Louisbourg harbor. All of the iron armaments at Stadacona, Louisbourg and the destroyed French forts, also would be smelted to become useful. Smelting such iron would be far, far more productive, than beginning with raw ore, that often contained less than 50% of iron.

Nearly every pound of those astoundingly many tons of already nearly pure iron, would be converted to hundreds-of-times-stronger steel, in beams for the beamways, for steam engines and importantly, also for constructing immensely stronger, steamships and steamboats.

Chief Lady Annie was helping the Healthors with casualties, both friend and foe.

King Tully said to the Chief, "Isn't it amazing that we've seen so many men die, along the Ohio River, and Lake Champlain, and Louisbourg Harbor, and now here. None of us is crying about it. It's an awful thing, this damnable war, Sire; it's an awful thing."

"Yes, my friend; war always has been, and always will be, gory. But we have a right to do what's necessary, from our point of view. We have very great military power, and I tell you, I intend to use it," Chief Odin told him.

"Chief Odin? You're going to use your power for what?" Odin's longtime friend, King Elias Tully, asked.

"You'll see, my dear friend. But first I have some thinking to do," the Chief sighed.

Odin looked back and could see the house fires were spreading.

Entire towns all over the world were burned down flat to ashes, now and then, for no one on earth had found a way, to stop a major conflagration in cities, once it had begun. Even the giant city of London, in 1666, had been burnt to ashes... only to be re-built, with the crazy cow-path-way layout, it had always been.

But Odin reasoned that in this "innovation nation," that problem would also be whipped.

The Nobles pulled out of the river, just over 1,700 survivors of the English attacking fleet. They could never know the exact number of soldiers, sailors, and marines, the Lowdown Loser had in his forces − plus those 187 attacking on horseback. The records and the record-keeping Yeomen that could have enumerated their personnel were destroyed with the ships. The best guess of the attacking English casualties, was probably about 9,000 soldiers − not the 15,000 the French had claimed Loudoun had on hand − plus perhaps, another 9,000 marines and sailors had died, in that great fiery catastrophe, their ill-thinking commanders had led them into.

Chief Odin had to gasp at the thought, that they had possibly killed a ghastly, 18,000 *British sailors, soldiers, and marines.* They had died due to the extremely gross incompetence, of their commanders.

Nearing sunset, the Chief and Chief Lady and others, toured the town on horseback, to see the fire damage.

The street on which they had lived, was a lengthy, block-long building, of 25 joined row houses. Their entire block, along with other similar blocks, was totally gone.

That particular block-long fire had only been stopped on both ends of the block, by "bucket parties," throwing water on the adjacent buildings, of row houses around the corners, that weren't yet burning. Two schools in the center of those blocks also were burnt flat. Other complete blocks were reduced to sorrowful ashes, too.

There were no townsfolk harmed by cannonballs – including King Croghan's mother and daughter, nor Montour's 2 wives and children—thanks to being evacuated to safety, by Nehi Bushnell and others.

But by the next evening, 78 houses, in total, had been lost, along with 2 taverns, 2 schools, 1 general store, and the new Congregational Church.

A witness told of seeing a large, sparkling mortar bomb, as it plowed through the church roof. It then exploded and put the new wooden church ablaze.

But none of the all-important mills, the arsenal, the steel mills, boatyards, and shipyards, or the mint had been struck; for they were further upstream along the Housatonic.

Chief Odin's parents invited him, Chief Lady Annie, and Kings Croghan and Montour, to dinner. King Copley was engaged in developing his coppix of the English fleet, before and during its dramatic destruction. Chief Odin and his wife, would stay at least one night, until shipbuilder Uriah Hayden, returned with their new Odin-ShipOne "home."

They were well into the meal, with Odin's younger brother, and sisters, at the table as well, before King Andrew Montour, arrived at the front door with a man in tow.

Nehi Bushnell asked them both to come to the table, as they must be famished.

As they squeezed in 2 more chairs, Montour introduced the man.

"Chief Odin and everybody, this is English Army Major General, the Baron Charles Hay. His uniform is drying out yet and is being cleaned; that's why he's in buckskins. He was found floating on a door in the river. He had been a prisoner of the Loser, Lord Lowdown."

"Excuse me, King Montour!" Lord Hay laughed as he sat down. "That is so funny and yet so appropriate, that you'd call Earl Loudoun that! That fits him perfectly! *The Lowdown Loser!* And how very grand are your Chief's ideas of forming a new nation, and giving the greatest of high titles to your leaders!"

Baron Hay was handsome, of medium height, thin, graying and maybe 50 years old.

"As I said," King Andrew went on, "he was a prisoner on one of those ships, and most luckily when it blew up, he was able to grab his cabin door to hang onto. Sire, I'd best let him tell you why he was the Lowdown Lord's prisoner. He's the only British officer of much rank that survived the battle today."

The Baron Hay proved to be a bitingly sharp fellow and showed obvious intelligence.

While he hungrily forked down the perfectly done beef roast, bread, carrots, and potatoes, he told them he had come from England on July 11th, in that year of 1757, with Admiral Holburne, in the Admiral's flagship, to Halifax harbor. He said he had long years of experience as a British soldier and was to command troops, in the taking of Louisbourg.

Other ships joined Holburne's fleet until it was about as numerous as the French fleet, anchored at Louisbourg. Many officers reckoned, they could certainly defeat the enemy, whether the French ships were inside, the protection of Louisbourg harbor, or not.

But to Lord Hay's dismay, Lord Loudoun had his men growing vegetables, on land next to the town of Halifax, instead of training for, and heading to battle, despite the great preparations for the siege. Loudoun was not *positively certain,* he could meet with success, it seemed.

Lord Hay had let his displeasure with the lack of action, be known loudly, and as a result, Loudoun had him arrested, and locked up aboard ship, to wait for a court-martial in England, for insubordination.

"Chief Odin," Lord Hay added with a bit of trepidation, "I really wanted that court-martial, to let King George, and our government, know what sort of cowardly numbskulls were in command over here. My only fear was, I would never make it to the trial alive, to tell the truth. For, however, that crowd of Loudoun's may have been thick in the head and faint of heart, they knew the stakes for them. Thus, I was certain they would have me poisoned, at the least.

"In truth, I possibly could not have had any influence with the King either, as it was his son William, made the Duke of Cumberland, that got those unqualified politicians, appointed as land and sea commanders. I can't believe even one of them was up to his responsibilities.

"What has been a terrible calamity, for the British Army and Navy today, is for me, so very sadly, sort of a blessing. At least, I'm alive, to tell the truth of the Louisbourg fiasco; the fiasco King Montour tells me you Nuworlders took care of, so grandly," the English Lord said.

The man was certainly a fabulous catch, Chief Odin thought.

The Chief told him, "Baron Hay, you shall very soon have an opportunity to tell the King of England, the facts, and no one is going to poison you or harm you in any way.

"While you were talking Baron, I decided what must be done. We have business to attend to here for a few days, and then we will take you to London. And we will do that as no one has ever done it before; on a new, huge, and steam-powered, steel OdinShip. We'll take other British survivors, too. Our Kings and I have much to discuss before we leave. So, rest easy. Make some notes, so that you are certain your facts are straight. Is that good, Baron Hay?"

"Yes, Chief Odin, that would be very good indeed! And a kindly Sergeant of Marines aboard the ship I was prisoner on, smuggled a few NUWORLD NUZ to me over time, so I've read of your Ohio valley campaign. Also, I've been told a little about your amazing campaign to the north. I must say, Chief Odin, that speech you made in Philadelphia was truly, truly beautiful. If I may be so bold sir, that was the very best speech I ever read. Yes, sir, the most remarkable speech ever I have read," Lord Hay repeated.

"But now, I have some serious thinking to do. I've only read the Nuworld State Constitution and your Coronation Address briefly, and I must read them thoroughly. To create a State that's a Monarchy, a Commonwealth and a genuine Democracy, is the most amazing thing any human being could conceive. In the British Isles, we don't get to choose our Overlords. We just don't. I'm beginning to think that's our big problem, right there. Yes, Chief Odin," he said as he again looked up from his plate, "I also have some thinking to do."

"Thank you for that, Lord Hay. My wife and I are quite exhausted. If all of you will excuse us, we'll head for my fine brother Ezra's room, as he said he would sleep on the sofa tonight," the Chief said.

❧ 21 ❧

On Wednesday morning, September 7th, 1757, Chief Lady Annie and her mother-in-law, Sarah Bushnell, raked through the ashes of the Bushnell's burnt row house. They recovered only a few dishes, and a teapot, that had been found short years before on the Caribbean Seafloor. All of Chief Odin's four hundred or more treasured books were destroyed in that awful fire.

Notable shipbuilder Uriah Hayden proudly gave the new Chief, and his Kings, a tour of, the new 400-foot long, 40-feet wide, "Nuworld OdinShipOne," named "LOUISBOURG."

The lettering LOUISBOURG was painted in large, white letters – outlined with black—along the bright-red, iron-oxide-painted, oaken sides and rear.

The inside of Odin's ship was different from the 5 other newly launched vessels. It was furnished elaborately for the new Chief of the new innovation nation, the Nuworld State.

Five other steam-powered vessels, the master shipbuilder Uriah Hayden had completed, were named for victories: NOS STADACONA, NOS MONTREAL, NOS CROWN POINT, NOS TICONDEROGA, and NOS DUCAIN. Below their names were their numbers.

Those 6 large steamships, had been named for victories over French forces; but they would not name any ships after battles with their native countrymen, the Nuworld Asians.

Hayden planned to build many, many more of those ships and, in the future, was to build an additional huge new shipyard in the State's new capital of OdinCity, on the lower Ohio River. Greater and greater amounts of steel would be available soon, from the smelting of iron cannons and iron balls, for building stronger ships and boats.

Oak had long been the most used shipbuilding wood since it was strong. However, Odin assured everyone that the present ship designs would be superseded soon. He felt certain almost all new ships and riverboats would be built entirely of steel in the future, as soon as the Metals Realm could make steel plentifully.

Long Island, near Connecticut, was re-named "Odin Island," after the late great Chief of the little Pochaug Band, Odin Bushnell had grown up next to. There were surely endless numbers of islands, in the world that were "long"; but there would only be that one island, with the distinction of being named for so important a man. Also, "Long Island Sound," was from then on, to be called "Odin Bay."

Hayden's new shipyard and a steam engine factory would be part of a gigantic "city of machinery," in the Nuworlders new capital city. It would be served by multiple beamways, to easily move materials to the mills there, and their finished goods from that and other ports, and to places near and far, around the world. There would also be a steamboat building yard there.

Nehemiah Bushnell explained to them on the new OdinShip tour, the centrally located boilers in the hull of the ship. Also, there were hot water heaters, steam condensers and pumps for water, air, and the exhaust gases coming out of the bottoms of the boilers. On the ships, those exhaust gases were to be pumped through, a double-walled "nose," extending out from the points of each prow, and the bottoms, to "lubricate" the steel hull, against the frictional cling of water.

Odin Bushnell had wrestled mightily with his imagination in

deciding how best to propel the new OdinShips. Huge wheels similar to those on the OdinBoats would be efficient, he reckoned. Mounted on the prow sides, just aft of the point of the ships, the 2, 32-foot diameter wheels, would reach 15 feet down in the water, to the ship's bottom. Each wheel would grab 20 "slice-of-cake" buckets full of water, and compressed air, to blast the water backward.

The rear of the hulls was pointed – but only underwater—much like the prows were, to allow the rushing water to fill in the "ditch" left in the ship's wake. So, Odin designed a rudder for both front and back of the hull, to make sharp turns possible, with the help of adjusting speed on the 2 wheels.

To Odin Bushnell, it was a matter of action equals reaction.

Inside the hull, each wheel was turned by a double-acting, compound steam engine, consisting of 4 large, and 4 small cylinders, mounted like a big X on the hull wall. Crankshafts turned a single crank, which turned each wheel. They were larger, more powerful versions, of the proven engines in the OdinBoats. These engines used the steam twice; first in the small cylinders, then, although the pressure was reduced, in the larger cylinders. That gave double use of the steam.

Odin expected that the bubble-filled water along the sides, would absorb wave energy to such an extent, the 40-foot-wide ship, wouldn't roll much in a storm.

In the pilothouse during the tour of the OdinShip, King Rittenhouse told of the various instruments, and controls, which he had designed, and his men had made in his shop. The British General Baron Hay was truly attentive, as he learned about the OdinShips.

Odin, a pretty good mathematician himself, emphasized that Rittenhouse's mathematical calculations were responsible for taking much of the guesswork, out of the machinery design.

The group, with the English Major General, gravitated to the front of the ship, where the Chief mentioned, that since the wheels would be pulling water from under the waves ahead, he reckoned those waves would be much weakened.

Shipbuilder Uriah Hayden mentioned, "Chief Odin, the engines aren't yet broken in, so we held all of the OdinShips to 27 nauts. And that Sire, right there is faster than any sailing ship ever moved! Yes, Sire; much faster!"

The much smaller OdinBoats could speed at a maximum of 19 nauts.

By noon they had gathered in the large knotty-pine-paneled dining room, where a celebratory meal was waiting for them. The meal had been made by 12 newly assigned Noblewomen, to the Chief's huge OdinShip.

The NuworldOdinShipOne would for some time be the home, and office, for the Chief and his Chief Lady. At times, the ship would accommodate a few Kings as well. It was thought the Chief's government business, would be conducted for some time, aboard his vessel next to the site of the new Capital City. They hoped to begin building that city soon, about 100 miles north of the Ohio Gulf, on the lower, mile-wide Ohio River. The Chief, the Chief Lady, and their hoped-for-children would live on his OdinShip until buildings had been constructed ashore.

Chief Odin planned to tour as much as possible, in both his OdinBoat and OdinShip, all over the Nuworld State. He would visit and speak to the Princes, the Mayors and especially the people. He hoped to encourage them in their innovations, a concept unknown to most people of the world, for many centuries, of almost no human progress. Oh, except for the inventions of religions, insisting that men and women should aspire to nothing more, than personal humility.

There were 12 well-furnished suites, consisting of office, dining room, kitchen, sleeping room, closets, shower, and privy, for each suite. Each of the privies even had a flusher. Human waste was flushed down into a huge tank, which in turn, could be emptied far at sea.

Of course, there was an ice room to keep food fresh, a main kitchen and rooms for the crew. Unlike other ships though, there was plenty of empty, unassigned space in the ship.

The 5 other OdinShips were more modestly made and were adaptable for transporting either a full BattleForce of 2,000 Nobles or a great deal of freight. All 6 of those ships also had an OdinCart with 3 horses to pull it, down a ramp from the side, and out and about.

There were brilliant OdinLamps all over the ships. They achieved their brilliance from Odin Bushnell's observation that burning lime, in iron furnaces, produced an abundance of bright light. So his whale oil lamps, molded of glass, with their glass "chimneys," had lime-infused wicks, that burnt brilliantly. They produced far more-light than the old, smoky, oil lamps.

Before boarding English prisoners to return to England, to make use of that extra capacity, King Montour, Baron Hay, and others questioned most of the 1,700 prisoners individually, to see who actually wished to go back, and who might wish to stay and become prosperous Nuworlders. Just over 900 of them wanted to return to duty, with the English Army and Navy, and to return to their families in England.

During a lunch with the Kings, Odin discussed his plans for the London trip.

They would take NOS LOUISBOURG for the Chief and Chief Lady, and for Kings Croghan, Montour, Copley and King Doctor Gale; plus, Baron Hay, Ezra Stiles and his wife would also go with them, with no official duty but reporting for his NUWORLD NUZ, and as a friend of the Chief.

Under the command of King Montour, 3 Battle Forces would go.

Battle Force *Dreadnots* would go on STADACONA, to rob a long list of English banks, goldsmiths and trading houses, in the mile-square, ancient old City of London.

Battle Force *Bravehearts* would go on MONTREAL, to rob the Tower of London.

Battle Force *Valiants* would go on CROWN POINT, to gather up King George and many notables from London's West End, and bring them to a meeting with the Chief. King Eyre was to accompany the *Valiants,* as he knew pretty much who-was-whom in London.

Two of the Forces would bring with them axes, picks, sledges, and explosives, to open "difficult" doors of those places to be relieved of their gold, silver, and gemstones.

King Paul Revere nearly stripped his factory of the newer, more powerful OdinRockFlamers, for possible use to burn London down. The threat of burning down that town would be a most powerful bargaining tool, Odin reckoned.

Some of the OdinRocks had to be left, to defend Stratford, in case of an attack; however unlikely it might be.

Whatever wealth they gained in London, would hopefully compensate for the losses the British inflicted on them and would help to pay for the return of slaves to Africa. The Nuworlders would also be training, and arming, some of the repatriated slaves, in their own Battle Forces, and suggest proper government to them.

"At that meeting with King George and other English government notables," Chief Odin announced, "I will inform them that they shall sign the Treaty of Peace, we have printed up, or we shall burn the entire London town down, to ashes. War or peace, it's up to them. Let's all put our heads together, and consider the terms we must insist on.

"Also, we've all talked about the evils of slavery, and now we can do something about it," Odin said. "I'll create an Africans to Africa Agency, and I suppose that brave Virginian, George Washington, might be most qualified to be the head of it. He has slaves of his own. We know he's a brave man. I've read that Washington now plows many acres of farms, much of it growing that poison called tobacco. He obviously has much experience, with Africans, and with their management. He was also a partner in the Ohio Company, whose claims to the Ohio valley lands, we most certainly have made moot," the Chief said.

Kings Croghan, Montour, and Eyre, all agreed that King of the Fuels Realm John Armstrong, should take an OdinShip up the Potomac, and propose for Washington, to be the Prince of returning all enslaved people, to freedom in their native continent of Africa.

Further, he was to emphasize to Washington, that much of the manual labor required of slaves, would in the future, be performed by machinery. He was also to inform him that the cotton-growing Southern area, was likely to become "*Clothier to the World.*"

In the future, with the advent of endless innovations of steam-powered machines, easily tilling the earth; of such machines to plant, cultivate and pick cotton; another device called the OdinDeseeder, already invented by Odin himself, to remove seeds from cotton bolls, in addition to the OdinStitcher sewing machine, already in use. Finally coming, were steam-powered air pressers, to provide prest air to spin thread, weave cloth, and to power OdinStitchers to sew cloth into garments.

They were each somewhat familiar, with 25-year-old Washington's sense of integrity, and a deep craving for fame, from even before the time, of the Britisher Braddock's march to calamity. Each would write him a letter, urging him to apply, for the extremely difficult task.

During the lunch, the Chief also created Kings of Benjamin Franklin, for the Science Realm; Israel Pemberton, for the Elections Realm; and John Armstrong, for the Fuels Realm.

A bit later, the Chief met with Kings Rittenhouse and Franklin. They discussed Rittenhouse's brilliant invention of the ritt system, of sending messages through the air. They talked of doing the same through wires, for privacy. Also, King Rittenhouse thought it might be possible with vibrations, varying the flow of electricity, to send such as music and voices, through wires, and possibly, through the air.

TICONDEROGA was to load up with supplies for Louisbourg, Stadacona, and Montreal. The ship must get to those places, before the blockage of ice, in the Gulf of Canada, and in the Canada River, prevented the movement of all shipping, except for OdinBoats.

Of extreme importance, they on the TICONDEROGA were to gather up cannonballs, mortar shells and brass and iron cannons, for smelting at Stratford. The mill there would be making steel plate, to build the sturdy OdinShips. Much steel would also be needed for the production of engines, tools, and beamways, to transport people and freight over land.

Three supply OdinBoats would be sent to Prince Bradstreet, in the far-off west.

King Armstrong would take DU CAIN on the Potomac mission. Major George Washington, Esq., would likely get quite a start, to see the big, bold name on the sides of that vessel, pulling up on the

Potomac River, to his rented estate called Mount Vernon. Washington had nearly lost his life more than once, near that French Fort Duquesne. He had his own battles against the French there in 1754, and in 1755, helping the "parade ground General" Braddock, and helping to save as many British, and Colonial fighters as he could.

King Paul Revere spent a happy hour soldering on, 13 more colorful gemstones on the Nuworld Crown, 1 each, over of the *now-former* English Colonies. Being soldered in place on the gold Crown, they could be easily moved to correct positions when Regions were officially established. Added to the 5 gems for the conquest of Ticonderoga, Cadillac, Montreal, Stadacona and Louisbourg Regions, Chief Odin's headgear was beginning to *really shimmer*.

Odin and Annie went aboard each of the 4 OdinShips to steam to London, to talk to the Nobles, to assure them of the very great importance, of their assigned missions.

In a nation founded by Noblemen and Noblewomen, slavery could not possibly be tolerated. Their intention was to right a terrible wrong, and would force the slave-profiteering British – and American and other slavers—to help finance the safe, and hopefully successful, the return of the former slaves, to a life of freedom and prosperity, on their huge and rich, home continent.

The entire group worked on the Peace Treaty wording of the document.

Ezra Stiles was most helpful and would accompany the Chief, to have his printers print many copies of the Peace Treaty document, on the way over the Atlantic. He would also report events, for his NUWORLD NUZ. Stiles insisted that he would continue to record news events, to attract readers to his Church of Happiness messages, in his newspaper.

Also coming along was Benjamin Eads, of the BOSTON GAZETTE, and William Bradford, for the PENNSYLVANIA JOURNAL AND WEEKLY ADVERTISER.

King Benjamin Gale, said the Chief needed his care, and that he had to come along.

They also took along, 6 each of printers, coppixers, and ritters; plus, 15 Healthors, as clerks, cooks, bakers and of course, nurses.

They also gathered 300 copies of the latest NUWORLD NUZ and a good supply of quality paper and some parchment.

The NUWORLD NUZ would show the full draft of the Constitution, and of Chief Odin's Coronation Address, as well as reviews of all of their battles and some of the casualties.

King Clark, as the Vice Chief-of-State, was asked to assign various Kings left behind – with a Band of Nobles as Guards—to speak to gatherings of people, and Colony Assemblies, about the new State's Constitution, and to gauge their enthusiasm to a be part of it. There could be no turning back. The Nuworld Nobles had defeated both the French and the English powers, so the Nuworld State was the established power then, on much of the Nuworld continent.

All of the Colonies were benefitting, from the spread of Nuworld's silver nu, and no one could be not influenced, by the new prosperity, and the fame of the Nuworld Noble's accomplishments. But with an understanding of human nature, all of them knew there would be people objecting to any change in their lives, even if it was obviously for their own long term good.

The 4 OdinShips bound for England steamed in line out of the Housatonic River, into Odin Bay (formerly, Long Island Sound).

It was Saturday morning, September 10th, 1757.

The weather was good, and the Odin Bay waters were calm.

They were soon into the choppy Atlantic, and Chief Odin and Chief Lady Annie went up to the prow of the OdinShipOne. They looked down at the froth being created, around and behind the nearly hidden wheels. The upper half of the wheels was behind painted sheet-steel.

It was that froth which in effect, lubricated the bottom and sides of the hull. The cling of water to the hull was a definite drag on any vessel, not so equipped.

They could see that the waves ahead of them, were suddenly calmed by the wheels pulling water from under them.

Annie had a question. "Odin darling, what happens when these ships meet fish or whales or porpoises? Won't they get killed by the wheels?"

"That could happen, my sweet," he answered. "But sound travels 5 or 6 times as fast in water as it does in air. So, any creatures ahead of a ship should have more than ample warning by the noisy wheels, and the turmoil of water being thrown backward. They'll dive out of the way, I'm quite sure. I do believe whales, or anything else ahead of our ships, will suppose there's a dangerous monster coming at them, so they'll just naturally dive out of the way.

"Also, smells seem to move fast in the water, and the odor of burnt air and whale oil, should be repugnant to such creatures; so, I expect them to stay away. Hopefully, we also won't have hulls covered with barnacles and such, because of the stink of oil smoke in those bubbles."

It was obvious the OdinShips were moving very fast so, they went up to the pilothouse, to visit Captain MacDougal, and to see the two types of instruments, that measured speed.

"Sire," the Captain smiled, "we're going faster than any human has ever gone before, lest he's jumped off a very high cliff! We've got her going to 31 nauts, but she'll go faster when I open her up after the engines are more broken in. Your Pop's orders, Sire."

The 3 other OdinShips, were following in LOUISBOURG's wake. Although the sea was more and more choppy, there was neither roll nor up-and-down pitch, to the ship, what with much wave energy being absorbed, by the gas-bubble-saturated water.

"Odin," Chief Lady Annie said, when they were alone again, with a solemn look on her face, "I'm beginning to get ill. It's not from seasickness or my pregnancy, but from thinking about all the people that would be killed, if you burn London down. Your Forces have already killed, so many thousands of men. But they were warriors who would certainly kill you, and your Nobles if they had had the opportunity. This is different because the people of London seem to me to be innocent civilians. Have you thought of that?"

"Oh yes, my dear," her husband answered. "I have thought about it some. But you see, this is war brought on by the English, not by us. It's their fault entirely. The Oligarchs there we hope to deal with, own the British Government, and they also own most of the land in the British Isles. But most importantly at this time to us, *is their properties in London.*

"Whatever small sentiment they might have for their countrymen, *they will not relish having the sources of their incomes destroyed. That's the rents on those London apartments and stores properties.* Thus, I feel very confident, they'll agree to our Peace Treaty, almost no matter what it contains. Events, of course, can always go terribly awry, but we expect to have them by the throat. Therefore, I think no Londoners will be killed, although there just might be a bit of displeasure with our thieving," Chief Odin grinned.

"I hope you're right. But you seem *always* to be right. I and everyone, are so very much in awe of you sweetheart, for all you've accomplished. And maybe now, such feelings are mostly because of these OdinShips. They are some sort of miracle; it seems to me. But of course, none of this could be at all possible without your escape, from the brutal English Navy, 3 1/2 short years ago," his darling wife said.

"Yes, you're right about that. But actually Annie, they aren't miracles. My ideas are just the culmination of a lot of bold thinking, and hard work by many, many others, as well as myself. But you say you and others are in awe of me? By golly Annie, I'm kind of in awe of me, too!" he chuckled.

She smiled. "I'm so glad you're happy. Everything seems to be going your way."

"Oh yes; so far, so good. But it will be some time I think before people understand that the value of our money, is backed by metals still in the ground and salt, and I'm quite sure even petroleum, yet to be pumped out. We even have an apparent great wealth in coal, which we can transform into coke, for our iron smelters. We might run out of gold and silver eventually, and that's what people think of as money.

"When we were on the way home from bringing up treasure near Jamaica, in 1755, we sailed easterly, a little north of Cuba. We went near the south of Florida and then sort of close ashore on the east of that Spanish possession.

"Well, I had the idea we might see more shipwrecks on the

way. So, during daylight hours, we always had two of us looking out the 'see the sea scopes.' Sure enough, we found two such wrecks, with cannons strewn about on the sea bottom. Also, in the wreck south of Florida, we also saw, a great many bars of silver laying there. We were so laden with weight on that OdinRaft, we didn't dare bring up more, than a single pound of silver, off the sand there.

"Anyway, we were careful to make notes of the two locations, so that someday, we can retrieve that precious treasure for our people, also. I'll charge our Nobility to bring that stuff up, someday, since we should be able to easily locate those two sites.

"But for now, we're going to try to put a big scare, into those Spaniards, who are now living in the Nuworld. We hope to have them want to ship the gold, silver, and gemstones they've stolen, back to Spain. Then we'll try to take it, probably in Havana, Cuba, when their treasure fleet is gathered there. Well, we don't know exactly how that's to be done yet, but we're thinking about it, so we'll have another supply of bullion. It's a big secret, of course," he told her.

Then the Chief added, "Here's another big secret, my sweet. I've got King Thomson to get up a group of men, and maybe some women too, to change our language. The English language is so full of contradictions, and loaded with spelling errors... well, like all those soundless 'g's' and 'h's.' Also, they make and F sound, as in rough enough to be tough. That makes learning the language more difficult than it should be. I think I should ask the English if they'd like to help make our mutual language better."

"Wow! My husband sure does want to advance things! Change the language! Wow! What a challenge that has to be. But then, future generations of children and... oh yes, all those Asian peoples who have no written language now... wow! We might come up with an easy to learn the language yet, so that everyone in the nation, could easily communicate with each other. Odin that is really a great idea!" Chief Lady Annie said.

They could feel the tempo of the throbbing engines, picking up their pace sounds, so they went forward to the pilothouse again.

"Captain MacDougal," the Chief said, "we can feel the engines going faster. How's your speed now?"

"Sire, we're almost at full speed. The instruments show 40 nauts. She'll do a bit better in time so we should have you, and your Nobles, in London exactly as you predicted; in 72 hours or so, from the time we left Stratford."

"Odin!" Annie gasped. "You actually knew how fast your ships would go?"

"Oh now sweetheart, it was only a guess. That's the truth. I reckoned they'd be speedy, but there was no way to predict with precision.... well, it was just a guess, I tell you," he said.

There was little time to rest.

The Chief and the several Kings present devoured the maps of London.

King Croghan was to go in London, with King Eyre and the *Valiants,* so he could practice his diplomatic skills, on those they "kidnapped," for a most important meeting with Odin.

The Nobility King Montour said they counted just over 2,000 older OdinRockBlasters, and 4,400 of the newer, mostly OdinRockFlamers. With the new maximum range of 3 1/4 miles, they could, with those 6,400 OdinRocks, easily set the entire city of London ablaze, if necessary.

The new Chief spent the first evening, and nearly the entire second day at sea, discussing his views on the future with Stiles, of the NUWORLD NUZ, and Benjamin Eads and William Bradford, of the other papers. Odin expected they would give much publicity in their publications, to what he had to say.

After talking for some time, about the great importance of science – the methodical, cool and logical search for truths – and that every citizen ought, to a degree be a scientist, he went on with some of his thoughts for them.

"I think the reason we have so many religions on earth," the Chief began, "is that every human is in fact, divine. It could very well be that every one of us is a God or a Goddess. We are all creators, are we not? Can a horse bake a cherry pie? No, because only humans are creators, including creators of religions. Animals learn very little;

they make their nests, and do all else, strictly by instinct. Just think of human's inventions of clothing. It's really is amazing.

"Priests and preachers love to insist, that we human beings should be humble. They say we must get down on our knees, and beg forgiveness from some magician, for being what we are. Well, whether we might believe somewhat, in some religion or another, we must absolutely believe in ourselves. Each of us and all of us can do so very much good in our lifetimes. I feel certain, that what men and women can conceive, they surely can, with persistence, achieve.

"Gentlemen, I don't want to belabor the point, but I think each of us ought to be our own best friend. Naturally, we all have lots of friends. But we must respect, admire, and love ourselves. We must absolutely love our awesome, creative, and wondrously ingenious selves.

"Also, there never has been a cause as great as ours. We serve in this cause as an unexampled fight, for what is so very right and reasonable; for all of our people, everywhere in our perfectly wealthy Nuworld. People of other continents can handle their own problems.

"Now then, among the problems we must confront, are the situations in our Southern Regions. We can understand that the Southern planters, will not be terribly grateful to have their inexpensive, enslaved workers taken away," Chief Odin told them. "Some of them will expect compensation for losing their so-called property; but they will certainly be disappointed in that, and ought to be grateful, that their sins against humanity, won't be more damning than that.

"And many of them will be disappointed to learn, that their growing of the poison, called tobacco, is very much disapproved of. Tobacco cannot possibly be anything but harmful to a person's body. That it could be a helpful medicine, is very certainly stupid nonsense.

"I've done some reading, about that really useful fiber called cotton; how it is grown, etc. I was astonished to learn it is difficult, to pick the cotton bolls when ripe; yet even the children of slaves, are required to pick cotton. It is slow and quite tedious work. Therefore, I have begun to conceive a machine, to pick the stuff. I'm rather certain such a machine must be large and complicated, and steam-engine-powered, and we know how to do that.

"Another surprise for me is that picking the seeds out of the cotton bolls is slow and difficult. A slave might pick the seeds, out of only a mere pound of cotton, in an entire day! A mere pound of it! So, I've also conceived a machine to de-seed the stuff; and that, gentlemen, was pretty easy to do. I'll have draftsmen make the drawings of these, and other inventions, as soon as we get back to our Nuworld State. I expect to encourage men to form companies, to make those things, as soon as can be done and in great quantities.

"In the future, I expect great quantities of de-seeded cotton, to be sent to a factory near the fields, where it's grown. There, the cotton can be spun into thread, by prest-air-powered, or maybe steam-powered, machinery. With other prest-air-powered or steam-powered machinery, it'll be woven into cloth.

"Beyond that, other shops can transform the cloth, into the clothing of every sort, with the sewing machines I invented. Those OdinStitchers can be powered by prest air, so that sewing together garments, is fast and cheap. Cotton is the easiest material to wash really clean.

"No longer will housewives have to waste their precious time, spinning and weaving, to clothe their families. Housewives can in the future, dedicate more time to their husbands, to their children and just possibly, even have a little time for themselves," he said with a grin.

"I feel very certain cotton clothing, bed sheets, and all sorts of cloth can be made, to be quite inexpensive, for our people, and for folks everywhere in the world. What I envision is that in our State, we shall have cotton growers, and cotton millers, to become clothiers to the world.

"I've also begun to think about machines to harvest wheat, oats, rice and even corn – although the Nuworld's corn – really, it is *maize* —is so very different a grain.

"There are plows, and cultivators to think about, and machines to pull these things, in fields, and to pull wagons. Can machines replace horses? I am very certain machines can do very much, to lighten the burdens of mankind. I do know you have to feed a horse, whether he works for you or not. That isn't true of machines.

"We now know how to make nails, screws, and bolts in quantity and cheaply. Our Metals Realm will be doing that, on a very large scale, to sell to our people and to others everywhere. That venture alone should bring good revenue into our Treasury," he told them.

T he new Chief went over the assignments, he had given to each of the Realms, assuring the 3 "reporters" that those Kings, had for a long time been planning, in every spare moment, for fulfilling those new responsibilities.

Odin thought to himself that he must conceive machines with which to fly. To have such machines, obviously will be of great assistance in war; that's why his work on flying machines, must be held absolutely secret.

He was careful not to say out loud, how it was to be done. The subject of flying often popped into his head. It was more than simple curiosity. *He felt he had a need to fly.*

After a few minutes of quietly scratching out notes, a hand went up.

"Yes, Mr. Eads?" Odin asked the Boston newspaperman.

"To me, it's a stunning thing that you've invented so many things. Most especially, your invention of the steam engine.... Sire, how did that happen?" Eads asked.

"Well now; it's about time someone asked me about that. Yes, that is a very good question sir," the inventive Chief of State David Odin Bushnell said.

"It happened shortly after we 14 members, of the Nuworld Company, returned from the Caribbean, with those tons of Spanish treasure. I was sitting in our parlor, thinking about the next kind of ship we should have. My darling mother, had a meal of white beans with bacon and molasses cooking, in her heavy cast iron pot, hanging in the fireplace. The water was beginning to boil. The heavy iron cover on the pot was being lifted up, by the expanding steam. Steam would escape, and the cover would fall back down on the pot.

"Now then gentlemen, you and I know endless thousands – oh, surely, millions of men and women—have watched this exact same thing happen, but thought nothing of it. But I grasped the significance of it then because I do constantly think, of innovation. Over a few days – no, maybe 2 weeks—I put together the means, by confining steam in cylinders against pistons, to use this force of nature called steam, to move ships, and power sawmills, and much else.

"Now please, let me emphasize that the brain in my head, has no more potential for thinking of new ways to do things, than any other man's or woman's brain. It's really pretty much a matter of believing in oneself; it's a matter of self-confidence. That is that we have a natural ability to create good things if only we will practice it.

"A really good example is a creative concoction invented by the Chief Lady. Just today, she told me she was inspired by the ice cream freezer, I invented, to mix foods for cooking. She, with her Noblewomen pitching in, is going to mix beef she's ground, with the grinder I invented. Mixing it, she's going to add mashed potatoes, chopped carrots, chopped onions, some flour, salt, and pepper. She'll then make them into half-pound patties, fry them and put them on freshly baked buns, for everyone to try. You newsmen might want to try them too, and report to your readers whether Chief Lady Annies' idea, is good or not.

"By the way, she said she'd also try mixing in eggs, with the rest of it, and then you'll have an entire meal in your hands, with every bite," he added.

The Nuworld Chief of State paused for a minute, before continuing, as the 3 were busy making notes in "short-hand," of what he told them.

"I suppose all religions insist, people should strive to be humble, and that pride in oneself is somehow a terrible sin. Oh yes, they insist that those men, who wrote that big fat book, those centuries ago, possessed all the knowledge, there ever could be. But that is very certainly nonsense, as has been repeatedly proven. Oh now; enough about that," Chief Odin said.

"One other thing. I've discussed with King Thomson of the Education Realm, to gather up ingenious men and women, to comb away the absurdities of our language. Maybe just correcting the spelling of our words, and having a single sound, for each letter in our alphabet, might be sufficient. How ridiculous is it, to have only 5 vowel letters for 18 sounds? Maybe we need a lot more letters to work with," the Chief told the reporters.

"And gentlemen, swallow this idea if you will: maybe we should come up with a different alphabet than the cobbled-together Roman alphabet, we've been stuck with," he grinned, seeing the shocked looks on their faces. "Come on, gentlemen, there must be many alphabets in use, around the world. I've suggested to King Thomson, that he and his staff, look all of them over, to perhaps incorporate some strange alphabet letters, into ours. Or, it could be that we could simply add some kind of marks to our letters, to alter their sounds.

"After all, that's what our alphabet letters do: they picture sounds in words.

"Certain marks could add, say, an h to a t, to make the th sound. Others could alter an s to make sh... well, there's really very much, that could be done.

"For numbers, I wondered, even as a child, why we have arithmetic using 10s instead of 12s as the base. Obviously, 10 squared is 100, whereas 12 squared is already a 44% increase. Twelve is more divisible that 10. Six is wholly divisible twice, but 5 isn't divisible at all. That should be worked on to see the considerable advantages of the 12 number base instead of the 10s base. I expect King Thomson's people are already juggling, with that sort of thing.

"Well gentlemen, I hope you will encourage your readers, to experiment with letters and numbers; they should then suggest their good ideas, to the Education Realm. Maybe you could print examples made up, by your talented typesetters," Chief Odin said.

"I cannot emphasize enough, that we are engaging in a beautiful experiment, with our government, and we could also experiment, with lots of other things," Chief Odin said.

William Bradford spoke up, with much excitement in his voice.

"Chief Odin Bushnell, I for one, shall most certainly encourage my readers, to please try some ideas for themselves, and to contact King Thomson about them," Bradford said.

"Mr. Bradford, I assure you that it's just a matter of believing in one's own ability, to do such things. Once you discover you really can create... well, just as I did in that single week in April of 1754, when I conceived of an improved sailing ship. I was only 15 at the time, so I've been rather in awe of myself, ever since! You create all the time, of course, because of your newspaper. See there? You actually are a creator, Mr. Bradford, and according to that very good man next to you, that makes you a God! How about that? Ezra Stiles is a really intelligent fellow, and if he thinks you are rather like a creative God; you must really be that!"

All 3 men had a look of wonderment, on their faces, so Odin changed the subject.

"In our Capital City, much space should be devoted to laboratories, including experimental farmland, and orchards. And everywhere, ceiling fans for cooling must be installed in houses, stores, factories, and offices. The power for them could come from piped-in prest air. Such air should be provided the same, as pure water by every city, which also must provide sewer pipes and proper treatment of wastewater. Trash dumps must be provided by every city.

"Very importantly," Odin continued with his talk, to the 3 newspaper publishers, aboard the Nuworld OdinShipOne, "King Benjamin Gale and his Healthors, have inoculated every Noble with the mild Cowpox, and not one of us, has contracted the deadly Smallpox. As a result, he and his collaborative doctors, are envisioning immunizations, for other diseases such as measles. There are many other diseases, they might succeed with, using either dead or weakened forms of those sickness-causing microbes."

"Also of the greatest importance," he told them, "was that the innumerable Asian tribes, will be in great shock, at the terrific war power of the Noble Warriors, including Asian Nobles. They also might be amazed to be correctly called Asians. It is of the greatest importance to immunize them, against European diseases, which are so dangerous to them."

The Chief assured them, he would see to it that men and women, would be encouraged to explain to the many Tribes, of the good intentions of the new government. They must tell them of the necessity for educating their children, for getting proper medical care, and better housing. The Asians must also be assured that they are equal citizens to everyone else and that they have the same rights. They should strive to learn, how to read and write, so that they too, could read their constitution, and of course, vote.

"The Asians too," the Chief said, winding up the meeting, "like everyone in the nation, should be assured of their natural genius, for creating things, such as the ingenious canoes, kayaks, and teepees, that advances the conditions of life for them, and for everyone."

Odin authorized the printing of the Peace Treaty. A few copies were to be printed on parchment, and 100 more copies on paper.

Stiles had brought 300 copies of his NUWORLD NUZ also, with the texts of the Nuworld State's Constitution, Chief Odin's Coronation Speech, and tales of their battles.

They received a coded ritt from Ambassador Hazelwood, that claimed King Frederick of Prussia was "all atwitter," to meet Chief Odin. He said it was arranged to have France's King Louis XV, at the French port of LeHarve, "by any means necessary" on Wednesday or Thursday.

King Croghan of the Diplomatic Realm, had asked Hazelwood to arrange all that.

It was certain millions of Europeans, must be in wonder of the warrior King Frederick, since he had won so many stunning victories, against 4 larger nations, and had captured great territories. His forces had the very great advantage, of having the accurate, long-range and quick to re-load OdinGun, over those armies with the awfully inferior musket. The Nuworlders had not offered the Prussians to buy their OdinRocks; but they had in use 1,000s of cannons of their own, and 1,000s more of the big guns, that they had captured.

Just about dawn on Tuesday, September 13th, the Chief and Chief Lady, came up to the pilothouse after a hearty breakfast. Both were dressed in tan buckskins, brass hats, riding boots, and they wore their Odin2Guns, with handles holding 50 automatically re-loaded shots.

Captain MacDougal was wiping the sleep from his eyes, as he relieved the mate, who had piloted the ship through the English Channel, during the night.

"Sire," MacDougal said, "we've just entered the 27-mile-wide estuary, of the River Thames, from the North Sea. The river will narrow, as we go upstream to the west, and it will take about 2 hours, to get to London. We must slow to about 20 nauts, because of the ship, barge and boat traffic. That speed will seem like we're merely creeping along."

Odin could see that his LOUISBOURG was trailing the other 3, as those OdinShips, would be docking at the Custom House Wharf in London, on the north shore of the Thames. The LOUISBOURG would unload the British prisoners, on the opposite shore, to the south.

All of the Nuworld steamships flew very large British "double-crosser flags," so long as they were in the river. That was to hopefully avoid being shot at by English warships or forts. They would only raise the beautiful "gold and blue" Nuworld circular brass flags when docked.

In the next 40 miles going upstream, they saw three OdinRafts, heading downstream. They had been built no doubt, in the Nuworld, in Hayden's or other imitating shipyards. There were, of course, many other vessels of the older style, and slower, sailers, barges, and boats.

Nearing London, they, at last, saw a British warship, perhaps of 74 guns. Men on all those craft simply stared in disbelief, at the overly large ships, mysteriously moving faster upstream in the Thames, than any of them could sail at sea, with the best of winds.

The huge OdinShips had no masts, no miles of rigging, nor acres of canvas, yet they moved fast! It had to seem magical, to those watching such ships, speed by for the first time and with each of them leaving huge, frothy wakes behind.

The leading OdinShips were cleverly clearing the way ahead, by flashing their keg lights up and down and side to side, plus tooting the Hoppy Organs with music, seen as well as heard. The smaller craft scampered toward the shores when being alarmed by the huge red vessels.

OdinShipOne, tied up at the Deptford Shipyards, on the south bank, while the 3 other OdinShips, proceeded a bit further upstream and went to the other side of the Thames.

The LOUISBOURG disembarked the nearly 900 prisoners, from the accommodating holds and the more comfortable suites, in about an hour's time. Some of the Englishmen still had to be carried ashore into the shipyard, on litters, by their fellows. Baron Hay was seen to be especially attentive to the English Navy and Army veterans, as he helped them disembark.

Interesting to the Chief, he was told the tireless Major General Baron Charles Hay, had been speaking with his soldiers aboard, and endlessly discussing things in secret, with most of the 900 English soldiers and sailors, being given a quick ride home. He also was full of questions, with many of the Nuworld Nobles aboard.

All of the prisoners had their uniforms cleaned, and were given underwear, gifts of an OdinRazor, a bar of pretty good soap, tooth powder, toothbrush, washcloth, and a towel. During the 3-day voyage, they had been well fed and had showered, with warm, fresh-water. For some of them, it was for the first time in their lives. It seemed none of them recovered their white wigs, which had been lost in the Housatonic, when they leaped for their lives, into the river.

Deptford Shipyards was the principal yard, of the English "Royal" Navy. It had been established away back in 1513, by England's King Henry VIII.

Interesting to Odin, it was where the ambitious giant of a man, Russian Emperor Czar Peter the Great, had learned about shipbuilding, during his 7 months stay in England in 1698. Odin had read that Czar Peter was even taller than himself, being about 6-feet-6, or maybe even another 2 inches taller. Chief Odin was *merely* 6-feet-4 inches tall, the same as his "knee-high" father, Nehi – Nehemiah —Bushnell.

If London was to burn, Deptford shipyard, with its great piles of timbers, boards, and ships under construction, would also make a great wondrous fire.

With the English prisoners all repatriated, they then cast off OdinShipOne from the shipyard and headed upstream, and the little distance across, to the north bank of the Thames. Standing on deck, Odin could pick up the sharp crackle of Odin2Guns, being fired intermittingly; *but thus far, thankfully, the Chief could hear no cannon fire in response.*

The Nuworlders knew that most common Englishmen, were forbidden to own guns; only the Aristocrats had that privilege; among countless other rights. That there were very, very few guns of any kind, available to that huge population in London, was an undeniable advantage for the Nuworlders, in their raiding assault on the one-mile square, "City of London."

At the Custom House wharf, there was about 40 feet of paved space, between the river's edge, and the sizeable Custom House building itself. It was where imported goods were routinely unloaded, and taxes assessed.

Overlord Whiting's MONTREAL was tied up at the quay, just short of the impassable London Bridge. Overlord Boone's STADACONA was aft of that ship. And Overlord Biddle's CROWN POINT was secured, outboard of MONTREAL.

As the Chief had a few bites of cake, to end his short *fast*, they made *fast*, his *fast* OdinShip, and *moored, or docked*, at the *wharf*, or the *quay*, behind the STADACONA. Ah, such was the English language!

Although he had not heard much of it, Odin stared in disbelief at nearby London Bridge, connecting the north and south shores of the Thames. The long bridge was covered river bank to river bank with buildings, that apparently were shops, houses, and apartments. All the buildings on the bridge, were simply helter-skelter, as though done with no pre-planning whatever. Rich English oligarchs were collecting fabulous rents, from off that bridge, Odin reckoned.

The stone arches of the bridge were too low, to the Thames River surface, to let anything but the smallest watercraft pass through. In case the Nuworlders were to burn London town down, all those wooden structures on the bridge would make a tremendous giant fire, also!

The air was so foul from the stink of the city, and the sewer of a river, it almost took one's breath away.

They knew that London had a population of 750,000 or so humans. There were also, some 20,000 horses; 1,000s of cattle; sheep, dogs, cats, rats – no doubt, 1,000,000s of rats and mice – and birds beyond numbering, large and small. They were all dropping their poop and urine everywhere. That, plus trash, garbage and even human waste, were routinely thrown into the streets, and into the river. All of it added up to an incredibly filthy place, with swarms of flies, constantly multiplying by planting their eggs, in the overly abundant, nurturing nastiness.

Only when there were exceptionally hard-pouring rains, were the streets more or less washed clean. Then that awful run-off poured more extreme filth into the River Thames.

London, with its many 1,000s of housings, had no provision for bathing or for flushing away human waste. The Chief vowed his State would do things very differently.

The new OdinShips were at the edge, of the ancient square mile, called "The City of London." The town had been started, at least 17 long centuries before, by Roman Legions. That was just about the time the Jew Jesus of Nazareth, was found guilty of something or other, and crucified in Jerusalem, as 1,000s of other malefactors were. A new branch of the Jewish religion was begun, with magical happenings reported as being absolutely, supernaturally, true.

After all that time, it was said some of the old Roman walls and gates, still to that day, stood here and there in London.

King Montour came over from the STADACONA to see the Chief.

"Sire, I do believe everything's going about as planned. I can see in the distance that our Nobles have gathered many horses, carts, and wagons, besides what we brought with us. But I don't know yet how their confiscations are going," the Nobility King said.

"Off to the west, my King Montour – doesn't that sound like our Nobles doing a bit of shooting?" Odin asked. "It might be that King George's Horse Guards, are putting up a fight."

"It sounds like it, Chief Odin. But I have not heard a single Odin-Rock exploding over there, although I've heard a number of them blasting, up Lombard Street and at the Tower. We'll know something, from each of our Battle Forces shortly," King Montour said.

Each of the 4 OdinShips, had 1 Combat of about 65 Nobles left on board, to guard the vessels.

Overlord Boone's Battle Force, had 24 Combats, totaling about 1,800 well-armed Nobles, to conquer the Tower of London. Boone was to become King of the Police Realm when they returned to the Nuworld.

Various river craft were coming up too close, in their curiosity about the OdinShips. So, the Chief had 3 Arch Barrons, each send an OdinRockBlaster into the River, to drive them away. The huge geysers and loud booms created were plenty convincing, and the river craft did scurry away, *immediately.*

To Chief Odin, the news from his Noble Battle Forces seemed slow in coming.

By and by, a Noble on horseback brought a note from Overlord Daniel Boone, that his *Bravehearts* had secured the Tower of London, had wounded but not killed, and disarmed 22 of its guards, and had locked up the rest. They were then loading up wagons, with their plunder.

Shortly after receiving that note, along came a parade of carts and wagons, by Overlord Whiting's *Dreadnots.*

The total number of Whiting's well-armed Nobles, dedicated to relieving the rich of their wealth, was about 1,800. The *Dreadnots*

Healthors were, of course, to remain on their ships. The *Dreadnots* wheeled their vehicles – including their 3-horse OdinCarts—onto the Custom House wharf and then toted the stuff up the MONT-REAL's ramp, laid on the paving.

As Odin congratulated his Nobles for their thievery, he noted that much of the loot, besides gold coins and bars, seemed to be in silver – bars, coins, and utensils. Yet England was supposedly having a severe shortage of that metal. Ah, he surmised that it must be that the big money men, were hoarding the stuff; and therefore, running up the "value" of it as a result!

The Nuworlders were helping them create a *genuine* shortage of silver – and of gold—but Odin supposed, *the money men would not be grateful*, for the Nuworlders' assistance.

King Andrew Montour had a long list of places to be robbed, and he checked them off as each of the 125 Band Overlords, reported results of their assignments.

Topping the list was the Bank of England, and alert officers of that business saw what was coming, and locked their doors and their vault. Three of the explosions heard, were OdinRockBlasters knocking doors asunder, and making a mess of that establishment.

Also among *Dreadnot's* responsibilities – mostly along Lombard Street – were the Royal Exchange, Child's, Hoar's, Martin's, East India Company, South Sea Company, Hudson's Bay Company, Russia Company, and the Levant Company. The favorite target, the Royal African Company, which profited so terrifically, from the cruel enslavement of 1,000,000s of Africans, was also robbed. This last building was left in complete ruins from OdinRockBlasters, but only after they had loaded an entire cart with their records, correspondence, and much gold and silver. Those records could be invaluable in finding those guilty, in the slave trade.

England had actually fought brutal, bloody, and expensive wars – with plentiful English and other-side casualties—to gain a monopoly in the slave trade. The Brits won the legal-by-treaty right, of selling dark-skinned humans to light-skinned humans – "Blackies to Whities," some said—in the colonies of Spain, France, Holland,

Portugal and of course in their own, American and Caribbean Colonies.

Chief Odin thought it to be the greatest of ironies that the slavers named their company, *The ROYAL African Company*. It was as if they were so very ignorant, to not know the word "royal" – along with other words – sprang from the ancient root word "ruth," meaning "caring." They had altered the true meaning of that word "ruth," to mean presently, "ruthless."

The London merchants obviously loved the wars, that were so costly in human misery, and life, but so financially profitable to them. They eagerly loaned money to the English government, in order to finance the death-dealing, horrendous violence of wars. That so many humans sadly lived miserably and died young as a result of slavery, obviously bothered them not at all.

Mostly on Lombard Street, in that ancient square mile of The City, were also 40 or more banks to be robbed, with or without the use of OdinRocks, or the shooting of the resisters.

The Nuworlders thought it quite considerate, of England's richest moneymen, to concentrate so much of the nation's portable wealth, in one convenient place, for the wholesale robberies, going on that day.

The Chief had instructed Overlord Boone, to be certain to take all of the Royal Regalia from the Tower of London, including the King's Crown. None of that regalia was ancient, since "Lord Protector" Oliver Cromwell, a little more than 100 years before, had sold all of the old "Royal" paraphernalia. Any the Nuworlders found at this time would have been made for the Godforsaken womanizer, and Pope of the Church of England, King Charles II, in 1660 and later. Chief Odin vowed to melt and sell that "Royal" stuff, to show his contempt for their government.

From the Tower Mint vault, Nobles also brought to the STADA-CONA, much gold, and silver, in bars, sheets, coins and silver objects. Treasury King Abraham Clark would be pleased that his vaults would be "bulging," much more than before!

Odin received a note from King Croghan that Overlord Whiting's Force had "kidnapped" from the wealthy West End of London, some 100s of "big wigs." They included several admirals, generals, government officials, and most importantly, King George II himself. They had been taken to Westminster Palace, where the *Parlormen Parleyed in Parliament*.

Croghan said the detained important Englishmen, were angrily and impatiently, awaiting the new Chief of the Nuworld State's arrival. While waiting, the captured ones were also reading the NUWORLD NUZ accounts of the French, and the English navies, disastrous encounters with the Nuworlders. The Chief's coronation speech and the Nuworld State's new Constitution were also being read there, as well as a recapitulation of the many Noble's battles to win the war.

King Montour arranged for a "parade" to accompany Odin to his meeting with them. King Copley showed up and said he'd like to take his coppixer with him, to that meeting. He had to admit to Montour, that he didn't feel like picturing the robberies, and the loot from them.

The Chief and Chief Lady watched as a Noble drove their Odin-Cart, pulled by 3 huge, white-faced, dapple-skinned Percheron mares, down the rearward side ramp of the OdinShip. All 6 of the OdinShips were equipped with the same cart, 3 big horses and the stable to maintain them in.

The OdinCart floor was a massive 8-feet wide by 12-feet long. The 2 wheels were 6 feet in diameter, with the springs and axel suspended, so that the bed was but 18 inches off the ground, instead of being more than double that height. Getting on and off the cart, and loading and unloading it, was far easier for being so low. The 4 shafts going to the sides of the 3 horses were strapped to them, so they held the cart level at all times.

For this occasion, seats were held fast on the cart bed, so that more than 12 could easily ride on it. Chief Bushnell and Chief Lady Bushnell preferred to stand on either side of the Noble driver, hanging onto the "dashboard," so as to wave at the people on the way to the Westminster Palace. King Doctor Gale, King Copley, and red-coated Major General Baron Hay and his 2 aides, also rode on the Chief's OdinCart.

Most carts, wagons, and buckboards, had some sort of "dash-board" in the front. That was to ward off mud, dirt, and dung. Without the dashboard, those in the vehicle were bound to get splat-tered, with all sorts of nasty stuff, "dashed back," from their horse's iron-shod hooves.

Following close behind the OdinCart marched 200 Noble warriors.

Beside their OdinGuns, the Band Overlords carried OdinRock-Cannons, and their Nobles carried 2, 18-pound OdinRocks each, in their AndyPaks, strapped to their backs. The young leader of the world's newest nation was certain, they could overcome any resis-tance, that might be offered.

For this occasion, Chief Odin wore his "blues," as did his Chief Lady. Her many-pleated, knee-length skirt and her stockings were white. His blue trouzer had a gold stripe down each leg; the pressed creases were sewn in. He had by then, 2 rows of gleaming medals on his chest. The raised, gold-embroidered letters, on his shoulders, showed his rank of CHIEF and his collars told of the NUWORLD STATE.

Chief Odin also wore his Nuworld Crown, with the 14 equal-sized gemstones on the platinum band of it, and the 18 small regional gemstones, flashing colorfully in the sunlight. His gold-like Odin2Gun was holstered for this occasion, even though he was formally dressed.

The merely-knee-length, beautifully pleated white skirt on the Chief Lady, was bound to raise the eyebrows of men, and to-the-ground-skirted women, in the crowds lining the street. The Chief Lady too had a chest full of well-earned medals.

Literate Londoners were by then, aware of events in "their Prov-inces"; some of them up to the capture of Quebec, and were aware of various name changes, such as "Quebec" to "Stadacona." But they were quite ignorant of the great disaster falling on the French, at Louisbourg, and the even greater calamity for the British, on the Housatonic River. Only the latest issue of the NUWORLD NUZ covered those truly historic, earth-shaking battles, and the formation of the new nation, the Nuworld State.

Chief Odin was told he had been famous in London, for a year, from his previous year's exploits, in destroying the French hold on the Ohio valley. That and his Philadelphia speech had made him something of a hero, to thousands of Londoners.

Surprisingly, London's SPECTATOR MAGAZINE was so bold, as to report accurately on the arrest of Abraham Clark, and Earl Loudoun's humiliation in releasing him. Even reported was every word Duke Odin had spoken, to Lord Loudoun, and the obvious fright of the "Commander in Chief of all British Forces in North America," while urinating down his leg!

That magazine had also printed Duke Odin's surprisingly famous, Philadelphia speech, and more astonishing, his story of bad military rank names and all about his sense of Nobility.

That was certainly a daring public report, in such an oligarchical country. Surprisingly, the English actually enjoyed a fair degree of press freedom. It was said England's "middle class" had grown much richer in the last 50 years and were *increasingly politically aware*.

As the tall, muscular and handsome Chief, and the incomparably pretty Chief Lady, rode that cart on, they could hardly avoid noticing, that the air stank awfully, and was quite smoky.

Distilleries, breweries, gin mills and every sort of little business, were burning coal inefficiently, for the heat necessary in their operations. The streets were uniformly dirty breeding places, for biting flies, which were a constant irritant as those, and other insects, buzzed around everyone, all the day long and through the night.

The crowds of people along their parade route were silent, it being a scene, unforeseen. Many of the English knew something about the Nuworlders and stared at them with curiosity, but no resistance was offered.

✸ 2 3 ✸

Westminster Palace was a quite large building, and obviously 100s of years old. It seemed to be well weathered.

Kings Croghan and Eyre, and Overlord Biddle met Chief Odin and his Chief Lady Annie, on the grounds of the Palace. They knew it was where, 558 members of the Commons, and the 200 or so Lords, plus Church of England Bishops, met separately.

It was said King George was seated, on the Speaker of the Commons' throne-like chair. He was said to be eager, to meet the "infentor" of the OdinRazor, the OdinLamp, etc.

Croghan gave his Chief a broad grin, when he told him, "Sire, we've got the Spanish Ambassador in there, too. I'll be careful he doesn't get away, so I can go to work on him."

Odin thought: How perfect! He had told his Nobles, that they should brashly gather up all the Spanish language dictionaries, maps of Spanish territories and such, in book stores, when they could; but to be careful to pay for those things. The news of that intense interest, in their language and colonies, should give Spaniards something alarming to think about.

King Eyre said he guessed, they had inside about 250 Members of the Commons, and perhaps 24 Lords, and several Bishops.

The arrogant "First Minister to the King" William Pitt, was inside and was acting outraged, at being forced to come. He had blatantly claimed to be, "in command of the Government," while his ally, Lord Thomas Pelham, the Duke of Newcastle, "bought votes for the Government," in Parliament. Both of those dignitaries were designated, "Secretaries of State."

George II, the dull-headed Duke of Hanover, was crowned King of England (and laughably, also King of France!) at the age of 44, some 30 years before. Shockingly, George had said in his heavily accented English, that he hated England and everyone in it! And more besides! He visited his beloved Dukedom in the German part of Europe often but also relished the privileges, the fawning – and unearned – respect, and especially the wealth, bestowed on him as England's monarch. He had got that ticket to wealth, authority and privilege, by being fathered supposedly, by the previous King, Hanoverian George the 1st.

The Nuworlders heard King George hated William Pitt with a passion because Pitt had loudly objected to British troops, being sent to protect his Dukedom of Hanover in Germany, from the great onslaughts of the Prussians, under King Frederick. But Parliament had forced Pitt upon the King, as his main—or "First"—or "Prime"—Minister.

As the Nuworlders entered the Commons part, of Westminster Palace, they could see seats were almost filled. But almost no women were there. A wide aisle in the center of the big room led to a large table covered with a fancy cloth. The raised Speakers' Chair was just beyond that table, with the homely old King sitting on it. He and the rest were gaping at the formally-dressed Chief and Chief Lady, plus those accompanying them in buckskins. The Nuworlders were stared at, as though they had just dropped down from the moon.

However, some in the room hardly looked up, from the NUWORLD NUZ they were holding. They were reading the lists of English officers and men known to have been killed, and ships lost, on the Housatonic. Baron Hay had put himself and 3 Navy Yeomen to work, quizzing every survivor for names of ships and men killed. The list had no order to it, but by the persistence of those making it, they had named every warship, most of the much smaller troop transports, and nearly a remarkable 13,000 men; although more than that had surely been killed, it was thought.

At the head of the list was Earl Loudoun, and his French-spy-whore, at Stile's insistence. The accompanying article revealed, how the pretty blonde stood by the Earl, as they were both blasted to bits, by the awesome OdinRocks, fired at the very poop deck, they were standing on.

Stiles had the list printed in his NUWORLD NUZ. The list took an entire page and three quarters, and it was being read eagerly by those then, in Westminster Palace. From the Louisbourg disaster, no such list was made up; although the French, very much yet in shock as they sailed away, could have done that – but without a printing press—during the voyage to France.

George had half a dozen large, fancy medals on his red-coated chest, and Odin remembered he might, in fact, have earned one of them. English so-called "Royalty," actually wore inherited medals, in addition to other unearned privileges.

George had been in direct field command, of English and Allied Forces, fighting the French, at Dettingen, Bavaria, in 1743; that was 14 years before. His apparent courage there had helped to ease the dismay, the English felt for his insulting cantankerousness.

George's wife, Queen Caroline, and his oldest son, and Heir to the throne Frederick had died a few years before. It was said both King George, and his Queen violently detested their erratic, and surely insane, son Frederick, and felt no remorse when he died.

Their other living son, William, made Duke of Cumberland, had badly commanded the troops, that lost the Hannover Duchy to the Prussians. The frequently inept commander, returned to England, in disgrace, to reside at Windsor Castle.

King George's young grandson, Frederick's son, also named George, had a wife and an expanding brood of children. He was the not-very-bright Heir to the English throne that those in the British Isles had to look forward to.

Ezra Stiles asked Chief Odin, "Sire, have you written what you intend to say?"

The Chief leaned over to his long-time associate. "No, my friend; again, I'll be like the fiddler at a dance, and play it by ear."

Stiles grinned, knowing Odin was hardly so careless, as to merely make things up as he went along, whether written down or not.

Chief Odin and Chief Lady Annie, King Croghan and his Queen Molly, King Eyre, King Copley, King Doctor Gale, and Overlord Biddle; Misters Stiles, Bradford, and Eads; all took ordinary chairs, in the aisle just inside the hall, facing old King George. The Chief's 12-Noble Guard Band stood behind them, with Odin2Guns in hand, obviously "at the ready." Two other well-armed Bands were also there, to the left and to the right.

Seemingly forever self-confident, King George Croghan stepped forward, and raised both of his hands, to hush the crowd. In the light of the hall, King Croghan's title, spelled out in gold, sparkled nicely on his buckskinned shoulders.

Only then did King Copley rise to begin making coppix of everyone, and everything in that old hall. Somehow, the man and his apparatus seemed hardly to be noticed, for the time the Nuworlders were there. Coppixing was so new, it had not yet come to Europe.

"King of England, George the Second; Ladies, Lords, and Gentlemen," he roared out. "I am George Croghan, recently appointed by our Chief of the Nuworld State, as the King of our Diplomacy Realm. Most of you have just this day been informed of our new nation and of other news. I shall introduce our Chief of the Nuworld State, Odin Bushnell, to you in a few minutes.

"But first, you should very much want to hear what your own, British Army Major General, the Baron Charles Hay, has to say," the diplomatic one said, as he waved a hand toward the small, thin, 50-year-old, but handsome man, in his bright, blood-red English army uniform.

Lord Hay seemed nervous, as he stepped to the middle of the aisle. He nodded to Croghan, and bowed to his own sovereign, and to the new Chief, as he doffed his tricorne hat.

"Your Majesty," the Baron said, addressing King George, "may recall I was ordered to meet with His Majesty's Commander, Earl Loudoun, for the purpose of leading troops, in the taking of France's Fortress Louisbourg, across the Atlantic Ocean. I arrived in Halifax harbor, aboard Admiral Holburne's flagship, on July 11th, last.

"It was a disgusting shock for me, to see that instead of preparing to assault Louisbourg, as ordered by Your Majesty, Earl Loudoun was actually idle. He had your soldiers planting vegetables, instead of training for the battle. Of course, I spoke loudly, and clearly, that we were ordered to take the French Fortress Louisbourg, and not cultivate cabbages!

"I urged action, and Loudoun took unbelievably extreme offense, at such criticism. Although I was a fellow general, in the same Army with more – very much more—experience at war, than he had, he arrested me, Sire. Loudoun charged me with insubordination and had me locked up in a small room, on Holburne's ship. I was to remain there, I was told until I was returned to England for Court Martial.

"But I was absolutely certain, I would be poisoned or thrown overboard, by that dull-headed crowd, so the truth would be buried far at sea, as has so often happened before.

"Your Majesty's fleet, and all those assault troops, at last, sailed not for Louisbourg, to do battle with the French, but they retreated like dogs, with their tails between their legs, to New York harbor. The cowardly Loudoun could not believe, he had overwhelming force, to ensure a victory. The fleet was anchored at New York, for some weeks, until it sailed one last time.

"The next thing I knew, I could sense the ship, was again under sail. I heard the ship's guns firing, shaking the very timbers of the ship. Instantly, that firing was followed by the most awful screams! In the blink of an eye, I found myself in the water, clinging to the wooden door of my cabin. Everywhere around me, Your Majesty's warships were burning, and blowing up, sky-high! I saw screaming through the air, the Nuworlder's rockets, called by them OdinRocks. The Nuworlders were blasting, and burning, our huge warships! Within just minutes, every one of our ships was totally destroyed! Transports and all! *All of them were destroyed in minutes.*

"Shortly, Nuworlders in boats came to haul myself, and the other few survivors, of that most astonishing of calamities, to shore.

"That very evening Your Majesty, I was taken by their King of Nobility, to the Chief of State of their new nation, the Nuworld State.

"I told Chief Odin the truth, as I have told you, Sire. The Nuworlders have brought me, and about 900 other survivors of that disaster, home. About 800 other English survivors, chose to enjoy the liberties, and the opportunities for prosperity, in that new and innovative nation. They will not return to England. I talked to them myself, and I assure Your Majesty, they stayed of their own free will. That Sire has got to speak loudly, of their feelings for your Army, and for your Navy, and the grossly incompetent commanders we had over there.

"As unbelievable as it may seem, Sire, we came to London, on their new steam-powered, steel OdinShips, not in the rather usual *72 days'* voyage, but in *72 hours*. It's hard to believe, but the voyage required, a mere 3 days time, across the wild Atlantic Ocean.

"Chief Odin has told me, that our two nations are now at war, and he shall have a Peace Treaty signed by Your Majesty, this very day, or he shall burn his Majesty's entire Capital of London town down, this very night!

"No treaty agreement and the Nuworlders will most certainly burn our London town down Sire, this very night," the English General repeated, putting his strong voice on each word.

The sound of 1,000-people breathing in all at once was awesome.

"Your Majesty, as an old soldier, I know military power when I see it.

"I have witnessed the destruction, by the Nuworlders, of 29 of your warships, 57 of your transports, and many 1,000s of your soldiers, sailors, and marines, in no more than a matter of minutes — *86 English ships destroyed, in no more than a matter of minutes, sire.* I wish to assure Your Majesty, with no treaty signed, they very certainly can, and will, burn London town down, to mere rubble and ashes, this very night!"

Again, as 1,000s gasped at his words, Lord Hay bowed again to his King, and to the Chief, and hurried over to a bench to take a seat.

King Croghan jumped up, and again raised both of his hands, to still the crowd.

"King George, Ladies, Lords and Gentlemen," King Croghan roared again, "I now have the very great privilege, of introducing the conqueror of New France... the amazing destructor of forts and fleets.... scientific inventor without peer in the history of the world.... our unequaled friend.... the exalted leader of the Nuworlders, CHIEF OF THE NUWORLD STATE, ODIN BUSHNELL!"

Odin nodded his thanks to Croghan, for that colorful introduction, and stepped briskly forward. He stepped more nearly, to the center of the hall.

Tiers of seats were to his left and right, and the German King of the United Kingdom, was sitting bug-eyed and attentive, straight-ahead 5 or 6 paces.

There was no doubt the young, tall, muscular and handsome master of the new nation, had the undivided attention, of the crowd of wealthy and powerful men. At every breath, the medals on his chest flashed their gold, silver, bronze and blued iron, shiny beams.

Chief Odin figured this was no time to criticize that audience and their government, as was so certainly deserved.

King Elias Tully had said to him, "Sometimes you have to get ahold, of the old cow barn shovel, and spread it on good."

But Chief Odin thought he shouldn't spread the smelly stuff on, too obviously thick.

"King George," he roared, filling the hall with his powerful voice, "we Nuworlders have tried to comprehend, why your forces would attack us; allies in our war with France. We had, of course, prepared the defenses of our small city of Stratford, on the Housatonic, in the *former* English Colony of Connecticut, in case of an assault... *by the French; but not by the English*."

The Chief was especially careful to let them know, Connecticut was *formerly* a Colony. Saying that he hoped he got through to them, those colonies over there, were no longer English.

"We knew the French might relish destroying our various mills, shipyards, ironworks, gunpowder works, and arsenal. We supposed they would want to rob our rich treasury.

"It turned out, it was your own, pathetically incompetent commanders, who had such evil visions against the allies, friends, kin and solid customers, of the British Isles.

"We feel with some confidence, such orders to attack us, to burn our homes, our churches, our schools, our mills and all that, could not have come from you, sir.

"However, anyone on earth might castigate this or that facet, of the government of the British Isles, no one can imply your Kingdom, is without honor."

The Chief hoped he hadn't shoveled that on too deeply.

"I won't speculate on your commander's very faulty reasoning, that they could easily defeat us with bombardments, of red-hot-shot, from your 22 ships-of-the-line and 5 frigates; plus, they had 2 bomb ketches to throw, their fire-filled hell at us. But it was proved once again, that red-hot-cannonballs are at least as dangerous, to the sender, as to the receiver.

"Your British fleet burnt down 78 of our new, and much-loved homes, 2 of our children's very-much-prized schools, 2 taverns, 1 store, and 1 truly beautiful new Christian Church. They did all that with a single broadside, from those ships. That was all I allowed, before returning hell upon them with our deadly weapons.

"I wished this new and obvious enemy to fire the first shot. That was all I permitted, sir.

"They got off 1 broadside, and that sealed the death warrants for about 18,000 of your subjects, and for all of your ships present that day, on our Housatonic River.

"They should have known about the 5 French warships, Nuworlders obliterated in the Caribbean, last winter, with our terrifically powerful new weapons. They must have had knowledge of our victories, north of the Hudson River, this summer. How could they be so blockheadedly stupid, as to disregard those known facts of our military power?

"However, your commanders could not have known, before they

sailed from New York, about our absolute destruction, in Louisbourg harbor of the Island Battery, the Lighthouse Battery, the Royal Battery, 18 large French men-o-war, and 5 frigates. All of that was accomplished, only a few days before the English attack on us, in merely, *8 1/2 minutes*.

"We did that, *with a single Battle Force*, on 8 steam-engine-powered OdinBoats, including my own OdinBoat.

"Another of our Battle Forces, with their 7 OdinBoats, crawled through, and conquered the town of Louisbourg, and its defensive walls, within 1/2 hour, at the same time.

"As if the attack on us, on the Housatonic River, wasn't idiotically stupid enough, your commander sent in, almost 200 cavalrymen, to charge into the other side of our town, with drawn swords. We suppose they were to happily lop off the heads, of any innocent Nuworlders they might meet.

"Within a few minutes of beginning their hell-bent ride sir, they were all riddled with shots, from nearly 2,000 of our Odin2Guns, of the Battle Force, sent to protect the town from that direction... *of course*. Not one of them survived, that senseless charge to oblivion.

"It's true; our honorable Nobles there were somewhat well hidden, behind a stone wall, and took those English cavaliers, charging toward our innocent town, pretty much by surprise.

"But still, *attacking with drawn swords, while making themselves perfect targets high up on horseback,* was ignorantly suicidal. They were all slaughtered quickly, to the last rider. It is simply impossible they didn't know, about the rapid and accurate firepower of our handguns. Yet, they charged at an entire Nuworld Battle Force, on horseback, incredibly making themselves perfect targets, for our highly accurate sharpshooters."

Chief Odin paused to let all of that sink in.

It seemed the bags around the ancient King's eyes, were bulging out even baggier.

Glancing left and right, Odin reckoned there could be skepticism, as though he could be exaggerating or even lying, about those tiny short times it took for victory.

"Our sincere hope is that we shall never again, need to create so much death, and destruction, as we have lately been obliged to do.

"But I assure you, King George, if we must, we shall very certainly, on all occasions, apply all the deadly force necessary, to win the day.

"Most assuredly, we absolutely could use all the deadliness, we have available, to win the day, on this particular occasion as well.

"Of course, all of us Nuworlders understand that you in England, and probably in most of Europe, must think us of the Nuworld, much too brazen and bold, to call those men and women in our Nobility, *Noblemen, and Noblewomen.* In this Old World, one must be *born to such titles.*

"But George, since I have the incomparably great honor, to be the leader of the Nuworld, *I am the one to make the rules. In the Democratic Commonwealth Monarchy, of the Nuworld State, only those who actually earn such honors shall ever have them.*

"And you must understand, that since we have such brave and intelligent Nobles, and since we furnish them with such powerful weapons, the total conquest of our entire continent, is only a question of how soon, that goal shall be accomplished.

"Now then; we have printed a Treaty of Peace, for you to agreeably sign today, to end this ugly war between our 2 nations, that your own incompetent commanders have begun.

"You have heard from your truly excellent and outstanding, Major General Lord Baron Charles Hay, what the consequences absolutely must be if you refuse. *As all the many Gods on this earth are my witness sir, we shall do as we promise.*

"You may have heard that we have, 2 extremely powerful Battle Forces right now, robbing your banks, your trading companies, your goldsmiths and your Tower of London."

There were more astonishing sounds of air being sucked into 100s of lungs.

"As I have said, the people of these Sceptered Isles have been an honorable people, most of them priding themselves in being charitable, God-loving Christians, with you as their Pope."

Again, he hoped he hadn't shoveled the stinky stuff on too awfully deep.

"And yet amazingly, your prideful Christian nation has made brutal, bloody wars to gain a monopoly in the buying, distributing and selling of human beings; humans not different from all other humans, except for being from Africa and with dark skin.

"The Golden Rule is much more preached than practiced by this country, it would seem.

"Whatever happened here to the phrase, 'Love thy neighbor as thyself'?

"I assure you, sir, whatever riches may be gained in our actions today, shall be partly in compensation, for the losses your fleet inflicted on our town. But such wealth as we take back with us shall mostly pay for the education, feeding, transport, and establishment of Africans, back to freedom, and their self-made prosperity, in their natural, rich home continent of Africa.

"It is so surprising that you, King George, as the Head of the Christian Church of England, should personally profit from your shares, in the slave-trading, Royal African Company. Do you deny this, sir?"

The old King seemed not to understand the question and did not reply.

"George the Second," Chief Odin roared out with measured words, "King of this United Kingdom of Great Britain, I ask you again: *Have you, or have you not*, profited from your shares, in the Royal African Company's, trading in slaves?"

The old man suddenly stood up. He teetered a bit and seemed unsure of himself. He steadied himself with a hand, on the arm of the chair. He stood tall with his chest puffed out.

"Chief of the Nuworld Odin, sir! Yes, yes, I do admit to such shameful profit! I am sorry to say that many in England have become very rich, through trading in Negroes.

"In this country, which prides itself in the glory of many freedoms, we enslave, we put to chains, and we apply the lash, to those of a different race of men.

"Chief Odin, do you believe we can end, this horrible practice?" King George asked.

That was the surprisingly remorseful admission, Odin could hardly have hoped for.

"Yes, George; yes, we can and yes, we shall! We can cooperate in ending that evil business, and we will work out the details later," the Chief said.

"But what of the slaves presently held, on your islands of Jamaica, Barbados, the Bermuda's and the Bahamas?"

"You will see in the Peace Treaty, our King Croghan is about to present to you, that you must cede to us, all of the territories you now claim, in our Nuworld, north of the Equator.

"We shall take full responsibility then, for the repatriation of all those African slaves, your people and our people too, formerly owned.

"Also, I must add," Chief Odin said, "we must not ever again have Light-skinned people, nor Tan-skinned people, nor Brown-skinned people, nor Gray-skinned people, nor Black-skinned people, condemned to slavery again.

"You have allowed your own citizens to become slaves, for some years as indentured servants. That must stop. We will gladly bring them over to our shores, for free. And we shall bring them quickly, safely, cleanly, and even respectfully, in our steamships; both people of the British Isles and of Europe. For those of good character, and with plenty of ambition, we will loan them money, so they can get a good start in our *Nuworld, our Free World, our Brightest Rich Part, of the Whole World.*"

Chief Odin especially enjoyed speaking his famous phrase, with strength on every word.

"I must add that prior to the arrival, of so many foolishly arrogant, English Army and Navy officers, and your money-grubbing politicians, to our shores—and before your wicked Navy wrongfully enslaved, so many of our young men—the people of our Nuworld had great, nostalgic affection for England, and almost everything English.

"I fondly hope, and I do expect that good trading relations and true affections can be restored, in a fruitful peace between our 2 nations. I sincerely believe your countrymen, and ours, will find it far more happily profitable, to have free trade, and peace between us, than to continue this violent, bloody, ugly war.

"Please sit still now, and listen closely to King Croghan. He has much to add," he said.

Chief Odin returned to his chair, next to Chief Lady Annie, noticing that 100s of pairs of eyes, were taking in the truly perfect blonde beauty, of his porcelain doll.

Croghan spoke loudly but soothingly, directly to the old King.

The crowd left, and right was listening, and watching as though at a stage play. It seemed their somber attention, was riveted to each speaker.

Holding the printed parchment up, Croghan said, "I shall read the explicit, and uncomplicated provisions in this Treaty of Peace, for Your Majesty's kind consideration:

"The Chief of the Nuworld State, and the King of the United Kingdom of Great Britain, do mutually pledge, to make no further acts of war, against the other, after this date; such as the killing of the other's Citizens, the destruction of Cities, Towns, Villages, Estate Houses, Castles, Palaces, Apartments, Stores, Ports, military and naval forces and shipping, etc."

(Chief Odin had insisted, on listing some of the Oligarch's, vulnerable properties.)

"In exchange for that pledge by the Nuworlders, the United Kingdom pledges here and now, to abrogate all its (by whatever name) grants of land on the Continent—heretofore styled North America, but forever after to be called the Nuworld—and adjacent islands, north of the Equator. This includes those grants by appointed British representatives and governors, etc. The United Kingdom does here and now, cede to the Nuworld State, any sort of claims it has made in the past, to all and every such territories, in the Nuworld.

"There can be no exceptions whatsoever.

"Companies based in the British Isles that may have had claims, to territories on said Continent of the Nuworld, such as the Hudson's Bay Company, shall from this date be dissolved.

"Particularly, the United Kingdom shall dissolve the Royal African Company, as both nations signing this Treaty today, do pledge to cease enslaving humans and to end slave trading.

"Within 5 years, the Nuworld State pledges, to return to Africa, all slaves now employed on former English-ruled Caribbean Islands, as well as on the Nuworld continent.

"Seven years is so very sadly, the present life expectancy of the average, cruelly-treated, and malnourished slave, on the Caribbean Islands, formerly claimed by the United Kingdom.

"Further, the United Kingdom shall not impede, the transport of its citizens to the Nuworld State, who may wish to emigrate there, for a more happily prosperous life."

That was the last line in that straightforward document.

"So, you see King George, this Treaty relieves your government, of all responsibility to make laws, or provide protection for the people, on that Continent, or on those islands, across the Atlantic Ocean.

"This Treaty will save your citizens, and your government, great amounts of money—money that you can much better lavish, on the good people of all the British Isles.

"Such is the simplicity of our Peace Treaty, sir. Now, our Chief of the Nuworld State, has some very important additional things, to mention to you," King Croghan said.

King Croghan sat down, and Chief Odin took his place again, on the aisle.

"King George, as a friendly nation, your people may like to share, in some of our inventions. The more brilliant of our present inventions, by the King of our Ritting Realm, David Rittenhouse, is a system of sending messages, through the atmosphere, over long distances.

"That is how we were able to communicate, with our Ambassador to Prussia, who has arranged a particularly important meeting.

"I shall meet tomorrow, with King Frederick of Prussia, and King Louis of France.

"We will steam over to the French port of LeHarve, beginning tonight, whether London is to be burnt down to ashes, or not.

"You sir, are invited to that meeting. You may like to discuss with King Frederick, the future of your Hanover Duchy.

"The Spanish Ambassador is also cordially welcome to accompany us.

"Another matter is that your people will be officially invited to join with our people, in improving the English language. Our Education Realm has already begun that important work.

"Sir, do you or your Ministers have any questions now?" the Chief asked.

Proving that he was paying rapt attention, King George immediately hollered to a tall, skinny man on the front bench to Odin's left.

"Mr. Pitt! What have you to say about all this?" George asked. "And I want to know, who ordered the unforgivable, and stupid attack on the Nuworlders, that Loudoun made?"

Chief Odin had noticed that man Pitt, and the man next to him, he had been told was Lord Thomas Pelham, the Duke of Newcastle. Both seemed in shock at what had been said.

Pitt stood and bowed to King George – but not to Chief Odin. It was a subtle snub, and it was noticed.

"Majesty," Pitt shrilly said to his King, with an unpleasant scowl on his long face, "I merely suggested to Earl Loudoun, that if the Louisbourg affair was not then attainable, he should get his just dues, from the extraordinarily impertinent, damnable and ignorant provincials, who, with no authority whatever, foolishly and scandalously, gave sacred Noble titles to altogether undeserving peasants.

"Not only that, but they have lied damnably, about the great casualties among their enemies, caused by mere pistols, and how few hurts they had of their own. All such of their claims are clearly impossible! That mad statement of destroying the French fleet and 3 powerful gun batteries, in a few minutes is quite the tale of nonsense!" Pitt screamed contemptuously.

There it was, finally out in the open, the resentment Nuworlders knew, had to be boiling among English "aristocrats," about the Nuworld Nobility.

But the untitled William Pitt was not actually of the aristocracy; he inherited his somewhat considerable wealth, through robberies by his grandfather in India.

Most English titles of nobility came down even then, from William the Bastard, Duke of Normandy, who had conquered England in 1066 – 691-years before—by killing the rightful English King Harold, on the plains of Hastings. Then he rewarded his French followers, after their ravaging, raping, pillaging, slaughtering-of-landowners, with grants of land and inheritable titles.

They were rightly called knights – the Saxon word *k-nig-hts* – those evil *k-naves* whose long sharp *k-nives* brought *night* – death's darkness – to their victims.

It was amazing to Odin that they would insult Sir Isaac Newton with "knighthood." Newton had brought much light, to the subject of light, ending the darkness of understanding, about that subject. Plus of course, Newton made big strides forward, in mathematics.

Rather than answer Pitt directly, Chief Odin roared out his words to King George.

"Your Mr. Pitt, sir" he shouted, unholstering his Odin2Gun, in a menacing fashion, and noticing from the corner of his eye, that men around Pitt were scrambling away, "has bragged that he had taken command, of the English government, of the English Navy and the English Army, and that he and he alone could save England! And yet he knows nothing of war! He knows nothing of the weapons of war!

"How could he not know that Frederick of Prussia, has won victory after victory with the OdinGun, similar to this one?" he shouted, holding the golden-hued weapon up for all to see.

"You give that King very little credit, for his great military genius, methinks!" Pitt screamed that out in a sneering way, acting with hollow bravado.

"King George, let us educate your insubordinate subordinate. I could shoot him in the face, and he'd have chopped liver for a brain!" Odin shouted.

Then, first seeming to aim at Pitt's head, but swiftly lowering his yellow brass gun, he put a shot into the floor in front of the man. KA-BOOM!

"Or I could shoot him in the neck, and practically decapitate him instantly with this gun!" Odin roared matter-of-factly, *again raising and then lowering his weapon to shoot into the floor. KA-BOOM!*

"I could also shoot a hole in his chest with my Odin2Gun, and you could almost put your fist right through him!" he said very loudly.

He put another shot into the floor, in front of Pitt. KA-BOOM!

Only after the third shot into the floor, did he look to see what damage had been done. Odin was surprised, to see three jagged holes through the thin oak flooring, and on through the pine planking, under that. He could actually see into the basement of Westminster Palace!

He could also see through the gun smoke, that Pitt had fainted, and fallen backwards onto the seat, where he had been. As he re-upholstered his Odin2Gun, he called out behind him.

"King Doctor Gale, would you please bring Mr. Pitt around? He doesn't seem to have enjoyed my teaching," the Chief shouted out, with a sober look.

How silent that hall was just then! People all around seemed to be stiff with terror, seeing a demonstration of a weapon that was fired repeatedly, without being reloaded!

Odin noticed with each shot, that the dull-headed old King merely jumped a little, from the stupendous noise bouncing around in the hall. But George seemed to be numbly unafraid, true to his reputation for unmindful bravery, unlike most of the others present in the hall.

King Doctor Gale grinned, and whispered to Chief Odin as he came by, "Sire, you sure do make a racket with your lessons!"

As Gale poured water from his canteen, onto the limp Pitt's fore-head, it seemed not to have any effect. He didn't stir. He didn't moan. The doctor said there was no pulse. Pitt's unseeing eyes and mouth, were wide open, giving him a startled look. The Doctor slapped his face, shook him, and lifted his arm to see it fall limp.

Finally, he said, "Chief Odin, it would seem you frightened this man to death! Just like that old General Webb, at Fort Lyman!"

But Daniel Webb had obviously been a sick old man, and Pitt

had seemed healthy, although high strung, skinny and pale. Four men hauled the limp form away.

There was no pity from King George, who was known to thoroughly detest the man.

He shouted down to Lord Pelham, "Good riddance, I say. Newcastle, I want you to look over that Peace Treaty, right now!"

The Duke nervously glanced through the document and, displaying little emotion over the death of his partner in government, handed it up to his King, while nodding his approval.

The Duke of Newcastle bowed graciously, to the shooter.

"Chief of State Odin of the remarkable Nuworlders, I am no natural philosopher or scientist, so I have no questions about your inventions. It is enough for me to understand; the power you have in your fabulous weapons.

"But my question Chief Odin is this: you have in our – *no sir, in your Southern Colonies* – many thousands of Negroes enslaved, and you have merchants there involved in the slave trade; won't this be a big problem for you? And oh yes, mayn't you have some difficulty with taking land away from them, sir?" the Duke of Newcastle asked.

"Excellent questions, Duke!" Odin smiled at him while speaking loudly, so all in the hall could hear. "Let me answer your Lordship's last question first.

"You see, we won't exactly be taking land away, from any of our citizens – oh no, quite the opposite. We will put it to – oh, say a large planter claims to own, 10,000 acres – we will put it to him, that we are giving him 1,000,000s of acres!

"Also, he and every one of us shall own tremendous, endless forests! And mines beyond counting, producing gold, silver, copper, iron, coal, salt, and so many precious things!

"You and I know a truly selfish man, will not wish to share all we offer, with the other citizens of our State, their children and to the furthest grandchildren. He might not care a whit, about the education, health, and welfare, of anyone but himself, and his own family.

"We understand that, and we will deal with such men, as well as those who have better hearts and brighter heads.

"Regarding returning Negroes to their natural homeland, we can be sure, there will be more than a little objection to this by some. Present slave owners will fear being financially ruined, and no one likes that prospect; no more than those innocent people, who were not just financially ruined but lost everything that mattered, from being enslaved.

"Those dark-skinned people, as human as any other peoples on earth, not only were financially ruined, but cruelly lost their freedoms, their natural dignity, their self-respect, their self-confidence, and often their health, friends, family and too often, they lost their very lives.

"We think there is not much comparison as to the losses borne, by slaves and by slavers, Lord Pelham," Chief of State Odin told him.

The Duke smiled. He seemed to have recovered quickly, from the death of Pitt.

"It is perfectly clear to me Chief Odin," he said, "why you were elected to be the Chief of the Nuworld State. All of us have read and pondered your especially beautiful Philadelphia speech. That remarkable speech was a genuine gem, Chief Odin," the Duke said.

"Thank you for those compliments," Odin said. "Now, King Croghan will have our Nobles pass around copies of the Treaty, we have printed for the information of everyone here."

The hall soon rustled with people reading the paper copies of the 4, calf-skin parchments, meant for the State and the Kingdom.

The reading time was short, and there seemed to be little chagrin, over losing the costly and troublesome, North American Colonies.

The loss of the English pride in being an "Empire," might be another matter, when time allowed them to reflect, and the Nuworld's 3 powerful Battle Forces, were no longer near. But the English still had newly successful battles, with the French and the Dutch, for control of the rich sub-continent of India, and the many 1,000,000s of *actual Indians* living there.

King George was royally gracious when introduced to Chief Lady Annie, King Croghan, and his Mohawk Queen. He narrowed his eyes when introduced to King Eyre but apparently didn't recognize him. He remarked, though, "Dare was a fort, ofer dare, wid dat name."

Odin noticed that when George was introduced to Annie, the old lecher removed her clothes with his eyes. He had been getting away with that, his whole privileged adult life.

King Croghan very soon, had the parchments ready to sign.

King George, 4 of his ministers, then Chief Odin, Kings Croghan, Copley and Eyre, all signed the documents.

Chief Odin wished to add some popularity to their King, so he said softly to the Duke of Newcastle, "Your King George has just saved your London town, from being burnt to endless piles of rubble."

Newcastle said nothing but solemnly nodded agreement to the Chief.

Servants were sent to fetch fresh clothing, for the King and his ministers.

Then the parade in reverse was underway, back to the OdinShips, with King George standing upfront on the OdinCart. People along the way waved, and bowed, and even curtseyed, to their King, standing next to Chief Odin and Chief Lady Annie. He waved back graciously. The old lecher actually looked rather majestic.

24

OdinShipOne's ramp wheels were laid down on the Custom
House Dock, for easy walking up into the ship. Wheels
were necessary to allow the large and small ramp's movements, during tide level changes. Bundles of rope were dangling
between the ships and the wharf, to prevent damage from the two
rubbing together.

King George marveled at the sight, commenting on the size of
the ships, and the huge white letters on the bright iron-oxide-red,
sides of the OdinShips. Chief Odin advised the old King that
STADACONA was the original and proper name for the captured
city of Quebec.

George expressed surprise that there were no masts or sails, or
rigging above the weather deck. There was only the little square
pilothouse, with the beautiful, 4-feet wide, circular, bracketed, brass
Nuworld flag, swaying with the breeze on a pole.

Chief Odin explained to King George that the British ensign
would soon go up, and the Nuworld flag would come down until they
were beyond the Thames River forts. That was so as not to begin a
shooting war, with those forts. It was captured French maps of the

Thames River that showed the Nuworlders, where those English forts were.

Most of the carts, wagons, and horses were gone from the wharf, having been returned to – or at least made available to – their Londoner owners. The huge OdinCarts and the horses for each OdinShip had been returned to the ships, and the loot safely secured and stored away.

Chief Odin took his guests on a tour, of the boiler room amidship, and then showed them the steam engines, that turned the huge bucket wheels upfront. He briefly explained how the boiler, engines, and pumps worked, but the guests surely grasped little of it.

They next climbed up to the pilothouse slowly, as the 74-year-old King George, was easily winded. He was, for that time, a very old man; and he looked older than being only 74.

After Captain MacDougal spoke of the instruments there, the group went forward to the prow, just as the vessels began to move out into the river, away from the wharf.

They could feel the throbbing of the engines, and the guests allowed as how the OdinShip, seemed to be a gigantic living thing.

In the dim light of the smoky evening, they could see the water boiling, in the wake of the other OdinShips, they were following, downstream on the Thames River.

The huge metropolis of London town began to fade in the distance. It wasn't burning to ashes, as it most certainly could have been.

Chief Lady Annie joined them on the prow and announced dinner would soon be ready, and that the gentlemen had just enough time to wash up.

King George was escorted to a kingly suite, as were his ministers.

Chief Odin and his Chief Lady ducked into their apartment, and checked their formal raiment, with their hard-earned medals and all. He kept his Crown on over his black waves, and she combed the gorgeous curls of blondeness, crowning her beautiful head.

King Montour stepped in to say, "Sire, you simply cannot believe the gold and silver, we put aboard our OdinShips this day! Tons and tons! Our State is now very much richer!"

"Well King Andrew," Odin replied, "we promised to spread Treasury Valts, all over our country, to loan working money to men, for starting businesses, and building houses and such. We'll also need to make loans to cities, so they can begin, providing necessary services. We'll need probably a lot more, to back our paper money, by mining silver or stealing it – as the English have done. But of course, much of that loot from today must be dedicated to helping the Africans back to their homeland. Please keep in mind, my friend, we can never have too much silver, so we must try to capture a Spanish treasure fleet.

"Also, dear King of the Nobility, please spare me a little time later tonight. I'd very much like to have your opinion on something, I've been thinking of," the Chief said.

"Of course, Sire," King Montour said. "And I should mention too, that Baron Hay disappeared immediately when we left Whitehall Palace. Nobles have told me, that he seems to have gotten a pledge of allegiance to him, from those prisoners we brought back. He seems to have told them that every Irish man and woman, and the Scots, Welsh and English, are all one British Isles people; and every one of them must be treated as such. He's got some kind of plan going, Sire, but I don't know what to make of it."

"That's very interesting," the Chief replied. "But, I must think it's the business of these people and none of our affair."

In the knotty-pine paneled dining room, Chief Odin made sure the Chief Lady headed the table. He was seated to her right, with King George to her left.

Nuworld Kings – now in their formal blues, medals and all—and English ministers, were seated beyond them, and further down were the ever-curious newspapermen.

Spain's Ambassador to the United Kingdom was seated next to King Croghan, and that invited diplomat seemed in wonder of it all.

Chief Odin explained to his guests, the reasons on his crown for the 14 beautiful large gemstones, that represented the courage, and most especially the generosity, of the 14 men who gave most of their hard-earned, and really great fortunes, to the new nation. Then he explained the reason for the 18 glittering little gems representing Regions, on his Crown.

As the diners were beginning to devour their delicious clam chowder, they could see the liquid sloshing in their bowls. A sudden strong wind was having fun with the 4 OdinShips.

Captain MacDougal soon appeared, and informed them, that all of the OdinShips were gathering on the lee of the south shore, to ride out the howling storm. They were still about 20 miles from the sea.

Some light rain was also pelting the vessel, and Odin mused to himself, that except for the wind, London town might not have burned really well after all.

"Very well, Captain," the Chief said, "but we have an appointment in LeHarve."

"Aye, aye Sire, but hopefully by morning, the storm will have blown itself out, as usually happens here," said the good ship's Captain.

The guests enjoyed the tale, of the Nuworlders recovering from the Caribbean Sea floor, the made-in-China "Blue Willow" dishes they ate from. But all of them were accustomed to eating the choicest foods, from the finest dinnerware, anyway.

They had all read of the Nuworld Company's recovery, of the tons of treasure from the Caribbean Sea sands. But Stiles in his NUWORLD NUZ had been careful not to reveal how it was discovered, through the "see the sea scopes" and the cranes, and so forth, with which it was brought up onto the 1st of the OdinRafts, 2 years before, in 1755.

The visitors were astounded with a lobster dinner, brought along alive in the ice room.

When they had finished with the tiny huckleberries in the ice cream, Chief Odin thought it a good opportunity, to speak about slavery. He, at last, noticed that King Copley wasn't present, so he must have become extraordinarily busy with "developing," after making so many coppix that day, of London, and of the events at the Whitehall Palace.

But first, the Chief made the error of asking King George as a courtesy, about the battles of Dettingen in Bavaria. That was where English, Hanoverian, Hessian, Austrian and Dutch Coalition Troops, under George, had beaten the formidable French, 14 years before.

A man more excited in relating his experiences would be hard to imagine. Apparently, no one had asked the 74-year-old King George, to tell the tale for a long time.

England's German monarch, George II, recalled every single move of every unit, no matter the country they were from. That was remarkable for a man so old and considered by many, to be quite the dullard.

Proudly, George had been wounded but not grievously.

King George was amazingly long-winded, and talked in his bad English, *for 3 hours.*

The old King had been born to a life, of easy privilege, but was prideful to have endured the hardships, and inconveniences on actual, death-dealing, fields of battle.

King George finally "ran out of air," and they all retired to their suites.

Chief Odin noticed that his guests were too shy, to inquire about the medals on his chest, as well as those on the Chief Lady, King Croghan, King Montour, King Copley, and King Eyre. Among the last ones Odin won for bravery, at Fort Eyre, was the gleaming, Eleven Feathered Gold Crown for Courage, with a tiny ruby on it. Others gleaming in yellow gold on his blue jacket were the Eleven Feathered Gold Crowns for Leadership. Those were earned after the Fort Eyre defeat of the French. It was largely Grand Duke Odin's planning that helped to defeat every fort and city in their conquest of Canada.

The Chief visited King Montour in his suite.

"Well, my friend," Odin said, "I've been thinking that our Nobles ought to have an identifying number, and their name, put on them. That would be so if, in battle, they were killed and maybe their jacket was gone, and their face was no longer recognizable, they could still be positively identified.

"Those dead French and British fished out of the waters after those battles, could have been easily identified, if they had such markings. And in the future, when citizens ask for their money in our Treasury branches, or when they're voting, they could be positively identified if they had their name and oh, some sort of birth number on them someplace," Chief Odin said.

After considering markings on a hand or elsewhere, the 2 decided on the underside of a person's left forearm. They thought a "birth number" should be the year born, the month, day, and a 4-or-even-6-digit time of day, of one's birth. That would be 10 or 12 digits, in a person's birth number. Someone duplicating that number with the exact same name would be extremely unlikely, Odin supposed.

It would be definitely rare, that there were duplicate numbers, since there were 1,440 minutes plus 60 seconds in every minute, in a day to choose from! Above the "birth number," would be their first, middle, and last name. Marrying women could keep their maiden name; it would be their choice.

People would only need to reveal those permanent marks to identify themselves. Ordinarily, their clothing would hide that information, probably from age 18 on. But when voting, when withdrawing money, from their Treasury accounts, people must be positively identified.

Maybe the time to put that identifying information on a person would be at birth, the Chief thought. As the arm grew, so would the markings grow.

The Chief told Montour to say nothing about those marks just yet since he was going to revise the calendar. Birthdates for people would change for everyone, with the new calendar. It could be tried first in the Nobility, to see if Nobles objected, and the reasons for objecting. The Chief and that King would be the first, to have the markings pricked under their forearm skin. Surely, Chief Lady Annie would bravely be the first example, for Nuworld womenfolk.

Annie woke Odin, well before dawn the next morning. They were pleased that the storm's wind had died down a lot, and the rain had ceased to fall. Looking out, however, they could see a starry sky, was mostly hidden by gray clouds.

They showered and dressed in their formal blue raiment, but he left his Crown behind as they headed for breakfast.

They could feel the heartbeat of the engines, telling them the big wheels hugging the hull, near the prow, was throwing back great amounts of exhaust-gas-bubble-filled water.

King Croghan caught Chief Odin in the hall before they ate. "I believe Sire, I've done well with Spain's Ambassador. He was amazed at how much I knew, about the defenses of Havana, and I assured him, you could take that place in a quarter hour! But I told him we merely wanted Florida but didn't wish to kill even a single proud Spaniard in taking it.

"Also, I assured him you would soon possess Louisiana and would insist on having the entire continent north of the south edge, of the Rio Grande outlet into the Gulf; then straight west on a line to the Pacific.

"There are practically no Spaniards above that line I told him, as it is all desert and we knew California was not an island, but a peninsula, and that must be included. He and I have signed the agreement I made up, which of course will have no effect unless agreed to, by Spain's King Ferdinand the Sixth. But it's a start, Chief Odin," the great diplomat said.

"Wow! My King! You are a piece of work! The Spaniards will think us dangerous and unpredictable neighbors. King Andrew showed you his captured maps of the place, then? I mean, those we discovered at Fort Duquesne and in Canada?" Odin asked.

"Oh yes Sire, and King Montour has lots of information – oh, such as how profitable it is to the Spanish Crown, for them to bring to Spain, Cuban tobacco, which they process in Spain's factories; oh, and the shipbuilding there in Havana, with Cuban mahogany, a very precious wood. He has been gathering much intelligence, on Spain's Empire," Croghan said.

"I must say, you have done extremely well, my friend," Odin said. "That ought to light a fire under the rich Spaniards in the Nuworld, so they'll ship their treasure back to Spain, so we can steal their plunder on the way; that is if we're smart enough and are very lucky."

Just then, the Duke of Newcastle came by in the hallway and greeted them.

"Chief of State Odin, Chief Lady Annie and King Croghan, good morning," the Duke said. "I spent much of the night going over your Constitution, and find it a most remarkable statement of the government. It's unlike anything I've ever read before. It is truly brilliant. I must admit, I do wish we of the British Isles had such a government as you have. Time will tell if you are successful with your experiment. I feel in my gut, we are about to have a revolution in England, at least. Among other things, 3 scribes for the SPECTATOR MAGAZINE were in the crowd at Westminster, when you demanded a Peace Treaty and all that.

"When they print all they heard there, I venture when Londoners read it, the uproar will surely begin, and a violent revolution will be exploding, throughout our country. Lucky you of the Nuworld, Chief Odin; you've already got it just right," the sad-looking Duke said.

"Lord Pelham," the Chief grinned, "as you said, it is an experiment and one that can be changed from time to time, as our Royal Sovereign Electors themselves, decide it should be. What did you think of the fact, there is to be nothing like your Parliament, where to get things done you have to buy votes, one way or another?" the Chief asked the Duke.

"Chief Odin, buying votes has been my awfully tiring chore, for 30 years," the Duke of Newcastle sighed deeply and walked away.

That Duke seemed not to be puzzled at all, at the concepts of Democracy, Monarchy, and Commonwealth, all in one State.

Chief Odin was as surprised as anyone that Newcastle expected a revolution to happen.

On Wednesday, September 14th, 1757, the English Channel was surprisingly, almost calm, after such a howling storm. The ship's barometer showed they were in a high-pressure area, and that seemed to clear away most of the early morning clouds.

They reached LeHarve, France, just after high noon. It was a port dedicated to serving their navy, as well as their fishermen, and their merchant marine.

The ritts to Ambassador Hazelwood, telling of the peaceful mission, had forewarned the French, so that their warships and fortifications, didn't send a shower of iron balls, onto the extraordinary OdinShips, flying the unfamiliar circular brass flags.

They docked, the ramps were laid down, and well-armed Nobles in buckskins and brass Nuworld hats poured out in neat formations. King Copley and his assistants, seemed inconspicuous, since they were making coppix, one after another, both in London and then here, in France. Those not aware of King Copley's invention had to scratch their heads, wondering what he was doing, putting his eye to a kind of sight on that "3-legged-box."

Other Nobles lined the rails of all 4 of the OdinShips.

Frenchmen would most certainly be amazed, to see the huge names, of their former New France, fortified cities, and forts, on the Nuworld vessels.

King Montour – fluent in French – soon reported to his Chief, that most of the French people still didn't know, that all of New France – except Louisiana—had been lost to them. There were no "freedom-of-the-press" newspapers, in France, to inform the people; not one.

Chief Odin had to wonder how the French people would react to their incompetent King's great losses in the Nuworld. Might they think of revolution?

The ritts shown by Hazelwood were apparently greeted with skepticism; but of course, their King and his ministers, knew of the Ohio valley battle results over there, for France.

But King Montour said the French King, and his ministers should be convinced, when they saw the several coppix, of their disaster, and a few of the names of lost ships and also, a few names of their top officers, the Nuworlders would report to them.

The ships returning to France, from both Stadacona and Louis-bourg, loaded with returning French people were, were supposed to be, still somewhere at sea. Or, they perhaps had gone to another French port. After all, it had been a short sailing time for them, and they could have been captured, or gone into the briny deep; or merely held back, by often contrary winds.

King Andrew Montour also said the town was in high excite-ment, anticipating the extraordinary arrival of their Monarch, as well as the conquering Prussian, King Frederick. Added, were England's King George and even the Nuworld's Chief of State Odin. But it was the steaming in, of the OdinShips, with those huge painted names, of conquest on their sides and rears, that caused the greatest astonishment, he said.

Also, King Louis' coaches were said, by advance riders, to be quite close, so Odin, Annie, King George, and the rest should meet them, at the foot of the ship's ramp.

King Frederick was said to speak French, almost exclusively, instead of his native German language, he supposedly used rather poorly.

About 36 cavalrymen rode up. *King Montour said they were Prussians, not French.*

Ambassador Hazelwood was among them. He leaped off his horse, and he ran up to Chief Odin, smiling ear to ear.

"My Chief!" Hazelwood shouted, his eyes gleefully sweeping over Odin, from his amazing crown to his blue woolen raiment, medals, and black shoes. "I am so very pleased to see you once again! And our dear Chief Lady Annie! How lovely you look!"

She was indeed lovely, in her blue raiment with medals, and many-pleated white skirt.

The Ambassador whispered an astounding bit of information to Odin.

"My Chief, you might as well know; Frederick loves boys and young men, and he will think you quite pretty!" the Ambassador said.

You could have knocked Odin down, with a blade of grass. A warrior king who loved his own sex? But then, Alexander the Great of ancient Macedonia – conqueror of the then known world— reportedly had similar sexual inclinations.

A loud clatter of hooves on paving stones brought another string of cavalry, followed immediately, by 6 fancy carriages. They were both Prussians and French. All of the French wore swords on their left sides, and the Prussians wore their golden OdinGuns, holstered on their right sides. The French riders had little brass pistols, mostly stuck in their belts.

Again, Chief Odin had to marvel to see modern warriors, actually bothering to carry swords, as though expecting to make war, with steel blades instead of death-spouting guns.

A large, fancily gilded carriage leading, with a 6-horse team of prettily caparisoned white horses, stopped directly in front of Odin-Ship LOUISBOURG's ramp, what with Ambassador Hazelwood waving frantically to the driver.

Colorfully dressed coachmen-guards, jumped down off the rear of the splendiferous, thoroughly gilded coach. They opened a door and put a little bench on the ground to step out on. Behind that one, other carriages had also stopped to discharge passengers.

King George unexpectedly darted forth the few paces, to the lead carriage, and enthusiastically greeted those emerging – 3 men and 1 woman.

Hazelwood whispered to the Chief and Chief Lady, "King Frederick is the one, King George is speaking so animatedly to; in French, of course. That woman is Madame Pompadour, with King Louis, and she is his principal mistress; she's extremely influential. She sure is pretty and so very elegant. That man last out of the carriage is Britain's Ambassador, Sir Andrew Mitchell. King Frederick regards him as a friend; he's a smart man, too," Hazelwood said.

All 3 of those Kings were wearing similar tricorne (3-cornered) hats, while Chief Odin stood there under his glittering, solid gold Crown. When he nodded to someone, they could see the "picture" of the Nuworld, prettily embossed on the top of his Crown, much like the brass hats all of his Nobles wore. His 2 shoulder patches were like that, and the 4-foot diameter brass "flags," also pictured the Nuworld.

Frederick's clothing was somewhat like the others,' but he wore a dark blue coat, buttoned almost to the neck. He had no ammos on his chest, although he wore the fancily engraved, gold-plated Odin-Gun, Odin had sent to him. It was holstered in the fancy leather, Odin had sent with the gun, along with the also fancy leather tether, over that King's shoulder.

The Prussian Autocrat seemed to be an average sized man, but a little stooped over.

King Montour came close to his Chief, taking Hazelwood's place. "George is haranguing Frederick, to get to hell out of his Duchy of Hanover," he whispered. Their arguing was all babble to Odin. "Frederick is telling him this is not the time or place to discuss it, but George is getting madder," King Montour told Chief Odin.

Ambassador Mitchell and the Duke of Newcastle stepped forward, and they came between the two fuming Kings. Frederick immediately composed himself and took King Louis' arm as they came toward Chief Odin. It was as if those 2 were great friends, and their countries were not at the time, in a vicious war, killing each other's soldiers.

Madame Pompadour took Louis' other arm. She was dressed in seemingly many yards, of pretty green silk. Yet, she was fashionably, very nearly bare-breasted.

Ambassador Hazelwood made the formal introductions, speaking in both English and French – although it was said, his use of French was not terribly good.

That took quite some time, because of so many ministers to introduce, and because the Chief could not understand most of what was said.

There was much contrast.

George II was 74 years old and had been England's Monarch (so-called) for 30 years. Frederick at age 45, had been Absolute-Autocrat-King of Prussia, for 17 years. Louis XV had succeeded his great-grandfather, the 14th – "Louis the Great," the "Sun King" – and had been the King of France, since the unbelievably young age of 5 years, 42 years before. Chief of State Odin Bushnell was barely 19 and had been the head of the Nuworld State, *for all of 16 days.*

King Frederick acted extremely happy to meet Chief Odin and practically jumped at him and embraced him! That King had enormous blue eyes that sparkled with intelligence.

Odin was shocked to see and smell, that Frederick was actually unclean. His uniform coat was messed with tobacco snuff and dirt, and he had obviously not bathed or put on clean clothing for some time. The Absolute Autocrat Frederick, ruling over 1,000,000s of people, apparently felt he had no need to impress anyone, with cleanliness or his appearance.

Louis XV of France also stank, from never sinfully bathing, for his entire life, as his Most Catholic Majesty then, was expected not to do.

There was the obligatory trek, to the boiler and engine rooms, with about 24 guests; they were of anxious to see for themselves, the magic that made OdinShips move.

Chief Odin explained the workings of the machinery briefly; Prince Montour interpreted his remarks in French, remembering the guests were not curious engineers.

The whole entourage followed the Chief, to the weather deck and front of the ship, where he had them bend down to peek at the big wheels, mounted nearly to the prow. They could at least see a bit of the slice-of-cake buckets there. He didn't bother to explain how the wheels worked. They could see the rudder on the prow, but they couldn't see the rudder on the rear.

They then ventured to the pilot house. Captain MacDougal had barely begun to speak of the instruments, when a very excited Frederick asked King Montour, to take them for a demonstration ride. "Well," the Chief said, "Why not?"

Nuworld OdinShipOne, LOUISBOURG, was soon cast off from the quay, and MacDougal showed off his newly acquired skill, in moving away and out from the port, into the English Channel. Luckily, both the wind and the waves were moderate, under a few white rabbit-like clouds, in a blue bird's sky.

"Sire," the Captain asked Odin, "shall I open her up to full speed?"

"Captain, why not show them the effect your ship has on waves head-on and coming at you from the sides? You might do some fancy short, and quick turns, to show how well she responds to your will. I'll tell King Montour, and he'll tell the others. Then you can let this big thing fly fast, whenever you wish," Chief Odin said.

As the crowd stood on the prow, the Captain plowed into waves of about 4 or 5 feet height. King Montour explained that the wheels, were pulling water from under the waves, and to an extent, flattening the sea, in advance of the ship. Then with waves coming at them from the sides, he pointed out that the water there, was full of gas bubbles and spongy; that made the water no longer incompressible and was therefore not transmitting, much wave energy to the hull.

The voyage was short, no more than about 10 miles out, with sharp turns, slowing and speeding up to 42 nauts, and then back to the harbor and quay, in about an hour. Both King Frederick and King Louis, were beside themselves, with having traveled faster than they had ever dreamed possible, according to King Montour.

Chief Lady Annie held Madame Pompadour close to her, as the French whore was "dramatically" terrified.

King Croghan's Queen Molly, seemed to think the Madame's "acting," was amusing.

The Nuworld OdinShipOne, had LOUISBOURG painted on it in huge letters, letting the French know that fortress city, was no longer theirs. They wouldn't know STADACONA, was Quebec to them, but MONTREAL and CROWN POINT would be familiar.

OdinShipOne wasn't even tied up yet when King Frederick unexpectedly asked if they were for sale.

Taken by surprise, Chief Odin blurted, "King Montour, tell Frederick, I can only refer him to the shipyards, that are building them. But you surely understand that we Nuworlders have great need for them. I will certainly recommend to the builders, that they consider his needs as well, when they send over an ambassador to us, with specifications and of course, the payments."

Odin's answer was interpreted by King Montour. Frederick nodded; he understood.

Chief of State Odin, didn't have to be told King Frederick, would be having plenty to do in consolidating his territorial gains. The Prussian Autocrat then had far greater land, and subject peoples, than before the war began against him, by four larger nations.

A few dozen OdinShips would add to the potential prosperity, in Frederick's new Empire. He had gained ports by then into the Atlantic, the English Channel, the North Sea, the Baltic Sea, the Adriatic Sea, and the Mediterranean Sea. The Adriatic seaport had belonged to the conquered Austrian Empire and led into the Mediterranean, along the west coast of Italy.

It would be smart to have the Prussians as friends, Odin felt. Of course, they would only need one OdinShip, to take apart the machinery, and duplicate it or improve it, he knew. So it would be well to get a large order, for the initial sale of ships to foreigners. So he added "they are only to be built and sold by the dozen," he told King Montour to tell the others.

Kings and ministers were excitedly making soft noises, very strange to Odin, in that odd French language.

It was awhile before he grasped that King Croghan, and King Montour, had been given orders for 12 OdinShips, for King Louis. But this order was given secretly by Pompadour, in exchange for ceding, the gigantic territory of Louisiana, plus the few Caribbean Islands and the territory of French Guiana, which was south of those islands. Those acquisitions were fabulous beyond dreaming, for the Nuworld State.

Chief Odin thought that a great move, on the part of King Croghan, as it might reinforce Pompadour's position in France. The Diplomatic one whispered to his Chief that it was far better to have her to deal with, than a tough minister who might actually be competent.

Odin reckoned his father, and shipbuilder Uriah Hayden would almost fall over to hear how nonchalantly, they had added to their engine and shipbuilding businesses, by the order for 12 OdinShips for France!

He knew Europeans would quickly try to duplicate his Odin-Ships, and also attempt to improve upon them, and of course, the steam engines as well. What none of them could know, was that Odin Bushnell always, finally settled on one design for something, after considering many other possible designs.

Since no one asked for more OdinGuns, he knew they had their European arsenals at work to imitate them, or better them also. He hoped those Europeans would not notice the slight difference, between the original OdinGun and the fabulous, "automatic reloader" on his hip.

Pretty soon, everyone was seated for the dinner prepared by the Noblewomen aboard.

Nuworld Kings and the foreign ministers could arrange themselves at other ends of the tables since all Peace Treaties were not yet being fully agreed to. Prussian and French ministers were wrangling over details of the agreement, to end the war very badly lost, by France.

The guests were complimentary on the meal, but of course, they were all accustomed to the very best food. Only the ice cream brought up from OdinShipOne's ice room, and loaded with tiny blue huckleberries, might have been unusual for them.

Odin thought for a bit that he might show them King West's painting, of the proposed Capital City they were going to build. But no, he'd keep such a plan quiet.

However, the Nuworld Chief did stand and give a speech complimenting everyone at the table, and everyone's wonderful countrymen besides. He emphasized how much better was peace in the world, rather than war.

Ambassador Hazelwood interpreted, as Odin proceeded in his talk. The Ambassador also pulled up a chair to near the Heads of State, so he could interpret for them. Now and then, he smiled broadly, as he snatched a morsel off either King Frederick's or Chief Odin's plates. Everyone got a chuckle, out of Hazelwood's antics.

By and by, Frederick asked how Odin got his title, merely as Chief, as though that King thought it was denigrating.

Odin responded – to Hazelwood – that the complete title was Chief of the Nuworld State; and that there could not possibly be a greater title, honor, and responsibility, than that.

Frederick asked, through Hazelwood again, to what extent the Nuworld "empire" was intended to go.

"You may tell our friend King Frederick, Ambassador," Chief Odin said with a sober look, "we shall never be an empire since we shall never have subject colonies, nor subject peoples. We shall confine ourselves to the Continent of the Nuworld, and the near islands; that includes all of those beautiful islands in the Caribbean Sea."

Of course, what Odin left unsaid, was just how far he assumed that Continent extended. But any of them there, had merely to look at the Nuworld flag; his shoulder patches; or even his Crown; to see for themselves that it was to extend to the Equator, from the North Pole.

Frederick then said, as interpreted by Ambassador Sir Andrew Mitchell, "Chief Odin's greatest invention by far, was his invention of his Nobility and secondly, his inclusion of women in that Nobility."

"Chief Odin," the British Ambassador confided out loud, "King Frederick is considering following your example, even though he will surely have trouble with his Junkers, who inherit their titles. He has, Sire, admired that move of yours several times to me."

Chief Odin felt this was no occasion to disavow the Nuworld Nobility as his invention, although he had made that clear before. His explanation of the Nobility had been printed in all 24 Nuworld newspapers, he knew. Lately, he was told his story of that had, surprisingly, been in London's SPECTATOR MAGAZINE, also.

Frederick also told Mitchell, to repeat it to Chief Odin, "That it was another stroke of genius of Odin's, to paint each Noble's name on their uniforms so they'd always be obligated to keeping that name, Noble. He was also impressed with the unit names, he gave to the various parts of his Battle Forces," Sir Andrew relayed to the Chief.

Although King Croghan was as smooth a man as could be imagined, he still had to patiently wean the French ministers from their insistence, on changing nearly every word in the Peace Agreement with the Nuworlders. The French officials finally accepted it, as it had been printed up, after a nod from Madame Pompadour.

The French also made an agreement with England, giving up some trading rights in India.

The matter of ending slavery, was easier to solve with the French, than anticipated since the English had already agreed to that; at least the English had agreed on paper, and then the French did so, as well.

Among the French, Madame Pompadour showed by far, the greatest grief over the loss of New France. She seemingly shed pints of tears, when King Montour told her of the French ships and men, doomed at Louisbourg. That King also told her of the flotillas bringing French folks back to France from what had been Quebec, and from Louisbourg. The French present at the table seemed gratified to hear of those returning Frenchmen and women.

The English King exhibited no emotion whatever, over England's losses.

Of King Copley's many coppix, he had only "developed" and printed a few of them, with ships blowing up at Louisbourg harbor, and at the Housatonic River. Copley's pictorial evidence showed the Brits and the French, a bit of visible proof of their losses. That his 6-by-9-inch coppix were, in fact, real, he demonstrated by showing King George, sitting in the Speaker's Chair, in Parliament, and Chief Odin speaking there, only a single day before.

Those coppix intrigued the Europeans, and they wanted to know about Copley's invention. He told them he had a coppix school, just then being established, in Stratford, and his instructors would accept students from everywhere.

Of course, the students would need to purchase their own equipment, and silvered glass plates and print papers, Copley was careful to mention, without specifying the costs.

Chief of State Odin reckoned, the English would be pulling their hair out, when they realized how much gold and silver had gone away forever, on those OdinShips. *But the Oligarchy still owned the British Isles; including all those rent-producing, London properties.*

But like a bolt out of the blue, it hit the Chief... with all that gold and silver cash gone from those banks, etc., how could English workers get paid? And if they're not paid, how do they pay their rents? They'd have to pay London's workers, with paper notes, which could not possibly be trusted the same as "real money," in the form of precious metal coins. Could the lack of actual silver and gold money, spark a revolution there? The Chief had no way to know.

Surprisingly, nobody brought up the subject of fishing rights just then, so the Nuworlders avoided it, too. Later, Chief Odin would declare none, but Nuworlders could fish in Nuworld waters – which he would extend, as far from Nuworld shores, as he wished.

European Empires could have all the Nuworld sea food they might wish – but they would have to buy it, from Nuworld fishermen, instead of stealing Nuworld lobsters, cod, whale oil, etc. In turn, Nuworlders would promise, not to take any creatures of the sea, from European waters.

Having learned the French government profited amazingly from Nuworld fisheries, the lack of that great income would surely spark really big problems, for the French King also.

The meeting continued through the night – although King Louis fell asleep in his chair – with much coffee and many snacks served.

King Frederick insisted that this was the very best time, for the French and him to talk of treaties, right there in LeHarve. So they did, and peace was established to end their war.

Odin learned that Frederick kept a couple of France's provinces, for the iron ore and coal they contained. He wouldn't wish to return such potentially rich resources, to a powerful enemy state. Also, he refused to discuss the Hanover matter, "at this time," he said, much to the chagrin of the frustrated old King George.

As dawn came upon them, King Frederick again embraced Chief Odin and raised his hand to actually swear, that the greatest of friendships existed, between his and Odin's States.

Just as the Chief insisted they must do, the rising sun was barely shining on the waters of LeHarve, than they said their goodbyes, and the 4 Nuworld OdinShips steamed away.

They dropped off King George and his ministers at Brighton, to face the wrath of an angry nation, across the English Channel from France. The Duke of Newcastle was seen to ride away at full gallop, the moment he could grab a horse. He seemed to be parting ways, with old King George, who rented a "coach and 4," for the trip to London.

Much later did they learn, that a mob of revolutionaries was expecting George, outside of Brighton. They yanked the King of England out of his carriage, and clubbed him to death!

As they sped their OdinShips, out of the Brighton harbor, all of the Nuworlders, were glad to be on their way, as they had so very much yet to do at home.

The Nuworlders would brave the turbulent Atlantic, that Great Ocean Sea, on the way home to "Life's great challenges and life's glittering rewards, in their Nuworld, their Free World, their Brightest Rich Part of the Whole World!"

Both "Kings of France" had kissed the Nuworld continent goodbye. The Nuworlders had combed those snakes, right out of their hair.

❧ 2 5 ❧

As OdinShipOne steamed away from Brighton, England, Chief Odin felt he needed a nap, after spending much of the past 24 hours, with the Kings of England, Prussia, and France. His beautiful wife joined him, and they snoozed until lunch time, at midday.

He told Chief Lady Annie, about the possibility that England could have some troubles, besides the troubles from the Nuworlders. She seemed not very impressed with such notions.

King Andrew Montour came by the Chief's suite, and he was invited to join the Chief with a cup of coffee.

"I thought I ought to let you know, Chief Odin," that King said, "that Ambassador Hazelwood whispered to me that the Prussians, and probably the Russians, are making guns similar to the OdinGun."

"Of course, my friend," the Chief said. "We could expect them and others to do that."

"Now Sire, my question is, why don't you have King Revere go ahead and make the firing of our Odin2Guns completely automatic, right away?" King Montour asked.

"That is a very good thought, my friend. You and I can understand that in battle, every split second can count; it's the enemy being made dead, or us. But I do maintain, it's best to do that only when a potential enemy is becoming equal to us. King Paul and I have discussed it, and he asserts he can re-make our weapons superior to all others very quickly, when the need arises," the Chief said.

"Now then, my friend, I want you to begin a recruiting drive just as soon as we're back home. I want you to think about taking Havana, and a Spanish treasure fleet soon. I think instead of you taking control of the Caribbean Islands next, you should prepare to take Mexico, then the islands," the Chief said.

The two men discussed taking Havana at length. They were sure Spain's King and the very rich Spaniards in their conquered Nuworld territories, must soon have learned of the success of the Nuworlders. Therefore, worrying about being attacked, they would most likely soon ship at least some of their tons of gold, and their tons of silver, back to Spain, via Havana.

They noted that the Spanish Ambassador at LeHavre had suddenly disappeared. He would surely have the assistance of Spain's French ally, in getting quickly home to Madrid and his King. When the Ambassador told King Ferdinand VI, what he heard in London and LeHarve, and what King Croghan had proposed and said to him, surely Spain would react quickly to such dire news.

King Montour told the Chief he would dispatch an OdinBoat, with plentiful food and drink, to the area near Cuba, so they could send ritts back to their King when ships were spotted going to Havana. He would have installed on the OdinBoat, some sort of elevated lookout platform, to enable them to see further than from that low vessel.

As King Montour gulped down his cup of coffee, and made ready to leave the Chief, the Chief told him, "Friend Andrew, we can be glad Kings Frederick and George, aren't men of the sea, or they would have pushed us hard, to sell them OdinShips quickly and in great numbers. Those two are actually soldiers, after all, and don't seem to realize how important, dominating the seas can be. Well, we shan't be so blind, for we can certainly understand what our needs will be, with such a far-flung nation, with so many beautiful islands. King Andrew, brilliant friend, you and I will be conferring again."

Chief Odin asked a secretary to find the 3 newsmen aboard, to have them come to a meeting in his knotty pine paneled dining room.

Soon, Ezra Stiles, Benjamin Eads, and William Bradford came in, and took a seat at the Chief's dining table, along with Chief Odin's two secretaries.

The Chief remembered that Stiles had his NUWORLD NUZ, being printed not just in the original town of Stratford, but then in Philadelphia and soon, in a southern city. He distributed his papers far and wide, by men on horseback and thus, was rather more influential in the Nuworld State, than some of the more nearly "local" newspapers.

And now, Stiles was starting up a new "religion" that he called "The Happiness Church." Odin thought it was going to be rather interesting, to see how Stiles revealed religious lies of imagined magical – or supposedly, supernatural – acts, and compared them to the truth he was to propagate. He had told Odin that the Catholic Church, was very adept at spreading "propaganda," and he would have to try matching their efforts.

But immediately in the meeting, religions were not discussed at all. Rather, all 3 of the newsmen were excited about Chief Odin's ideas, on the English language. The newsmen had played with the possibilities of changing the spelling, they said.

"That's the thing about new ideas; they're exciting; they make you want to come up with even more great ideas," Chief Odin said. "Now, I'd like to know whether you agree that the old and picturesque Roman alphabet we have now can be expanded. It's extremely important, because of perhaps a million, or even more Asians in our nation should learn our language. Also, many Europeans that will be coming to us will be illiterate, and it would be a blessing to make it easy for them also to learn, not just to speak English... if we wish to continue calling it that... but to read and write it also. And of course, it would be nice to make learning reading and writing easier for the millions upon millions, of children yet unborn in our nation.

"By the way, I thought about vowels and consonants. Isn't it interesting that the vowels O, E, I and U sound exactly alike in words worm, werm, wirm and wurm? And with the fifth vowel, an A, warm is close to the same sound. That points out to me that our language is truly complicated, and we should try to make it less so.

"I'm going to suggest that we stop writing in any form whatever, what those religious old Catholic Monks in their Monasteries, thought was a good idea, with cursive writing and with so-called, 'lower case' letters. It seems to me, that if we have a completely uniform way, of simply writing and printing of what's called, 'capital' letters, our language ought to be far easier to learn, and perhaps even to write for each of us.

"Here, let me print a few words, as I think they could be done," he said and proceeded to print with the pencil from his pocket, 'HERE IN THIS GOOD SHIP, WE STEAM ON.' We could slant the letters in our printing a little or a lot, to emphasize words.

"It seems to me if we print everything as plain as we can, by hand and in books, magazines and in newspapers, everyone could learn our language easier, with such consistent letters. I'm asking you to put that idea in your newspapers, and I shall most certainly take it up, with the Education Realm.

"I'm going to insist that every possible object, in our ships and boats, at least, be labeled that way. People seeing such words must automatically learn them, seeing them every day. That could be important lessons on ships and other things, for babies, for immigrants, and for our Asian peoples.

"We know people of the sea use different words than landlubbers. We must use the latter's words for floors, instead of decks, for walls instead of bulkheads; and so forth.

"Oh, and that reminds me, we might still have but twenty-six letters, to make a great many more, than twenty-six sounds. So here's another idea: I'll ask King Thomson and the other brilliant men and women, in the Education Realm, to consider making small marks on the top, bottom, left and right sides, and all four corners of letters. Those eight altering sounds could, in some hopefully logical, and consistent way, make those letters more accurate, in the way they would be pronounced. You gentlemen might also want to publish that idea.

"For example, a C could be marked with a tiny line to show it should be pronounced as though it was the extremely common CH. Also, the same mark could be used after a P, for PH and after a T for a TH. We wouldn't need to bother printing the H, you see.

"There must be hundreds of examples like that, in our language. But I'll not bother about that; we can just leave it up to the experts in language, diligently working to make our tongue far easier to learn and to use. As we all know, a big part of what makes humans far, far superior to other creatures, is our ability to communicate so very well," the Chief said with a big sigh.

"And that reminds me of something; that reminds me to have you fellows in your papers, suggest to your readers, that some genius needs to invent ink pens, with the ink in them, instead of needing to dip a goose quill in an inkwell, again and again, endlessly. All of us can see the immediate benefit of so handy a device, especially if you could snap it into a shirt pocket. They might have pens, hold different colors of ink, too. Oh; and they could even put alcohol in the inks, so they will dry quickly, not freeze and not need blotting.

"And, why not make pencils that don't need to be sharpened endlessly, ending up with shavings and graphite-clay... *it is not lod in pencils*... all over the floor?"

The three newsmen made notes right away, to suggest those ideas in their newspapers.

"You fellows will want to interview our Treasury Realm's King Clark, about his efforts to spread Treasury Valts around our nation. By now, he most certainly has plans to do that, and our people should be made aware, of his very important activities," Chief Odin said. "Our Kings are mostly going to have to reside in and do business from their OdinBoats. I have had a ritt sent to King Clark, to have all of our Kings meet me at Stratford when we get there.

"All of you know that we plan to have our capital city, begun rather soon. None of us have seen the site, which is on the lower part of our fabulously great Ohio River system. That river, with its many major branches, reaches into much of our continent. Thus, we expect the Beautiful River to be the primary means, for people and their goods, to get around over a lot of our Nuworld State. You will remember, that King Louis XV of France just ceded to us, the French claim to the extremely vast lands, they called Louisiana. Well, it seems from the maps, that the fabulous Ohio River system, drains all of that territory, and a great deal more.

"On some of the French maps we captured at Fort Duquesne, I saw a great crescent bend in that river, which suggests a great place for our nation's government compound. King West, King Eyre and I at least, will be going there shortly, after we're back home. This presents an enormous challenge; building a great city in such a wilderness.

"The French built a village next to that crescent, beginning in 1718, that they call New Orleans. It's named after the Duke of Orleans who was, at the time, substituting for the child king, Louis XV. The notes on the map say, there are floods there sometimes, so that means we must build up the land. We can do that by dredging the river bottom; that is, we can make the river lower, and the land higher that way. The current of the river might power our dredges, of which we will need a large number, up and down the river, to pour soil onto both shores."

"Sire, did you name OdinCity after yourself?" William Bradford asked.

"No, sir, I definitely did not name it at all," the Chief told the newsmen. "It happens that after I told my fellow members of the Nuworld Company, that I thought that was the ideal, centralized location for our capital, they unanimously agreed within minutes, that it should have my name on it. I would hardly be so self-centered as to name it for myself, but that others have done so, I feel is a terrific compliment. Like everyone else; I do enjoy approval from my friends."

"Thank you, Chief Odin," Bradford said, "for that explanation. We, of course, assumed you would not name it for yourself, like your many inventions."

"Gentlemen, I want you to know I am not in the slightest bit embarrassed by naming my creations after myself. I most certainly do hope and expect others to do the same. Coming up with useful innovations is very much needed now... now that we here in the Nuworld, can be free of religious restraints, practically forbidding new ideas. Why religions concentrate their ideas on an imaginary life after death, is beyond me. When a person dies, he is no more; he can no longer do anything for, or to anyone again, good or bad; that seems to me to be so obvious."

The Chief scratched his chin, thinking, then added, "I've mentioned to King Montour today, that our Noblemen and Noble-women ought to have a birth number – as I call it – put permanently with ink, under their skin, on the underside of their left forearm, for lifelong permanent, and positive identification. And now, thinking a bit further with that idea, I do believe every Nuworlder, should have such identification, as well.

"I believe I'll make a law stating that at birth, everyone in our nation must be given a birth number... oh, by the attending physician or midwife. It would consist of the year, the month, the day, the local hour of the day, the minute and... oh, I think, when we have them numbered, the Region or foreign nation in which the babe is born. That number, together with their first, middle, and last names, would very certainly be unique... just as every person is absolutely one of a kind, anyway.

"A further use of that birth number would be, as a Treasury Checking Account number, and as a Savings Account Number. Additionally, that birth number would identify each Royal Sovereign Elector, when voting. I'll take that idea up right away with King Pemberton of our Elections Realm when we get back to Stratford. The notion of crowds standing up, and raising their hand to vote for one or another, is neither a good nor an accurate way to vote. Think of how an Elector, might vote for 6 or maybe 10 Jurors, in their city?

"The first annual voting will take place this coming summer, so we'd best come up with useful ideas, to help our King Pemberton.

"As I have said, my friends, I do believe both men and women are creators, and therefore Gods and Goddesses. How can we not love our wonderful citizens, who are so endowed? Of course, I certainly must love them. We are all capable of great improvements, for all humankind. Now, if you will excuse me, I'm going to see if my darling wife is feeling better," the Chief said.

Odin found his wife sipping tea, "to settle her stomach." Odin suggested they go out on deck to get some fresh air, so they did. The wind was actually moderating, but being out of the west, the speed of the OdinShip made the light breeze seem much stronger than it really was. The Atlantic at the time was actually rather flat.

A large, white bird was gliding into that bit of wind, not far from the ship.

"I think that's an Albatross," Odin told his wife as he pointed to it. "They are said to fly continuously for weeks, or even months at a time, without landing. But I imagine they must sit on the water, in the black of night, and sleep. We can see his wings are not flapping. That means, even the soft wind going against the underside of his wings, and pulling off the air over them, keeps him up there. I've noticed that pretty often as a youngster when I was watching seagulls staying in one place, in the wind, while moving but slightly. I must make some sketches for my Pops; sketches of the flying machine I want him to make. I'll do that after dinner this evening."

The wind bothered them, so they also visited the pilothouse to find the instruments were showing the ship was plowing the waters aside steadily, at 42 nauts. The Captain told them he expected they would be back in Stratford early Monday morning, September 19th, if the weather stayed as calm, the rest of their way, back to their home port of Stratford.

Both the Chief and his Lady made a point, of visiting with the Noblewomen, to compliment them on their cooking and cleaning. Their guards, the Noblemen, were also complimented for their steadfast attention to duty. The ship's library also provided them with books to read.

Those 2 dined alone and the Chief Lady, stayed with her husband as he began to sketch his flying machine-to-be. He had the thing pretty much pictured in his head, so he put the design on paper quickly.

"You see here, Sweetie," he said, "this is the first of several sizes of machines, I want for our Nobles to ride into battle with. We'll eventually have many of these machines in use. I think there should be 2 pilots up front, as a precaution, as you see here," he pointed.

"Behind the pilots, I want to have 6 seats on each side, to carry a 12-Noble-Band. Those seats and seat-backs can be swung up, when not in use. With the seats out of the way, the machine could haul things. The machine will have 4 small wheels, spread out on it, to move around, on the ground or on a ship's deck," he said while sketching them.

"With Nobles aboard, they can see from above, what the military situation on the ground is, wherever they may be," he told her. "OdinRockCannons could be mounted on the bottom of the body, to fire OdinRocks, by the pilot, at an enemy fort or ship, for example. Maybe in time, one or more Odin2Guns could be mounted in the nose.

"The entire bird would have to be made of high carbon steel, for now, I think, with some small windows. The steel would be lacquered to prevent rust. Mounted under, and forward of the wings, on each side, will be a very new kind of motor I've only got inside of my head.

"A steam engine would have too much weight for this bird. So I've conceived, what I call, an OdinMotor. Here; I'll draw a picture of it as though it was cut through, end to end, down the middle of it," he said as he began sketching.

"These *OdinMotors...* will look something like a long barrel, inside another barrel, with the casings fastened to a bracket, extending down and forward from the wing. In those brackets, feeding those motors will be the fuel oil piping and electric wires for controls. The pilot can turn the engines up or straight ahead, by hydraulic oil under pressure, with levers beside him.

"There must be a small electric motor on the central shaft of the motor, to begin spinning it inside these motors. King Franklin has claimed he knows how to make one, that will also generate electricity. Spinning that shaft will get prest air, spurting into the fire area. That's where mists of oil, are to be mixed with that air. We'll have sparks there to get a fire going. That oil-burning would probably be so hot that it would melt the metals there. So, the oil will flow along the inner side of the burning area all around, cooling that metal, and there'll be cooling air on the outer surface of the burning area. Do you see here where that cooling air and the cooling oil comes in?"

"Ah, yes, honey. Yes, I see that" she answered him.

"Oh, I didn't point out that half of these angled blades you see in the air pressor and in the rear power part, are on fixed wheels. Every other wheel is attached to the central shaft, and the other wheels stay fixed in place; those just deflect the air and gasses to the moving wheels. Anyway, you see that the greatly expanding, hot gasses will turn those wheels, and thus that shaft, which in turn I expect will raise this machine into the air, with the motors turned up. When the pilot gradually turns the engines to the front, the tremendous hot exhaust will force the craft forward," he told her.

"And with that, my dear darling wife, I will be flying much like an eagle, but without all that darn flapping of wings," he said with a big smile.

"Well, that sounds wonderful honey, but it could be dangerous, because of that hot exhaust. Anyway, what will the wings be made of, Odin?" she asked.

"Well, the wings will be strengthened by hollow steel – but thin – wing box beam, going from wing tip to wing tip, across the top of the rectangular body," he said. "Fore and aft braces will form the shape of the wings, to provide lift. Another similar box beam will go from the front to the rear. The wings and the body both would be covered with thin but strong steel sheets. This craft must be as light as possible, and yet strong enough to fly. Someday we'll find lighter metals to reduce the weight of the bird, increasing its capacity for people and for freight.

"Those wing and front-to-back hollow beams have to hold compressed air, from the 2 motors, because that air has to come out of nozzles on the nose, the wingtips, and the rear. A leveler device with regulated air coming out, to keep the bird level when going up or landing. I'll devise controls by the pilot, to use that same air, out those nozzles, to steer the bird with.

"Suppose the pilot wants to go to the right. All four of those nozzles will be pointing counter clockwise, with the air blast turning the plane then, to the right. I must draw hundreds of details for this before we get back to Stratford. I'll ask my Pops to start-up companies of a great many men to make every detail, in order to get the first bird in the air. I'll want the first one, and the Nobility will want, scores of them in time. So will the Geography Realm, and maybe every King, want a bird for their use.

"The craft will have a compass, and a few other instruments, which King Rittenhouse's people can make for us," he told her.

"What will you call your machine, honey?" she asked. "What about OdinBird?"

"Ha! OdinBird, eh? Well, that sounds just fine to me!" he laughed.

He continued to sketch in the details of his flying machine, while she watched and occasionally asked another question.

By and by they called it a day, and went to bed to enjoy some fun time, before nodding off to sleep, with her head as usual, on his shoulder, as they cuddled and snoozed.

The Chief and Chief Lady Bushnell, woke Sunday morning, September 18th, 1757, to hear the wind howling, and OdinShipOne seeming to fight the Atlantic, in its progress toward the Nuworld and home.

For the first time in some days, Annie felt well rested and full of vigor. She got out of bed before her husband did. She made them a breakfast of toasted and buttered bread, and oatmeal loaded with raisins and walnuts. The ice-cold milk for the oats was still good, but it was near to becoming soured. The boiling coffee gave their suite a welcome aroma.

They dressed again in their buckskins and headed up to the pilot house. Captain Count MacDougal was there and told them of "the tiny squall we're going through."

"Actually Chief Odin," MacDougal said, "you can see well ahead of us, that there's blue skies and I think, an easy sea. We should be arriving on the Housatonic about dawn tomorrow."

Chief Odin looked back of them, to see the OdinShip STADA-

CONA following in the LOUISBOURG'S wake. The MONTREAL and the CROWN POINT were just ahead of them. The 4 vessels changed positions in line about every 2 hours since those following had a smoother ocean – an easy sea, says the Captain—to ride than the first in line.

Again, the Chief had the newsmen called to his dining room. When they and a secretary were seated, Odin was about to speak, when Eads of the BOSTON GAZETTE spoke up.

"Chief of State Odin," he began, "all 3 of us are truly amazed at your invention of a new weapon called the Odin2Gun. We can hardly accept that you thought it up in a single day."

"One thing you gentlemen might want to remember is that your Chief of State has a long habit of telling the truth. As a young boy, I occasionally experimented with twisting the truth to suit me. Both of my parents lectured me on the importance of being trustworthy. They stressed that being worthy of other's confidence, was exceedingly important, throughout one's life. And of course, I thought of weapons now and then; hardly just on one occasion.

"What I want first to talk about, is a new law I am issuing tomorrow, September 19th, in this year of 1757.

"It was only 5 years ago that the English government ordered us, Colonists, to use Pope Gregory's Catholic Church calendar," the Chief said as he continued. "It seems strange that such an Anti-Catholic government as England would order the use of such a bad method of keeping track of days, weeks, months, and the years of our lives. They could easily have brought to life a rational, really accurate calendar. Well, they didn't do that, but we most certainly will.

"Beginning December 21st, of this year, we shall begin using a new, and a perfectly rational calendar. That day is the Winter Solstice, as you all know, and that will be our New Year's Day. That day is a very good time for parents, families, friends, and lovers, to hand out presents, to celebrate the beginning of each New Year. It is a good time to count accomplishments for the year just past and to institute plans for the coming year. In 1760, and in every year divisible by 4, except the Century mark, will be a Double New Year's Day.

"I've heard that in Germany, some people cut down a pine tree each winter, and stand it up in their house. They do that so the nice smell of pine will overcome the stink, of unwashed bodies and unlaundered clothes. That's while their windows and doors are shut tight against the cold weather and the fresh air outside.

"That could be a good idea for us. We could bring a little pine tree into our house, well before New Year's Day. We might decorate it with something, and put gifts on the branches, for our loved ones. The gifts would represent the love we have for each other.

"Very well now. The day after the single or double New Year's Day will be the beginning of the first month of the year, which we are to call Month 1. After that, will be Month 2, etc., continuing to Month 12, instead of memorializing those ancient Roman gods, etc.

"The 1st and 2nd months in each quarter or season is to have 30 days each; the 3rd month in each quarter is to have 31 days, totaling 13 weeks of 7 days each, and 91 days total for the quarter year; or, season.

"There will be 4 quarters in each year, consisting of Winter, Spring, Summer and Autumn Quarters. Each quarter year will begin on a 1 Day and end on a 7 Day. You will see we will no longer be silly and celebrate, the imaginary old Norse Gods every week, nor the old Roman Gods and who the devil ever, each month. We're going to be rational with our new calendar. Our new calendar will only mark the passage of time, and not honor old saints and such, that might not have been good folks in fact.

"King Croghan of the Diplomacy Realm is to suggest the use of this reasonable calendar to other nations, and mention that their religious calendars, could still be continued in use for religious purposes only if need be.

"A calendar is a way to keep track of days, months, seasons, and years. I hope you gentlemen will suggest to your readers that they might want to come up with a different way of keeping time, with big clocks and little clockets, too. A problem we will have in keeping sun time as now, with clocks and clockets, is that we will have a great deal of traffic on our seas, lakes, and rivers, going east to west, and west to east. Also, we will be traveling swiftly on beamways someday, east and west, plus of course, north and south. Our Transportation Realm, I assure you, is right now working on getting steel beamways laid, throughout our nation.

"I'm going to help establish 3 or 4 private companies, to make clocks and clockets. Those clockets should have a strap of some sort on them, so they can be held on one's wrist, instead of needing to fish it out of a pocket, when we want to see the time. I'll have the Nobility issue a wrist clocket, to every Nobleman and Noblewoman. It will be very interesting to see how well clock and clocket companies make them, competing with others, as they will need to do.

"Now then, since time has been kept by the rotation of the earth each day, relative to our sun, time changes for us, when we go east or west. Thus, perhaps we should have one clock time for all time pieces, each day, no matter where in our Nuworld we might be.

"Tomorrow morning, we will be unloading the loot, we took from England's richest men. We took all that stuff as punishment, for their fleet killing a few of our Nobles, and for destroying some of our homes. Some of that wealth must go to returning Africans to Africa. We will be simply getting it off of our OdinShips, and into our Treasury building, without counting it.

"Later, Treasury King Clark is to give us an accounting of it, and we might or might not make that public at the time. I'm telling you, gentlemen, this, to ask you please, not to get too specific in your reporting of our Nobles, wheelbarrowing the stuff into that building.

"You will notice while you're there, watching the unloading of those riches, that we have 2 Battle Forces still right there, along the Housatonic. They are there to guard against attack by any sort of force, wishing to rob us. King Montour is also going to make that area his prime training ground, for additional Battle Forces. When our capital city is well underway to being built, both the Treasury and the Battle Force central training place, with be transferred there.

"I expect King Eyre of the Geographic Realm, will be producing a variety of maps of our State soon. I'll ask him to have mats made, that typesetters can print maps from, for our newspapers. Maps are pictures, and they are worth words, far beyond counting.

"Oh yes, and I'm going to have King Eyre's people make great numbers of world globes, for distribution to all of our people. I feel quite certain, Asians living in their little tribes, have no idea whatsoever, of what our planet actually is like. Probably most of our Euros don't either.

"The Geography Realm is already making those circular brass maps – or I should say – pictorial flags, of our Nuworld nation. We expect those will be helpful to everyone, to understand their place on this earth. And therefore, we can say, how beneficial such a great territory can be in resources, for everyone living in the Nuworld State.

"We want all of our people to learn, what a great nation they live in. We want them to understand that everyone has unlimited opportunities, to enrich themselves and their fellow citizens, in our Nuworld, our Free World, our Brightest Rich Part of the Whole World," the Chief said with a grin on his face.

Chief Odin had made that phrase famous, and he was aware that most of the 24 newspapers in the nation, repeated it fairly often.

The Bostonian Eads had his hand in the air.

"Yes, sir, Mr. Eads," the Chief said.

"Sire, to me, your organization of the State government seems beautifully complete, except for one thing. I would think there should be a Realm just for our Asian peoples. After all, their culture, their languages and so forth, are so different from us Euros, that..."

The Chief raised his hand to cut Eads off.

"No sir, we are not going to treat any of our citizens, as though they are foreigners, in their own country. Remember, Asians and Estimos came here from Siberia... that should be spelled Sib Aria, for it obviously means, 'Siblings to the Aries—the Euros.' Est-imos obviously means 'Eastern people.' I am convinced most of our Asians, will melt right into our society, and our culture, within a generation or 2 or 3.

"Our Asian folks have advanced little because they have either been nearly constantly at war or forever worried of attacks by other tribes. Even so, their canoes, their kayaks and their portable homes called teepees, are remarkable inventions. It's that damnable war culture, that has dulled their ambitions to be creative, like they could be, and should be. I hope you gentlemen will repeat that in your papers. No, Mr. Eads, I can visualize great advantages for us all, to be one people in our Nuworld State," Chief Odin said.

The NUWORLD NUZ publisher, Ezra Stiles raised his hand to speak.

"Chief of State Odin," he began, "I've had a bit of time to think about the new, so-called religion, I'm starting up; 'The Happiness Church." I originally thought that we would be countering the lies of other religions, with their supposed magical happenings. But no Sire, we're going to be positive, not negative. We'll have music and dancing. We'll have joke telling, and lots of laughter. We'll have fun with tall tales, of story-telling, every Sunday... well, what we'll soon call every 7 Day. What do you think of that, Chief?"

"Well now, I think I'd like to go to your church now and then... or maybe, really often, just for the laughs. But isn't that what taverns are for, Mr. Stiles?" he asked.

"Sire, taverns are mostly meeting places, alright, but they've all got alcoholic drinks to sell, and people do drink too much; they get drunk, and they get stupid. No sir, the Happiness Churches, won't get people drunk. There'll be not a thing there for sale, even, I don't suppose. Contributions of money will be strictly voluntary. The basic intention of my church will be for people to have a good time, and to be reminded of their natural powers to do good," Stiles said.

"That sure sounds different from other religions where the idea seems to be, to scare the hell out of folks, so they'll behave themselves. Also, it seems to me that priests and preachers must get great feelings of power, from scolding people for being human. For myself, Mr. Stiles, I'll be very interested to see how your *new religion* develops. Now, if you gentlemen will excuse me, I have some thinking to do, the rest of this day," Chief Odin said.

26

C hief Odin found the sketches he had made, of what his Chief Lady Annie had called, an "OdinBird." He spent precious hours, making additional drawings, of countless details in the machine. He showed glass on the front, and on the side doors by the pilots. He located fuel tanks. The swing-down seats and the straps to hold in the dozen Nobles were shown. He drew sections of the wings, to imitate the contours of bird's wings.

He then spent a lot of time, refining the drawings of his Odin-Motor. A multi-bladed fan would be needed in the front of it, to blow air into the air pressor and also, to blow air in around the fire circle, to cool that iron and then as it was allowed inside, to cool the burnt air-oil mixture to a safe temperature. Ah, he realized as he showed this feature, that water might also be shot in to cool the fire, thus creating steam. Hey! Water expands fantastically as hot steam! Water can expand with heat, certainly more than a thousand times over!

Chief Odin immediately saw a new source of power if his Odin-Motor employed steam. Thus, with a bit of time spent for lunch and dinner, he devoted intense work, to designing parts of the OdinMo-tor, including casting by the lost-wax method, of the many-bladed

388

steel wheels needed. He also showed further details of the burning chamber, that wrapped all around inside.

When the 4 OdinShips arrived that Monday morning, September 26th, 1757, at Stratford on the Housatonic River, the Chief was well-rested, and very much ready to meet with his father, to tell him about both, the OdinBird and the OdinMotor.

So while the gathered Nuworld Kings and the Chief Lady, were watching the unloading and storage of the London loot, and the Slave Trading records from London, into the Treasury, Chief Odin and his pops, Nehi Bushnell, had OdinShipOne's dining room, to themselves.

"Pops, you know I have for a long time, thought it would be a good idea if we could find some way to fly like the birds," the Chief told his father. "Now, I've finally got it all, in these sketches I made for you. If you possibly can, I'd like you to begin this venture right away."

His father was flabbergasted, at the great detail, Odin had put into the drawings. He studied them for a while, until he finally told his son, "Chief Odin, all of this is very surprising. But I can see you have learned to draw, better and better.

"It so happens; I have had 3 new mill buildings built," his Pops said as he continued. "I've tried to anticipate our needs for the future making of machines. I can use the largest 1 of them for the OdinBird, and a smaller 1 for the OdinMotor. The 3rd building is for the OdinHorse you conceived for us; that project is coming along quite well.

"Casting those bladed wheels for the motor will take some experimenting and learning, but following your exact instructions here, we'll get it done. I'll have our best men working on these 2 projects. What about you? What are your plans for dinner tonight? Your mother and I would love to have you, and your Chief Lady Annie, come over to our house."

"Pops, thank you for that invitation, and of course, we'll be there. We're to have a meeting of our Kings for lunch today, here in this room. Also, I do hope George Washington is here to become a Prince. He's to head up the 'Africans to Africa Agency.' Tomorrow

I'm steaming up to Boston on some business. Then I'll go to Manhattan. We'll then steam to Philadelphia to speak and to spend some time with the Chief Lady's folks. From there, we'll go to one of the larger southern cities, to find a King of Farming. Then, we're heading for the site of our proposed capital city, down there on the fabulous lower Ohio River system. We won't spend much time there before we come back to Stratford, I suppose," Odin said.

"Well son, you knew you'd have lots to do, as the Chief of the Nuworld State. I feel certain your success will continue, unabated. Well, I'd best get started on these 2 new projects for you. If successful, would you figure to have only a few, or a great many OdinBirds built?" Nehi Bushnell asked.

"Pops, I expect the Nobility Realm, will be the first to require many of them. They will be very useful in the taking of hilly Mexico, and our many Caribbean Islands. The Geographic Realm will need some. Every city Mayor will want one or more, especially for their Noble Police-Fire Fighters. Every King might have one for his own use. Oh yes sir, you'd best figure to build many OdinBirds, of different designs and sizes. Besides use on the OdinBirds, I don't know what uses might come about for the OdinMotors. But as OdinSteamMotors, replacing the reciprocating OdinSteamEngines, there could be a considerable need," the Chief said.

"The other thing is, Pops," the Chief said, "that the fire coming out of those motors, would, of course, set the wooden deck of ships to burning. We'll have to have steel covering for those decks, that won't burn.

"You can have a crew of men on that bird-rising-landing project, and have them prepare to make the layout on wooden ship's decks, to receive all that steel. Also, we'll have to have water on hand, to put out any fires that might be started, at any time," the Chief told his Pops.

With a bit more of personal chit-chat and a grand hug, Nehi Bushnell left to get started in those new ventures.

The Nuworld Kings then began arriving onto OdinShipOne, built of welded steel.

Of the Kings to attend, King Clark of Treasury was the first to be greeted by Chief Odin. Clark was full of excitement, after seeing tons of silver and gold, pouring into his Treasury.

Following him to be greeted and shake the Chief's hand, were Kings Pratt of the Metals Realm, Chalker of Glass, Putnam of Forestry, Allen of Transport, Croghan of Diplomacy, Montour of Nobility, Revere of Supplies, Thomson of Education, Gale of Health, Copley of Arts, Tully of Commerce, Rittenhouse of Ritts, West of Building, Eyre of Geography, Armstrong of Fuels – who introduced George Washington to the Chief—then Franklin of Science, Pemberton of Elections, Boone of Police and Trent of the Big Works Realm.

There were no Kings appointed yet for the Farming Realm, the Insurance Realm, nor the Chemistry Realm. And King Morgan of the Hunting Realm had not yet arrived from Louisbourg. The three newsmen were again aboard OdinShipOne and sat across the dining room.

After each of the Kings took a chair, at the huge dining table, Chief Odin remained standing to speak to them.

"Dear Kings, I will first have a couple of important things to tell all of you about. Then I'll expect a brief report of what, each of you has so far got done. After that, we can inform Mr. Washington, of what's involved in the Africans to Africa Agency. If he accepts that demanding assignment, I'll make him a Prince. In the meantime, Mr. Washington, you and I can be assured we are midst an extremely able group of Kings here.

"Gentlemen," Chief Odin went on, "I have invented a flying machine, that my wife calls an OdinBird. Also, I invented an Odin-Motor to power it. Just before you came here, I went over all the details of those with my pops. He has agreed to make both the flying machine and the motors. It so happens, he has decided anyway, to sell his steam engine business to the employees of that company, and he has had the foresight, to have several mill buildings built. So he has the necessary places to take on both projects. He may have a time to get workmen for those jobs.

"Here's an overall sketch of that machine with the new kind of motors. Please pass it on around the table. I am very much convinced that my bird will go straight up in the air, such as off the deck of an OdinBoat, or an OdinShip, or of course, off the ground. Then those same motors will propel it forward, and I suppose, at some speed. You'll see I've designed this first OdinBird, to have seating for a Band of Nobles. In a fight, they can see, through small windows, the situation they'll face, before they are even on the ground, to confront an enemy. Also, I am inclined to believe any enemy, will be very much in awe of our Nobles, coming at them this way.

"The other thing I want to mention may not amount to anything. But it could be important to make writing, reading, and communications of every sort, easier and more efficient than it has been with the old Roman alphabet. King Thomson of Education, will be particularly interested in this, but I'm asking each one of you brilliant men, to convey your own thoughts to King Thomson, please. Here, I'll show you on this chalkboard, an idea or two.

"The ancient Roman alphabet has but 26 characters to represent a great many more sounds; incredibly, there are only 5 letters to represent 18 vowel sounds. I thought last night that we could easily modify the sounds, of each letter with marks on them. Oh, say the letter A, could be marked with a tiny line, up, down, from each side, or angled from the 4 corners. So a particular letter could actually represent 8 sounds, or even more if different sorts of marks are made! Our 26 letters could possibly represent 100s of sounds, with marks made on, or about them! How about that?" the Chief said.

"King Thomson, I hope you and your people, can make such markings on that alphabet useful, to make the English language more easily learned, with corrected spelling, too. For example, a mark atop the letter T could mean the sound we now get by using TH. King Thomson, you and your talented crew can take it from there.

"I've heard there are advantages to the 12-number base system. It's obvious that 10 squared is 100, but 12 squared is 44% more and cubed, it's even better. If any of you have ideas on revising our system of arithmetic, please pass your thoughts on to King Franklin. I suppose the Science Realm, should explore the possibilities, and the advantages, with such changes in the interesting field of mathematics.

"To institute such a system with all the refinements, King Thomson and his associates, could surely make, to our alphabet," Chief Odin went on, "would be a burden for all of us who are literate. We're so accustomed now to the old ways, and we would have to change. But from our difficulties, we would all be rewarded with the fact, that millions of our present countrymen, and immigrants who are now illiterate and add the millions upon millions of persons not yet born, who could master our language better. Well, we must think ahead to the welfare of those who need a system of writing, that is more reasonable, and easier to use than the one with the crazy spelling, we have all inherited.

"Oh, the other matter is that, as you all saw, we were successful in gaining recompense from the English, for the attack by their fleet on us, right here. We have a Peace Treaty signed by King George and another, by King Louis. Both the English and the French, have ceded their claims to any and all territory in the Nuworld, above the equator, to the Nuworld State. Three excellent newspapermen were with us, on that very profitable voyage, and they will have all the details in their papers.

"Oh yes, speaking of newspapers, I must remind everyone, that every first of each month, beginning on the first of the new year, I expect to have a progress report, from each Realm. Perhaps it would be best for the State, to print your full-page reports in a magazine, and depend on the Transportation Realm for delivery, to all who would subscribe to it. Possibly, we wouldn't charge subscribers. Newspapers would of be primary subscribers to our magazine," he said.

Then he told them about the new calendar he was declaring to be the law, that very day.

"Enough about those things for now," the Chief said. "I'll sit and let's all hear of the advancements made in each of our Realms. Let's just go around the table, beginning with our King of the Treasury Realm, who has been made especially happy this day, with all that wealth pouring into his Realm."

"Ah, thank you, Chief of State Odin," King Abraham Clark said with a huge smile. "I know each of us must be brief, so I will, too. We will be weighing all that loot, and converting bulk metal to nu coins. I expect to report our total take, from the French in Canada and Louisbourg, from that we got from England, and the total in our vaults, within about three weeks. My Treasury has yet to compile, the contributions by the 14 Nuworld Company partners, also.

"I definitely will not meltdown any of the British Royal Paraphernalia. We might wish at some future time to return it, for good relations with them. Although, from what Mr. Stiles told me, England might by now be having a revolution; they might want a government like ours, and not want anything to do with that so-called, *Royal* stuff.

"Also, I expect to report the functioning of Treasury branches, or Valts, in about eight cities quite soon. One last thing; Chief Odin, I am very certain the Treasury Realm can best handle the insurance business, instead of having another Realm. Every Treasury Valt can logically have an office for insurance. That's where money will be transferred daily, anyway."

"Thank you, King Clark," Chief Odin said. "We notice the English insurance companies have lots of competition, and one has to think, that keeps their rates somewhat reasonable. No sir my King, I want Insurance to be a separate Realm. That Realm will have a far larger backing in money, than any private companies, could possibly come up with.

"Also, I've thought the Transportation Realm could take care of the postal business; but now, I'm not so certain. King Pemberton will, of course, have something to say about this, but I've thought the best and easiest way our Royal Sovereign Electors can vote, rain or shine, storms or fair weather, would be to receive ballots by mail. They could take plenty of time to decide which candidate or candidates, should be voted in to particular offices. They could mail in their very secret, marked ballot. Upon receipt of each of those, the Treasury Valt would immediately add the proper compensation to that Elector's account.

"I want a Mutual Insurance Realm, that will pay insured

customers, part of the annual profits, by returning a portion of their payments back to them. It would be, in fact, a non-profit enterprise by the State. Also, Mr. Robert Morris of the Willing & Morris Company in Philadelphia, told me, some time ago, that he knew quite a lot about insurance. I'll see him in a few days and find out if he's available for that Realm. Insurance, we all know, can save folks after the disaster of a husband dying, or a fire, or a lost ship... from all sorts of tragedies.

"King Clark, your Treasury has more than plenty to account for already; especially with your Valts all over the country, and training men and women for that extremely important work. As for private banks to compete with your Treasury Branch Valts, you have said we should be wary of them, and we shall."

"Fair enough, my Chief," Clark said and nodded to his left, for King Pratt of the Metals Realm to speak.

"Chief Odin," King Pratt began, "we have been very busy this past week, hoisting those hundreds of English cannons, off the Housatonic bottom. Next, we're concentrating on bringing up cannonballs. We've been converting cast iron, to hundreds of times stronger steel, and from it, rolling it into one inch and half-inch-thick sheets and framework, according to Uriah Hayden's requests. He's using your invention of welding, with those OdinConeWelders.

"King Montour has assigned a Combat of his Nobles, to accompany my men to search south of Lake Superior, for the possible great deposit of iron ore the French notes hinted at. Also, north of Lake Erie, the French indicated metals were found. We know there's copper ore somewhere up there, as well. They will also try to find a good route, for a beamway south to the North Ohio River, so that iron ore can be beamwayed, and barged down, to OdinCity, etcetera.

"We have virtually exhausted local iron ore here, and are now starting to make a large stock of steel plate and frames for ships, out of all that cast iron in the river," King Pratt said. "Also, we expect to get much more iron when the Ticonderoga gets here from Stadacona."

"Excellent, King Pratt; excellent," Chief Odin said. "Now, King Chalker?"

"Chief Odin, you'll remember I've been producing several kinds of glass, since shortly after we got back from our treasure hunt. In addition to the sheet glass we make, we are selling now many thousands of especially strong glass bottles, jugs, jars, cups, dishes, bowls, and even some small buckets. We've so far distributed most of our stuff, as far north as Portsmouth and as far south as Philadelphia, by ship. People have gone crazy for our products, and it turns out to be quite profitable. We mostly turn sand and lime, into useful things and at the moment, I can tell you in this year of 1757 so far, we've made a profit of just over 20,000,000nu!"

"Wow!" Chief Odin exclaimed. "King Chalker, I've always known you to be an excellent man, and you've proven it for everyone to know. I hadn't realized you could do so very well so very soon. Thanks for that report. Now, King Putnam; how is your Forestry Realm doing at this time?"

"Chief Odin, we've been particularly busy, experimenting in making paper, bleached or not. I think we've got the right way, now to do that, and we'll instruct the forestry departments of every Region when they get organized. We'll keep on for now though, making and selling paper, until the Regions can do it. Also, we've finally had success in stripping logs, of thin sheets, to make plied wood. I can assure you Chief, that has got to be a profitable thing for Regions to do," King Putnam of the Forestry Realm said.

"That's great, King Putnam. You know the Transport Realm could be handling Postal Services for a while. I think, when Regions are organized and utilizing their forests, I'll want you to take over the Postal business. I feel sure it might eventually be separate from Transport. Now, King Ethan Allen of Transport, what's happening with you?" the Chief asked.

"Sire, I now have three private companies established, to begin making beamway steam engines, beamway carriages, and beamway freight cars. I'll get yet another company to make those huge Odin-Boxes, although that might be done by Regions. Once they get going with their projects, we'll get competitive companies established. We have yet to receive a single beam to lay down, but our sawmill has halved many thousands of logs, to lay the beams on, when we get them. We haven't got the tar necessary to coat them yet. Also, I've got King West to design beamway stations, that can also accommodate postal, Valts and insurance services," said the King of Transport Allen. "He also said he'd include other State offices in some of his designs."

"Thanks for that, King Allen," the Chief said. "Now, King Croghan?"

"Sire Odin, I had planned to take Diplomacy Realm's first Odin-Ship to England, to bring back immigrants from there, after posting Ambassadors, in several North European countries. But with King Clark's warning about England, perhaps being in revolt, I'll stay clear of the British Isles, until we know something. Instead, I'll try first for some immigrants from Holland, Denmark, and Norway," King Croghan said.

"Very good. Now, King of the Nobility, Andrew Montour," the Chief said.

"Chief Odin, I'll begin a recruiting campaign right away, as you ordered. Also, I expect to establish a temporary training camp, with tents only, on that State Compound you decided should be at the great Ohio River Crescent, next to the village of New Orleans. I'll have our Esquires cut down the trees there, for their exercise.

"I am confident that for the defense of our Nuworld, that location for our capital is by far, the most difficult for any future national enemy, to safely get to. And Sire, I shall shortly give you a list of the Battle Forces we have, where I intend to employ them, and I'll include the new Battle Forces being formed, and where they could be employed."

"Wow! Excellent, King Montour," the Chief said. "I will certainly welcome your report. Thanks for that. Now, King Revere?"

"Sire, for the Chief's and the King's houses on that State Compound, I think the furniture should be of Nuworld design, strictly. I've begun to make sketches myself, and I hereby invite others with a desire, and a talent, to design assigned pieces. We understand that the houses and the furniture for them must be uniform for the two dozen or more, King's houses. The Chief's house is to be unique... indeed, King West's design for that house seems sure to be revolutionary," the King of Supplies Paul Revere said.

"Thanks, King Paul," the Chief said. "Now, King Thomson, what's new with you?"

"Chief Odin, I now have 26 men and women, hired to correct English spelling for our Nuworld Dictionary. Also, I've hired an experienced builder, to design a variety of school buildings; he's not a graduate architect, but he's a great draftsman and very talented..."

"Hold it right there, King Charles," the Chief cut in. "On the way back from Europe these last several days, I've almost exploded with language ideas. On the morrow, we are to steam up to Boston, where I've promised to speak, and I'd like you to accompany me, so we can discuss some of those new ideas. Will you do that for me, King Charles?"

"Aye, aye, Sire. It will be a genuine pleasure," King Thomson replied.

"Thanks. Now, King Doctor Gale; what's new with you?" he asked.

"Chief Odin, we have so very much to accomplish in the Health Realm... but we will not allow that to overwhelm us. Because our dear Asian peoples have no immunity to the Euro diseases, I have right now, nineteen dedicated Doctors, and medical students, working to understand those invidious illnesses and trying to make immunizations for them. Their efforts, I am very certain, could save a great many precious lives; Asians and Euros alike, Sire."

"Excellent, King Doctor Gale. Thanks. Now, King Copley?"

"Sire, I tell you, we are trying everything possible to make coppix printable in newspapers, et cetera. It's frustrating, but my associates, and I are making some progress. Although I'm hardly an athlete, I do think we should create sports teams someday, most especially in schools. Also Chief, we must have music, and painting taught, to all children in our schools. We are humans, and as such, the arts are important for each of us to absorb."

"Thank you, King Copley. Now, King Tully, what progress have you made in creating commercial law? I know you've been working on that."

"You are so right, Chief Odin. I do believe I'll have a complete set of commercial laws for you to examine, and approve or disapprove, within a couple of weeks. I'm being careful what I select from English law, since their standards of justice are fairly often, unjust."

"Good. That's good, King Elias. King Rittenhouse, I've seen you smiling as though you are making great progress with your ritting invention. Very well, what's what?" the Chief said, with a big smile coming from him also.

"Chief Odin, you're quite right. My associates and I are now managing to break down electron frequencies such that, we will very soon be able to adjust each ritting device, so that messages can be sent and received, in privacy. As we all know, at present, every ritt sent can be received by all. And quite another thing, is that I'm fairly confident we shall soon also be able to talk privately, over a similar system to ritting. I don't want to discuss that further, Sire. I just want you and the other Kings to know, the Ritting Realm has been rather busy."

"Wow! King David Rittenhouse, you are a wonder! Very well; all of us will try to contain our curiosity. All of us do understand, those fast and reliable communications would most certainly be a gigantic advantage for our people, over those in backward countries who have it not. The ability to communicate in great detail helps to distinguish us humans from the animals. Now, King Benjamin West, what's happening in your Building Realm?" the Chief asked.

"Sire Odin, I want you to know I have been working on the designs of the Crown House, and the two dozen King's houses. Before I have anything like complete building plans done, I'll have sketches for everyone involved, to comment on. I'm heading in the morning for the site of OdinCity, and I know others will be doing the same. We should be there in our slow OdinBoats when you get there, with your faster OdinShip," King West said.

"Thanks, King Ben," the Chief said. "I would like you to remember that the safety of our Kings in their houses is paramount. Also, it would be nice to see an occasional tip of the hat, to the Greek founders of Democracy, in those houses. King William Eyre is next."

"Chief Odin, I have begun designating Regions and Cities, on crude maps beginning at the edge of the Canada Gulf. Obviously, Sire, that terrain is rather tortured, and there are times that I wish I was an eagle, so's I could see the land below. But of course..."

"King Eyre, I wish to assure you, that you'll soon be able to do that very thing. You and your associates will be able to fly all over our nation. You'll be able to coppix the lands, from up high, too. My Pops has begun, this very day, to execute my designs for a flying machine – an OdinBird. The power for it will come from a new kind of engine, I call an OdinMotor. I first thought to employ steam engines, for that machine, but they are much too heavy for that purpose. So, I invented a new kind of motor, which all of you will see, by and by.

"Now, King Armstrong; what are your plans for the Fuels Realm," he asked.

"Sire, I have not a thing to report, except that I shall also steam my OdinBoat, down near the site of our capital-to-be, in the morning. I'm awfully curious about a so-called petroleum spring, shown on a French map, near the proposed Capital. Also, I'm taking drills, boilers and other equipment with my crew and me, in case it's really there. My Queen, bless her, does not wish to enter that swampy wilderness, as she hates mosquitoes."

"Mosquitoes sure can be a nuisance, alright," the Chief said. "Well, we must find out what can be done about them. No one enjoys their bites... and the possibility of them spreading diseases into us. Ah, now King Benjamin Franklin; what do you have for us?"

"Sire Odin, I really do enjoy calling you 'Sire,' for you surely are the father of our nation. What I have to..."

"King Franklin, the truth is, there are *14 fathers of our country;* the 14 dedicated, courageous, and very generous partners, in the former Nuworld Company. That is one of the very good reasons for embellishing our Nation's Crown, with those 14 large gemstones. Now; you were about to say?" the Chief said without a scolding tone.

"Please excuse me, Sire," Franklin came back with, unabashed. "You know I am fascinated with electricity and magnetism. Thus, experimenting practically night and day, for some time now, I have finally conceived an electric motor, that can also generate electricity. I do suspect my invention can be useful, in your creation of a flying machine. I shall work with your father, and see if it's applicable. Also, I am thinking of using electricity for lighting. After all, lightning produces light, but only in flashes. I shall keep you informed, Chief Odin."

"Thank you, King Franklin, that sounds promising," the Chief said. "Now, King Israel Pemberton; have you made any progress yet with your Elections Realm?"

"Sire Odin, I've been working on scheduling various annual dates for elections. But now, with a new calendar, I'll have to change everything. I should soon have that done, with the new dates, Chief," Pemberton said.

"Good; thanks for that," the Chief said. "Hunting Realm's King Morgan is on the way here, and I've not appointed anyone to the Farming, Insurance or the Chemistry Realms yet. I'm beginning to think Chemistry might be responsible, for finding things like clays, sands, lime et cetera, because making glass or ceramics like bricks, is a chemical process. Well, so is making steel, a chemical process. Anyway, King Daniel Boone, I know you've had no time yet to get things done in your Police Realm. And you have just arrived, King William Trent; have you thought about your Big Works Realm yet?"

"Oh yes, Sire; very much so," King Trent said as both he and Prince Lamb had left their posts as Prince of Montreal, and Prince of Stadacona, and hurried by OdinBoat from Canada.

"I am really fascinated by how we can control the river banks, in the lower Ohio River, at and near our OdinCity," King Trent admitted. "I think I know just how to do it. It consists of building wooden panels on the banks of the river. When each panel is perhaps, say, twenty feet wide, and long enough to completely cover the bank to the river bottom, we can have a crane lift it and slide it down the bank. The wooden panels will stay in place, and so long as they're kept wet, they won't rot. There's a great deal more to it than that, like using wooden pegs to secure each tongue-and-grooved plank, to half logs and each panel to a panel downstream from it," King Trent told them.

"That sounds like a terrifically clever solution, King Trent," Chief Odin said. "Also, if we had a Realm King, with advanced knowledge of Chemistry, he might be very helpful in that other chemical process, called making concrete. We must look for someone with real ability in that field, my Kings. I think even buildings, and especially people's homes, might be made of indestructible, fireproof concrete, that even the fiercest hurricane couldn't blow down.

"One more thing before we adjourn from this," the Chief said. "I feel now that we must print that magazine I spoke of, with each Realm's report on a page of it, and publish it monthly. We'll figure out how many words are allowed on each page for your reports, for the Chief Lady's report, and my report to the Royal Sovereign Electors, of our beautiful Nuworld.

"Now, if George Washington is actually willing, to have the really great task, of taking the Africans in the Nuworld, back to their homeland of Africa, I'll create him a Prince. What say you, Virginia Colonel of Militia George Washington?" he asked with a broad smile to the man, just then standing up to speak.

Washington had a mouthful of bad teeth – a common thing then —so he spoke with hardly any smiling at all. Rather than opening his mouth, he seemed to barely part his lips to talk.

"Chief Odin, I very much want that task. I understand, I think, the difficulties involved, and I do very much grant, that great injustices have been done to those Africans, here in the Nuworld. I will treat them with respect and have a kind understanding of the anger, most of them must feel. With our Treasury Realm providing the funds, I shall see to it, that all of them are properly fed, clothed and sheltered. King Armstrong also told me, I should create several Battle Forces of their most able men... and Sire, women as well. I shall also search diligently for those, who might become worthwhile leaders for them," Washington told the Chief.

"Excellent! Here; King Montour has your uniforms; both buckskins and formal blues. Let's put the blue one on you George... there, you are from this moment on, for the next five years, a Nuworld Prince. Congratulations!" the Chief said with a huge smile.

All of the Kings gathered around the new Prince, shaking his hand and patting his back. King Montour then began to tell him about the organization, and the principles of the Nobility, that Prince Washington was to follow. He would have at first, one steam-powered OdinShip, to gather up perhaps three-thousand Africans at a time. He would need probably three such ships, to continue picking up, feeding, clothing, lecturing, etc., those former slaves, and take them home to Africa... the actual destination to be decided by their leaders.

King Clark spent some time with Washington, explaining the procedure for drawing necessary funds from the Treasury, from time to time, accounting for it, and would give him a large safe to keep his funds in. He should get Africans, to fulfill the bookkeeping task, so those folks would know of the money spent on them. He was happy to hear of the many records taken, from England's Royal African Company; King Clark would make sure he got the entire cart full.

The Prince would begin his unquestionably difficult task, in Boston, where the Chief was headed the next day to speak. He could take command of TICONDEROGA at that port. The name on the sides and rear was to be changed to AFRICANS TO AFRICA AGENCY, # 1.

Afterward, Chief Odin and Chief Lady Annie walked – with their guard band of 12 Nobles – to his parent's townhouse in Stratford. Their "townhouse" was almost exactly like the several hundreds of others, hastily built in the city. Unlike other towns in the Nuworld and indeed, the entire world, all of those new houses had piped in fresh, filtered city water, and privies with sink, bathtub/shower, and a flusher. Wastewater ran through sewer pipes which emptied temporarily, far out into Long Island Sound... newly re-named, Odin Bay.

The number-one failing in their city had been not to make provision for fighting fires, including large faucets on street corners and big hoses. Thus, when the English bombarded their town with red hot shot, they lost very many homes and other buildings. Also, the streets in Stratford were not yet paved.

27

The Chief and his wife had a good meal, and a grand time, with his family. They were all especially attentive, while Annie told of their experiences in London and in LeHarve, France. They were especially curious, about the dealings with the 3 Kings over there.

Returning that night to OdinShipOne, his whole family trailed along with them, since they wanted to take the opportunity, to spend a night aboard. There was more than plenty of suites for the 2 sisters, for brother Ezra, and the parents, to have them all enjoy *warm water* showers, instead of their usual cold baths, before going to bed.

While they were all eating breakfast the next morning, a Noble came with a ritt from Ambassador Hazelwood, who was at the moment, in Amsterdam, Holland.

The Chief was startled to read, that the citizenry of both England and France, were involved in violent revolutions! The total of "Royal Families" in both countries, had been *assassinated, by mobs gone mad! Even all of the Royal's children were butchered!*

Hazelwood said he heard Baron Charles Hay, was attempting to calm the crowds of rioters, and the old soldier did seem to have a steadying effect. Rumored also was that the Duke of Newcastle, Thomas Pelham, was attempting to form a government. The Nobleman-by-birth Baron Hay was even trying to establish a Nobility, like the Nuworld's.

The Hazelwood ritt would, of course, be received by every newspaper in the Nuworld. Very soon, everyone who could read would know what was happening over there.

The Ambassador said England's riots began, when the SPECTATOR MAGAZINE printed stories by notable men, that losing England's Nuworld possessions, not putting Louisbourg to siege, and losing the disastrous battle with the Nuworld Nobility, was completely the fault of the stupid King George II, and his even more stupid, and much too influential son William, the so-called Duke of Cumberland. Those two had chosen impossibly incompetent commanders to serve over there, and those sorry wretches created calamities for England!

Chief Odin was astounded to read the Ambassador's, brief account of London's SPECTATOR MAGAZINE demanding a new Constitution, *exactly like the fair and wonderful* Nuworld State's Constitution! *It was a free press exploiting its power!*

"Well," the Chief said with a sigh, "those countries are having problems we can do nothing about. We have our own problems to take care of, and that's what we will do. I expect Ambassador Hazelwood will keep us informed. My dear family, I do thank you sincerely, for bringing back some dear family times, but duty calls Annie and me, to steam up to Boston. Have a great day, all of you!"

Just in time before cast-off, Prince John Lamb came aboard. He had agreed back in April that he would join the Chief as his assistant, as soon as the Montreal Region, seemed quiet enough, to turn over to the new Region Prince—his Battle Force Overlord. King William Trent of the Big Works Realm, had a similar agreement; he was also aboard then, on OdinShipOne.

Also aboard was Education King Thomson, and Prince Washington, for the short trip to Boston. The Chief was to give a speech for the first time there. Kings Revere, Copley, and Putnam were from that town but were left behind to tend their duties.

Chief Lady Annie and 2 Noblewomen secretaries listened as the Chief, 2 Kings and 2 Princes discussed language changes, as well as the Africans to Africa Agency problems.

OdinShipOne arrived in Boston's harbor in the early afternoon. A fair-sized crowd was on hand to greet them as they docked next to the TICONDEROGA, which they learned had arrived shortly before. On the dock as the Chief and Chief Lady stepped ashore, was King of the Hunting Realm Daniel Morgan, to greet them, along with a number of Boston's notable men.

At the dock, were 29 mostly female Africans, who were graciously handed over to Prince Washington. Each of them had an identical bag, holding all their possessions. That Prince was off to a fair beginning in his task, since he had 43 of his own former slaves, yet housed on the DU CAIN. He was to take over also, the TICONDEROGA, and change the name of those new vessels, to AFRICANS TO AFRICA AGENCY, Number 1 and Number 2. The Chief had assured him that at least a 3rd OdinShip would be assigned for his use when needed.

A ticklish issue was weaponry for the Africans. The Chief had told the Prince he would gradually allow the Nobility, to turn over the thousands of original OdinGuns and ammunition; but the need for the extremely powerful OdinRocks was open to question for the time being. The Nuworld Nobles would soon all have the new Odin2Guns. The Africans would, of course, need Battle Forces, to assure a place for them on that continent. The Chief told the Prince they should be Nobles, one and all, to help restore their self-worth. They would all need new and appropriate clothing, be supplied with plenty of good food, *and every book possible, they could get for them, to learn and practice reading.*

Nobles lowered the large ramp near the rear of the ship. The 3 huge Percheron mares pulled out the 12 by 8-foot OdinCart, to the astonishment of those notables on the dock. The OdinCart was practically covered with chairs, which were quickly filled with Kings, Princes, Nobles and the well-dressed gentlemen of Boston.

They drove to Boston's "State House," with the Chief and the Chief Lady in their formal blues, medals and all, standing up front, and waving with broad smiles to the crowds along the street. The Chief wore his Nuworld Crown and would keep it on until they returned to their ship. His Crown was somewhat heavier than a similar brass hat, being of gold and platinum.

The big room in the State House was nearly full as they entered. A couple of Nobles wheeled in the heavy 6-foot-wide slate board from the Chief's ship; it had been made somewhere in Wales and intended for classrooms. They got it up on the small stage, in the front of the room. Chairs were there for the Chief Lady, the 2 Kings and the 2 Princes to sit and listen, as the Chief spoke.

First, the Chief introduced his wife and the 4 "extremely important men in the challenging work they are doing, for the benefit of all Nuworlders."

"Ladies and gentlemen!" he then boomed, as he noted very few women were present.

"I had intended to talk to all of you, about our Nuworld Constitution. But I think you might be interested to know that England and France are presently in revolution. We are informed that a London magazine over, there printed a copy of our Constitution and my Coronation address. With their fleet's destruction by us, and ah... other things, the result is, *those Englishmen are in an uproar because they want a Constitution and a government exactly like ours!*

"Riots are happening also in Paris, with those folks also in an uproar, it seems.

"Most people don't realize that our Constitution was created over several years, mostly by 14 Nuworld Company partners, eager to set down rules, that were best for all of our people.

"I'm quite certain your Boston newspaper and the 23 or so other newspapers around our nation, will soon be giving us, all of the facts of what is, and has been, happening to those lands that so many of us, or our ancestors, came from.

"Instead of politics, I'd very much like to talk to you about a business many of you, or perhaps just some of you might be interested in. That's why we brought this slate board and chalk sticks here," the Chief said while pointing to the large blackboard behind him.

"All of you know, I have invented steam engines; they power our OdinBoats and our OdinShips, as well as other things. What you wouldn't know is that I have also invented what I call, an "Odin-Horse." It is a machine to do the work of horses; do that work better, more dependably, and over time, probably a lot cheaper. We have to feed horses every single day, whether they do any work or not. And we have to clean up the messes they make, all the darn time! An OdinHorse only needs to be fed some kind of oil when it works for you; period.

"That machine is right now being made by a company my father, and a fair number of workers have begun. When that outfit gets well started, my father will sell his shares to that company and start another enterprise. You must have heard of the great success, several companies have had in Stratford. Very importantly, *every worker in those companies owns shares in their company*. The principle is, our Treasury will loan the necessary money to the employees, to buy shares in their company. Everyone, therefore, shares in the profits, and that of course means, everyone works their best at making a success of their commonly-owned enterprise.

"You might want to do the same. Also, Commerce Realm King Elias Tully has printed a small book on starting and running such a company. You'll want to read his book carefully.

"Now, I'm going to draw on the blackboard, and tell you some of the details of the OdinHorse, being made in Stratford now, as we speak," the Chief said as he picked up the chalk.

Explaining as he drew, he talked of the steel frame necessary, the 4 large wheels and their dimensions of 5 feet diameter and 1-foot thickness. Instead of spokes, the wheels had boards enclosing both sides flat so as to prevent mud and such from accumulating. The front wheels did the steering. Their tires were of bent wood, with 3-inch square oak "grippers" across them, 2-inches apart, all around each wheel. The grippers were held to the wheel with inset screws, so the grippers could be replaced when worn out.

The 3-cylinder steam engine laid flat just below the frame, was fully enclosed, with the piston in each cylinder being pushed forward and back by steam. The connecting rods came out both ends of the cylinders to turn, the fore and aft crankshafts, which were a part of the axels, to power all 4 wheels.

The Chief drew the driver's seat, and the steering wheel, and spoke of the controls.

"However," he told them, "I do recommend you buy your engines, boilers and steam coolers, from the steam engine company, at first. With experience, you can begin to make your own engines. The coiled brass tubing in the boiler is by far the most difficult to make; it nearly drove those of us crazy, trying for it full time, for about 3 weeks, until we got it mastered. When you examine a boiler, you'll see our difficulty in getting it just right.

"Now, what I highly recommend you make, here in Boston, isn't the OdinHorses, but vehicles vaguely like them, but for the transport of workers, or families, or with multiple seats to haul lots of people, and also those with a box on back, to haul goods. You could also make a vehicle with real power to haul large wagons – or you might call them, trailers.

"I shall mention to my father, that a group of you Bostonians, could be visiting the OdinHorse mill, to see the production line there, as a model for what you might begin to do here. Mind you, *millions of such vehicles, are going to be needed in the years ahead.* That is why I'm suggesting, some of you folks might want to grab this opportunity, with all of your might, with all of your imaginations. You must have competition, so I'll be telling those on Manhattan and those in Philadelphia shortly, the exact same thing I've told you, good people, here today."

The Chief continued to describe details of possible vehicles and answered their questions.

As the Chief and his companions filed out of the Boston State House, they shook hands with the people. They climbed back aboard the huge OdinCart, drove back to the docks and steamed out of Boston Bay to sea, to return overnight to Stratford.

Prince Washington was left behind with his Africans, on the former TICONDEROGA. King Morgan came along on OdinShip-

One, to take over a new OdinBoat, he would live on and conduct, his Hunting Realm business from... for perhaps 2 years or more.

King Daniel Morgan's concern just then was when the Chief would declare Nuworld fishing limits and how far out. But Chief Odin insisted there was no point in doing that, until they had the means for the Nobility, to enforce their laws at sea.

The whole group had suggestions to King Thomson, about improvements to the language. Everyone agreed that the Chief's idea of marking letters, in at least 8 ways, to alter their sound, was good. They were agreeably surprised, he would suggest one form of writing or printing their letters, as capitals letters were then done. The Education Realm King seemed to soak up all the new ideas with aplomb. Everyone agreed; King Thomson had a delicate task, in boldly altering the language.

They all had fun in discussing whether Nuworld Treasury branches should be called "banks," "vaults," or "valts." King Thomson insisted that rivers and even piles of snow have banks; people ought to keep their money secure in "valts"; that word was the most nearly right.

Prince John Lamb kept himself busy making notes, while King William Trent kept mostly to himself, while also making many notes, about what might be done in building the new and hopefully very grand, OdinCity.

They all were just completing a nice dinner when they docked in Stratford. The Chief got a note off to his Pops that groups from Boston, Manhattan, and Philadelphia might soon be nosing about his OdinHorse mill, to study their techniques, of building their work vehicles.

That next morning, OdinShipOne steamed for Manhattan. The crowd the Chief spoke to, repeating his Boston talk, was listened to by a smaller, but even more enthusiastic crowd. After visiting with some of the people there, they steamed out onto the Atlantic, and then up the Delaware, to spend a couple of days at Philadelphia.

This time, Chief Odin gave his talk on the same oaken wagon, in the same intersection, as he did when he gave his famously memorable, "Philadelphia Speech." The crowd there was larger than at any talk he had given and equally responsive. Even Chief Lady Annie was impressed with that throng, as they were absorbed in watching the Chief draw on the slate.

The Chief and his lady had dinner at Robert Morris' estate and the 2 men spent at least an hour discussing the insurance business. Morris, however, was astonished that the Chief insisted on a non-profit variety of insurance, "Since it was to serve the people, not make a profit off of them." Nevertheless, the man was as happy as a fellow could be, to be made the King of the Insurance Realm, beginning that day.

The new King pledged to settle his business affairs in the Willing & Morris Company quickly, and get himself up to Stratford to take over an OdinBoat to live and work on.

After spending some time with Chief Lady Annie's family, they again steamed away, this time for the Gulf of Ohio and the Beautiful River; O! Hio! A stop along the way would be made at Charleston, South Carolina, to check out a possible prospect, for Farming Realm King, named Henry Laurens.

Laurens had been heartily recommended by King Daniel Morgan, and a ritt had been sent to Laurens and his wife, via the Charleston newspaper, to please meet Chief Odin that next day, and come to dinner aboard his ship. The Chief told him in that ritt that he was being considered, for the position of King of the Farming Realm.

In case he was selected, the Chief had a Noblewoman aboard, make a formal blue jacket for the man who had been described as "average" in size. The Lady would embroider his name on each arm, and "FARMING REALM" on the collars. Red silk sleeves over his shoulder straps would announce his rank as "KING," the same as had been done for King Robert Morris.

Aboard beside the Chief and his Chief Lady, were Big Works Realm King William Trent – whose Queen stayed behind—and of course, the Chief's Chief of Staff, Prince John Lamb. That Prince and his Princess wife would be permanent "guests" aboard Odin-ShipOne, with their own splendid suite of rooms. The Princess was, like the Chief Lady, "with child"; her baby was due in 2 months; she was having a remarkably easy, and untroubled pregnancy.

Chief Lady Annie's and the Chief's child wasn't due until February or March. Two of the Noblewomen aboard claimed to have helped several women giving birth.

Also coming along, were Ezra Stiles and his pregnant wife. Stiles would report on the voyage, and on the location for the new capital city, by way of ritting to his *Nu World Nuz*. Therefore, all the newspapers in the Nuworld would receive his reports. The more powerful E-cells aboard, were necessary for ritts to reach satisfactorily, to and from Ambassador Hazelwood in Europe.

Even before they had cleared Delaware Bay, an Autumn storm was creating a riotous Atlantic Ocean. Steaming south along the Virginia coast and beyond, OdinShipOne plowed through waves, churned up by winds heading straight north. Passing the North Carolina coast though, brought an easier sea and just at dinner time, they pulled into the calm waters of Charleston harbor.

Sure enough, Henry Laurens, his wife, and little son were waiting for them on the dock there. Others had also gathered at the dock, to see a large ship without masts, rigging or sails.

The Laurens family was welcomed aboard. As they all settled down for dinner and began eating, Chief Odin hardly touched his food. Excitedly, he informed the prospective King, some of what was involved, in the management of the very important Farming Realm.

Among other matters, the Chief mentioned that countless machines must be invented, to assist farmers in producing more. "We'll have a meeting in the hall here, and I'll describe a machine needed for the harvesting of cotton," the Chief said.

"To me," he continued, "it's truly astonishing that farmers are still harvesting their wheat, and other grains, with a sickle, as was done I suppose, 2 or 3 thousand years ago. Even with a horse pulling it, a harvester could easily be produced, to harvest wheat and the straw, far, far more efficiently than has been done all this time. I'll give you sketches later if you wish."

"Chief Odin, I know a thing or 2 about business," Laurens said, "and I know you could become extremely rich, making and selling such an invention."

"My friend, I am already the richest man on earth, having the job I was elected to do. One reason for creating the Nuworld State, by my partners and me, *was to ensure every Nuworld citizen can become far richer, in many ways, than they otherwise could.* I expect sir, you will always remember that statement, for it will be a large part of your task, as it is for all of our Kings.

"On the morrow, at the meeting in the hall, I'll describe a machine of the greatest importance, for some enterprising men and women, to get busy inventing and making. I hope you will listen carefully as I explain it. If you still desire to help our people get richer, I'll create you a King of Farming, in front of all your friends there. Do you agree, Mr. Laurens?"

"Yes, Chief Odin, I do. You know I had a pretty good business education in England, and I've had some years of practical business experience, here in Charleston. I do believe I could also be helpful to farmers, in teaching them the ways of business, that could benefit them, I think greatly," he said.

"Excellent, sir," the Chief said. "That was one of the reasons King Daniel Morgan recommended you to me. Well, I hope you won't change your mind in the hall in the morning."

Shortly after that, they all retired for the night. Come the morning, they all joined for a hearty breakfast, before climbing aboard the 3-horse OdinCart, and heading for the hall. The Laurens had brought much luggage, in anticipation of approval.

As usual, people along the way stared in open-mouthed astonishment, at the largeness of the cart, and the unusually huge, dappled, white-headed Percheron mares. Again, chairs were arranged for the dignitaries as they rode, and for the Noble band of guards for the Chief.

As expected, the meeting hall was well packed and entirely by men. There was a small stage up front, and it had chairs there to sit on. But right away, the Chief refused to sit and acted anxious to get on with his agenda.

The Chief, Chief Lady Annie, King Trent, and Prince Lamb, all were "wearing their blues," with their chests gleaming with gold, silver, bronze and iron medals. Chief Odin also proudly wore his unique-in-the-world, Nuworld Crown.

Chief Odin Bushnell stretched out his hands, to silence the crowd, and roared out, "Gentlemen, let me introduce those of us here, visiting the good people of Charleston today."

He first pointed out the Nobles, dressed in buckskins, and each packing an Odin2Gun, telling the audience they were guarding him, the Chief of State of the Nuworld. Then he introduced his wife, Princess Lamb and her husband, and the Prince as Chief of Staff for the Chief.

Then he pointed to King of the Big Works Realm, William Trent, and told of his responsibility, in creating bridges over rivers, and dams to control flooding, throughout the fantastic Ohio River system.

"I must mention," he went on, "that King Trent has already devised a way to cover river banks, so they won't be torn away. Also, he pointed out that water seeps through the soil, along a river, which wets the land, far from the river itself. His wondrous method of covering riverbanks will prevent that seepage, also.

"Most of you have probably read our Nuworld State Constitution, and understand the reasons for it. We are fortunate to have Prince George Washington, a Southerner like yourselves, and an especially courageous man, to head up our Africans to Africa Agency. He is presently, and respectfully, gathering Africans in the north, and will be doing the same here, in time. But I came here not to talk politics, but to consider a shining prospect, for King of our Farming Realm.

"Now, your native son here – Mr. Henry Laurens – is that prospect. He comes to me, highly recommended. But before he formally accepts that position, I want to mention to you folks gathered here, and to him, an important idea, for these southern regions. I want him to know about the very great importance that Realm has, for all of our people; most certainly, for those who choose to earn a splendid living, by working our farmlands... *with machinery*.

"The climate, the soil, and even the rainfall seem perfect here for growing cotton. I visualize this area of the Nuworld as becoming, the *clothier to the world... I repeat; the clothier to the world...* because you can not only grow that most easily cleaned fiber, but you can process it completely, from seed to untold billions of yards of cloth, going into clothing, bedding, tenting, sails, and so many other things.

"You might as well know, I have already invented and patented, a cotton de-seeder. I've made a drawing of it and registered it with the Patent Agency of the Commerce Realm. But I've stipulated that any Nuworlder may make, and use that cotton de-seeder, for free. The Patent Agency will happily furnish a copy of my patent drawing for a small fee.

"With that de-seeder, anyone cranking it could remove and save the seeds, from a pound of cotton, in only a minute or two! Nowadays, I understand it takes a slave, an entire day to remove the seeds from a pound of cotton!"

The sounds of amazement from the crowd showed they were paying close attention.

"Some of you, gentlemen might want to add your ideas to mine and form a company, with every single worker in it, owning shares. That's very important, because our Treasury will not likely loan money, to any company owned by one, or by only a few men. The Nuworld Treasury is extremely rich, and will loan out as much silver as necessary, to help finance worthwhile enterprises, from houses to very large companies."

Then the Chief proceeded to tell them of a "Cotton Harvester," powered with a steam engine. It would be about 10 feet wide, so as to travel on roads and yet, harvest 3 rows of cotton at a time. There would be vertical spindles with straight wires sticking out, along the front of the machine; all of them would spin to snatch cotton bolls. Those spindles would throw the cotton bolls back, into a 10-foot-wide de-seeder, with many, many spinning, toothy discs. The de-seeder would have the seeds, fall into a hopper below, while the fibers would be tossed back into several spinners, to wind the fibers into large-rope-like rovings; which was done at the present time, inside a mill, instead of in the field.

"You wouldn't waste time and effort by putting the cotton into bales; no, you'd have those several rovings, piled up in the rear of your machine, ready at a mill, to be spun into thread. At the mill then, the thread could be woven into cloth, it could be washed, dyed or printed, and then sewn into unlimited kinds, of clothing and bedding, too," the Chief told them.

"You know that is an awfully brief description of the Cotton Harvester you all, with your collective genius at work, can build. Your company or companies probably wouldn't want to sell them to farmers, because they'd be too expensive, and only used briefly each year. But your company could have teams of men, contract to do that harvesting and afterward, service and make improvements to those machines, in your own harvester mill, year after year. It could most certainly be quite profitable, for everyone concerned in the cotton business," the Chief said.

"Now, with that out of the way, I must ask Mr. Laurens if he would still like to take on the really great responsibility, of heading up the Farming Realm?" he asked.

"Yes, my Chief, I most certainly will do my very best, for all of the farmers in the Nuworld!" Laurens stood tall and replied, most seriously.

Chief Lady Annie jumped up off her chair, bringing the lovely blue jacket, embroidered with HENRY LAURENS on both sleeves, and FARMING REALM on the collars. She and the Chief then helped Laurens, get the jacket on. When Queen Laurens had buttoned it up the front, the Chief then slid the red silk with gold lettering, sleeves onto his shoulder straps, announcing to the world, that the man was now a King.

Very loud applause, whistles, and stomping throughout the audience indicated Charleston's approval, of the promotion for their native son. King Henry Laurens waved happily to the crowd, as tears of joy wetted his cheeks.

"Good people," the Chief shouted as the people listened, "King Laurens and Queen Laurens will accompany us, as we briefly visit the spot on that vast, and beautiful Ohio River system, where we anticipate building, what could eventually be, an extremely large, central, Nuworld State, capital city. My guess is, that area could be ideal for growing cotton too, what with the rich soils, the plentiful irrigation water, when rains fail, and an especially long growing season. Goodbye, and good luck!"

Merrily shaking everyone's hands within reach, the Chief and companions made for the OdinCart, and on to OdinShipOne. Lining up along the ship railing, they waved to the crowds until they had gone nearly out of the harbor, back into the then-calm, Atlantic Ocean.

The Chief and Annie went alone to the prow, where they stared at the coastline. Captain MacDougal had been asked by the Chief, to stay close to the coast when he could, so they could study the land as they went by.

Pretty quickly, they were looking at the newest, barely settled, former English Colony, Georgia – named remarkably, for the recently killed, King George of England. The Carolinas were named for then King Charles – "Carol" in Latin—when they were settled. Virginia had been imaginatively named for the "virgin" Queen Elizabeth. She never married, but it was known she had many lovers. Many knowledgeable people, declared Elizabeth was the best King, virgin or not, England ever had.

The two Bushnells stayed entranced, with the increasingly tropical coasts they were passing. Just at dusk, they were about to go inside for dinner. Then the Chief told his wife a secret.

"Annie, when we had our OdinRaft so fully loaded with treasure, we had to stop diving for more. We would have loved to haul home, those tons of iron cannons and balls, left behind, but we durst not. It was early in June of 1755, and we were aware hurricane season would be soon upon us. Half a year before, in mid-December, we had sailed directly from the end of Long Island – now Odin Island—straight for the passage between Cuba and Haiti, on the way to near Jamaica, and our bringing up of treasure.

"So, loaded as we were with treasure, we set sail in June, to the north, cutting through the Yucatan Channel, between Mexico and Cuba, into what we now call the Ohio Gulf. We took a course toward Florida, staying clear of Cuba, and in fact, we never once saw any ships – or even fishing boats – up close.

"Just for curiosity, when we got near the shallow, and clear waters, of the Florida Keys, we kept two partners during daylight, looking out those 'see-the-sea scopes,' that had been so very useful. Of course, we had heard the Spanish had suffered many wrecks, trying to get their thefts of Nuworld treasure, home to Spain, where their souls could absolutely be saved, and sent to heaven, by gilding their churches with precious metals.

"Anyway, Elias Tully and I happened to have the duty down there one day. Both of us spied things laying on the seafloor, in fairly shallow water. We hollered up to drop the anchor and lower the sails, as we saw something curious. In my amazement, I flew up to the weather deck, threw on my diving mask, and jumped in. Annie darling, it was a most astonishing sight. Those things on the sea bottom proved to be silver ingots; *hundreds of them!* There were other things there made of gold, but I only grabbed a single silver ingot and brought it up.

"Well, everyone else also got a good look at those tons of silver, and we weighed anchor and sailed onward. Of course, we most carefully fixed our position. We knew we would return someday when our Treasury Realm needed more treasure. We had already begun to plan for a new nation, to make good use of our great fortune.

"A few days later, still looking through those see-the-sea scopes through the bottom of our OdinRaft, we were close to the east coast of the Florida peninsula, when Rittenhouse and Revere, spied some treasure on the seafloor. We stopped; Paul Revere went down there to take a look. He came up declaring he had found another wreck, with much scattering of, as he said, quite a few bushels of gold bars, coins, and jewelry.

"Again, we carefully determined the exact location of that find and sailed on home. We only saw those two wrecks, but we've heard there are many more, to hunt for someday," Chief Odin told his wife.

"Honey, do you still have those scopes?" she asked.

"Yes my sweet, we removed them from the SARAH BUSH-NELL and stowed them in our Treasury. But when I send some men – probably trustworthy Noblemen and Noblewomen – we'll have 3 much larger scopes, so as to look to each side and straight ahead. I think I'll rig up very bright, OdinLights also, so they can see even better," he said.

"Well, when King Clark gets his Treasury Valts established, in many places, there'll be a whole lot more silver to make nu of, for him. Honey, you might have to do it sooner than you think," she supposed.

"Yes; so it would seem. But we got a fair amount of silver, from the French at Stadacona, a bit more at Louisbourg, and frankly, astonishing tons of that precious coin metal, from London. Also, King Clark will be minting gold coins, to sell for silver; for whatever the exchange rate is, from time to time," he said. "Even so, I might arrange to have those 2 treasure hordes brought up, sooner than I had supposed.

"By the way, King Clark is going to reveal the value of what we found in the Caribbean and the amount we spent for our war, against the French; right up to the establishment of our Nuworld State. He'll reveal the 5% each of us partners ended up with, and the balance in the Treasury up to the day of the revelation. That is, he won't specify how much came from the French and how much from the English. That'll remain a secret."

"Hey sweets, our baby is getting hungry inside of me," she said. "It's almost totally dark, so let's get in there and get ourselves fed!"

Steaming along at 42 nauts, OdinShipOne had, on the morning of September 28th, 1757, taken them to the southern tip of the Florida peninsula. They got well beyond the islands called "the Florida Keys" there, by noon and were heading northwest, beyond the west coast of that tropical land. Captain MacDougal had their ship steaming for the "South Pass," which was the final outlet of the extensive Ohio River system, into the Ohio Gulf. He told them they had yet to go, perhaps another 600-nautical mile, to the planned location of OdinCity.

That Noble Count MacDougal, also said it would take at least 16 or 17 hours because he should probably go slower in the river, so as not to have waves wash too severely on the banks. To that, Chief Odin told him, all of them on board, would like to go slowly enough, that they could study the lands, they had never before seen, on each side of the river.

Indeed, the Captain and his mate were excellent navigators, for they arrived at the mouth of what was presumably, the South Pass of the Ohio River outlet into its Gulf, right after breakfast on the 29th of September. The O! Hio!, the Beautiful River there, Chief Odin supposed, was probably about a nautical mile wide.

✤ 28 ✤

And as they had heard, the water flowing by was a light, dull orange color, from the remaining extremely fine silt, the water carried to the Gulf, from great distances upstream.

Again, the Captain informed them, because of slowing a bit, it would take about 3 hours more to span the 100-miles, to the place all of them had read about, but never yet seen.

Gathered on the foredeck to take in the scenery, were the Chief, Kings Trent and Laurens, Prince Lamb, and the nosy one, Mr. Stiles. The Chief Lady was feeling a little woozy, she had said. She had just finished giving a tour of the boilers and engines to King Laurens, his Queen, and Catherine Stiles, the Ladies' Reporter for the *NuWorld Nuz*.

The further upstream they went, the larger were the trees on the river banks. That told them, a lot of the silt in the water was being dropped and gradually adding, in effect, to the length of the river, into the Gulf.

"King West is already up there, where the city is to be built," King Trent told the Chief. "I'm going to insist to him, that the Chief's House, and all of the King's houses, be built with concrete if we ever figure how to make it like the Romans did. Every 10 years or so, Frenchmen have told me, there's a hurricane hitting this place. So everything built here should be resistant to terrific winds, and also to fire."

"Well now King Trent," the brand new King Laurens put in, "all you have to do is find a mountain of limestone, which centuries before, had a volcano in it, as the Romans found. You have someone pound that limestone into fine powder, as they did with slaves back then, and there's your concrete cement. I'd have to guess though, that there are not any such volcanic mountains around here," he ended with a shrug.

King William Trent seemed amazed at what he had just heard.

"Where the devil did you ever hear of such a thing, King Laurens?" Trent asked.

"Oh, don't you know; I was given a rather intensive, day and night education in London," he answered. "In one of the books about ancient Rome I read, a limestone mountain outside of that huge city was mentioned, as the source of the famous concrete cement, that they actually built buildings with. I recall that some-body wrote, in fact, concrete was re-constituted rock – because it's made from rocks – but the size of any man-made rock, is actually unlimited."

"King Laurens, you shall be my well-educated friend forever!" King Trent spit out with a huge smile. "Why, I can see right now how to make that cement. It was the very great heat of the original volcano, that transformed the limestone chemically, to make it a cement when it got wet. I remember reading someplace, that they called it *hydraulic cement,* because it would even cure, and become rock-hard, underwater.

"Wow! All we have to do is find limestone – hell, that's really plentiful. We'll put that limestone, in some kind of furnace to burn it, and it will melt, just as is done right now, in our iron smelters. But instead of joining with everything that's not iron, and floating on top of the melt as slag, we'll melt it by itself, let it cool and then crush it to a fine powder. We won't enslave anyone to do it; just make the machinery to do that, by cracky!" the now King and former Battle Force Overlord, as well as Prince of the Stadacona Region, said.

"I can see a bit of rain ahead," the Chief cut in. "We'd best get inside, rather than stay out here, and get wet."

They trooped inside and sat at the dining table. The Chief provided King Trent with paper and pencil to draw on, which the King did.

Reporter Ezra Stiles was, of course, "all ears." He habitually memorized every word spoken, anywhere near him.

"We'll build a kind of round tower of steel, and line it with burnt-hard clay bricks. We'll even make them with tongue and grooves, on the four edges. King Phineas Pratt can help us with that. That's where we'll load in broken up pieces of limestone. Below that tall area of stone pieces, we'll have terrific heat flowing through holes in the outer wall, and going out the top of the tower. On the bottom will be molten lime, flowing out an open trough, going into the top of a laid flat, long revolving barrel," King Trent said as he sketched fairly well on the paper.

"We will just have to guess at first, about dimensions, particularly about the diameter and length of that rotating barrel," Trent said as he continued sketching. "That barrel will have very many short iron partitions, oh, about 7 inches apart, circling all around, just with... oh, say several thick iron rollers, between each partition. The barrel being slanted down-hill, as it rotates, those rollers will continually fall and crush the cooling limestone finer and finer. Also, that burnt lime can easily fall through the large hole in the partitions, that the rollers cannot. So, little by little, our concrete cement will cool and become very fine and ready for use.

"It'll flow out of the low end of that long barrel and into... oh, perhaps easy to handle 50-pound bags, ready for use in fusing together for all time, sand and gravel, into any size rock we might wish. Hooray!" King Trent exploded.

Everyone was smiling at the obvious genius, who just described his invention.

"King Trent, I can only see a single error in what you said," claimed the Chief. "It can't be 'concrete,' for that word seemingly means 'with' and 'Crete,' an island over there in the Mediterranean Sea. The name of it has to be corrected from now and forever, to

'TrentCement,' to make 'TrentRock' with; that will be among our dictionary changes. We'll mix water, sand, gravel, and TrentCement, to make TrentRock. Naming it for the brilliant King of our Big Works Realm makes the greatest sense in the world. There can be no argument about that TrentCement and TrentRock, I do here and now declare!"

Then the Chief added, "Prince Lamb, please make a note of that change, to King Thomson, for his new dictionary; he has a couple of dozen folks working on it. You'll want to furnish him too, with an accurate description of what TrentCement, and the resulting mixture making up TrentRock, we'll be using, in extremely fantastic quantities."

The Chief rubbed his chin for a bit and then added, "Also, King Eyre, I've thought of this before, but now I'm much more certain— we need to have your Geographic Realm to also search throughout our nation, to find good sources of lime, clean sand, and clean gravel, for TrentCement, TrentRock; oh, and for the Glass and Metals Realms as well.

"Also, we are going to have a terrific need for TrentRock as well, as for millions of miles of streets and roads. We could use billions of cubic yards of gravel also, for overtopping the present soil of our capital city. Both geography and geology are Greek words for the study of the earth. I do believe we must have your Realm, King Eyre, do both surface and subsurface studies of our lands, to learn what treasures our part of the world, holds for us, and for our endless generations ahead," the Chief said.

"Ha, ha!" King Trent laughed. "Only billions of cubic yards for our city, Chief Odin? That could very well be an underestimate, I do believe. Well, Sire, we'll soon be able to judge our needs a bit better; that's for sure. Oh, maybe I should be embarrassed, but I certainly do thank you for naming that stuff after me. That's good to reward all of our inventors that way, as you have done for yourself."

"Indeed yes, King Trent," Chief Odin replied. "We shall continue that practice."

"Wow!" Ezra Stiles said. "All of this really must be, in all of our newspapers!"

The group of men looked out to see OdinShipOne had gone beyond the falling rain, so they went outside again, to look over the terrain on each side of the "Beautiful River."

Just at noon, on Saturday, September 30th, they came to the village the French had called "New Orleans." The village was on the beginning of the downstream bend, making the crescent, Chief Odin had decided to build the State Compound on. The ground there did seem a little higher than it was beyond the bend, making the gently curved crescent.

The OdinShip's crew tied it to a tree, and an old man said to be the "Major de Place," came on board. It had to be far and away, at 400-feet long, the largest ship the man, and his people had ever seen. He looked around at everyone, and everything, in wonder.

King Laurens had learned the French language well, so he interpreted the old man's words. The Chief knew also that Prince Lamb and King Trent were both somewhat proficient with French; enough to understand it fairly well, with their duties in Montreal and Stadacona.

Kings West and Eyre had stopped by the day before, and talked a bit with the Major de Place, the old man said. King Armstrong had visited with the old man 2 days before that. But they had mostly asked questions of the French there, and failed to mention a huge capital city for the Nuworld State, was to be built there. The old man was surprised at that statement. He said that ground was often wet and occasionally flooded in the spring, from the melting of snow, far upstream, to the north.

King Laurens told the Major de Place, that Chief Odin had, at the port of LeHarve, met King Louis and his Mistress Pompadour; that King had ceded Louisiana, and all other of France's New World possessions, to the Nuworld State. It was done in exchange for 12 OdinShips, like the one he was standing on.

Laurens confirmed that the Nuworlders had conquered Canada, and Louisbourg also. The Major de Place told them, he had long been a resident of Quebec and was surprised by the name change to Stadacona.

Oh yes, King Laurens told him, at that meeting, King George of

England was there, as was King Frederick of Prussia. Frederick had taken a couple of French provinces, too. And, sad to say, he told the old man, they heard revolutions were going on, in both France and England, because of their disastrous defeats in that war. They hoped to hear more by ritt, that night... and of course, ritting seemed monstrously far-fetched, to the old man, so he reacted with disbelief.

The head of New Orleans village had practically just gone ashore off OdinShipOne when indeed, a quite long ritt came again from Ambassador Hazelwood. Although it was still daytime there, in Europe night had come, so the high-powered ritting was successful overall that terrific distance, as though "the signal," bounced off something, high up in the sky.

The Nuworld's Ambassador to the Prussian Court, was yet in Amsterdam, at the behest of King Frederick. He had, just that day, been visited by the English Ambassador to Prussia, Sir Andrew Mitchell, coming fresh from London itself. Hazelwood said, in the confusing days all around them, Mitchell seemed to be, the only man who could be completely believed, in his tale of the English revolution.

After more than a week, after the assassinations of all English "Royalty," and rioting, pillaging, and deviltry of every sort, a government had at last been formed. The former English Baron and Army Major General, Charles Hay, had been elected by a small number of important men, as *the Chief of State, of the British Isles!* His Vice Chief and King of the Treasury Realm was none other than the former Duke of Newcastle, Thomas Pelham! Chief of State Hay, was having a referendum for *all men... and all women... aged eighteen or better, on every piece of the British Isles, to vote yes or no, to adopt the Nuworld Constitution!*

Chief Hay had also declared the money system, for the British Isles, was going to be much less awkward than the old pounds, shillings, and pence, by using their nation's initials, bi. Bi of any amount, was to be equivalent to, and the same value as the nu, in the Nuworld.

King Eyre would later comment that the Brits couldn't buy much with their bi, since the Nuworlders had steamed away, with much of their silver and gold. Perhaps though, there was more of the precious metals, in the British Isles, than in just that square mile of the City of London, they had so thoroughly robbed.

Ambassador Mitchel was certain the constitution referendum would pass *because it was so perfectly written!* Newspapers and the chief instigator of revolution, the SPECTATOR MAGAZINE, were being snapped up and devoured by every English, Welsh, Scot, Irish and Cornish man and woman capable of reading, the ritt said.

Mayhem was continuing unchecked in France, the ritt claimed, with no government yet being formed. It said the Catholic Church "authorities," were attempting to bring order to the reigning chaos, throughout that country. But priests too were being murdered, they said.

Apparently, for the time being, the Prussian government was having very few problems, in controlling their own, and their conquered peoples.

All of them aboard quietly considered what the ritt from Ambassador Hazelwood had said, as the Captain moved the OdinShip slowly upstream, along the 4-miles-long, gently curved crescent of riverside land. As they came around to the further bend, in the Ohio River, they saw King Eyre's and King West's OdinBoats, against the river bank and tied in place. The Chief knew King Armstrong had also come to this place, but his OdinBoat wasn't there.

The sun was about to go down by then, so the Chief asked the other Kings to join them on OdinShipOne, for a talk, and for dinner. Neither of those Kings had brought their Queens to this spot, just yet.

Those 2 Kings had worked on a plan for the State Compound. They showed the Chief and the others, they had drawn a large acreage lot along the river, in the center of the crescent, for the Crown House. Twenty-eight plots had somewhat smaller lots, for Kings Houses, east and west of the Crown House, over the 4-nautical-mile wide crescent.

Inland from the Crown House, would be a large lot, first for a "Public Plaza," then another for the Justice Realm, housing both the Justices, their offices, and a courtroom. Similarly, in front of the

King's Houses, would be lots for their administrative offices. Beyond them, would be their Colleges, with housing for students, so that altogether, those Colleges would make up, the Nuworld State University- the NSU. The Chief had stated that in every King's Administration Building, and in every College, he would expect experimenting to be going forward, towards improving the services of each Realm.

Between the State Compound, and the business center of the city would be a 4-mile-long park, in pieces, because of necessary streets cutting through it. They expected over the years, it would be filled with many statues, acknowledging the greatest of men and women, in the Nuworld, in most fields of endeavor.

"Chief Odin," King West said, "I've only begun to design the King's Houses. I understand they are all to be equally alike, even to the furnishings. I've got the second floors designed, with 3 large suites, each with a privy, where they can walk into their large dressing room, on the riverside of each house for the family; there'd be a matching 3 suites for guests on the north side. There'd be 3 fair-sized balconies on each side, and a smaller balcony at each end of the central hallway. The residents could look out to see things all around them.

"There'd be a curving stairway, in the center of that central hall. At the roof over that stairway, will be an 'oculus,' a glass dome for light, and maybe ventilation. It will show our Nuworld painted on it, like the far larger dome, over the Crown House.

"I figure each King's House should be about 66 feet long by 36 feet wide, with a full basement below. That would make each King's house be 4,752 square feet, plus a basement.

"On the first floor would be a grand kitchen, a family dining room and a larger one for formal affairs, plus a sitting room.

"There'll need to be a fine office-library for every King in his House. That's as far as I've got with the King's Houses, and only have a vague idea of the needs for the Crown House," King West informed the Chief and the others.

"If I may inject a few thoughts about all of that," King Trent put in, "King West, you'll want to consider that there are occasional hurricanes here, with terrific winds and amazing rains. I've talked in Stadacona, with some Frenchmen, who've experienced houses being blown around here, as though they were mere paper boxes. You'll want all of those buildings in the State Compound, to be able to withstand whatever might come at them. You'll want really strong shutters at every window, to be locked shut during such times. Those buildings must not be built of wood. Think of the horror, of any of them burning down, possibly with the family roasted."

"You seem to have a lot of ideas about architecture, King Trent," King West said in a friendly way.

"Oh no, my friend, I don't have any ambition to involve myself, into your field," King Trent answered. "But during every day since our Chief decided, this spot should be our capital city, about a year ago, I have thought about it. I've visualized every street being paved forever with... very well, with TrentRock. Sidewalks also should be wide and paved smoothly with it. Under every sidewalk should be a trench for drainage water. There could be sections of such walkways to be lifted out, so that men could get under the walk, and add or modify services to homes and other buildings, now and then.

"Your King's Houses could be built with the same stuff, last forever, be strong against all hazards, and be naturally, fireproof. You could pour the steel-bar-reinforced-TrentRock, into steel forms, that could be re-used, one after another, for each identical house. You should have a full basement, under each of those houses, for a large water heater, that could furnish heat and hot water throughout the house. You'd want fans on the ceiling, of every single room for cooling breezes," Trent said just as the Chief raised his hand to interrupt.

"About those basements, King West," the Chief put in, "I do believe you should figure to have very large doors, for steam-engined vehicles to enter and leave. At Boston, Manhattan, and Philadelphia, I spoke to encourage people, to form companies to make vehicles similar to the OdinHorse, which is being produced right now. They could make vehicles for the King's families, to get around the city on or out into the country. They could drive such machines to go shopping or visit friends. King West, you might consider those King's

Houses, might keep as many as 4 kinds of vehicles in their basements. Of course, the Crown House will also require such vehicles in its basement."

"Wow!" the Building Realm King said. "My Chief, I'm getting more ideas all the time for this State Compound."

"Well, you might also think about the possibility of building structures to considerable heights, with TrentRock. Think about an inn, let's say, or an office building, in your central section of the city. Using steel reinforcement inside TrentRock, you could move your steel forms up, floor after floor, to as high as you'd wish to go. Ten stories? Twenty? How about all the way to 30 stories high? Of course, no one would want to climb that many stairs, so you or some other genius, would have to invent a cage, let's say, that could rise and descend with passengers or whatever. Then it would be a ride-cage or something; eh? Think of the experience people could have, riding up and down *on the outside of high buildings.*

"Why should priests and preachers have all the glorious buildings, higher than all others in a city? Since we are to build a unique city, we should consider lots of things," the Chief said.

"By the way Chief," King Trent said, "since you've suggested we might use the river current to power some sort of machine, to dig out the bottom of the river to fill in the land, I've thought of going all out with a steam-powered rig.

"After we've sealed off the river banks like I suggested, I'd say we could have steam engines on barges, driving 3-foot diameter screws, in a like size pipe, to gouge out enormous amounts of soil from the river bottom, to pump it onto the land. We need so very much soil up there, and a rig like that would get it up there in a hurry. Your idea of lowering the river to raise the land is exactly what's needed, I think. Of course, we've gotta drain away all that water that rains on the soil, the buildings, and the streets, too."

"Hey, my friend; that's great thinking!" said the Chief. "That's the kind of thought that will get the job done and quickly, I have to say. Well, my Kings," he said, glancing at all of them, "I know we have your brilliant minds at work on this. Let's have dinner, and on the morrow, we can all go for a walk all over the State Compound area and then take a ride on my OdinCart over to look at that water the French call, Lake Ponchatrain."

The next morning, the OdinShip had to be moved upstream some ways, to where the river bank was more easily lined up with the big ramp, that allowed the huge Percherons to haul the OdinCart ashore. Then the Chief, the Kings, the Chief Lady, and Queen Laurens, all strolled through the forested and bushy area destined to be the State Compound.

The species of trees were quite variable. Many of them there were oak, with "Spanish Moss" dripping from their limbs.

The ladies were wary of possibly lurking snakes, as they were walking among such thick bushes. Thus, they fairly soon got on the OdinCart for the ride to the lake. Three Frenchmen were hanging around just then, so they were invited to ride along with them.

The French maps indicated the lake at that point, was about 9-nautical miles from the river, at the crescent. There wasn't even a trail to follow. The horses pulled the cart this way and that, on the way, dodging trees and the larger bushes.

At the lakeshore, they noted they could not see across the lake. Someone said it was about 25-miles to the other side. The Chief saw that it was shallow and King Eyre told him they had those same Frenchmen, residents of the nearby village, canoed them out some distance. They found the lake seemed to be uniformly, only 10 feet deep.

"Wow!" the Chief exclaimed. "Only 10 feet deep! That means it can be filled in so that we can build here, a really large city. King Trent, I'm sure you'll find a big hill over there that you can level, to barge the dirt over here. In time, you can fill that lake entirely so we'll have plenty of room for people's homes, and mills to work in, and schools... well, and all the rest. That lake has got to go! We have more than plenty of water to look at, in the Beautiful River."

Several of them scooped up a handful of the water. They found it tasted a bit salty, indicating seawater on tides, got mixed in with the freshwater, a lake should consist of.

Back on the OdinCart, they had not gone back but 1/2 mile, when the right-hand Percheron jumped to his left, against the shaft and the middle horse. They instantly saw it was a sizeable alligator, with his mouth opened wide, threatening that horse. He was laying on the ground, within about 10 feet of the far larger animal.

"Chief Lady Annie," the Chief said, "here's your opportunity to show what a tremendous great shot you are. Which eye do you want to shoot out first?"

"Oh, I'll try that right eye, my dear," she said ever-so-calmly as she lifted her Odin2Gun out of its holster.

In seconds, she had shot the alligator's right eye to bursting, with its substance spurting out all over the ground. Then she exploded the left eye, the same way. All of that was done in an instant since she had practiced with her Odin2Gun, just as her husband had.

With each shot, all 3 of those giant Percherons jumped. Queen Laurens did exactly the same. Later, she expressed amazement that the Chief Lady would shoot the thing. She didn't know then about Overlady Annie, killing the French ship Captain, attempting to re-take his merchant ship, the Nuworlders had captured in the Caribbean.

The ugly beast's brain was doubtless chewed up, as his head slumped to the ground. His toothy mouth snapped shut. The Chief Lady re-upholstered her weapon and visibly shuddered at the sight of the eye-less alligator. Blood was pouring out of those eye sockets, over its head.

Several of the men, including the Frenchies, picked up the dead animal, and laid in on the back of the OdinCart, proving the beast was as long as the cart was wide: 8-feet. They would haul it over to the river. From there, the Frenchmen could take it to their home, to remove its valuable skin, and earn lots of nu, probably.

Returning through that dense forest, where their capital city was to be, they saw no more alligators. The French had doubtless reduced their numbers over the years. There were, however, plenty of squirrels scolding them, as they moved along under the squirrel's trees. Also, aflight the whole time, were numberless birds. They noticed especially, the tantalizing hummingbirds, as they constantly searched for yet another flower, to poke their long beaks into.

At the river, King Trent told the Chief, "Sire, what we must do here first, is cut every single tree down. We'll have to set up a sawmill, to utilize all that wood. We'll cut off all the branches, and the smallest diameter ones, we'll spread everywhere on the ground, to stabilize that soil as the dirt is pumped up, from the river bottom. We'll leave the tree stumps and roots in, too. Of course, we must also stabilize the riverbanks as I've described.

"While we're at it, we'll build little fish houses, on those wooden walls lining the banks. We could make their houses slanted, so that the smaller fish can rest inside from fighting the current, and also be protected from big predator fish, now and then."

King Trent showed him a sketch of a 3-foot-long plank, with angled sides, that was fastened low on the wooden wall on the upstream side. Swimming into it, little fishies could go into the house further, because of the slant, than big fish could.

"That's what I like about you, King Trent," the Chief told him with a smile; "you're always coming up with great ideas. By golly, I'll have to try fishing when we're living here. With your thoughtfulness, there should be lots of fish to fry in our kitchens."

"That's the idea, Chief," King Trent answered. "With lots of fish in the Beautiful River here, there'd be no excuse for any of us going hungry."

With such silliness behind them, the lot of them climbed aboard OdinShipOne, for a cruise upriver. A few miles up, they saw on the left bank, where surely King Armstrong's OdinBoat, had climbed up, and over the bank. They continued on and found a very sharp loop in the river, where the stream flowed to the west and then sharply came back.

"King Trent," the Chief said, "I'm sure you'll remember to straighten out the river here. You can barge that soil down and put in on our land somewhere. There could be other such loops too, where you can dig it out, and shorten river trips."

"Aye, aye, Chief," Trent replied. "I shall do that. Wow! Are you suggesting, Chief Odin, that I might be the founder of OdinCity, like my father did with Trenton, in Jersey?"

"King Trent, I do believe that's a very good idea," the Chief said.

"However, it should be understood that King West has the appointment, as Architect of our State Compound."

The Captain turned the ship around and tied it up to a tree beside the bank where the OdinBoat had climbed up and over. The Chief and his companions got up the bank and followed the trail of the OdinBoat, where it went through the forest, dodging trees.

They had only to go a 1/4 mile or so when they spotted a wooden drilling rig sticking up. There were King Armstrong and a crew of men. Every one of them was splattered with black oil. Armstrong's OdinBoat was off to one side, and a variety of tools and equipment was scattered around. The wooden, tapered rig stood up about 30 feet, the Chief guessed, as he noticed much of the wood had black oil on it. A sizeable pipe was sticking up out of the ground and was held up further in the structure.

"Obviously, King Armstrong," the Chief greeted the man with his hand out, "you've found the oil the French notes on the map said was here."

"Right you are Chief," that King replied. "My hands are oily, so I'd best not greet you as I'd like..."

"Nonsense!" the Chief came back with, as he grabbed the King's hand. "I shall treasure whatever oil you put on me, and I'll surely remember the smell of it. What a beautiful thing; to find we do have petroleum under our lands!"

King Armstrong was as excited as a man could be, as he told the Chief and the others about drilling into the ground, where a trickle of oil had come out to make a 5-foot-wide puddle. At 28 feet down, oil came out the top of the pipe. That had happened 1/2 hour before, and most of the men had been struck with oil, flying through the air, from that pipe.

Lately, they heard a bit of rumbling underground and didn't know what to make of it.

Just as that King began to tell the Chief about the "refining furnace" he had concocted, before he steamed away from Stratford, and had set up nearby, everyone heard and felt some vibrations under their feet.

King Armstrong shooed everyone away from the drilling rig, warning them that they might all get showered with oil.

Sure enough, in a few minutes, oil did burst out of the top of the pipe, stuck in the ground. Anyone who had stayed near would have been drenched in the black stuff.

That spurting of oil out of the top of the drilling pipe lasted but a few minutes. It seemed like such a waste, to everyone witnessing the oil splashing onto the ground.

"Chief Odin," King Armstrong said, "as soon as we found oil to be under here, I sent a ritt to King Pratt − of course in a code we had agreed on − in that ritt, I told him to proceed with the list of things I told him we would need for the near future."

"And that would be?" the Chief asked him.

"Well Chief, we're going to need large steel pipes and valves... lots of those... we'll need steel oil tanks, for fuel stations in the towns, we can expect to spring up all over the Ohio River system; and sooner, of course, more of them for our Atlantic ports. Importantly, we'll need quickly, a couple of steel oil tanker ships, too. I gave him a design for 200-footers, with the bucket wheels upfront like your OdinShips, for rivers and seas.

"You see that steel furnace refining rig standing up over there, Sire?" he continued. "I expect it can separate the oil from the ground, into heavy tar, lubricating oil, and fuel oil. We'll soon find out whether it'll work right or not."

"King Armstrong," the Chief took the man's hand again and gave him a huge smile, "I am so very glad I chose your shining genius, for the very difficult Fuels Realm. Now, I must hurry back to Stratford and take care of some of my business. I don't have to wish you good luck; I can see you make your own luck! I hope to see you again soon, my friend."

℀ 29 ℀

Back aboard OdinShipOne, the Chief asked Captain MacDougal how long it would take to get to Havana.

"Sire! You want to go to Cuba?" the Count asked in surprise.

"Well now; not quite. King Montour has placed an OdinBoat, just beyond sight of that island, to watch for Spanish ships coming from, and going to, Havana harbor. I want to stop there, on the way to Stratford, to encourage those Nobles, in their boring task of observation."

The Captain immediately looked at some charts. Pretty quickly, he told the Chief it was nearly 600-nautical miles from where they were, to Havana. Figuring a lesser speed while in the river, than the at-sea-speed of 42-nauts, it could take about 17 hours to that location.

That could be about dawn, the next day; a Sunday, October 1st, 1757.

They would then have to search near Havana, for that OdinBoat.

The long-recognized "hurricane season" was to be over in another month; in November. From that time, the Caribbean Sea would be swarming with every sort of sailing ship, until the next

June, from several nations... including probably, some nasty pirate ships. The Chief expected his Nobility, to someday clear that Beautiful Blue Sea, of all men inclining toward piracy.

"Good, my Cap-i-tain," the Chief said. "We'll drop off Kings West and Eyre by their OdinBoats, and then, let's go find our careful observers. After the Chief Lady and I meet with those brave Nobles, we should steam full speed for Stratford."

Before King West disembarked from the Chief's ship, Chief of State Odin reassured him, that he was to be the design master for the State Compound. King Trent was the one from then on, in charge of designing and building the adjacent city.

Almost as though scolding, the Chief then reminded both of those Kings, that they would need to learn much as they went along. He wanted King West to reflect Greek designs, where he could, to remind everyone, that the Nuworld State, was the successor to Pericles' concept of Democracy. He might use his imagination, as the ancient Greeks did, and have human figures, hold up the eight balconies on the King's houses.

King Trent would need to learn the principles of hydraulics very well, in designing earth moving machines; there would be plenty of need for them, the Chief said.

The Chief had his Noblewomen roust from sleep, the next morning, all of his important guests, before dawn. They ate their breakfasts and thus, just as the sun was rising up from the Atlantic in the east, they were all out on deck, watching for some sign of the OdinBoat.

Suddenly, they could just barely see land in the distance, ahead of them. Captain MacDonald declared it was the island of Cuba. He swung OdinShipOne to the west. They searched in that direction for about 1/4 hour, keeping the island barely in view. They neither spied any boats at all nor the city of Havana itself. So the Captain turned the ship to the east, keeping his speed up. Twenty minutes later they did see the Nobility OdinBoat. Sure enough, the roofs of buildings in a city could just hazily be seen, to their south.

The OdinBoat had a tower much like King Armstrong's oil-pumping rig, erected on its deck. Two men were on the top of it, with telescopes up to their eyes, looking in all directions.

OdinShipOne tied up to the OdinBoat. Chief Odin, Chief Lady Annie, Kings Trent and Laurens, Prince Lamb, Queen Laurens, Ezra, and Catherine Stiles, all went over to the OdinBoat, to greet and shake hands, with the 36 Noblemen, and Noblewomen, aboard.

Chief Odin went so far as to climb that wooden tower, to join the 2 Nobles up there. He took one of their spyglasses, and peered around, to see what they had been seeing. He looked too, at what had to be the entrance to the Havana Harbor, but the sea having a layer of haze over it, he could only faintly make out the shoreline itself. Nor could he detect any ships, or even fishing boats, out to sea.

They stayed for about 20 minutes. After assuring those Nobles of the importance of their mission, the far larger OdinShipOne, steamed away. Only then, did the Chief inform his guests that he and Nobility King Montour hoped to take a Spanish treasure fleet if one such actually sailed into Havana. He also told them, of how Diplomacy Realm King Croghan, had baited the Spanish Ambassador, ever so slyly, to that purpose.

Captain MacDougal told the Chief, it would take almost a day and a half, going full speed, covering the 1,400-miles, to Stratford. He said he would not bother this time with traveling within sight of land, but speed between Florida and the Bahamas, then to the northeast.

No sooner were they again on the way, when another ritt came from Ambassador Hazelwood. As usual, every ritt device could receive it.

The ritt offered "hearty congratulations," by Chief of the British Isles State, Charles Hay, for the brilliance of Odin Bushnell, in conceiving the incomparable Nuworld Constitution. Also, the people of those islands – even including the Irish – were celebrating the very new benefits of that document.

Chief Odin immediately replied with a ritt to Hazelwood, to please inform Chief of State Hay... and the SPECTATOR MAGAZINE... that *all 14 members of the Nuworld Company,* struggled to perfect that plan of government beginning in April of 1754, right up to the last battles for Canada, and the formation of the Nuworld State, on August 30th, 1757.

The Chief, of course, understood, that all 24 newspapers in the Nuworld, would also be receiving that ritt. He hoped some of them would publicize that message, so that proper credit would be given to all the men, represented on the Nuworld Crown, by those 14 pretty Nuworld 100-plus-carat gemstones.

The Chief and his guests spent most of their time during that voyage, to coming up with ideas to improve the lot of farmers. Their thinking was that farmers should think of themselves as business-men, instead of mostly growing food, merely for their own families. Since more and more men would be employed – even, *self-employed* – in building or making things, they would increasingly be customers, for food produced by others.

King West kept busy drawing details of the Kings Houses. They would be made of reinforced TrentRock. Instead of the usual wooden studs, and other framework, steel would be used. Between studs and under the roof, some sort of insulation would be used to keep cold and hot weather at bay. All of the TrentRock on outside walls would be covered with a variety of ceramic tiles, to provide texture and perhaps colorful decoration. Floors inside would also be tiled, with rugs here and there, to soften the looks.

King Trent was his usual self, concocting plans to control rivers. Among his ideas, were 12 large, swing-open-into-the-river gates, upstream of OdinCity, to divert some of the Ohio River, into a canal leading straight down to the Ohio Gulf. Gates could be opened one by one, as necessary, to prevent too much water, reaching the city itself. Farms could also be irrigated from that Gulf Canal, the King of the Big Works Realm reckoned.

The Noblewomen aboard outdid themselves that evening. They roasted and stuffed a large turkey, taken from the ice room. With it, was the usual complete Thanksgiving dinner, although that holiday was to happen later in the year. The meal and the business conversa-tion was much enjoyed by the Chief and all his guests.

The OdinShip was being jostled just before, the sun took a swan dive into the Great Ocean Sea. Chief Odin and his Annie ventured out to the prow, to see the Atlantic's waves somewhat higher than they had witnessed before.

That night, the Chief decided he would take aboard the Odin-Horse machine, to employ it as a replacement for the 3 large horses. Also, he would have those stalls removed, as well as the room full of their hay and storage for their oats; of course too, the large pile of manure would be taken away, to be used to fertilize a farmer's field.

The OdinHorse and OdinCart, would take up far less room, and still serve the same purpose of transport when the Chief and others needed it.

"I can't tell you how very anxious I am, to learn how they're progressing with both the motors and the bird. There is one very large disadvantage for the OdinBird though, and that's the very hot gas and air, blasting down from those motors. A pilot will have to be most careful where he puts down with his bird, so as not to start fires," he told her.

"Oh; I hadn't thought of that at all," she told him. "Well honey, why don't you design a bird using a windmill turning and blowing just air down, and not hot gasses. You've made successful windmills. Why not have one that blows air down to lift your craft up? That way, even with the same OdinMotor to power it, if it's horizontal, the hot gasses won't be going down to burn a deck or say a grassy field," she said.

She was altogether serious, he could tell, but he had to smile.

"Well, well," he said. "I don't get enough challenges from my job as Chief... even my dear darling sweet wife has to give me good ideas. Very well, that does make sense; getting a bird up and down without starting fires, is good thinking. Ah, what we desperately need to provide, at least for our Nobles, will be both OdinBirds and... *ANNIE BIRDS!* Yes, my dear; it's your idea, so I'll design an Annie Bird!"

"Oh honey," she said, "that is flattering. But wouldn't it be used mostly by Noblemen? Others too, but mostly it'll be flown by those brave men who'll have to conquer the rest of the Nuworld for us.

Sweetheart, I'd better ask you to call this new machine, an Andy-Bird. Please do that."

"No way, my dear," he said. "This idea came from you, a female, and it seems to me to be important for females all over our country, to know they can use their brains, as well as men. We can have women pilots, too. I cannot believe our Nobles will resent using our AnnieBirds, because that perfectly grand idea, came from the most beautiful woman in the world!"

He bent over the drawing paper and continued sketching... an *AnnieBird*.

The body would be much like the one on the OdinBird, holding two pilots upfront and having twelve folding seats behind them, to carry Nobles as guards, or going into battle; it could also haul stuff. It would have four wheels that could swivel, so it could be pushed around on a deck. He showed an OdinMotor mounted on the roof, with a shaft going forward, into a gearbox, which connected to a vertical shaft holding rotating wings. Another shaft came out the rear of the OdinMotor, to turn the shaft of the rear rotating wings. The rear wings would counter the tendency of the craft to rotate, opposite the turning of the front wings.

Chief Odin guessed the eight wings, fore and aft should be about six feet long. They would be attached at a fixed angle to two-foot-wide caps. Those caps would be turned by the shaft turned by the motor, or possibly, motors.

The "caps" to which the wings were attached, could be hydrauli-cally angled by the pilot's "control rods," mounted between the pilots. When going up, off the deck, the caps would be level, and then tilted to the direction, they wished the craft to go. The wings would be permanently angled so as to provide both lift and propul-sion of the AnnieBird.

Chief of State Odin Bushnell was a "detail man," and he continued well into the night to sketch every idea he could come up with, for the AnnieBird. He continued in the morning, adding a few ideas, to make the AnnieBird more and more nearly perfect.

Speeding from near Havana, Cuba, to the temporary capital of the Nuworld, Stratford, took every minute the good Captain of OdinShipOne, said it would.

They docked a little after high noon, on Tuesday, October 3rd, 1757.

Lunch had been served a little early, so Chief Odin, Chief Lady Annie, and their guests hurried over to the mills area. They first trooped into the new mill building, housing the company of men and women, making the OdinHorse.

They had completed just 2 of the machines, thus far. But on the production line, it was pointed out more of them were in various stages of construction. The company president, as he was called – wearing workmen's clothing like the others there – told the Chief that they already had orders for 27 more OdinHorses; the future looked great for that machine.

The steam engine itself consisted of 3 cylinders, slung horizontally between the rectangular steel frame. Inside the cylinders, were double-acting pistons, that were forced back and forth by steam from the boiler above. A converter in front of the machine was where used steam was cooled back to water, by air being sucked through by a fan. That water was then pumped back to the bottom brass coiled pipes of the boiler, to again be heated to high-pressure steam.

Crankshafts were connected to both the front and the rear axles, turned by the engine, driving the 4 very large wheels. There was a seat, a steering wheel, and controls for the operator, and a tow bar for pulling carts, wagons, plows, etc.

"Sir, has anyone tried out this rig, to see how it works?" the Chief asked.

"Indeed yes, Sire," he replied. "Every single one of us in this mill has driven it back and forth, to see if any of us could come up with improvements. Except for those wooden tires, we think it's perfect, just the way you designed it, Chief Odin. Someday, someone will come up with some sort of soft tires, that don't make so much noise on cobblestones, like those of wood."

"Thank you very much for the compliment," the Chief said. "I'll give it a try myself."

Chief of State Odin climbed aboard. Without any instructions except for his memory of what he had designed, he started the oil fire blowing down onto and through the coiled brass tubing, in the boiler, to make steam. That required but a minute or 2. Then he drove the machine to the far end of the mill building, and back again. He flashed big smiles, and waved at the company's *owners/workmen,* as they applauded him when going by.

He told the company president that he must pay them for the OdinHorse, and he would have a Nuworld Treasury check for it when they delivered it to his ship in a few days. Being the Chief of State, he was not to accept, such as a personal gift; it would belong to the State. He explained that the huge Percherons, and all their accommodations, would need to be removed, before the machine was put on board OdinShipOne, for duty in pulling the OdinCart. He told him they had to make accommodations also, for flying machines, he hoped could be delivered soon.

"Oh yes, Chief Odin," the man said. "Everyone in Stratford, I suppose, has heard your father and his company, are making Odin-Birds for you. But I don't think I've heard a single person agree that flying machines are possible."

"Sir, I do believe we'll all find out fairly soon," the Chief said, as he and his guests left.

In the next mill building, they got to see other *owners/workmen,* making bladed wheels of hard wax, prior to them being covered carefully and dried, step by step, in plaster. Then the mold was heated to melt out the wax, and finally, molten high-carbon-steel was poured into those molds, to make bladed wheels for the OdinMotors. They saw there were already 6 of those 5-foot diameter, new sorts of motors, tested and ready for use on the OdinBirds.

OdinMotors for AnnieBirds would be narrower, with no need to throw cool air back for propulsion; only for moderating the temperature on the inside.

"King Benjamin Franklin has been here several times, Chief Odin," the head man there told him. "He's most anxious, he said, to try OdinMotors for turning electric generators. It certainly seems like a grand idea to us here."

The Chief and his guests next went to the mill building where the OdinBird was being produced. Inside, they were warmly greeted by Nehi Bushnell, who gave his son a big hug of welcome. All of them then went to the production line, to see the first of the machines, to be nearing completion. The box beam for the wings was on the roof of the body and was extended left and right. Another framework was attached to that beam, to support the wings; that box beam also went fore and aft on the roof, to distribute compressed air through the 4 nozzles necessary to keep the Odin-Bird level, when going up and coming down. They could see the box beam was tightly made, to hold a large volume of compressed air.

The body itself looked nearly complete. Even the pilot seats and the 12 rear seats were installed. The 4 wheels were there. The wings, however, were still bare of the thin steel covering, that had to be welded on.

Other OdinBirds were in various stages of being made, along the production line.

"Your new sheet metal welder works beautifully," Nehi Bushnell told his son. "King Franklin tells us that when he's able to produce more electricity, we can wrap that welder's copper cone, in electrical-resistant metal strips, and keep the copper at a constant temperature. As it is, we can only weld about 40 dots, before needing to re-heat that cone."

The sheet metal welder was an adaptation, of Chief Odin's steel plate welder. Instead of heat blazing out of a hot copper cone to heat a couple of inches of steel on 2 adjoining plates, to make them extremely hot, and expand into each other – welding them permanently – he had an insert into the cone of a high carbon steel rod, less than 1/4 inch thick. The copper needed to be only at moderate heat to concentrate, the heat rays onto that rod, to make it white-hot. Pressing that rod firmly onto clean thin steel, against other thin steel, welded the two together.

Chief Odin could see the dotted steel sheeting on the body of the OdinBird, making in effect, the framing and the covering, one.

The OdinMotors weren't yet mounted on the OdinBird, either.

"My son," Nehi Bushnell said, "I expect we'll have your 1st bird ready for testing within a week... oh, possibly by Friday. We know the motors worked perfectly when they were tested, so we'll soon see how well they perform in the air."

The Chief told his "Pops" that he needed to have carpenters, alter the space on his OdinShipOne for the OdinHorse.

The Chief and his guests studiously inspected the details of what had been so far done, on the OdinBird. They chatted with the *owners/workmen,* and congratulated all of them within reach, on the goodness of their efforts.

Before they left, the Chief asked his father to please bring the family again, that night, for dinner on his ship... and that he had yet another project for him and his OdinBird Company.

"Wow!" his Pops exploded. "Yet another project, son?"

"Ah, but this one Pops, won't be very much different from what your company is now doing. I know you'll like it because the idea for it came from my darling Annie," he said.

"Well then, it very much has to be a great idea," he said with a smile to his daughter-in-law, standing there, and taking everything in that she could see.

The Chief then showed his sketches of the AnnieBird to his Pops and explained everything about the aircraft. They would adapt the nearly complete OdinBird body to the AnnieBird design, and begin working on it immediately, Nehi Bushnell said.

With that, Chief Odin and the rest walked the 3/4 mile to Uriah Hayden's shipyard. Hayden took the group over to the shipways. The outside of several new steel ships seemed virtually complete. But as they climbed aboard, they could all see carpenters – or shipwrights – were still installing pine paneling on some of the walls. Doors and windows were in place, but not a stick of furniture nor any rugs had been brought into the ship yet.

"Chief Odin," the shipyard owner said, "we've followed your original design faithfully. The hull is of 1/2inch steel, and the bottom is 1inch thick steel. So, these ships are really capacious. Also, they're light and have a shallow draft. The French will most certainly be overwhelmed by their 12 ships, I'm thinking."

"Mr. Hayden, you know we've been friends for a long time, and

I've always respected you greatly. You and your many, many workmen have done a perfect job here. We will need, however, some iron rings on OdinShipOne's weather deck, to tie down a couple of aircraft my Pops is now building. Also, we'll need access with hoses to the fuel supply for those aircraft. They'll not be steam-powered, but rather OdinMotor powered. You'll see them rather soon, I'm sure. I must ask you sir – how is your progress on those 12 ships for France?"

"Chief, we've got 6 of them completed and launched. It'll be about 3 more weeks until the rest are ready to steam away. You can see them there, in the river. They're done as you said, with the interiors incomplete, so the French can complete them as they wish. Shall we get these 6 to France right away?" Hayden asked.

"No, Mr. Hayden," the Chief said. "I want the entire 12 Odin-Ships to be taken over all at once. I'll have King Croghan of Diplomacy, arrange for crews, who can speak enough French to teach their people how to operate them. Also, I'd like him to accompany them, in his own OdinShip, so he can present them with his usual, beautiful friendliness."

"By golly, I'd very much like to go along with King Croghan; he's such a wonder of a man. You could not have appointed a better one than him, for Diplomacy," Hayden said. "Anyway, Chief Odin, my wife, and I need a vacation; we've worked long hours for a long time. By the way; she supervised the painting of your steel OdinShip. How about that?"

"Really? I'll have to congratulate her on doing such a good job," Odin said. "Please, Mr. Hayden, I'd like you and your dear wife, to join my family for dinner on our ship, tonight."

"Very well, Chief Odin," he replied. "Tell me what time, and we'll gladly be there."

Returning to OdinShipOne, Chief Odin was delighted to see both Kings Rittenhouse and Franklin there, waiting to meet him.

"Ah, Chief Odin," King Franklin said. "Both King Rittenhouse and I have good news for you, but his discoveries are more important than mine. He's first."

"Thanks, my friend," King Rittenhouse said to Franklin, as all of them walked onto the ship. "I really have come to an important break-through, with ritting, Sire. I'm finally able to finely separate ritts by frequencies, therefore making ritts private. With the new ritting device Chief, you can ritt to anyone with complete privacy, *and talk to each other, back and forth*. How about them apples, Sire?"

"*Them apples please me greatly,* my dear friend King Rittenhouse," Chief Odin came back with, to the scientist who was an original partner, in the Nuworld Company.

Both David Rittenhouse and Benjamin West had been recruited by Ezra Stiles, on a trip to Philadelphia, when the building of the very first OdinRaft was begun. Doctor Gale had gone at the same time to Boston, to recruit artist John Singleton Copley, artisan Paul Revere, and Rufus Putnam. The rest of the 14 Nuworld Company members were from the Old Saybrook area.

"I brought this for you, Sire," the King said, as he put a strap over Chief Odin's left shoulder, which held a finely made leather bag. "Inside, you'll find a ritting device; I call it a 'Rittalk.' You talk into it and hear back from the party you've rittalked to. Under that in the bag, is the necessary E-cell, to provide electricity. It's one of those lod-acid things which are so heavy. I'm trying to find a way to use the plentiful zinc metal, instead of lod, so it'll be much lighter. I'll also give you a charging device, so your E-cells will work for you. Also, you'll need the electrical power of your ship, to call much further, than you can now with the Rittalk. Eventually, I hope to be able to rittalk as far as Europe, and anywhere in the Atlantic, from here."

The Chief took the "rittalk device" from the bag, and saw it was an 8-inch-long, skinny box, made of fine wood. A series of tiny holes were on the "face" of it, on each end. There was a sliding metal arrow, that could be shoved to anyone, of a lot of finely printed names, in alphabetical order. There were about 30 names there, including his wife, his Pops and his mother.

"I'll be using numbers, instead of names, in the near future. Why not talk right now to King Montour?" King Rittenhouse said. "Actually, he is expecting you to rittalk him."

The Chief slid the indicator on the box to "Montour," and like magic, he could hear his King of Nobility say, "Hello Chief! So nice of you to rittalk me!"

"Wow!" the Chief said into the little holes in the box. "King Andrew; where in the world are you right now?"

"Sire, I'm at sea in my OdinBoat, off the coast of Charleston," he heard that King say almost clearly, into his ear. "I'm on the way to meet up, with the 3 Battle Forces I've positioned in the Florida Keys. They're waiting for word that a Spanish treasure fleet has sailed into Havana, so's we can take them. As you know, the hurricane season won't be over for another month, but I figure the Spaniards might get a little antsy, and sail early... you know, figuring we might look for them later."

"Well, that's our King of Nobility, always thinking ahead of the enemy," the Chief said into the rittalk device. "You might know it, but I stopped by your observing OdinBoat, and we enjoyed talking with them and giving them encouragement."

"Sire, they don't have the private rittalk thing yet, but I've brought along enough devices for my Force Overlords; that's all our brilliant King Rittenhouse had to give me. Are you going to stay in Stratford for a while, Chief Odin?" he asked.

"Yes, King Montour, I am," the Chief replied. "I expect to be here for a couple of weeks, or more. That will give me an opportunity to visit with all of the Kings that are here; importantly, I will also be able to visit with their associates too and encourage them in their extremely important work. Please keep me informed, by rittalking me, my dear friend."

Standing next to Chief Odin, and listening in on the rittalking, a man more pleased with himself than King Rittenhouse, would be hard to imagine. He was smiling, ear to ear.

"You have every right to be proud of this rittalk device, my friend," he said to the King of the Ritting Realm. "I expect to be near here for a while, so you and I will have some chance to confer about all of this.

"King Franklin of the Science Realm," the Chief said to the man. "What's happening?"

"What's happening, Chief Odin, is I'm making some progress with confining lightning in a glass tube, to light the nights of the entire Nuworld. I must admit, I don't have it nearly perfected just yet, but my very able associates and I are getting close, I do believe. We're close enough that I've told your King Trent, that he'll have to have electrical wiring into every building in every city... and not just for lighting; I expect for other things, too. Your OdinMotors will be generating electricity for lighting, and probably for running electric motors on fans."

"Well now, my friend," the Chief said to King Franklin, "your invention of putting lightning in a tube, sounds like a great marvel. I had thought we'd need to run pipes to every building to power fans with city-provided compressed air. But since you'd need electricity for lighting, you might as well figure it for motors on fans, too.

"We all must think how to chill, or even freeze foods, someway, without packing it around ice. Think of the difficulty it will be with ice, in our southern regions, and our tropical islands," the Chief said to all of them present.

"Sire, I do think that will be a good question, to raise with the Chemistry Realm, when you have a King for it," King Franklin said. "For one, I haven't the faintest idea of where I'd begin, with that very big problem. The spoilage of food, Sire, is a terrible waste."

"I'd like all of us to remember," the Chief said, "that worse than food spoiling, is that sometimes it's eaten anyway. People can and do get sick, from consuming bad food, and some die as a result. Every loss of life unnecessarily is the very worst heart-breaking waste of all."

Out of the corner of his eye, he noticed Ezra Stiles scribbling notes, as usual. What was being said – except for the talk with King Montour – wasn't at all secret, so it could be counted on, to be in newspapers soon.

That meeting broke up and a short while after, the Bushnell family and the Hayden's arrived, for a happy evening of dining, and conversation, mixed in with plenty of fond memories.

B eginning the next day, Wednesday, October 4th, Chief Odin kept busy all day long and into the nights, visiting with the "millers," as he called those working in mills, making things. In addition, he had talks with the men and women in every Realm, including King West's Buildings Realm, and King Eyre's Geography Realm, when they finally got back to Stratford.

King Trent accompanied the Chief and became fascinated with the OdinHorse. He talked with the "millers" about mounting a blade on the front of them, to flatten the ground. Others could have a large roller, to pack the earth down. Also, instead of the four large wheels as on the first OdinHorse, he suggested putting on a lot of small wheels, inside of a steel "belt" of hinge-like plates, so as to not sink into the soft, wet ground.

Chief Odin's Pops, as Supervisor over the OdinMotor, OdinBird and AnnieBird production, had everything proceeding smoothly. Those millers expected great success, with their aircraft and the motors for them.

The Metals Realm was turning out steel plates, and frames for the OdinShips. Six ambitious divers had already stripped the Housatonic River, of much of the cannonry and the countless iron balls. The TICONDEROGA had brought many thousands of cannonballs too, from Stadacona. More came from the walls of Louisbourg, with countless thousands of guns, and balls, yet on the harbor bottom.

The Glass Realm was experimenting with "floating," on melted tin, molten glass, to create window and mirror glass that would be perfectly clear. The Chief cautioned them that for a place like Odin-City, stronger, thicker glass would be needed, for windows due to high winds.

King Croghan of Diplomacy, asked for and received, another steel OdinShip, to steam away then, to transport his Ambassadors to European nations. All of those Ambassadors had the new Rittalks, so they could communicate with each other and their King, secretly and frequently.

King Revere had already supplied Prince Washington, 4,000 of the original OdinGuns, with ammos, to equip 2 Noble African Battle Forces. Also provided, were AndyPaks, shoes, underclothes and indigo-dyed, cotton garments for those Africans. By far, most of them were males, but the female slaves were also accommodated, with respect. Washington was at the moment underway to transport the first, of their 3 Battle Forces, to what was then called, "Guinea." That was said to be the closest part of that continent, to the Nuworld State.

His other Battle Force was continuing bringing in Africans, from the former Maryland Colony. That was an area where "plantations" were swarming with slaves. The Chief was informed that so far, very little violence had occurred, as slaves were surrendered, to the armed and disciplined African Nobles, as demanded by Prince Washington. Many a tear was shed, however, by slave "owners" whose enterprises were then without workers.

King Elias Tully had finally converted English commercial law, to what he thought more reasonable for those businesses, in the Nuworld State. Chief Odin agreed with his efforts and applauded his sharp friend of many years.

Building Realm's King West was greeted by the Chief, with suggestions about the 6 large and 2 smaller balconies, on the sides and ends, of the King's Houses he was designing. Chief Odin suggested sculptors be commissioned, to create in various ways, a figure – or partial figures – for holding up those balconies. For example, the Chief told him, he could have them make figures for the Metals Realm, representing 8 different activities in that Realm. Oh, for another example, the Hunting Realm King's House might show hunters and fishermen at work; or perhaps the magnificent horns of their quarry, supporting a balcony... but all in TrentRock.

Ah, King Benjamin West was an elegant artist himself, so he was greatly enthused by this. He supposed a possible total of 192 such figures could be created, by perhaps 24 individual sculptors, competing for the eternal fame involved.

King Daniel Morgan of the Hunting Realm, returned during that time with all of the oil tanks full, on a new, 300-foot-long whaling ship, he had designed. There would be plenty of whale oil for their steam engines until refined petroleum oil was available.

The 12 OdinShips promised to the French, by way of King Louis' mistress, Madame Pompadour, had their tanks filled and steamed away for LeHarve, at the Chief's insistence, since that was where they were promised. They were accompanied by King Croghan in his OdinShip. He would be bringing Ambassadors for not just France, but for other European nations. He would try for some immigrants to the Nuworld, in those ports. They hoped soon to establish an immigrant reception station, at OdinCity.

Chief Odin managed to visit every Realm during the 10 days after October 4th. Finally, on the 15th, the first of his 2 aircraft were tested and declared, ready to fly. It was the AnnieBird though since there were a few problems yet with the OdinBird, the broad-winged, two-motored aircraft, he had designed.

The AnnieBird had been tied down while being tested in the mill yard. Chief Odin got the ties off, went inside, buckled himself in, and tried out the controls. Waving everyone around to stand clear, he revved up the OdinMotor, and the craft left the ground. He held it to going merely straight up for some ways, before he angled the wing caps forward, front and rear. Obediently, the AnnieBird moved out away from the mill yard, while still gaining altitude.

There was more than plenty of noise, as those 16 short, extruded brass wings whirled rapidly around. The Chief climbed the craft higher and headed for his new OdinShipOne. He was astonished at the great view he had of the city of Stratford, the Housatonic River, Odin Bay, and the Great Ocean Sea beyond. In minutes, he found his OdinShipOne and eased the AnnieBird down on the rear of the weather deck.

By that time, of course, nearly everyone on the vessel was on the weather deck, watching the amazing flying machine, come by and set down. His Chief Lady Annie was beside herself in the excitement of seeing *her idea,* flying in.

The Chief turned the motor off, got out, and came around to open the right-hand door for his wife. She acted thrilled to be seated and buckled in, as he shut her door. He went around, buckled himself in again, and started the flying machine's OdinMotor again. Up, up and away they went, with the Chief hollering at his wife, instructing her how to control the AnnieBird.

He flew the craft back to the mill yard, where he had come from. There, he had his Pops sit in one of the rear seats, as the Chief again took the machine into the air. He flew it around the town – they located the Bushnell house from up there – and after a bit of a tour, returned it to the mill yard.

This time, the Chief took off with 13 owners/workers, that had been crucial in the making of the flying machine. They were, of course, thrilled at the experience. Chief Odin flew them around the city for a while and returned, again and again, to take others of the aircraft mill, up for a tour. Finally, he loaded in his bride again and took off for OdinShipOne. That seemed enough for one day, as he had Nobles tie the aircraft to the deck.

The next day, a Sunday, he flew around the town with both Noblemen and Noblewomen as passengers, and then crewmen of his ship. Captain MacDougal too, thrilled to have a ride.

Each time Chief Odin flew the AnnieBird, he got a little more experienced with it. By Sunday evening, he was satisfied he knew every aspect of handling the AnnieBird.

By Monday afternoon, October 17th, the problems with the Odin-

Bird had been corrected. It was rolled out to the mill yard. Chief Odin climbed aboard, buckled up and started both OdinMotors. He studied the gauges in front of him and, satisfied that all was well, fed a lot more fuel to the OdinMotors as the aircraft rose slowly up, up and away. Pushing a control rod next to him, angled the wing-mounted motors forward somewhat, and he gained both altitude and speed. Soon, the gauges show a wind speed of 120-nauts as the aircraft gained altitude.

He was cautious about pushing his motors too much until they were well broken in. As a gauge showed his speed was nearing 200-nauts, he noted he was above the ground at 4,000 feet! He might not have been that high up, crossing those endless mountains, the Alleghanys, back in 1756! He was already higher up and flying faster, than he had in the delightful AnnieBird, the 2 previous days.

He returned to the mill yard, set the machine down midst great noise, and again, took up his wife, his Pops and a host of passengers until the sun was about to vanish once again. On the last flight, with dusk closing in, he set the OdinBird down, on his OdinShipOne, at last.

The Noblewomen aboard created a quite special dinner, to celebrate their Chief's success with both aircraft. Everyone aboard, celebrated the grand events, with the Chief and Chief Lady.

About mid-morning the next day, Tuesday, October 18th, 1757, the Chief's rittalk buzzed. Putting the device to his ear, he found out it was King Andrew Montour rittalking him, again.

"Chief Odin," that King said, "I just got word from our observation OdinBoat, that they've just seen ships sailing into Havana harbor. It's just after sunrise here, and they think some of those Spaniards sailed in before they were noticed. They've counted 39, and they believe there's more than that. No question, my Chief, it has to be a treasure fleet. I'm taking my 3 Battle Forces, the 80 nautical miles from these Florida Keys, to there, beginning right now. I have very definite plans on getting ashore, with our Odin-Boats and conquering that fleet."

"What I have not told you yet, King Andrew is that I have 2 new aircraft aboard my OdinShipOne. I am quite confident that the superstitious Spanish will be mystified at the sight of them, flying around Havana. So, don't you even let those Spaniards know you are anywhere near until I get there. We're full of fuel and food, so I'll be leaving immediately. I should be there in about 30 hours or so, as this ship will be pushed to its limits," the Chief told him.

King Montour agreed to hold up at sea, short of Cuba, with his 3 powerful Battle Forces at the ready, in case the Spanish ships should sail out of Havana.

Newsman Ezra Stiles and his wife Catherine were called to come aboard. Two of the Nobles on board had coppix devices to record important events.

Captain MacDougal quickly had the ship steaming, out of the Housatonic, into Odin Bay and then, at full speed, heading south in the Atlantic for Cuba. Pretty soon, the gauges showed their speed at 44 nauts and a bit later, at 45 nauts; that was 3 nauts better than the speed they had gained before. The Gulf Stream flowing at about 3 nauts north along the "Eastern Seaboard," would actually slow down a ship going south. Thus, the good Captain steamed OdinShipOne out beyond, that vast moving sea current; that could help to get the Chief to Cuba sooner.

Meanwhile, Chief Odin had OdinRocks loaded, into the Odin-RockCannons, installed at the mill, on the bottoms of the 2 aircraft. The machines each held 10 OdinRocks. They had no other weapons other than the Odin2Guns, carried by Nobles onboard either flyer. Fuel tanks were topped off, and each machine was thoroughly checked. Several of the Noble Guards were assigned the extra duties, of caring for those mechanical birds.

Captain MacDougal produced for the Chief, several of his maps of Cuba and of Havana. Robert Morris of Philadelphia had already shared with Chief Odin, his observations of harbor defenses there, and important details of the city of Havana. Absorbing all of this, the Chief felt well prepared for the coming adventure.

Of course, during the trip, the Chief and King Montour were in frequent contact.

King Montour's OdinBoat was spotted by the Chief, while he was standing atop the pilothouse, at a little after high noon, with not a cloud in the purest of blue skies. They were then about 22 miles outside of Havana's harbor entrance.

It was Wednesday, October 19th, 1757.

As King Montour leaped over to OdinShipOne, the Chief hailed him and immediately began talking.

"My King, there is no time to waste. I'm going to fly that fixed-wing OdinBird there, over the harbor and city. I hope that will spook them a little; they might think it's the devil, or an angel, or what the hell ever. Meanwhile, you should order 2 of your Battle Forces, to go forward and crawl up on land, east and west of the harbor entrance, as you've planned. You should move your central Force though, just up to the harbor entrance. This ship will accompany that Force. I'll then land the OdinBird, back on the ship here, within sight of those onshore. Then we'll run over to the AnnieBird, and fly off in that. I'll want you to be with me, and my Nobles, in both machines, so you can judge the situation with the Spanish. All right, friend? *Let us now fly!*"

The Nobles and Stiles were already buckled in the rear seats, of the OdinBird as the 2 leaders climbed, onto the front seats. The Chief started the 2 OdinMotors and angled them straight up. With a terrifically noisy roar, the bird was quickly well above the ship.

He came in low, flying at nearly 200 nauts, directly over the harbor entrance, with soldiers visibly terrified, on both sides. He then "stood the OdinBird on its tail," roaring straight up from the center of the harbor, with a fantastic racket, surely shaking the ground itself. At about 10,000 feet, he turned the OdinBird over and came screaming down toward the largest sailing ship there – an easy to recognize Spanish galleon, with its ridiculously high poop deck.

Wasting not a minute, he first circled the entire, irregular harbor. Then he leveled his bird and headed for his ship. Again, he had the motors aimed straight up, as his craft remained level, and he settled it on the steel deck.

Everyone then bounded out of the OdinBird and ran across the deck to the AnnieBird. As soon as King Montour, and the Nobles, and Stiles behind them, were buckled in, Chief Odin had the Odin-Motor going to turn the 2 sets of 8 "golden wings." In seconds, they were in the air and again, flying directly over the harbor entrance waters.

He hoped the Spanish would be further mystified, by the transformation of one kind of flying machine, into one that was radically different.

The Chief had seen a rowboat in the center of that entrance, and it was obviously holding up a chain going from side to side, to bar entering the bay, with certainty, by any ship.

Stopping in mid-air, near the water, he shot off an OdinRock. *Whooooosh! Screeeem! Ka-booooom!* That OdinRock luckily hit the little boat, and pieces of it flew all over the place as a great geyser of water erupted into the air.

The projectile had apparently also broken the chain in half too since it was not seen then.

The Chief flew then into the harbor. Just as quickly as he got there, he gained some altitude, and then fancily dove the AnnieBird down and again, circled the harbor, noting that all of the Spanish ships were either tied up to the long, curving quay, or tied outboard of those who were against it. He pulled the craft up, to gently set down on the dock, next to the largest Spanish galleon. Oddly, there was a long unoccupied space at the dock, in front of that ship.

Sure enough, the dock and ground beyond for some ways were covered with wooden planking. That wooden surface would surely have caught fire if the OdinBird was landed there.

Everyone got out of the AnnieBird, each of them holding his or her Odin2Gun at the ready. Stiles, as usual, was the only one unarmed, except for pencils and paper. The Nobles gathered behind the Chief and their King, those 2 standing expectantly, facing the largest of the Spanish ships. All of the Nobles backed those 2, and obviously alert and ready for anything that might occur. King Montour had a white cloth on a stick, indicating – he hoped – it was to be a peaceful meeting.

Spaniards were peeking at them, silently in awe, from behind ship railings. Whoever may have been on the wharf there, had scattered to hide somewhere.

Three men came slowly down a kind of stairway, from the largest ship. One of them was elderly and had a bunch of medals on his chest. He looked to have a navy uniform on. Thus, he was an Admiral. Another in an apparent Army uniform, wigged and showing medals, was probably a General. A younger man was well-dressed, as though a civil authority of some sort. The 3 men stopped a pace or so in front of the newcomers, looking them over and also looking, in open-mouthed fascination, at the then-stilled, bright-orange-painted, AnnieBird.

Chief Odin and the rest, wore the usual Noble brass hat, made as though a half-globe of the Nuworld, but with a brim all around, to shade one's head. They were all in buckskins.

"Aha," the civilian Spaniard said in slightly accented English, and with a faint smile, "you must be the Nuworlders, we have heard about recently."

"Ah, so you do speak English!" the Chief smiled back. "Yes, sir, you are correct; we are of the Nuworld. I am Odin Bushnell, Chief of the Nuworld State, and this is King Andrew Montour. He is the King of our Nobility. And you 3, sir? Who might you gentlemen be?"

"This, Chief Odin, is the Admiral commanding our King's fleet," the civilian pointed. "This other is the General Commanding our King's Army here. I am appointed by the King of Spain, Ferdinand the Sixth, as the Governor Generale of Havana and of Cuba. My name is Fondesviela y Ondeano Filipe, Marques de la Torre. That's a bit much for English speakers, as I found out during my Embassy time in London. If you will simply call me Marques Torre."

Just as the Governor Generale finished saying that, a stupendous ringing sound came from a nearby church. The sound was practically deafening. Much offended by the racket, Chief Odin whipped out his Odin2Gun and aimed for the offending noise. He couldn't actually see the bell, high up in an elaborate bell tower. It seemed to be about 300 yards distant. He could only see the top of the bell, as it was strapped to a support above it. He aimed and fired as rapidly as he could; probably, he got off 8 or 9 shots. He could see the straps snapped and the huge bell made a great crashing sound, as it tumbled down into the church.

The Admiral, the General, and the Marques appeared to be

astounded, by the extremely rapid firing of the Odin2Gun, to say nothing of the distance, and the great bell being silenced.

Without looking down, the Chief re-upholstered his weapon and nodded his head as if to say, well, that's that.

King Montour nudged the Chief and nodded toward the high ridge across the harbor.

The Spaniards nervously glanced around also, and they too noticed a Battle Force's 7 OdinBoats appearing side by side, amazingly atop that ridge.

"Marques Torre," the Chief said, "that's one of our 3 exceptionally powerful Battle Forces, we brought here today, to take Havana, the island of Cuba, and that fleet. They landed on the beaches over there and climbed that hill. We have an identical Battle Force right now, going around the city walls to enter the far side of the harbor. A 3rd Battle Force, and my own huge steamship, made of the strongest steel, is waiting for King Montour's order, to come into the harbor entrance.

"I want you to please tell the Admiral and the General here, all of that and add this: each of our Battle Forces is staffed with 2,000 Nobles; that's a total of 6,000 Noblemen and Noblewomen. Every one of them, are equipped with a gun like mine; an Odin2Gun, we call them. They can fire them very rapidly and have exactly 50 shots in their handles, 200 more on their chests, and plenty more in their AndyPaks. You must have seen what happened to the harbor chain boat, when I shot it with just 1 of 10 OdinRocks, that I have under my AnnieBird there," he said as he pointed to it.

"Each Battle Force is equipped with thousands of those OdinRocks, and could easily blast to nothingness, every one of your ships. They could easily destroy all of Havana's fortifications. We have totally destroyed a large and thoroughly modern, French fleet at Louisbourg, and captured that fortress-city. We have also absolutely made matchsticks of an even larger English fleet, also very modern, that attacked us. We conquered Canada, too. Both England and France have conceded all of their former territories in the Nuworld, including all their islands in the Caribbean, to us. Please tell that to the Admiral and the General," Chief Odin said.

Wow! The reaction from the Marques was extraordinary, as he rattled on to the other Spaniards, fearsomely, and in very rapid Spanish, what Chief Odin had said. The wide-eyed, wrinkled Admiral, reacted as though being struck with fists. The General was more stoic.

When the Marques finished, he turned back to the Chief, anticipating more information.

"I want everyone on this island to know, we have no ill will toward Spain, nor any Spanish soldiers or sailors," the Chief told him. "But this is Nuworld territory. It is, and forever shall be. We have no desire to kill any person here, whatever. That fleet and these fortifications must surrender to us. We shall remove all of our precious metals, and our gems from those ships, as well as every sort of weapon. Then we shall give the Admiral and his fleet, and every soldier, free passage to return to Spain, unharmed. Please, Marques Torre, tell that to them," Chief Odin said after he had rattled all of that off.

The Marques actually smiled, as though in relief. He then proceeded to inform the Admiral and General again, in his staccato Spanish, what he had been told. The Admiral then said something to the Governor Generale.

"Chief of State Odin," the Marques said, "the Admiral wishes to be assured... that you really do mean none of King Ferdinand's 53 ships will be taken or destroyed."

"I do absolutely guarantee that... if we meet with no resistance. We will need some help from his crews, in removing his cannons, and cannonballs and gunpowder; even every other sort of weapon, right down to muskets, pistols, knives, and swords. They must be put on the dock before they can leave. Our Nobles must have free access, of course, on every ship, to recover as I said, our Nuworld treasures. Any man, of any rank, shall be instantly shot, who interferes with our mission here. Also, all Spaniards, military or civilian here, will be permitted to return to Spain, unharmed, with those ships. But all weaponry must remain.

"Why? I shall be honest with you. It is because we need the iron, to make steel for our steamships. My own steam-powered ship, made entirely of steel, is outside the harbor now, and I do now invite you, Marques Torre, and the Admiral and the General, to come and see it. My wife, the Chief Lady of the Nuworld, is aboard and awaiting my return. Please, Marques, ask the Admiral and the General, to come along with you, to see my new steam-powered steel ship."

The Marques turned to the older Spanish commanders and rattled off what he was told to say. They nodded their assent, though wide-eyed. The 3 Spaniards turned and waved, to the crews remaining on the ships, and walked the small distance to the Annie-Bird. Three of the Noble Guards were left behind on the dock, as the 3 guests were strapped in.

Chief Odin started up the AnnieBird's OdinMotor, and they were soon rising up and over the harbor, cluttered with the unfamiliar Spanish ships. From up there, they could see the Battle Force, that had gone around the town, getting their OdinBoat bottoms wet, easing into the far side of the irregular harbor.

At that altitude too, they could plainly see the great number of well-protected fortifications, on both sides of the entrance, and Spanish cannons, forbidding entry to the harbor.

Doubtless, both the General and the Admiral studied with fascination, the menacing 22 OdinBoats, and the giant steel OdinShip, they could see below them.

The afternoon was waning, and as there was no outdoor lighting for them and precious little of it indoors, Chief Odin was in a hurry and landed on his ship. Then the Chief had the Captain move into the harbor, to dock at the space in front of the largest Spanish

The 3 Spaniards, of course, looked about them in open-mouthed wonder, at the marvel of a steel steamship, as the Captain moved to dock it, at the open space on the wharf, before the largest of the Spanish oaken galleons.

King Montour took them on a short tour of the boiler room, and the magic of steam engines driving the 32-foot diameter bucket wheels, on each side of the prow. Each of the Spaniards understood King Montour's French rather well.

That gave Chief Odin the opportunity, to gather up the 3 surrender documents, he had the printers on board, print with several copies of each of them. He felt now that his presumptuousness had been well rewarded... that is if he could convince all 3 of the big wigs, to sign.

When King Montour brought the 3 Spaniards up to the Chief's knotty-pine paneled dining room, they were introduced to the breathtaking beauty, of Chief Lady Annie Bushnell. That King said of her, exaggerating not a little, that she was the brain behind the AnnieBird.

But then a Noblewoman who was fairly fluent in Spanish opened up a large book whose pages were covered with coppix. She showed those coppix to the 3 guests. She explained the first of many coppix, were of French forts burning in the Ohio valley, in 1756. Then on and on, she pointed out the Ticonderoga and Crown Point forts, being destroyed and finally, she pointed to the destruction of the French fleet at Louisbourg, and the English fleet, on the Housatonic.

She showed real sadness, telling the 3 Spaniards that the French were thought to have over 15,000 sailors, marines and soldiers killed, at Louisbourg alone. The English were thought to have lost about 18,000 men, on the Housatonic. She also itemized the various kinds, of ships they lost, in both of those one-sided "battles."

"Two of our gallant Noblemen here, have used their coppix device, to picture your fleet in Havana's harbor, but they haven't yet finished them," the Noblewoman told Marques Torre.

Fires had been hand-colored on those coppix, to add to the drama of them. Naturally, the 3 Spaniards were highly impressed with those pictures, even if they might have some doubts.

Chief Odin had them get down to business right away. He gave the 3 surrender documents to them to read. On each of the single pages, one column was in English, and another was in Spanish. That was thanks to that Noblewoman aboard, who was fairly fluent in Spanish.

He told Marques Torre that there was to be no negotiation and no dissent. It was either the 3 would sign their appropriate documents, or there would be hell to pay. They signed, and each of them surrendered their beautifully-made swords.

The Chief Lady invited each of them to dinner, but not that

night. All of them had much to do before darkness set in; they would have a friendly dinner on board, the next night.

King Montour in the meantime, rittalked his Battle Force Overlords, so they would all be in the harbor before dark, and prevent any ship from entering or leaving.

Most especially, his Nobles were to tie up to and swarm onto the Spanish ships, swinging their OdinLanterns by their handles, to look for and recover every speck of gold, silver, and gems they could find.

Poor Ezra Stiles; he was wearing out his pencils, with all the notes he had to make.

The Nuworlders accompanied the 3 Spanish men, onto the dock.

The Chief and King Montour wanted to give the Spaniards not a minute more than necessary, to hide that treasure bound for Spain, and never to be seen again. Or, he feared, they might dump it all, into the harbor mud, if the treasure wasn't seized immediately. Those 2 would hold their OdinLanterns up, watching as Nobles brought gold bars, and zillions of silver bars, both gold and silver coins, gold and silver jewelry and satchels full of precious stones, onto the dock. That loot was to be loaded on the OdinCart, being pulled along by the OdinHorse machine.

It seemed virtually every sailor on those Spanish ships, understood the danger to them personally, if they refused to cooperate; and cooperate, they did. They seemed to be universally in awe of the Nuworld Nobles, with their Nobility ranks plainly printed on their shoulder strap sleeves. Surely, some of them saw the reasonableness of the Nuworlders, recovering their treasures from the Spanish invaders... most especially with those ultra-fast-to-shoot-again Odin2Guns on every Nobleman's and Noblewomen's hips.

By OdinLantern light, the OdinHorse pulled the OdinCart back and forth, on the dock, accumulating some tons of treasure, on its eight-by-twelve-foot bed. Nearly at midnight, the OdinCart was again up the ramp and nestled securely in the rear of OdinShipOne.

Bright and early Thursday morning, swarms of Nobles were again filing, onto the Spanish galleons, some of them large 3-deckers, relieving those who had muskets, pistols, and swords, plus their ammunition. The day also was filled with piling, not just those personal weapons, but also uncountable cannonballs, up to 30-pounders in weight, and over 3,000 cannons, of various sizes. Surprisingly, some of those Spanish cannons were still fancily made of brass.

These were merely off the ships since the weapons in the forts could stay in place for a while. There were also the fortifications in faraway Santiago de Cuba, to take over, on the other, the eastern end, of the island.

While they were at it, the Nobles also removed the cannon mounts from those ships. The wood they were made of was well-seasoned oak and would make excellent charcoal for the iron furnaces to come, for Havana or elsewhere.

Also, every bag of gunpowder was removed from the ships and piled on the dock. It was then doused with water, so as not to be explodable, by someone wishing deviltry. It could be dried by King Revere's arsenal. Perhaps it could be improved or at least, used to blast tree stumps or other such purposes.

They could not get all of those cannons, and cannonballs off on Thursday. It was thought, much of Friday would be needed to finish the job, even with the surprisingly friendly cooperation of Spain's sailors. King Montour guessed, that part of the reason for the help-fulness, was that their ships would sail a little faster home, without all that weight of iron.

Chief Odin estimated that the value of iron seized was at least equal in value to that of all the treasure from aboard those 53 Spanish ships. Busting up those cast-iron cannons and mixing them, and their balls, with limestone and charcoal, into the tops of their furnaces, was far more fruitful in making steel, than working with the best of raw iron ore.

On Thursday night, Chief Odin, Chief Lady Annie, King Montour, Ezra, and Catherine Stiles, all entertained 20 top Spaniards in the OdinShipOne's, ample dining room.

This time, the main fare was lobsters, fetched from the ice room. Apparently, the guests were pretty much unfamiliar, with that northern Atlantic seafood, but they enjoyed it anyway, smothered in fresh melted butter as it was. They were also served corn-on-the-cob, baked candied yams, fresh bread and had for dessert, strawberry ice cream. The General was especially enthused about the meal but had to voice his surprise that the Nuworlders supplied no wine.

"Ah, but we are all much too young for such spirits," Chief Lady Annie told them, with her usual broad smile of perfect white teeth. Her teeth were indeed, rarer those days for an adult than every sort of alcoholic spirits.

Wine or no wine, the Spaniards seemed to enjoy the dinner, and the interpreted conversations, by Marques Torre. They left holding OdinLamps to light their way, seeming quite friendly, with the oil-burning lamps having been a gift for each of them.

On Friday, they completed getting onto the dock, every last bit of armaments, from all 53 Spanish ships. They had provisions for the journey home to get aboard. Also, there were a few hundred "Habaneros," as they called Havana's residents, that wished "to go home" to Spain, to get settled on various ships. The roughly 4,000 disarmed soldiers also had to be accommodated on the increasingly crowded vessels.

King Montour estimated that about 11,000 Spaniards would be sailing away the next morning, Saturday, October 22nd, 1757. That was surely a better fate for them than being blasted to tiny bits, settling on the bottom of Havana harbor, as food for every creature of the sea.

That Friday evening, Marques Torre invited Chief Odin, Chief Lady Annie, King Montour and Stiles, and his wife, to have dinner with him and his family, in the Governor General's Palacio. Curious about the man, they agreed.

Accompanied by a select Noble Guard, they arrived to find the Marques, had a young wife and 2 pre-teen daughters. They all sat around an enormous heavy table. The fare was completely unfamiliar, but the chicken enchiladas, the bread, the many fresh vegetables, and the coffee, were all excellent. They were offered wine but begged off from that experience.

"Chief Odin, I want you to know, my family and I wish never to return to Spain, but to become Nuworlders. I have sent a personal letter to King Ferdinand, explaining my reasons for this. He will be

astonished I know, that people in the Nuworld are never to be domi-
nated by the Catholic Church, or any other religion. But they can
believe or not in any religion, as they wish.

"I told him, Chief Odin, that you informed me, you believe not
in one God or in 3 Gods, but that Nuworlders are creators, and
therefore, millions of Gods and Goddesses reside over here. King
Ferdinand is an intelligent and well-meaning ruler, and I know he
will be in a state of shock when he reads what I've sent him.

"I also enclosed a copy of the Nuworld Constitution, and your
beautiful Coronation Address, Mr. Stiles gave me. I trust the
Admiral can get all of that, directly to the King, and by-pass those
priests near him, who would, of course, destroy such sacrilegious
information.

"Chief Odin, I am at your service, to play any role you wish of
me. I do believe I can be quite useful to the Nuworld cause, here in
Cuba and in Mexico, where I have also served," the Marques said. "I
suppose Mexico is next to be conquered by you, and I wish to assure
you, you will love the Mexican people just as my family and I do,
Sire. You will also appreciate the mining of endless tons of silver, in
Mexico, for your money called nu."

After drinking a little more coffee, the Marques added some
fascinating information.

"No one can help but admire your OdinBoats, that can climb out
of the water and crawl along on land. And that Sire reminds me of a
study made in Nicaragua, of a possible way to get ships back and
forth across, from the Caribbean to the Pacific Ocean. There are
rapids, at the least, in the way. But your OdinBoats could easily
climb out of the San Juan River, go around such obstacles, and get
back in the river, go across Lake Nicaragua, and thence down a few
miles of land, to the ocean there. Chief Odin, I am very certain of
that," Marques Torre said, and produced a map of "Central America," as it was then known.

In great excitement, the Chief and King Montour studied the
map and could quickly see that transiting, that 90 nautical-mile
stretch of mostly water, sea to sea, was surely practical. But those

OdinBoats might have some rough going, in and out of the water, so they should be made of nearly indestructible steel.

That night, Chief Odin had his rittalk to his ear, telling King Phineas Pratt of the Metals Realm, to immediately get built, at least 14 OdinBoats, in steel, for 2 Battle Forces. They would cross to the Pacific, and complete the conquest of Mexico on the Pacific side, and go up and down the west coast of the Nuworld, from there. They must be equipped to do some whaling there, to guarantee fuel supplies. They'd also need fishing equipment for their dinners.

In time, of course, that inter-ocean route could be canalized as necessary, for every size and design of the ship, going east to west or west to east.

The Marques also revealed that Cuba had an extraordinary iron mine, with the very hard metal nickel, mixed with the ore, near to the east end of the island. The Chief would fly them there in his OdinBird the next day, to bring back samples of that ore, for making excellent steel.

He was so very pleased with the new citizen of the Nuworld, that he made him Prince Torre, and put him on the payroll, as the assistant to King Montour, in the taking of Mexico and all that terri-tory, north and south of there. He renamed Nicaragua's San Juan River, as the Prince Torre River, too.

Oh yes, and there was the little matter too, of getting occupied the Caribbean Islands and lands, right down to the equator.

The Nuworlders stood on the Havana dock that Saturday morn-ing, October 22nd, 1757, to wave goodbye to the 53 Spanish ships struggling, to fill their sails with air, and get out of that harbor, and out of the Nuworld.

Oh, but those they left behind, all had so very much more to do, *in our Nuworld, our Free World, our Brightest Rich Part of the Whole World!*

ABOUT BILL BARRONS

Born 1926, in Cadillac, Michigan, the oldest boy of fourteen kids. Survived the Great Depression and joined the Marines the day after I turned 17. Could hardly wait to go fight those nasty Nazis and Japanese. Served 2½ war years in the Marines. Got married, went to college, had kids, re-joined the Marines in 1949, in time for the Korean War. I became a Marine Second Lieutenant but was a Platoon Commander only for a short while as my sick wife nearly died and I had to resign to care for my family. Became a Telephone equipment engineer with AT&T in Chicago. Then was a kitchen and home remodeling designer for 22 years. Retired at age 69 and began to research and write novels. At age 93, I'm still at it!

Bill Barron's Website: williambarrons.com

williambarrons.com

f

Cover design by DJ Rogers
justwritedesign.com

iCrew Digital Publishing is an independent publisher of digital works. We support the efforts of authors who wish to independently publish in the digital world.

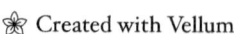 Created with Vellum

BOOKS BY WILLIAM BARRONS

Marine Corps Daze

Nuworld at War

The San Diego Police Homicide Detail

The .22 Caliber Homicides

The Nude Beach Homicides

The Coldest Cold Homicides

The Forever Homicides

The Red Hot Homicides

The Homeless Homicides

The Rawhide Homicides

The Hellish Homicides

The Holiday Homicides

The Chief's Homicide

The Hatchet Homicide

The Cadillac Detective

Visit WilliamBarrons.com

www.ingramcontent.com/pod-product-compliance
Lightning Source LLC
Chambersburg PA
CBHW072333020726
47506CB00004B/872